SOAR TO THE HEAVENS ~~WITH THE STAR P~~OT AND RISING ~~...~~

*RITA Award ~~...~~
*P.E.A~~...~~
*PRISM Award Winn~~er ...~~ ~~(...~~ Fiction Romance)
*Sapphire Award Winner (Best Science Fiction Romance)
*Best Alternative Romance—All About Romance
Annual Readers' Poll

"Fans will not be disappointed! *Contact* is exhilarating [and] unique."
—*Romance at its Best*

"…Splendid visual imagery, natural dialogue, and superb characterization…[*Contact*] will wring your emotions and touch your heart [and] leave you breathless."
—*Romance Reviews Today*

"Drawing on her unique credentials and front-line perspective, Susan Grant has delivered a story of unusual depth and power."
—All About Romance

"*Contact* is a superb military science fiction romance loaded with action."
—Harriet Klausner

THE STAR PRINCE
*Winner of the Dorothy Parker Award for Excellence
Romantic Times Reviewers' Choice Nominee
*Winner of the 2002 Colorado Award of Excellence

"Susan Grant [takes] readers on an exotic exhilarating adventure…Ms. Grant proves she has a true gift for storytelling."
—*Romantic Times*

Ms. Grant keeps "the reader amazed and entertained…. An out-of-this-world story you don't want to miss!"
—Scribes World Reviews

MORE PRAISE FOR
AWARD-WINNER SUSAN GRANT!

THE STAR KING
*RITA Award Nominee (Best Paranormal)
*P.E.A.R.L. Award Winner
(Best Futuristic Romance, Best Sci-Fi)
*Best "Other" Romance Award—All About Romance
Annual Readers' Poll
*Sapphire Award Finalist
*Writer-Touch Readers' Award Winner

"Drop everything and read this book!"
—Susan Wiggs

"Excitement, action, adventure and wonderful romance!"
—*Romantic Times*

"It has an air of exuberance that is worthy of any swashbuckling futuristic. Evocative and exciting!"
—Mrs. Giggles from Everything Romantic

ONCE A PIRATE
*The Francis Award Winner (Best Time-Travel)
*Two-time RWA Golden Heart Finalist

"Grant's background...brings authenticity to her heroine."
—*Publishers Weekly*

"The best romance I read this year!"
—*The Romance Reader*

"A delightful, sexy story [that] you won't want to put down. A real winner!"
—*Affaire de Coeur*

"*Once a Pirate* is a fast and rollicking adventure. Following [Grant's] career as she hones her craft will be a pleasure!"
—*The Romance Journal*

A CHILD'S CONVICTION

Barb's eyes swerved to the television. What she'd thought was a commercial was in fact a news broadcast, a special report. The reporter was standing in an airport terminal building, a chaotic scene behind him. "Again," he said grimly, "reports are unconfirmed—a Boeing 747 bound for San Francisco has disappeared from radar. United Flight 58 departed Honolulu International Airport at twelve thirty-eight a.m. Two hundred seventy-one passengers and twenty crewmembers are onboard. . . ."

Barb's hand went to her throat. Suddenly there wasn't enough air in the room to breathe. . . . Tightly, she said, "Honey, shut it off."

Roberta glanced up and her brows drew together. "Are you crying, Grandma?" the little girl asked in a serious voice.

Barb flopped onto the couch and hugged her close. "Mommy's airplane got a little lost. There are brave rescuers looking for her right now. Try not to be scared."

"She's not in the ocean."

Barb moved the child back and searched her face. "What do you mean?"

"She's in the sky." Roberta moved her hand in a sweeping motion over her head. "High up. Not in heaven. In the sky."

Other *Love Spell* books by Susan Grant:

THE SCARLET EMPRESS
THE LEGEND OF BANZAI MAGUIRE
THE STAR PRINCESS
THE ONLY ONE (Anthology)
A MOTHER'S WAY ROMANCE ANTHOLOGY
THE STAR PRINCE
THE STAR KING
ONCE A PIRATE

CONTACT

SUSAN GRANT

LOVE SPELL   NEW YORK CITY

LOVE SPELL®

May 2005

Published by

Dorchester Publishing Co., Inc.
200 Madison Avenue
New York, NY 10016

If you purchased this book without a cover you should be aware
that this book is stolen property. It was reported as "unsold and
destroyed" to the publisher and neither the author nor the publisher
has received any payment for this "stripped book."

Copyright © 2002 by Susan Grant

All rights reserved. No part of this book may be reproduced or
transmitted in any form or by any electronic or mechanical means,
including photocopying, recording or by any information storage
and retrieval system, without the written permission of the
publisher, except where permitted by law.

ISBN 0-505-52499-6

The name "Love Spell" and its logo are trademarks of Dorchester
Publishing Co., Inc.

Printed in the United States of America.

Visit us on the web at www.dorchesterpub.com.

A special thank you to the following individuals, without whom this book would not have made it from mind to paper: Catherine Asaro, who makes discussions on dying in space disturbingly fun; Charlotte Wager, a wonderful bookseller and person who didn't mind reading in a pinch; Rose, another great lady who said that lovely word, "yes," when I'd asked the same thing; the Thursday night readers group at the Book Barn, always willing to share the "opinion from the trenches"; Theresa Ragan, for those treadmill brainstorming sessions and pity parties; my loyal readers, the ones who have stuck with me from the very beginning; and Chris Keeslar, whose teaching, encouragement, and badgering continues to make me a better author with each new book.

CONTACT

Chapter One

The thunderstorm appeared in front of the Boeing 747 without warning. At 33,000 feet on a calm, clear night over the Pacific Ocean three hours out of Honolulu International Airport, it should not have been there.

"It always happens during dinner," grumbled Brian Wendt, the captain of United 58, the redeye from Honolulu to San Francisco International. "There wasn't anything on the radar five minutes ago."

First Officer Jordan Cady set aside her half-eaten meal and leaned forward to adjust the weather radar display. On an otherwise black screen loomed a bright oval with crisp edges and a solid center soaked in hues of magenta, red, and yellow. A radar return of that size and color indicated an intense, isolated storm cell. "It's about sixty miles off the nose," she said.

Captain Wendt lifted his dinner tray off his lap and slid it onto the empty cockpit seat behind him. "So much for an uninterrupted meal. Get us a heading around it."

Jordan typed the request to veer off their assigned flight path to air traffic control, using one of the three cockpit keyboards. UAL 58 REQUEST 100 NAUTICAL MILES TO THE LEFT FOR WEATHER.

As the captain lifted the hand-microphone to his mouth and transmitted over the PA, "Ladies and gentlemen, fasten your seatbelts," Jordan scrutinized the radar screen. Other than the bright, multicolored blob, periodic sweeps of green speckles showed a storm-free sky, an ideal night to fly over the Pacific.

A chime announced the incoming message from ATC: clearance to skirt the storm. The captain turned a knob connected to the autopilot, banking the 747, while Jordan lowered the lighting in the cockpit and peered into the night.

One good peek outside is worth a thousand sweeps of the radar. That was an old saying among pilots of the modern era. And it was usually right. Far below, tiny puffs of clouds glowed in the light of a quarter moon. Below the clouds, the sea was smooth. No lightning flashed on the horizon. Nor did Jordan see any towering cumulus clouds to back up the radar's warning. Yet, on the odd chance the thunderstorm was too far away to be seen or was obscured by wispy cirrus clouds, standard operating procedures dictated that they circumvent it. Common sense, too. And whatever common sense Jordan wasn't born with, she'd learned. Sometimes the hard way.

For eight years, she'd been flying around the world, and through more bad weather than she cared to remember. Even one-million-pound jumbo jets couldn't risk flying through thunderstorms. She knew—she'd read the post-accident reports of those who'd tried. There was no faster way to end up as a smoking hole than to think you could outfly Mother Nature. Hail punched holes in hulls and snuffed out engines; lightning knocked out electrical and communication systems; extreme turbulence wrenched off wings. Jordan preferred her life to be less exciting.

A lot less.

She had enough on her plate as a single mom who juggled flying for a living with raising a six-year-old. Flying paid the bills. But every heartbeat, every breath, every cell in Jordan's body was devoted to her daughter. That wasn't to say that at thirty-two she wasn't proud of her accomplishments—graduating flight school, getting hired by the airlines, making sure she was good at what she did—but existing as one of the many anonymous cogs in United Airlines' global transportation wheel was fine with her. Unlike her retired fighter pilot father or her fire chief older brother, she didn't go looking for action. Dull as it sounded, glory was not her goal. Maybe the limelight might have appealed to her, once. But these days, her idea of adventure was braving the Saturday afternoon checkout lines at Costco.

The captain aligned the aircraft on a safe heading. Jordan reached for her dinner tray and balanced it on her lap. "I don't care how many times we have to go around phantom thunderstorms tonight, Brian," she said. "Nothing's going to ruin my mood. The minute we land I'm officially on vacation."

"Big plans?"

"Two weeks in paradise—Colorado. My family owns land along the Front Range. Two hundred acres."

Brian whistled. "Ranchers?"

"Not even close. My father's a retired Air Force officer . . . went to the Academy in Colorado Springs, class of 'sixty-six. Started buying the land when he was a freshman, and kept adding acreage a little at a time." A wry smile played around her mouth. "Until he met my mother, who wasted no time telling him he was insane if he thought she'd leave the suburbs for the wilderness. But Dad couldn't bear to part with the land. So there it sits, undeveloped. Waiting. . . ."

For me, she mused, conjuring an image of aspen-covered foothills, the glorious backdrop to the property. By now, the slopes of the Front Range would be pure gold. If it wasn't for needing the money, she'd quit flying, move to Colorado with her daughter, and never come back. Someday, she'd find a way to make that dream come true.

"So," she said wistfully, "camping's the plan. My daughter Roberta and I. Poor kid—Boo, I call her—stuck in the wilderness for two weeks, while I drone on and on about the ranch I want to build and the horses I want to raise."

Luckily, Roberta was into horses. They were on her backpack, her socks, her bed, and in plastic miniature form all over the house.

"Horses." Brian perked up. "I didn't know you rode."

"Well, actually, I don't."

He gave her a funny look. People always did. She smiled sheepishly and tore open a packet of vinaigrette, sprinkling it on her salad. "It's a dream of mine, though." And in her dreams, she *did* know how to ride, flying across sun-soaked meadows with long fragrant grasses, the sun on her back, the wind in her hair—

A ripple of turbulence dragged her attention back to the radar. The glowing oval was in the same relative position. "That's weird." She leaned forward. "We turned left. The storm cell should have shifted to the right. But, look, it's still off the nose."

"It's a radar problem," Brian surmised.

"I'll write it up when we get to San Fran."

Then the airplane rolled abruptly to the left. Jordan grabbed her tray to keep it from sliding off her lap. Her mineral water spilled and salad dressing splashed onto her tie. "So much for blaming the equipment." Choppy air meant the storm was real.

Another call chime rang, this time from the cabin. Cleaning herself with a napkin, Jordan picked up the phone. "Yes?"

"Jordan, Ben. How long is this turbulence going to last?"

"Not too long," she told him. Ben Kathwari was the chief purser, in charge of all eighteen flight attendants. He needed to stay updated on all aspects of the flight. "There's a little weather up ahead. But after that it's clear."

"Good. Find me some smooth air and I'll bring you guys a couple of frozen yogurt pops."

"Ooh. Incentive. You got it, Ben."

A sudden sharp jolt sent the captain's dinner tray careening off the rear seat and onto the cockpit floor. The smell of Thousand Island dressing mixed with the odor of overcooked steak. Ice cubes skittered over the carpet.

"Seat the flight attendants," the captain ordered.

Jordan made the announcement. "Flight attendants take your seats." Brian slowed the big airliner from the faster speed used for cruise to what was recommended to penetrate turbulence. Jordan turned on the ignition, lighting a continuous fire in the engines, insurance against all four huge turbofans flaming out should they plow into heavy rain or hail.

"Tell ATC we need"—Brian calculated the distance and direction they'd need to skirt the rapidly intensifying storm—"eighty more to the left."

Jordan busied herself doing what he'd asked. The bright oval shape had increased in size and clarity. But something had covered the slice of moon, making it impossible to see if something was actually outside, in front of the airplane. According to the radar, there was clear air to either side of the storm, which would allow the luxury of a wide girth as they went past.

A chime sounded. Jordan answered the incoming call and

passed along the message to the captain. "ATC says . . . yes. We can deviate."

Again they went through the routine of circumventing the storm. But the crisp-edged ovoid on the radar mirrored their evasive maneuvers, almost as if it didn't want to let them pass by. A crazy thought. Yet a flicker of unease prickled inside Jordan, a whisper of apprehension. It was that first hint of inner acknowledgment that something wasn't going right, that a situation might not pan out as planned.

Promise? Jordan could almost hear Boo's husky little voice, feel the girl's skinny arms in a death grip around her neck. *You'll come home, right, Mommy?*

Jordan winced, pressing her lips together. Her husband, Craig, had died five years ago, but she was lucky to have parents nearby who were happy to watch Roberta several times a month while she worked. Roberta loved staying with her grandparents. Never once had the child needed reassurance that her mother would return for her. Yet strangely Roberta had balked at this trip, a mere overnight to Hawaii. It was a short jaunt compared to the three-day trips Jordan typically flew. Had the child sensed that something might go wrong?

Jordan's spine tingled. Before 9-11, an airline job was fraught with the usual risks: bad weather, mechanical malfunctions, and air traffic control errors. Now, she was on the front lines in the war on terror—whether she wanted to be or not. She'd never wanted to be a soldier, or a hero. But it seemed that sometimes life had different ideas.

I promise, she had whispered into Boo's hair.

Jaw tight, Jordan scrutinized the sky ahead. She almost missed it at first. Black against black, looming in front of the plane, was an oval of the same relative shape as the storm depicted on the radar screen. It didn't look anything like a thunderstorm. It appeared . . . solid. "Is that an aircraft?"

Contact

"An aircraft?" Brian peered into the night. "What kind of aircraft?"

"I have no clue. I don't see any lights. Or wings." And it looked larger than their 747. Much larger. "I can try calling them on Guard."

"Do it," he ordered.

Jordan radioed in the blind on Guard frequency, 121.5, monitored by all aircraft all over the world. "Aircraft on track Bravo, this is United Five-Eight. Do you read?"

There was no answer, not from the known airplanes in the vicinity or any others. She repeated the call. No one replied.

It was deathly quiet. The moon winked out of view. The black shadow loomed. Jordan felt like a fieldmouse in the shadow of a hungry hawk.

"Do you read United Five-Eight?" she transmitted on the radio. "Do you have us in sight?" Slowly her hand fell away from the microphone button. "I don't think they can hear us. I don't know, Brian; I don't think *anyone* can hear us."

Promise, Mommy? Jordan gave her head a quick shake and tried to block thoughts of her little girl.

The object rushed out of the darkness. St. Elmo's fire slithered along the oval's smooth edges. Framed in blue-white streamers of electricity, the object yawned open like a nightmarish Venus flytrap. At five hundred knots, United 58 hurtled toward its shadowy maw. Jordan's thoughts bogged down in disbelief. Whatever was out there, they were going to hit it head on. Death would be instant.

"I can't turn away," the captain yelled, banking the airplane hard to the left. Several blinding flashes of light filled the cockpit. "Here we go."

No! The primal urge to survive exploded inside Jordan. She didn't think. She reacted. Her hands shot out. Her boots hit the rudder pedals. But she barely had time to brace herself before the shadow engulfed the airplane and swallowed it whole.

7

Chapter Two

"Terrain, terrain!" the 747's ground-proximity warning system protested loudly. "Pull up—*whoop whoop*—pull up!" urged the computerized voice.

Convulsively, Brian's hand shoved the throttles forward, as he was trained to do. Jordan's gaze jerked to the radar altimeter. God. The computer was right: they were only a few feet above the ground—and getting lower. Impossible. Just seconds ago, they were at 33,000 feet!

But they were alive, still *alive.*

"Max power," she shouted, backing up her captain. Her hand pressed against his, pushing the throttles as far as they would go.

Think. Think. She swerved her attention to the two main altimeters that read pressure altitude, not absolute altitude like the radar altimeter. She'd hoped to gain insight as to what was happening to their aircraft. No dice. The altimeters were headed in opposite directions.

One hundred thousand feet and climbing, read one. The other was on its way down to sea level. *Damn it.* The airplane was as confused as its pilots.

The 747's computer announced a set of altitude call-outs in feet issued only when the aircraft was landing: "Fifty . . . thirty . . . ten." There was a grating noise. Then a sharp deceleration threw Jordan forward against her shoulder straps.

The engines stopped running. The silence was thick. Suffocating. Impossible.

Her breaths hissed in and out. Jordan peered around the dim cockpit, tried to find something that made sense. Without engine generators to make electricity, standby power had taken over, powered by the aircraft's battery. All but the most essential electrical equipment was dead. The silence magnified the thunder of something huge slamming behind them.

The booming thud reverberated through her teeth and jaw. Was it a bomb?

Chimes from the cabin began ringing; every flight attendant on board the jet must be calling to see what had happened—or was happening.

"Tell them to remain in their seats," the captain said hoarsely.

Jordan reached for the phone with one shaky hand. But before she could lift the receiver to her ear, the entire aircraft plunged into darkness. Not even starlight seeped into the now oppressively black cockpit. The battery, their last remaining power source, had been snuffed out, too.

The glow-in-the-dark face of Brian's watch blazed like a full moon. Fixating on the light, she listened to the muffled sounds of passengers screaming from beyond the closed cockpit door.

It was dark. Silent. The people were terrified. Understandably. But without electricity, she had no PA, and no way to communicate with them from the cockpit.

Jordan and Captain Wendt dug their flashlights out of their flight bags that they kept next to their seats. Without the engines running, the airplane should have been plunging toward the ocean, losing air pressure at a rapid, eardrum-wrenching rate. But it wasn't. In fact, the airplane was so motionless that it felt like it was parked at a gate.

Jordan glanced around uneasily, trying to work moisture into her mouth. "It feels like we landed."

"Where?" the captain snapped. "The Pacific? We're not a hundred percent airtight. Where's the water?"

"Okay. No water. But we're not flying, either. Or at least I don't think we are. And if we're not flying, then *where are we?*"

Jordan and the captain swerved their flashlights out the forward window. Brian's indrawn breath echoed hers as the faint glow from their flashlights illuminated the area in front of them. But it wasn't the ocean. Or the nighttime sky. What surrounded the 747 looked like a ribbed, concave . . . *wall.*

Jordan's pulse surged. Her mouth went dry. The sight was so far removed from anything she expected to find that at first she was unable to comprehend, let alone accept, what was plainly before her. "We're inside something."

The captain made a sudden, strangled noise. His shaking hand flew to his neck and he fumbled with his tie.

"Brian! What's wrong?"

He tried to talk. Couldn't. His flushed face deepened in color. Then the hand at his collar became a twitching claw as his entire body stiffened. Was he convulsing?

Jordan threw off her shoulder harnesses and jumped out of her seat. With her fingers, she pressed firmly against the captain's neck. No pulse.

The thunder of what had to be multiple fists pounded on the cockpit door. Darkness prevented Jordan from seeing out the peephole. And the newly installed external video monitors were as dead as the engines. Outside the door might be hijackers who would hurt or kill the incapacitated captain.

What's closer—the stun gun or the ax?

The ax was within arm's reach, but Jordan was trained in firing the Taser, a super-powered stun gun capable of delivering a 50,000-volt blast from twenty feet away. Whipping the gun from its holster on the cockpit sidewall, she disarmed the safety switch. "Who's there!" she shouted, the weapon clutched in her sweaty hand.

"It's me, Ben. And Ann and Natalie!" the chief purser yelled.

Jordan lifted the heavy metal bar blocking the door. Then she pulled open the door, stepped back, and took aim. Three flight attendants lurched into the cockpit.

"It's just us," Ben gasped, his dark eyes slewing from the red laser on the stun gun to the slumped-over captain.

"He has no pulse—we need the defibrillator!" she told him.

"Natalie—go." The purser dispatched one of the women to get the emergency medical kit. The Automated External Defibrillator, or AED, could restart a heart, even after sudden death from a heart attack.

Jordan shoved the Taser into its holster. "Help me get him out of here." She raised the armrest on the captain's seat and shifted the man's legs away from her and the center of the cockpit. Then she lifted a lever, sending the seat as far back as it would go. Ben pulled Brian free of the seat and dragged the unconscious man out of the cockpit, where there was little room on the floor, through the open cockpit door, and into upper-deck business class.

In the dark, Ben laid him in the center of the carpeted aisle. The passengers fell silent at the sight of their captain illuminated by the beams of several flashlights, lying prone and blue-lipped on the floor. As they edged closer, Jordan saw the terror etched on their shadowy faces.

"Stand back!" ordered Ann, the other flight attendant who had come upstairs with Ben. She was short and somewhat plump, with a round, sweet face and Asian features—Korean, she'd told Jordan—but she could bark orders like a drill sergeant. "We need room! Stand back!"

There were thirty or so passengers on the upper deck. Jordan asked, "Is anyone here a medical doctor or nurse?"

The replies were all negative. Ann met Jordan's gaze. Her eyes broadcasted fear, but her voice was steady and calm. Like Jordan, she was calling on her extensive training to keep cool in the midst of chaos. "I'll go downstairs and find one," she said.

"Good. Are there enough seats down there to reseat these passengers?"

"I think so."

"Then take them with you."

Ann nodded. Jordan addressed the onlookers. "Go downstairs with Ann. You'll be in a better position to stay updated if we need to make announcements to the whole group."

As Ann herded her charges down the staircase to the main cabin, Jordan crouched by the captain's side. Ben had already started CPR.

Natalie returned to the upper deck. Like a salmon trying to swim upstream, Natalie pushed her way up the aisle past the passengers. In her arms was a case containing the defibrillator.

Urgently Jordan told her, "He's still not breathing."

Ben tore open Brian's shirt and yanked the man's undershirt over his head. Natalie readied the defibrillator. The AED led the flight attendant through the series of verbal prompts, telling her what to do. They gave the captain one shock. His body arched; spittle leaked from the corner of his mouth.

"Come on, come on, Brian. *Fight!*" Jordan clenched her teeth. Brian's heart didn't restart. Natalie raised the paddles.

"The unit says we can try again."

"Do it!" They were running out of time. Jordan's stomach clenched. Sweat trickled down her temple. Every second that ticked by stole precious oxygen from the captain's brain and increased the risk that he'd be permanently damaged by the attack, if not killed outright.

Natalie placed the paddles against Brian's chest. Her long, curved, red fingernails glittered in the beam of Jordan's flashlight. Again a shock blew through the captain's chest. *Come on, come on*, Jordan prayed silently.

Ann herded a man and woman down the aisle. "We've got doctors!" she shouted. "Two of them!"

Breathlessly the two doctors introduced themselves: an internist and a pediatrician. Specialists to cover all the bases, Jordan thought. They dropped to their knees and dug through the emergency medical kit supplied by the airline, while Ben and Natalie told them what they had done to try to resuscitate the captain.

Jordan stood, wiping her arm across her forehead. She couldn't let the captain's condition distract her from the safety of the rest of the crew and the passengers. The leadership role wasn't one she desired, or felt comfortable in, but here she was, in charge of almost three hundred passengers plus a crew of eighteen flight attendants.

Courage is accepting the challenge though it's easier to give up, her father would have told her.

Easier said than done? She'd find out.

Jordan strode back to the cockpit, where she could be of most use. Outside the forward windows, there were no stars, no sea. Where was the airplane? Weariness and fear clutched at her.

Think. Think.

She aimed her flashlight at the instrument panel. What good was high tech without power? Satellite navigation . . . radios . . . emergency signals—all were worthless.

She rubbed her temples. She was in a nearly one-million-pound 747 that had just been swallowed up by something even larger. But what was it? For years now, the fight against terrorism had been ongoing—and mostly successful—since the day of horror when four hijacked airliners were used as weapons against U.S. targets. Was this a hijacking, too? Had United 58 been snatched out of the sky? How had it been done? And who had the technology to pull it off?

Her skin crawled as she pondered the idea of aircraft swallowing other aircraft. She didn't think anyone had the know-how or equipment to do such a thing. But then back in 2001, on a sunny September morning, no one had thought anyone would use airliners filled with innocents as missiles, either.

A dull throb began behind her eyes. Stress? Or her body's first reaction to poison seeping into the aircraft, put there by those who'd captured them?

She shook off the thought. Paranoia never did anyone any good. It was time for her to take charge, whether or not she thought herself up to the task. If those who had "taken" them wanted to hurt them or use them in some horrific way, then she had to prevent it somehow, both to save those for whom she was now responsible and to make sure she got back home to her little girl. Her chest thickened, a wrenching of her heart. But she steeled herself against those softer feelings—they'd only weaken her when she needed to be tough, and weakness would sabotage her chance to bring this nightmare to a safe conclusion.

14

She rummaged through her backpack until she found a photo of Roberta and slipped it into her chest pocket. "Don't you worry; I'm coming home, kiddo," she whispered, pressing her hand over her pocket.

Grabbing her hat, flashlight, and the stun gun, she strode through the open cockpit door. As nonlethal weapons went, the Taser packed a punch. But to Jordan it seemed a flimsy weapon against such a monumental dilemma. It was like using a flintlock rifle to shoot a grizzly bear. According to other pilots she'd talked to the gun gave you two shots, but you'd be lucky to have time to load the second after firing off the first. She'd give her eyeteeth to have an air marshal onboard. Unfortunately, assignment of the marshals was random, and this flight had drawn the short straw.

Real short.

She took three steps and stopped. In the middle of the upper-deck aisle, the knot of people hunched over the captain had lost the intensity that usually characterized those trying to save someone's life. Jordan's stomach turned cold. "How is he?"

In answer, Ann drew a blanket over the captain's inert form.

Jordan crossed herself and hugged her arms to her ribs.

Ben made eye contact with her. "Now what, Captain?"

Captain, he'd called her. Ben's use of the title drove home the fact that she was now the commander of this ship. So did the shrouded shape on the floor. Grief for the loss of her flying partner mixed with an odd, loathsome, and entirely too familiar feeling. She'd tried, but she couldn't save him. *Damn you, Brian,* she cursed the now dead man. *You abandoned me. Left me alone, feet to the fire.*

Grimacing, she pushed her fears into the recesses of her mind and focused on her promise to get herself and everyone else out of this alive. She dropped her arms and squared her shoulders. "Ann, Natalie, Ben—let's talk."

15

They moved away from the two physicians filling out paperwork relating to their treatment of Brian. A futile, time-wasting activity, Jordan thought, considering everything else that was going on, but it would keep the physicians busy for a moment; any semblance of normalcy would go a long way toward maintaining calm among the passengers—for as long as it was possible.

"Okay," she began in a confidential tone. "We need to get going on some kind of plan. Then, Ben, I'll need you to pass on the information to the rest of the flight attendants. And keep the passengers calm and in their seats."

The shadow of Ben's beard stubble stood out starkly on his pale skin. "Right now they're too scared to do anything else but sit."

"That's going to change shortly, and that's why I need to speak to them. But not until we put a plan in action." Jordan took a breath. "We have to assume we were taken—kidnapped. Hijacked."

"Do we know that for sure—that we were hijacked?" Ann asked. All eyes swerved in her direction. "Well, we don't really know what happened, do we?" she insisted somewhat defensively.

Jordan directed a scowl toward the dark windows on the right hand side of the airplane. "No. We don't. But then, where are we? Inside something, is my guess. I saw it; there was a door, or hatch. It opened and we flew inside. Can I explain it? No, I can't. But it wasn't voluntary, us coming here. Wherever we are."

Ann cast a thoughtful and worried glance outside. "I've never heard of an aircraft this big being swallowed by something. Our training doesn't address this."

"Exactly," Natalie put in. "That's why I'm with you," she told Jordan. "We have to assume the worst."

Jordan folded her arms over her chest. "And that's what I'm doing; until we have proof otherwise. Our power is

16

gone. Our communications, our radios, don't work. That doesn't sound friendly to me no matter how you cut it." She met Ann's eyes. "But I appreciate the input. Don't stop feeding me information, gut feelings, anything. Please." Jordan needed them. More than they knew. "If we're going to get through this, it's going to be together."

Ann's lips compressed. "I have no argument with that." The others nodded gravely.

Jordan continued. "It seems to me that our efforts should focus on keeping our captors from boarding the airplane— maybe barricading ourselves inside somehow, until someone decides it's time to negotiate with us. *If* they plan to negotiate with us. Of course, I'm making the assumption that no one already onboard was involved with what happened."

Ben nodded. "They'd have acted already, made themselves known."

"Still, we'd better not take any chances," Natalie put in.

"Agreed," Jordan said. Silent, they listened to the sounds floating up the stairs from the main cabin below. The voices were agitated, frightened. But those of the flight crew rang loudly, reassuring everyone as well as calling out orders. She needed to get down there. What she'd say, she could only imagine.

She wrapped up her briefing of the flight attendants. "So. Our goal is to keep us in and whoever took us *out*."

"We can start by keeping the doors armed," Ben said.

"Good. Phase one—doors as defense." Armed doors meant that inflatable escape slides were deployed the instant the hatches were opened. The slides weighed hundreds of pounds and inflated in seconds.

"Ooh, yeah," Natalie said, her dark eyes glinting. "If anyone comes knocking, we're going to smash them like a bug."

"You got that right," Jordan agreed. "Now, get me an

17

accounting of what weapons we have onboard. Ask around; add everything you find to the arsenal." Security measures or no, it was likely that someone had sneaked a usable weapon aboard, even it if was only a nail file.

Ben turned to Natalie and Ann. "Have everyone tie up loose ends, put the carts away, lock up the liquor."

"Shouldn't we have the passengers don their life jackets, too?" Ann asked.

Jordan nodded. "There's still a chance that we might end up in the drink."

Collectively, they glanced out the dark windows. "When I'm done talking to the passengers," Jordan continued, "and you're done with phase one, I want one flight attendant representative from each area of the plane and any military folks onboard to meet in the cockpit to discuss phase two. We have a plane to defend, and we need to figure out exactly how we're going to do it."

They regarded each other in silence, crew members tasked with saving aircraft from a situation none of them could grasp.

Jordan spread her hands. "Are we clear on what's going to happen once we go downstairs?"

"Yes," they chorused.

"It isn't whether you win or lose," Natalie pointed out defiantly, "it's how you exude attitude."

"Well, we're going to win," Jordan told her, wanting to believe it with all her heart. Grabbing her flashlight, she led the way, descending the staircase from the upper deck of the 747 into the deeper darkness below. The three shaken flight attendants trailed her.

Shaken, indeed. Jordan bet she looked ten times worse. She'd never forget the sight of that dark hole engulfing the airplane, the feeling of helplessness in her inability to escape it. And the icy nausea as she wondered if those breaths she'd gasped would be the last ones she'd ever take. Oddly, her life hadn't flashed before her eyes. Only a powerful desire to remain alive.

At the bottom of the stairwell, she faced a stonily silent group of first- and business-class passengers. Some were tourists, judging by their resort outfits and wilted leis; others were businessmen, dressed in cotton shirts and trousers that looked like they belonged with suits.

Ann handed her a megaphone. All airliners had one or two. They were kept aboard to direct the passengers if the PA was inoperative, as in a case of total power failure—a rare event. When it came to an advanced aircraft's power supply, there were backups to the backups, which usually handled any emergency.

Not this time.

Jordan walked forward and centered herself in the aft area of the business section that bordered coach. There she could be heard if not seen by those in first and business class as well as the people seated in economy. The passengers' scrutiny was so intense that she imagined she could feel every eye boring a smoking hole into her uniform. She guessed they'd feel a whole lot better if she were six-feet-three, silver-haired, and possessed of an Oklahoma twang. But instead of the stereotypical airline captain, these people were getting a petite thirty-two-year-old blond, whose freckles and curly hair made her look even younger. But whether they liked it or not, or *she* liked it or not, she'd just stepped into the void left by Brian Wendt's death.

"Ladies and gentlemen, I'm Jordan Cady. I started out the day as your first officer. I'm now your captain."

That elicited more than a few murmurs. She took a breath and spoke over them. "Brian Wendt, the captain, is dead. He suffered a heart attack."

Passengers met the news with gasps. Some started to cry.

Oops. Too blunt. She needed to soften her approach. "I know you're concerned, so I'll try to explain what's going

19

on to the best of my knowledge. We never landed. But we're no longer flying, either." She cleared her throat. "As far as I know, we were taken involuntarily into something that now holds our entire plane. It could be a hijacking."

Some screamed. The few who were weeping began to cry louder. She probably was screwing this up. But should one sugarcoat the impossible: being snatched out of the sky?

"Your crew is well trained and in control!" she shouted above the noise. "We'll get you through this."

A lanky man with carrot-colored hair and an Irish accent stood on his business-class seat and shook his fist. "What are we going to do in the meantime—sit here like sheep and wait to find out?"

Indignant was how his question made her feel. But, somehow, her reaction came out sounding like determination. "No sheep here, sir. We're going to fight back."

There were a few whoops, mostly male, and the Irishman grinned approvingly. She thought of what her father would do, her brother John, too. They'd try to keep the crowd motivated and focused. Easier said than done. Fists clenched, she forged ahead. "We hope that everyone inside is on our side. But, should you see anyone waving anything that could remotely be used as a weapon—knitting needle, plastic knife, you name it—or if someone announces that this is a hijacking or that they have a bomb, every one of you should immediately throw things at that person. Magazines, books, pillows, eyeglasses, shoes. Anything to knock them off balance and distract them. Then we throw blankets over them and wrestle them to the floor. And keep them there." In the darkness, she made eye contact with as many passengers as she could. "Remember, there are only a few of them"—she hoped—"and almost three hundred of us. The odds are on our side."

Cheers met her off-the-cuff pep talk. Her confidence inched a little higher. "Three things to remember!" she yelled over the noise. "We don't panic. We stay in control. And we anticipate and prepare. Your crew is trained and capable of leading you out of this alive. But we need your cooperation to do that. Remain in your seats except when using the lavatories. We'll distribute food and water as needed, but conservation will be paramount until we better know our situation."

Hostage situations could take days, maybe longer, and she had no idea whether their captors would be willing to feed them.

"It's also going to be dark. There are only twelve emergency flashlights, with a battery life of two hours each. With no way to charge them, they'll be out of light in no time. So"—she met as many flight attendants' eyes as she could—"the emergency flashlights stay off unless we absolutely need them." To the passengers, she added, "If you have your own flashlight, feel free to use it. Just remember, we don't have extra batteries."

"What about cell phones?" someone shouted from the back.

She hadn't thought of the phones in the midst of everything. "By all means, use them! Has anyone been able to get ahold of anyone?"

There was silence. "They don't work," came replies. "No signal."

Her burst of hope faded. "Keep trying."

She turned to Ben. He was the purser, the flight attendant supervisor. He could take much of the load off her. "Get everyone working on what we discussed. Secure the exits and keep an eye outside. Use passengers you feel you can trust, if you find yourself shorthanded. I'll be in the cockpit for a while." Maybe there was something she could do there that she'd missed.

There was a disturbance from the rear. Two passengers made their way forward through the crowd. They introduced themselves—Father Sugimoto, a short, squat Catholic priest from Oahu, and Pastor Earl, a minister who looked more like an NFL linebacker, returning home from Hawaii with his choir and an entire church group from Detroit. "We're here if you need us," they told her.

"I do," she said. "Do what you can to calm everyone down." She dropped her voice to a private tone. "And the captain's upstairs. I . . . I don't know what religion he practiced, but something along the lines of last rites wouldn't hurt."

She turned away. Father Sugimoto stopped her with a gentle hand on her shoulder. "We are available for you, too," he said. The Detroit minister nodded along with him. Goodness glowed in their eyes—so at odds with the evil that she feared had detained their aircraft.

Jordan's fingers drifted up to the photo in her pocket. But she made a fist and dropped her hand. Somehow, she kept her own emotions and fears encased. "Thanks," she said. "I might take you up on that later."

As she walked away, she heard the minister's deep voice booming over the megaphone. He led the passengers in a general prayer, fit for a variety of religions, and followed up with a moment of silence for the captain. But it wasn't silent, really. Several people wept softly and infants howled. And Jordan's own heart thudded in her chest.

She trotted up the stairs. Where did that spurt of energy come from? It had to be from adrenaline. She stopped, breathless at the top of the stairs and wiped the back of her hand across her face.

Her body was damp with perspiration. Without ventilation, the airplane was beginning to feel stuffy and warm. The jetliner wasn't pressurized, and thus wasn't airtight. Suffocation wouldn't be a problem, but poor air quality would. Something would have to be done about the conditions onboard the airplane, and soon. Bad air, sick people, stagnant air—these were the makings of a big problem.

A problem that now rested entirely on her shoulders, she reminded herself as the passengers' distant voices joined together singing "Amazing Grace."

Chapter Three

On the bridge of the medium-sized starcruiser *Savior*, Kào Vantaar-Moray paced in front of a backdrop of stars stretched into threadlike streamers due to the ship's faster-than-light speed. With its winged target snatched from the atmosphere and now stored safely in the cargo bay, the *Savior* accelerated away from Earth, from whence its new cargo had originated.

Earth. Kào pondered the exotic if guttural-sounding word. It was the planet's name in one of its people's languages, according to the *Savior*'s eavesdropping linguist. And now Earth was destroyed. Its vast and varied population obliterated; its history, its culture, snuffed out.

A vague wrenching pulled at Kào's chest. *Running, terrified, the ground burning the soles of his shoes, he couldn't find his mother, his father, couldn't see, blinded by light that was as hot as fire and seared his eyes, his skin—*

Kào shoved away the memory imprinted in his mind

24

when he was barely three years old. Even years as a combat-hardened soldier couldn't erase the horror of what he'd witnessed as a child, that single snatch of memory: the complete and utter obliteration of his home world and his birthright.

Other than that single snatch of memory of escaping that fire, he had no other recollections, and none of his birth family, aside from vague impressions that hit him at the oddest times. His tender age at the time of trauma was the reason for the lack of memory, he'd been told by Commodore Moray, the man who had rescued him, adopted him, and raised him on a succession of starships, each one larger than the last. Since then Kào had traveled many roads.

Perhaps too many.

Residual adrenaline from the rescue kept him pacing the dais in front of the stars, despite his bone-deep—perhaps *soul*-deep—weariness. The two years in enemy prison had taken their toll. After four standard months spent recuperating aboard the *Savior*, he hadn't yet returned to his pre-POW physical state. What muscle tone and athletic ability he retained, he owed to the genetics of his hardy ancestors, not the exercise that was once his routine. Not that it mattered; in the war against the Talagars, he'd lost far more than his stamina.

"Here, son." The voice of Kào's adoptive father brought him to a halt. Commander-elite Ilya Moray handed him a fluted glass containing a mildly alcoholic juice beverage. "A little *zabeesh*?"

"Thank you, sir." Kào brushed one thumb over the delicate rim. The refined, cool glass felt odd in his hands. Prison was behind him, yet how long would it take before he again was comfortable in this world? A soft laugh escaped him. "Can you believe I have not tasted this drink in over two standard years?"

Moray didn't lose his smile, but Kào noticed the slightest

tightening of the man's lips. "You have not been amongst the civilized of our galaxy, that's why. All the more reason to drink."

"Commodore," called one of Moray's aides. "Incoming message for you, sir. Alliance Headquarters. Regarding the rescue."

"Put it onscreen." Moray threw back what was left of his *zabeesh* and let out a gust of air as he lowered his glass. It was typical that he'd made quick work of the drink and with such obvious pleasure. He was a big man with an even bigger gusto for life. Much more reserved by nature, Kào remembered as a boy feeling overwhelmed by the officer. But now Kào equaled him in height, at least, if not in bulk or outward enthusiasm.

A colonel wearing Intelligence Corps insignia appeared on the main screen as a three-dimensional image. The communication was two-way, allowing the colonel to observe the crew on the bridge of the *Savior* as clearly as they could see her. She was an older woman, regal and confident in a midnight blue jacket with silver braiding.

Kào had worn that uniform, but with lieutenant's stars on the shoulders and Space Force insignia on the breast. Now it was gray-blue Perimeter Patrol garb that he donned daily, stripped of any trace of military rank.

The officer introduced herself. "Colonel Anipa Frenton." She smiled cordially at the small crew manning the bridge— several ensigns, untried and young, and a pair of Moray's aides. Her gaze swept to Kào and stopped. Censure chilled her smile.

If Kào had any doubt that his actions in the war had disgraced his father, they were erased in that moment. He stood at attention, using his military bearing as a shield against the colonel's brief and penetrating scrutiny.

Her cool green eyes went to Moray, and her expression reflected forced cordiality before she gave in to her awe.

Moray was a living legend; his humanitarian efforts and exploration of the farthest reaches of the galaxy were celebrated. But even the commodore's staunchest supporters couldn't look him in the eye without thoughts of Kào intruding. Like microscopic cracks that weakened a battleship's hull over time, speculation and rumors over his son's reliability had chipped away at Moray's once-flawless reputation.

Colonel Frenton's smile was genuine now. "Commodore," she said. "It is my honor and a pleasure to deliver this message from Alliance Headquarters. You saved a previously unknown ethnic group from the brink of extinction. Congratulations to you, sir. Once again."

"I did so with the help of my crew," Moray replied humbly. He still glowed with the heady gratification of saving the Earth people, now homeless refugees. Clearly, he was a hero who enjoyed his work. "How we came upon this uncharted world was a fortunate miracle, a blessed accident, and I thank the Seeders for placing me nearby so that I could save them. As you know, Colonel, the *Savior* isn't a rescue craft."

No, it certainly was not, Kào thought. The *Savior* was a Perimeter Patrol vessel, one of a growing number of armed-to-the-teeth military battleships assigned to a new branch of the Alliance Space Force, created to protect the borders. Long hours and mind-numbing isolation mixed with true danger, it was one of those critical-to-peace duties that nobody wanted.

Kào flexed his jaw as he watched his father converse with the colonel. A man of Moray's status should have been comfortably situated in a high-level staff position at headquarters on Sofu—and no one could tell Kào that it wasn't because of his military foul-up that Moray had ended up here, instead. It was Kào's blunder that had his father working long hours patrolling the Perimeter, the boundary between civilization and the unsettled hinterlands, looking for rogue Talagar vessels eager to violate the "no-shoot" restriction imposed upon them in the recently signed peace treaty.

Kào glowered darkly. The Talagars, his former captors, were an ancient, fractious, isolationist people who'd continued the practice of human slavery and sexual servitude eons after both were banned by the Alliance, the democratically elected governing body of a mostly peaceful galaxy. Yet in the end, it wasn't the Talagars' cruel customs that had strained eons of peace; it was their aggressive expansion into new territory—attacking settlements, pirating trade routes. It was when a Talagarian slaver ship abducted and sold the husband and children of the Alliance's number-two leader that the long-boiling pot exploded and the galaxy had gone to war.

Ten standard years the bitter fighting had lasted, costing millions of lives. Finally defeated, the Talagars had come to the negotiation table sullenly. Their unrepentant attitude was what made such a risky business of patrolling the Perimeter—a duty that, though critical, was beneath Commodore Moray's status. Kào's father had insisted that he'd volunteered for the assignment, but Kào suspected it was forced atonement for his son's war record. Kào vowed to make it up to him at all cost.

Moray's cheer faded. "I'm afraid that the destruction of the planet was total," he informed the Alliance colonel, and went on to describe the reasons why. "We orbited briefly, and took the first vessel we encountered, leaving promptly afterward. It was too hazardous to remain. But we left viewing-buoys behind and observed the rest remotely. Standard safety procedure, you see." In a confidential tone, he added, "Having witnessed other such catastrophic planetary events, I know that impacts of this type and size trigger immediate and massive devastation. Be assured that once my science staff reviews the recorded data, I'll forward the full report."

"As your duties allow, Commodore," the woman said with grave deference. "There have been reports of at least one unidentified vessel in your zone of transit."

"Yes. I'm aware of it. We're attempting to trace its flight path. It may be Talagar. But I assure you that we will in no way let our unexpected guests distract us from our primary mission—protecting our borders."

"I have no doubt of that, Commodore." The colonel's mouth tightened. "Be careful. A cargo-hold full of non-Alliance refugees makes the *Savior* an almost irresistible target to a people devoted to slave trade."

Kào understood her concern. Most would rather die than be captured by Talagars.

He'd learned why, firsthand.

Grim, the colonel began typing on her handheld computer. "The refugees will have to be relocated as soon as possible." She stopped to take a message that someone handed her. Skimming the missive, she frowned before addressing Moray once more. "Commodore, I'll contact you once it is decided where to take the survivors. It may take some time before we know for certain, as we have other pressing matters."

"Of course. I will await your word." When her image disappeared, Moray turned to Kào. Gripping his empty glass, he smiled broadly. "Finally, fate has turned for us. Today has proved that. The rescue. Yes, indeed, the future will be bright. *Bright,* my boy!" He reached for Kào's shoulder and gave him a hearty squeeze. "The Earth craft practically flew under our very nose. We were meant to rescue them. It's another sign, you see. Perhaps the most telling of all. Our luck has changed."

"You deserve a change in luck, sir."

"You more than I. The war was a dark time for you, yes?

29

And your imprisonment . . ." He glowered. "We will live to see the day when your record will be cleansed of the matter, and all those involved punished for what they did. Trust me on this. If it's the last thing I do in this life, I will make it happen."

But Kào doubted that Moray would have any greater chance to expunge his war record than to find and punish those who'd imprisoned him: enemy soldiers who had long since scurried into the cracks and crevices of the galaxy, or had vanished forever, several of millions of casualties in a war everyone would rather forget.

"And we mustn't delay any longer on the subject of your marriage," his father went on. "I've already begun work on the matter."

"You're arranging a marriage?" At Kào's blurted response, several crew members glanced up from their duties, but swiftly averted their eyes when they met his cold glare.

"We may call ourselves modern men, you and I, but"—Moray winked—"there's nothing like the right mate to advance a man's career."

"I have no career, Father," Kào retorted dryly.

"Bah! You were robbed of it. We will put you back in play by returning you to society's eye. And we'll do that by finding you a well-placed life-partner."

Moray had attempted to steer Kào's life in subtle and not so subtle ways all his life. Manipulation-with-a-heart, Kào had dubbed it, for clearly the man acted out of love. He wanted the best for him. As for marriage? Kào hadn't given any thought to securing a mate and sharing a future with her. He had little enough to give to anyone at this point.

"The upcoming elections on Sofu will put friends of ours in influential positions, giving us the choice of several very eligible daughters," Moray went on. "Marry one, and your future is assured."

"Father—"

Contact

"Ah, but you're right, Kào. This is not the time to discuss it. Other issues demand our attention. A rogue Talagar ship. Unexpected refugees to relocate. We'll talk more of the future—*your* future—soon." Moray's narrowed gray eyes glowed with purpose, a reminder that once he set his sights on a goal, he usually achieved it, one way or another.

And if such were a devoted father's dreams for his only son, did Kào have the right to take them from him? The man had lost enough.

"If you no longer require my presence, sir, I will go." Kào's head ached and his patience waned. All he wanted to do was retreat to his empty quarters and the blessed solitude he'd find there. His father, though, had other ideas.

"Wait, Kào." Moray's thoughtful gaze shifted to the row of mission techs monitoring their stations for insidious signals that might indicate illegal Talagar activity. "I'm going to have my hands full, tracking that rogue ship. I'll have to put you in charge of the refugees, Kào. You'll be their primary intercessor, tasked with removing them from their craft, transitioning them to their new quarters, seeing to their needs. And keeping them out of trouble."

The liquid nearly sloshed out of Kào's glass. He'd do anything Moray asked of him. Proudly. But baby-sitting refugees? "Surely there are others on the crew better suited than—"

"An unemployed weapons officer?" Moray finished for him. "Perhaps. But if I cannot give my son preferential treatment, then what is the point of commanding this ship?"

His father's smiling words might mock the system, but Kào knew that principle infused every action he took.

Moray's gray eyes bored into his. "I need you on this task. I need someone I can trust."

Kào brought his glass to his mouth to hide the grimace he suspected tugged at his lips. Rolling some sweet *zabeesh*

31

over his tongue, he swallowed. "I'll get started right away, sir."

"Ah, I knew you'd want to! Security will assist you. Request as many guards as you think you'll need. I've assigned Ensign Trist Pren to the task, as well. She'll develop an instructional language program."

Kào's fingers tightened around the flute. Trist was a junior officer on the science staff. A skilled linguist and code breaker, he'd heard his father mention. But she was also one of the half dozen or so crew members of Talagar ancestry. Bearing the obvious hereditary traits of no pigmentation, white hair, pink skin, and red eyes, it would have been tough for her or the other Talagars to secure a position on a choice ship such as the *Savior* had it not been for Moray. The man had a habit of collecting outcasts and castoffs like lost puppies.

But they were an odd lot, the Talagar expatriates, and Kào found it difficult to interact with them—exacerbating his sense of isolation onboard the *Savior*. Moray didn't seem to have a problem relating to any of them, nor did any of the rest of the crew, so the difficulty must be Kào's alone. Social skills were not his forte. He was a military man, not a diplomat.

He *had been* a military man, he reminded himself.

A muscle in his jaw jumped. "Ensign Pren," he echoed as benignly as he could.

"Yes." Moray's eyes glinted. "She's a promising young officer, that one."

Kào hoped so. It would be distasteful, dealing with the woman. "Once the refugees are escorted off their craft, where would you like them put, sir?"

"Sublevel three. Empty quarters there are being converted into bunkrooms. It will be your job to communicate their situation to them without bringing on panic. We can't afford unrest. We must keep them safe. Unharmed." Moray regarded his son with knowing, sympathetic eyes. "They will have questions, these refugees. Answer them using your discretion. If any of their concerns involve proof of Earth's demise, the buoys we left behind sent back crisp images. The holo-recording is available for their viewing—and yours, if you so desire."

Kào kept his aversion to that particular activity from reaching his face. He'd seen too many worlds destroyed—his own, and those targeted during the war. "I think I'll pass, sir."

"Then the refugees will have to trust you on this point—they cannot go home."

"It's a fact they will soon learn." Kào finished his drink and handed the flute to a waiting aide. Then, bidding his father farewell, he strode from the bridge, his mind on his assigned duty.

If he worked it right, he could use the opportunity to repair some of the damage he'd done to his father's reputation. In fact, he'd contact the Science Academy on Sofu straight away and ensure that Moray received full credit for the discovery of the uncharted world and the rescue of the last of its people. Had it not been for his father's intervention, no one from the doomed planet would have lived. The military might already know of Moray's deed, but Kào would make certain that the civilians in the government, the true sources of power, were told. His father's name would again be mentioned with respect and admiration in the highest circles of the government.

As long as the refugees cooperated. But he saw no reason why they would not.

Immediately, Kào's mood brightened. Perhaps that had been Moray's intent in appointing him as primary intercessor, to distract him from dwelling on his time in prison and the incident that had led him there. Such a scheme would not be out of character. Moreover, although it pained him to admit it, he knew Moray was right. Jobless on an unfamiliar ship, he'd had little reason to wake each morning. Now, it seemed, he would.

Kào increased his pace. He kept his eyes straight ahead and acknowledged no one. He was focused on his plans for the day ahead: transitioning the survivors of a lost civilization to their new home . . . in the least troublesome way possible.

Barb Jensen wrapped a peanut butter and jelly sandwich in a plastic bag and tucked it next to a frozen juice box in her granddaughter Roberta's lunch sack, zipping everything in a Black Beauty backpack. "Honey, shut off the TV," she called from the kitchen to the family room, where Roberta had eaten her breakfast picnic-style. "We have to go or we're going to be late."

Barb poured a mug of coffee for the road, snatched her purse, car keys, and the backpack before it occurred to her that there hadn't been a response from the family room. "Roberta! Up and at 'em. We'll watch *Sponge Bob* later."

She walked into the family room, expecting to find the child transfixed by a cartoon episode. Instead, Roberta stared pensively at a toy horse in her lap, turning the toy over and over with her little hands. Without looking up, she asked, "Are they talking about Mommy's plane, Grandma?"

Barb's eyes swerved to the television. What she'd thought was a commercial was in fact a news broadcast, a special report. The reporter was standing in an airport terminal building, a chaotic scene behind him. "Again," he said grimly, "reports are unconfirmed—a Boeing 747 bound for San Francisco has disappeared from radar. United Flight 58 departed Honolulu International Airport at twelve-thirty-eight a.m. Two hundred and seventy-one passengers and twenty crew members are onboard. . . ."

Barb's hand went to her throat. Suddenly there wasn't enough air in the room to breathe. Tightly, she said, "Honey, shut it off."

The phone rang. Barb grabbed the remote, hit the off button, and ran into the kitchen. The caller ID read: *Illinois call.* Chicago was where United Airlines headquarters was located. The vise around her chest clamped down further. *No, please, not Jordan. Not my baby.*

She took a couple of deep breaths and shakily lifted the receiver. "Hello."

"Mrs. Jensen?" a woman's too-careful voice queried.

Barb wanted to say, *No, this isn't her, and this hasn't happened. It's a normal day, and my daughter will be home soon. Goodbye.* But of course she didn't. She'd been a military wife for most of her life. Just because Robert had retired didn't mean she couldn't still draw on that reserve of strength. "Yes," she replied, "this is she."

"Hi, Mrs. Jensen. This is Joanne Tierney from United Airlines. I'm sorry, but I'm afraid there's a problem with your daughter's flight."

Barb listened numbly as the woman repeated what the newscaster had said, adding little. The flight had disappeared from radar without any prior indication of trouble; search-and-rescue was scouring the ocean, searching for survivors; no, they had no evidence that a bomb or any act of terrorism had brought down the plane; United would call as soon as they knew more. "We're hoping for the best," Ms. Tierney finished.

"Yes," Barb whispered. "So are we." Eyes squeezed shut, she hung up. Then she wiped her damp, shaking palms on her pants and returned to the family room.

Roberta glanced up, and her brows drew together. "Are you crying, Grandma?" she asked in a serious little voice.

Barb flopped onto the couch and hugged the child close. "Mommy's airplane got a little lost. There are brave rescuers looking for her right now. Try not to be scared."

"She's not in the ocean."

Barb moved the child back and searched her face. "What do you mean?"

"She's in the sky." Roberta moved her hand in a sweeping motion over her head. "High up."

"In heaven? Oh, honey. No. They're looking for her. We have to pray that they find her. We have to, Roberta. We have to be strong."

Roberta shook her head. "She's in the sky." Her gaze turned inward, blue eyes focused somewhere that Barb couldn't reach. "I know, Grandma. I know she is."

Barb pulled the girl to her chest. She wept softly as she stroked Roberta's hair. Often, children could sense things adults couldn't. But if Roberta thought Jordan was dead, then Barb hoped with all her heart that she was wrong.

A vibration rumbled through the jumbo jet. Jordan caught the railing by the staircase and held on. Then the airplane jolted from side to side, almost throwing her off balance. There was a grating noise, and then it stopped.

The singing ended abruptly. People screamed. The baby's wailing went off the charts. And Jordan's heart thumped in her chest as she swung herself the rest of the way up the stairs from the main cabin. If this thing was going to start flying again, she'd damned well better be at the controls.

Upstairs it was dark. Eerie and silent. A blanket covered the captain's inert form, a shadowy bump in the middle of the aisle. Jordan stumbled over it, leaping into the empty cockpit. She sat in the captain's abandoned seat and waited, her legs rigid with pent-up adrenaline, her hands guarding the control yoke.

Come on—show yourselves. Bravado might not quell her apprehension, but it couldn't hurt. *I'm ready for anything you want to throw at me. Let this machine loose and I'll prove it!*

36

The ribbed wall in front of her cracked open like a giant clamshell. Blinding light streamed through the slit. Jordan's hand closed convulsively around the control yoke. She was too scared to scream, too fascinated to run. No longer was the airplane drowned in total blackness; no longer was there a question as to whether it was flying or not. The 747 was quite clearly locked in place on a giant platform in a featureless chamber of a size that defied comprehension.

Ben rushed into the cockpit. He stopped dead when he saw that the wall had split open, flooding the cockpit and the upper deck with a light so bright that he and Jordan had to squint. "What is that?"

Jordan's voice was still hoarse from shouting above the noise downstairs. "Whoever captured us has decided to say hi."

"We can't let them onboard," he said.

"You got that right." She jumped out of her seat. "Batten down the hatches!"

They bolted downstairs to the main cabin. Their urgency caught everyone's attention. "Phase two, people!" Jordan shouted. "They're coming, and we're going to keep them out!"

Ben and the other flight attendants spread the call to action through the plane. Passengers scrambled like ants as the flight attendants barked orders: "Pull the carts in front of the doors! Lower the shades so they can't see inside!"

There were enough military personnel to station one individual at each door. They were unarmed, yes, but three were young Marines—admin types, not combat soldiers, unfortunately. The others were reservists of various shapes, sizes, and ages. Jordan hoped that zeal would make up for any lack of experience and proficiency.

Natalie brought Jordan a straw breadbasket filled with an assortment of objects including several scissors, a pocketknife, two oversized nail files, and a set of brass knuckles. "Our arsenal," she said sarcastically.

The bounty of an eternally faulty security system, Jordan thought with equal cynicism.

"And of course there's me," Natalie said.

"You?"

"I'm a cardio-kickbox instructor. I guarantee I can kick some butt if you need me to."

Now Natalie's sleekly muscular body made sense. Jordan smiled for the first time in hours. "I have no doubt you can."

She grinned back. "Should we let the military folks have first pick?" she asked, lifting the basket of weapons.

"And give the civilian volunteers what's left over." Jordan peered into the darkness. "You never found any law-enforcement types onboard?"

"Not a one. Aside from that mall security guard."

"Well, I still say that the hijackers are going to have their work cut out for them if they think they can get inside this airplane." Jordan pondered something she hadn't considered. "Of course, they could use explosives. . . ."

Natalie pursed her glossed lips. "Why go through all the trouble to capture the plane whole only to blow it to bits?"

"It doesn't make sense, I know. I'm going to assume the hijackers wanted to keep us in one piece, and that's how I'm going to play my hand." She might not be a GI Joe, but she was a pretty mean poker player. Play her cards right and she'd see Boo again. Fold and—she winced. She didn't want to go there.

Jordan made her way back to the cockpit, supervising the well-orchestrated progress of readying the airplane for assault as she went. Ben, the purser and chief flight attendant, walked with her. Though he wore a brave face, his expressive dark brown eyes reflected the worry eating at him. She avoided meeting those eyes, or she might remember her own fear. His fingernails were freshly gnawed, and she saw him biting them whenever he thought no one was looking. And his once stylishly gelled black hair was a mess. Jordan realized then that her own hair had spilled out of her French braid. Corkscrew tendrils sprouted everywhere. Where the curls touched her skin, they were stuck to her damp cheeks and neck. She pulled off the blue scrunchie and started over, scraping the entire thick mess into a hasty ponytail.

"Oh, captain . . . my captain."

The slightly flirting, melodic voice caught Jordan's attention. It was the red-haired Irishman who'd insisted that they fight back. He walked to her, flanked by several other disheveled men she recognized from business class. "What are you going to do when they come aboard?" he asked in his brogue. "They will, you know. We won't be able to keep them out for long."

"You don't know that."

He shrugged. "Pragmatism is my middle name. If they worked this hard to net the oyster, they'll work just as hard to pry open the shell. You need someone like me to stop them." He winked and gave her a killer smile.

She hardened herself to his European charm. "Who are you, anyway?"

"Ian Dillon—but I go by Dillon." His hand was warm as he shook hers. "Senior Vice President of Network Global Technologies. Based in Dublin. Million-miler, many times over."

Jordan was so rattled, it took her a second to realize that he'd given her his frequent-flyer credentials. "And your area of expertise is?"

"For one, I can take normal electronic gadgets and transform them into what might be useful to us."

"Like weapons?"

"Like weapons," he confirmed.

She and Ben exchanged glances. Was Dillon's plan rash? Maybe. Would it save them? It could. Or it might cause a lot more of them to wind up dead than if they simply co-operated. But maybe there wasn't a right answer. Maybe she was going to have to rely on gut instinct and lots of prayers.

"Okay. We don't have a lot in reserve for defense. Anything extra will help. Go ahead and gather what information and helpers you think you need for manufacturing the weapons. Just don't take any chances with my crew or the other passengers." She held up one finger. "Any and all plans of action go through me. I make the final decision. The *only* decision, Mr. Dillon. This is not a democracy. Understood?"

Ben appeared vaguely unsettled by her monologue. She could see why: she was beginning to sound like a character from an Arnold Schwarzenegger movie. Dillon, on the other hand, didn't seem bothered by her abruptness. In fact, he appeared to approve. "Understood," he said. "Now, Captain, I'd like to requisition the defibrillator for defensive purposes."

"The AED?" Ben frowned. "No dice. We might need it if someone has a heart attack."

"We do have two," Jordan reminded him. "But, Mr. Dillon, the AED delivers a shock only if it detects that one is needed. You can't use it to shock someone, if that's what you're thinking."

Dillon's mouth tipped, and he jerked his chin in the direction of her holster. "Whatever I come up with will be better than that toy gun you're sporting."

The man was right. If they were going to fend off an invading horde, they'd need more than a single stun gun. "Do it," she said.

Dillon gave her a two-fingered salute and walked back to his huddle of waiting businessmen. Jordan departed in the opposite direction, her hand resting on the stun gun. Back in the cockpit, she settled into the captain's seat—*her* seat now—and watched for any changes in the wide-open wall in front of the airplane. The wall was still too bright to look at directly and too intense to see past. So she sat there, waiting for something to happen, which was the worst kind of waiting there was.

Her watch beeped, telling the hour. It was eight a.m. at Jordan's parents' house. By now, Boo would be eating breakfast and watching cartoons. Then she'd go off to school, expecting to find Jordan waiting to pick her up at three when the kids poured onto the playground. Only this time, Mommy wouldn't be there.

Jordan tipped her head back and closed her eyes. This wouldn't be the first time that her airline job had wrenched apart her family. Craig, her deceased husband, had wanted to be a pilot, too. But she had been hired by an airline and he wasn't. Her home life went to hell after that. Craig stopped working and started drinking. God, sometimes he'd seemed more like a high-maintenance child than a husband. Her father and brother had never acted that way. Big hearts and quiet strength, that's what they had, the kind of guys who were there when you needed them. Why she'd sought different characteristics in a husband, she'd never know. Youthful inexperience maybe; Craig's emotional volatility and chattiness had been a novelty after the more reserved men of her household. It wasn't until later that she realized the magnitude of her mistake.

She'd tried to help him work through his jealousy, feelings of inadequacy and depression, but it was made painfully clear that she'd failed when his drinking culminated in a fatal head-on with a parked car. Roberta was only nine months old.

It had taken a long time, but finally, after months of counseling and the unwavering support of her close-knit family,

Jordan capitulated, accepting that she wasn't to blame. Now this: *She* might die as a result of her job, leaving Roberta with no parents at all. What a nightmarish example of circularity.

A soft tinkling sound broke into her glowering trance. Music. She lurched forward and squinted outside. The white radiance obliterating the wall had transformed into a sheet of light, undulating in a rainbow of colors. A melody played. Inexplicably beautiful. Eerily foreign. And hypnotic.

She tensed. Were the music and lights designed to soothe? Were they purposefully mesmerizing to put her off guard? She noticed that when she averted her eyes from the colors, the effect was not as strong. She pushed away from the instrument panel. If the hijackers wanted to drug her, they were going to have to try a lot harder than this.

Ben and Ann burst into the cockpit. "We're all ready down below," the purser announced. His gaze flew to where Jordan still stared. "When the hell did *that* start?"

"Just now." The music faded into a husky female voice enunciating words in a monotonous beat, as if she were counting numbers and not speaking.

"It sounds like words picked at random." Jordan cocked her head. "And in several different languages."

Ann said, "I speak Korean. She just said 'best wishes.'"

"I heard 'olive tree' in Spanish," Ben said. "And also 'blue.'"

On and on the verbal presentation went, with no apparent pattern. "Earth" was repeated many times, but the monologue might as well have been gibberish, so unrelated were the string of words.

Jordan sagged back in her seat. "How could they not know what language we speak? United Airlines is a flag carrier. The stars and stripes are painted on the fuselage. You can't miss it."

The voice went silent. The music ended, too. Then two people walked onto a platform that she hadn't noticed before in the shadows off the nose of the 747.

So . . . these were the people who had taken them.

The man and woman were fit and athletic. The man was tall, and he had medium brown hair, while the woman's was so blond that it was almost pure white. Her skin was unusually fair, almost pink. Was she an albino? The woman stood too far away to reveal whether her eyes were red.

"Behind them," Jordan murmured. "There are more."

At least four burly men loomed in the shadows behind the couple. Bodyguards? Soldiers? They wore similar clothing to the first pair, which struck Jordan as uniforms. Crisp, blue-gray jumpsuits with thick black belts, from which hung various pieces of hardware, some with illuminated faces and other things with blinking lights. Communications equipment? Hi-tech computers?

She could hear Ben's breathing accelerate. "They're armed," he said. "All of them."

Jordan nodded grimly. "I don't recognize all of what they've got on their belts, but it's hard to disguise a gun in a holster."

"Six people, six guns," Ann muttered. "At least. There have to be others. Whatever this thing we're in is huge. Who are they? Or what are they? Russians? Scandinavians? A white-collar terrorist group that doesn't give a rat's ass about international borders?"

Jordan shook her head. "I don't know."

"This is bad," Ben whispered shakily. "Real bad."

Jordan glanced over her shoulder. *Don't fall apart on me, Ben. I need you.* "Stay positive, you guys. They're acting calm. We have to, also." Bringing a damp hand to her neck, she rested her fingers over her throbbing pulse, willing it to slow, willing herself to calm down, to think clearly. To do the right thing. "The presence of those weapons means that they're damned serious about what they intend to do with our plane—and us. And it also says that it's no accident that we ended up here."

"Wherever *here* is," Ann muttered.

Hijacked, Jordan speculated, in a plot that defied anything she understood about modern-day technology.

The white-haired woman outside raised her hands in an obvious greeting—not quite warm, but still welcoming. Jordan didn't see malevolence in the man's face, either. But still, the four stony-faced guards stood behind them.

"She looks like she's trying to be friendly," Ann said.

Jordan huffed. "Forget it. We're not taking the bait. Unless they use explosives, they're not getting onboard this plane."

The albino woman brought what looked like a handheld computer close to her mouth. It must have been wired to the speaker system, because simultaneously a familiar husky voice boomed, the same one that had accompanied the music. In a strong accent, the woman repeated Jordan's exact words: "We're not taking the bait," she crooned. "Unless they use explosives, they're not getting onboard this plane."

"Oh, crap," Ben blurted.

Jordan fell back against her seat. " 'Oh, crap' is right. They just heard everything we said."

Chapter Four

"That didn't go over very well, Ensign," Kào stated as he watched the refugees flee the cockpit of their vessel from where he stood in the cargo bay with the four security guards and Trist Pren. "What did you say to them?"

"I'm not sure. I merely repeated some of their conversation." Trist's colorless, almost nonexistent brows drew together. "I assumed they'd find it more comforting than words issued randomly."

"Well, it didn't. It frightened them. Look at their craft," he said. "It reminds me of the type of craft the Alliance flew eons ago, in the early years of atmospheric travel. If their civilization has begun manned space travel, they haven't gotten very far. They might not recognize that they've been taken onto a spacecraft. We'll have to try another way to coax them out."

"How about turning their ship upside down and shaking them loose?" Trist typed data into her handheld. "Or we can cut off all power in the cargo bay, leaving them to cower in the dark until they grow hungry and filthy enough to be lured out with promises of food and showers." She pursed lips that were dyed permanently lavender. "More realistically, let's inundate the ship with sedative gas and render the ungrateful boors unconscious."

Kào battled exasperation. It was hard to forget what those of this woman's ancestors' world had done to his home and family. The albino race had been the scourge of the galaxy for many years. They had imprisoned him. Now he was forced to cooperate with one of them to achieve his goal of helping his father. And although he was hardly a diplomat, her aggressive solution rubbed even his military-trained senses the wrong way. "No, Trist. That's not the way we're going to do it." Aside from its cold almost Talagarian expediency, her plan did not account for human fear, which would certainly soar higher with such induced helplessness.

A series of slams came from the Earth craft. The sound was muffled, almost below his hearing. "They're closing the porthole coverings."

Trist made a sound of annoyance. "Now we can't see inside the craft."

"No matter. We can still talk"—he started walking toward the Earth craft—"in person."

"How?"

"By knocking on their front door. A smile and a gentle tone will work wonders, you'll see."

"Oh, my God! They're *coming*!"

Ann's shout drove a spear of pure terror into Jordan's soul. She kept control somehow, saying calmly, "Which door?"

"One-left."

Jordan cut short the security inspection she'd been performing and headed to the door, where the Marines stood guard. Dillon-the-Irishman still hadn't turned the AED into a weapon, but he promised her he was getting close. Either way, it was too late. The aircraft was as impenetrable as they could make it with limited materials and time.

Her stomach felt wobbly and her head hurt. She tried to work moisture into her mouth as she gripped the Taser in her sweaty hand. Outside the small, scratched window in the door, she saw the tall man pushing a portable stand toward the plane. Behind him walked the albino woman and the four guards.

With a clang, the stand settled against the side of the fuselage. Down below, the woman made hand signals. She wanted the door opened. Jordan frowned. "In your dreams, lady," she muttered.

Clearly thwarted, the woman exchanged glances with the man. He tapped what looked like a touch screen on the ladder—pretty hi-tech for a loading platform—and the stand ascended. The guards remained on the ground level, watching the plane.

Jordan turned to Ann. "Throw the switch."

Ann smiled. "With pleasure, Captain."

With a grunt, Ann yanked on the door handle, cracking the door ajar. The movement deployed the emergency escape slide, as advertised. An explosive screeching hiss pinched Jordan's eardrums as the life raft inflated instantly and formed a slide. Rock hard, it plowed into the ladder-platform, throwing it across the floor and scattering their would-be boarders like toy action figures.

"Woo hoo!" Ann yelled.

"You got that right." Quickly, Jordan helped the flight attendant detach the slide-raft from the door. The discarded slide fell heavily to the floor as they pulled the door closed.

Ben shouted over the megaphone: "Flight Fifty-eight—

one. Hijackers—zero!" The passengers cheered, and the flight attendants gave each other high fives.

Ann was breathless, her eyes bright with triumph and adrenaline. Jordan suspected she herself looked the same way. "We can move slides from the other doors if we need to, Captain. I don't think they're going to try this one for a while."

Jordan peeked outside. "I agree. They don't look very good." Three guards were kneeling over a fourth lying motionless on the floor as the tall, brown-haired man and the albino woman wobbled to their feet. Blood flowed from the pale-haired woman's nose. She tried to stanch it with her bare hands. Her partner showed no outward signs of injury, but judging by his contorted mouth and surly expression, he was furious. And he turned his attention to Jordan.

Hard and obsidian-black, his eyes remained focused on her for longer than was comfortable, a formidable, discerning stare. But Jordan scowled back at him. *He* was the evildoer. *He* was the one who stood between her and getting home. No way would she feel sorry for the guy.

The man turned to assist his wounded partner, and the guards lifted their comrade to his feet. As a group, they limped out of sight. "Good. They're leaving," Jordan said.

Natalie and Ben had joined her. "I doubt they'll try the door again," Ben said.

"If they wanted to, they could try the other doors, one at a time," Jordan pointed out. "And if they force us to blow all the slides, we'll have none."

Natalie shrugged. "We'll have to stay one step ahead. That's all there is to it."

"Exactly." Jordan managed a smile. They were beginning to sound like a team. A good team. For the first time since plunging into this catastrophe, she felt that they might really have a chance at getting home safely.

* * *

At a cargo handler's station behind a bank of computers hidden from the refugees' ship, Kào took a careful breath to see how his ribs stood the expansion of an inhalation. They burned, but the act of breathing didn't bring shooting pain, the sign of broken bones. Unfortunately, he was quite familiar with broken ribs and the healing process that followed. It was nice to think that, this time at least, his ribs had remained intact.

He reached for his comm and called medical. "Heest is down. Yes—from the security detail. He's unconscious, bleeding from a gash on his scalp."

With medical personnel on the way, Kào peered at Trist's face. "When they get here, you go with them, too."

She shook her head and mumbled something moist and unintelligible from behind a blood-smeared cloth.

"No arguments. Your nose is probably broken."

She moved the sodden cloth aside. Blood gushed from her nostrils. "I'm fine."

"You don't look fine."

"Is that so?" Trist replaced the cloth. Her red eyes narrowed to slits. "What about you?"

Yes, what about me? He almost laughed. He hardly felt anything anymore—a blessed condition of the spirit. However, he kept that fact to himself.

Trist didn't press him for an answer. He imagined she considered him an enigma, and he was more than happy to maintain that belief.

Heavily she sat on a chair and made a sound of reluctant assent. "They could have tried to talk to us before they attacked. Why didn't they? What is their problem?"

"I don't know. I'm not from their world." *Or yours,* he thought.

"They won't be able to stay on their craft much longer. Their water tanks are halfway to empty, and once the water is gone . . . well, the hygiene problems will be obvious. We photo-sterilized them after the rescue. What microorganisms we didn't kill I assume we can treat. But what if I'm wrong? We could lose them all to sickness. Such fools they are!" She pressed the cloth to her nose. "Use the sedative gas, Kào. It will simplify the evacuation."

"Trist, in order to assure them that we won't harm them, they should leave their ship of their own volition. Their trust will make the coming weeks inordinately more enjoyable. For me . . . and for you." This duty would be a nuisance as it was, working with unruly refugees and a sullen Talagar. Kào didn't need more trouble.

Her reddish irises flicked to his. She didn't look convinced. But then her area of expertise was code breaking and languages; she worked with consonants and vowels, not people. In that respect, she was as out of her league as he was—a weapons officer handed the most peculiar of tasks.

Several crew members from medical arrived with a buoyant stretcher for the injured security guard. Heest, the guard, moaned as they fitted a brace around his neck and lifted him off the floor. His pink-white, almost transparent skin was chalky.

"Look at him. I'd reconsider the sedative gas if I were you," Trist said over her shoulder before she walked somewhat unsteadily through the hatchway.

Exhaling, Kào ran his fingers through his close-cropped hair. People were so complicated and exasperating. He was at his best when dealing with machines: computers that oversaw shipboard weapons systems and targeted objectives with cold, emotionless precision. If only it were possible to deal with life in the same way.

Ah, but he was trying. It was those around him who refused to behave rationally.

He dug his remote viewer from his belt and called up the live image of the exterior of the refugees' vessel. All seemed peaceful, but he had a feeling this was only the beginning of the trouble they'd cause him. And then there were the weeks, perhaps months, to look forward to before the refugees were brought to the starport from where they would be relocated.

But if he was to bolster his father's good reputation, he needed the refugee situation to conclude peaceably, successfully—and soon.

Trist had gathered data during the brief time they had orbited Earth. Using that database, and what she'd collected from eavesdropping on conversations within the vessel, she said she'd be able to create a program to teach the refugees Key, the everyday language of the Alliance learned by all in addition to their own local planetary dialects.

When she returned from her nose repairs in medical, she went immediately to work on her computer in a section of the cargo bay hidden from the refugee vessel. Paler than even her normal coloring, she put the final touches on the program she'd created as three security guards waited silently nearby. Heest was done for the day. Possibly the week.

Trist's face contorted—in concentration, Kào guessed, not from the newly fused cartilage in her bruised nose.

"Update me," he said.

"Almost there." She continued typing. "I've completed the alphabetic conversion—theirs to ours and back again. But I'll need both phonetic confirmation and access to their personal computers before I finalize my instructional lessons." She set a small rectangular box on the table. There was a soft whirring noise as a door in the container opened. From the shallow inner compartment she extracted two pairs of conversion-glasses, sleek and dark. "Using these, whatever is said is written down and translated into their language and ours—Key."

"I read the words off the inside of the lenses," he confirmed.

"Yes. The text appears to float in front of your field of vision, between you and your subject. Even if you turn your head, the caption will remain in sight. I have only a few of these glasses at my disposal." She shrugged. "Just as well. A handheld aural translator works better. But until I program enough handhelds—hundreds, it would seem—the glasses are our only choice."

"No matter. They will make communication possible. I, for one, would like to avoid further misunderstandings. I suspect you would, too."

Trist's fingers crept toward her nose, her expression souring.

"Initial contact with any people cannot be a hasty process. I'll have to take my time. I expect it will take a while to explain the situation. Then I'll have to initiate the evacuation. I'll call you before I let anyone off the vessel, though."

"You're going alone?"

"I'm going alone."

A guard of Talagar ancestry named Poul protested. Kào knew that he was thinking of his partner, Heest, in medical with a concussion. "But, Mr. Vantaar-Moray, you asked for protection."

"I know what I asked of you. But circumstances have changed. The refugees reacted the way they did only because they're overwhelmed and frightened. If they see I'm unarmed and alone, I believe they'll listen to reason. I have my comm. If I have any trouble, you'll be the first to know. Trist, you remain here at the workstation and monitor the Earth craft remotely. Poul, you and your men take a position from where you can keep a watch on the vessel."

Poul nodded curtly and left with the three remaining security guards. Kào took the container with the glasses and began walking toward the refugees' craft. Once in the main part of the bay, Kào commenced the plan he had plotted out during Trist's absence. Reaching for the nearest wall-mounted touch-screen computer, he entered a confidential access code followed by a lengthy command, and the interior and exterior lights on the Earth vessel flickered on.

Power, he thought. The gift of normalcy. It was one of the ways he hoped to show the refugees that he meant no harm.

A few window shades covering the portholes lifted but slammed closed just as quickly. Undeterred, he began walking toward the vessel. The blond woman—he'd get her attention first. She was the Earth people's leader—he was sure of it. Her expression of triumph as the inflatable device roared out of the hatch wasn't one he'd soon forget. Yet her actions could be interpreted as nerve, a willingness to fight despite overwhelming odds. Not only had her defensive measures led to cracking his ribs and breaking Trist's nose, she'd knocked out a security guard who had to be twice her size, all to defend her vessel, which she'd probably assumed—rashly—was under attack. But he was going to give her a second chance to act civilized.

If she didn't kill him outright, he'd try his damnedest to woo her and her compatriots off the ship.

Chapter Five

Inside the main cabin of the 747, the lights had come back on. Their captors had turned on the power!

Why? Jordan thought. Did they want to buy trust in order to lure their captives off the plane? They were armed; they could have easily chosen force to ferret the passengers out of the aircraft. But they hadn't. Yet. Still, she couldn't afford to take any chances until she knew what they were all about.

A burning smell surfaced, mixed with other, nastier odors—the result of stagnant air. Natalie swore. "The electricity—it turned on the ovens, too!" She sprinted away with Ann and several other flight attendants to secure the galleys, killing a potential fire hazard.

"I'll be upstairs," Jordan told Ben. "If the ovens work, maybe the radios do, too. I'll send out as many emergency signals as I can—and in as many forms as I can."

"Call if you need me."

Contact

"Will do. Meanwhile, keep minding the store down here."

"Sure," he said, tugging on the cuffs of his sleeves, something she noticed he did when he was nervous.

She paused by the stairwell to the upper deck, one hand resting on the railing. "You okay?" she asked him.

"Well." He swallowed twice. "I don't want to die."

She held herself very still. "None of us do."

He hesitated before answering. "I believe in heaven, an afterlife. You know. But what if there isn't one? I mean, what if your soul just blows out and you cease to exist?" He squeezed the handrail. His knuckles were white. "I don't want that."

As the mother of a child that she very much wanted to see again, Jordan didn't know what to say. It'd be easy to break down, to voice her fears, but she couldn't. She was the leader, and she needed to appear strong, confident, even when she felt like curling into a ball and weeping. "It's normal to be scared," she said tentatively.

He nodded, but she knew she hadn't convinced him, just as she hadn't been able to lift Craig out of his doldrums, her husband's constant state in the last years of their marriage. *Don't think of that. Not now.* Sighing, she rested her hand on Ben's forearm and squeezed. "Hang in there. Stay strong for me. I need you. You're doing a great job—a fantastic job. Keep it up."

His face creased into a haggard smile. "Thanks."

She gave him another squeeze and tried to return his smile. Then she pulled herself up the stairs.

Numb, she stepped around Brian's blanket-draped body and trudged into the cockpit. The instruments were indeed powered, and she intended to take advantage of that.

"This is United Flight Fifty-eight," she said into the radio handset. "Does anyone read?"

There was no side-tone, the sound in the speaker that

55

indicated the radio was working. She tried all the radios, and various frequencies, but with the same frustrating result. Her hand slid down to the console between the seats. Even if the radios didn't work, maybe the transponder would be functional and would bring help in their direction—wherever *that* was.

First, she dialed in "7500" on the aircraft's transponder, and followed it with the code "7700." The emergency numbers were used to alert air traffic control that they had both a hijacking-in-progress and an emergency. Only after transmitting her emergency messages did she notice that the tall, dark-eyed man was standing outside, in front of the plane. More importantly, he was alone. The goons who had accompanied him before were nowhere to be seen. The albino woman was absent, too.

Hands on his hips, he waited patiently for her attention. When he saw that she watched him, he withdrew his gun—or what she assumed was a gun—from his belt and laid it on the floor. A gesture of peace? Palm toward her, fingers spread, he raised his right hand. He paused, as if expecting her to respond.

She mirrored his gesture, and somehow withheld the powerful urge to show him her middle finger.

He brought his hand to his mouth and then pointed at her. He wanted to talk to her. Well, she could certainly do that without letting him inside, she thought.

Walking away, he disappeared from view under the fuselage of the aircraft. Then it hit her: Door 1-L. It was the only door that didn't have a slide! An unprotected entrance.

Her heart flipped in her chest, and she dashed out of the cockpit, leaping over Brian's body. Bolting downstairs, she shouted, "Take your stations!" The flight attendants echoed her call. Passengers and crew darted in all directions. The children—there were fourteen under twelve, three of those infants—took shelter in the bulkhead between economy and business class, along with three pregnant women to watch them.

The efficiency of their defensive preparations surprised Jordan. Many passengers had passed the hours sleeping, having succumbed to shock, exhaustion, and poor air quality. Others showed symptoms resembling those of motion sickness. Already the air was rank with the odor of feces and vomit. Before long, all their lavatories would be clogged and unusable. But when called upon to defend the plane, none of that mattered. "Natalie, Ben, we need a slide-raft at One-Left! *Now*—"

Mid-shout, she crashed into Dillon, the red-haired Irishman. He was slim, but he was as solid as a bank safe. She stumbled backward and fell hard on her rear. A businessman caught Dillon, but the AED he'd clutched went flying—into the hands of one of the Marines, Garrett Brown, who caught the defibrillator like a football.

From where she was sprawled in the middle of the first-class aisle, Jordan felt as if she were watching a screwball comedy. Unfortunately, her sense of humor was at an all-time low. Would this have happened to the typical, Hollywood-version, six-foot-plus, gray-haired airline captain with the Oklahoma twang? She doubted it.

The Marine, Garrett, helped her to her feet. Her chest stung and her eyes watered as she tried to catch her breath. Then he gave her the AED, and she balanced it in her shaking hands as Dillon apologized profusely. "I'm sorry, Captain. But I couldn't wait to tell you. It's ready."

Jordan's eyes shifted to the device in her arms. "You mean it works?"

Dillon grinned. "I had to cannibalize my laptop and a couple of cell phones, but, yes, I think it'll work beautifully."

"It'll shock someone?"

"It'll shock the bloody hell out of someone."

"Will it . . . kill someone?" she asked carefully.

"Depends on where you aim it and how long you hold it there." Dillon's singsong brogue made her wish he was describing purple horseshoes and four-leaf clovers instead of how to electrocute another human being.

The flight attendants had gathered around them. "What's going on?" Ben asked.

"One of them wants to talk to us. Again."

Frightened murmurs rippled through the crowd of eavesdroppers.

"This time he's alone. And I think we do need to open a line of communication."

The murmurs turned into shouts. Not for the first time, Jordan wished she was deep in the anonymous sea of onlookers and not in the spotlight—not the leader forced into making life-or-death decisions for all of them. "He's alone, and he made a big show of putting down his weapon. Now he's down there, waiting for us to open One-Left. Is a slide ready?" The folded and stowed slide rafts were heavy, but they were designed to be ported from door to door if necessary.

Ann called over the crowd. "It's ready to go."

"Good."

Ben tugged nervously on his sleeves. "Now what, Captain?"

Jordan sighed. "Conditions are poor and growing worse. So far, no one's come to our aid or answered our distress call. None of the cell phones work. The airplane radios don't work. We're trapped in this . . . thing, and we don't know how long they intend to hold us here. Do you agree?"

"Our water and food won't last forever," Ann conceded. "And the babies will need milk."

Ben echoed those concerns. "The rear lavatories and two forward ones are already full and locked. By the end of the day, we'll lose the rest."

"Then I say we have no choice but to talk to him." Grim, Jordan lifted the sunshade covering the window nearest 1-L. Through the inch-high slit, she saw the tall man waiting for her below the door, his arms crossed over his chest. At the movement of the shade, his gaze jerked upward. She snapped the covering closed and turned to her crew. "But no one says we have to let him come aboard. We can shout to each other through the open exit. Keep me covered with whatever weapons we have. If any of his buddies look like they're going to come aboard, or shoot, or set off explosives, we deploy the slide."

Natalie raised her hand.

Jordan nodded. "A question?"

"No. An idea: Let's take him hostage."

Jordan's jaw dropped. Natalie's flawless nut-brown skin was accentuated by dozens of tiny braids worn pulled back into a thick ponytail, revealing an open, pretty face that was totally at odds with her aggressive suggestion. "You want me to take him *hostage*?" Jordan asked.

"Well, yes. Not just you. We'll all help."

Dillon waggled the AED paddles. "Once we get him on the plane, we can incapacitate him."

A squeak bubbled up in Jordan's throat. She listened, stunned, as one of the two doctors offered, "I saw Valium in the emergency medical kit. Once you get him pinned, I'll give him an injection. It'll put him right out."

"And then we'll have one of them," Natalie summed up. "There's nothing like a little leverage."

"Leverage." Jordan snorted. "He won't be easy to over-power." She doubted the guy had an ounce of body fat.

"The stun gun," Ann reminded her.

"Right." Jordan almost blushed. In the quest for do-it-yourself methods of attack, she'd forgotten about the best weapon she had. She withdrew the gun from her pocket, testing the weight of it in her hand.

59

"The Advanced Taser—the third generation of Taser Technology conducted energy weapons," Ben said, as if reciting text. "Capable of sending a series of electrical signals called Taser waves or T-waves similar to those used by the brain to communicate with the body. Like radio jamming, the T-waves overpower the normal electrical signals within the body's nerve fibers."

Everyone stared at the purser as he droned on, a faraway look in his dark brown eyes. "The human target instantly loses control of his body and cannot perform coordinated action, falling to the ground." He lifted his brows. "I guess it'll do the job."

Jordan whistled softly. "That was almost word for word out of the training tech manual."

"It *was*." He shrugged. "I have a photographic memory. It comes in handy sometimes."

"Yeah. I bet it does." She stored away the discovery about Ben.

Natalie spoke up. "Once he's down, we have handcuffs to keep him there. Plenty of them."

"Exactly." The nylon cuffs were a staple of every aircrew member's suitcase. They used them for everything from quick-fixing broken seats to quelling unruly passengers. Jordan was pretty sure they'd be the first airline crew to use the handcuffs to take a hostage, though. "So we incapacitate him, cuff him, and drug him. Then we've got our hostage. At that point, we'll be able to negotiate for his release—and hopefully ours."

Everyone fell silent. Jordan pushed her hair away from her forehead. Was she doing the right thing? Hell, what was the right thing?

Her gaze drifted toward the still-closed door. The man was out there, waiting. He was probably wondering why she hadn't appeared yet. She blinked away an image of him lying bound and unconscious on the floor of the main cabin and forcibly replaced it with one of herself, back home, burying her face in Boo's hair. The thought fortified her.

"Ben," she said. "I've got extra handcuffs in my flight bag upstairs. Brian had some, too. Bring them downstairs and have them ready to go. Oh, and the crash ax, too. You'll find it in the cockpit, left side, next to the fire extinguisher." It was a heavy, sharp killer of an ax. She couldn't imagine they'd have to use it. But like Dillon's turbocharged AED, it would be a good deterrent and a welcome addition to the Taser.

Coolly she glanced at everyone in turn. "If this goes badly, we're dead meat—you know that, right?"

"We're dead meat any way you cut it if we don't do something soon," Ben said.

Ann wrinkled her nose. "Enough with the food talk. We've got too much of it rotting in the galleys as it is." They all laughed, despite feeling anything but lighthearted.

When Ben returned, Jordan handed the Taser to Garrett. Though he was an admin specialist, he was, after all, a Marine. "You know how to use one of these, right?"

"Yes, ma'am."

"When he climbs inside, nail him."

Garrett's hazel eyes sparked. "Yes, ma'am!"

"Everyone else, stand clear." The crowd backed up. Jordan said a silent prayer. Then she reached for the door handle with both hands and yanked it open.

Chapter Six

When the forwardmost hatch of the refugees' craft finally opened, Kào saw the blond woman standing in the opening. It was then he knew he'd been correct in assuming that she was the leader.

He slipped on the translation glasses. The other pair awaited use, protected in its case.

"I'm ready to talk," she shouted down to him.

Text scrolled in front of his vision: her words presented in his alphabet and language, Key, the common dialect of the Alliance. *I am ready to talk.*

Her smile was false. But he read no threat in her eyes as she gestured for him to come up to where she waited.

It made perfect sense; distance made it difficult to converse. Using aching muscles that disagreed with his demand for exertion, he wheeled the movable stand to rest against the vessel's gray and blue fuselage. As he rode the ascending platform, a headache reminded him that after all the months in solitary confinement, his tolerance for being among people, interacting with them, talking, relating, engaging, all waned after a few hours.

This never-ending day had called for a marathon of interaction. As soon as the refugees were tucked in their beds, he'd withdraw to the peace of the observation deck with its 360-degree view of the stars. There he found rare peace, private solace, the solitude he required before seeking sleep in his equally empty quarters.

The platform stopped level with the Earth vessel. Moist, stale air and a vaguely foul odor wafted from the open hatch. Conditions aboard had already deteriorated. No wonder: They had kept the exits sealed, leaving little ventilation.

The refugee leader stood just inside the exit. She was perspiring, and her white shirt was grubby. Epaulets on her shoulders indicated that the outfit was a uniform. Three gold strips on dark blue, a rank of some sort. Now that he had a better view of her, he saw that a smattering of freckles dotted her nose. Black was smudged under her eyes, appearing to have been rubbed off from a substance coating her long lashes. The purest of blues, those eyes were. Not the icy blue he often saw, but a warm color, like that of a tropical sea. He'd seen one once, a sea. Having spent more time on starships than he had on land, thanks to his adoptive father's career, he wasn't widely traveled when it came to planets. But once, on a stopover long ago as a boy, he'd visited an ocean, swum in it even. Ah, what a wondrous day that had been—

By the Seeders! Now was not the time for reminiscences; nor was it appropriate, or professional, to think of her as . . . *female*. Her disarming appearance might resemble the images his fellow soldiers had kept of their mates, women who waited for them at home, a different breed than the space-weary, battle-forged females Kào had worked with—

and slept with—during the war, but he knew better than to let down his guard. Heest was hospitalized with a head injury, Trist had a broken nose, and he'd suffered injured ribs, all because he'd underestimated the Earth leader, turning what should have been a simple transfer of refugees into a standoff. He would not miscalculate again.

In a traditional Alliance show of respect, he made a slight bow and spread his hand over his chest. "I am Kào Vantaar-Moray, emissary of the Alliance Perimeter Patrol ship *Savior*. I come in peace."

She squinted, as if trying to see his eyes through his glasses, and spoke slowly, as if not yet certain he could understand. "Take off your belt."

Translated properly—he hoped—into Key, her words scrolled across the lenses of the glasses. He unhooked his belt and laid it on the platform. He didn't need it; his comm was on his wrist computer, and he'd tucked the other pair of conversion-glasses in his chest pocket. "I brought a language translator for you—" He reached for his pocket, and she froze.

He showed her his empty hands. "I will not hurt you." He wasn't a gentle man in appearance, and particularly not since the war, but if his face couldn't convey his meaning, he hoped his tone would. "I come in peace. To help you."

The woman stepped aside, beckoned to him.

Through the hatch, he saw no people and no obstructions. In the back of his mind, he yearned for the reassurance of a pistol in his hand. But he saw welcome in the refugee leader's eyes, and worry in her drawn expression. He had to take the chance. The resolution of the situation—the way *he* wanted it—depended on her trust.

With one last breath of fresh air, he climbed inside the craft.

Light exploded in his eyes. His muscles seized, cutting

off his abruptly indrawn breath. The floor came up to meet him so swiftly that he never felt the pain of the impact.

Garrett and Ben dragged the unconscious hijacker away from the door and laid him on the floor in the first-class cabin.

"Get the cuffs on him!" Jordan shouted, pacing back and forth in front of the man's body. His lips were parted, but they had color, telling her that he was still alive. A miracle. The stun gun had caused his muscles to contract, painfully. Not only had it brought him crashing down to a fetal position, it had knocked him out cold.

"Bind his ankles, too." Her mouth was dry and her arms and legs quivered. She was flying high with adrenaline, unable to stop moving as she supervised her team immobilizing the hijacker.

They did it. They actually did it! But what would they bring upon themselves as a consequence?

She paced, wringing her hands. Strange, she'd never been a hand-wringer. But, hell, she had so much anxiety and energy spewing out of every pore, she didn't know what to do with it.

The men cinched the restraints around the hijacker's wrists and ankles. "Not too tight," she cautioned. Lord, she couldn't believe she actually cared if his circulation was cut off. The man was probably a terrorist, likely a murderer. And she pitied him? For crying out loud, it was a good thing she hadn't followed her father's footsteps and served in the Air Force. She would have wept over every target she had to bomb.

"There." Ben stood and wiped his hands. "Trussed and bound."

"And ready for interrogation," Dillon said, readying the AED.

"Put that down," Jordan ordered. "He won't do us any good dead."

Dillon shrugged. His contingent of business-class men looked disappointed. "But is he going to do us any good alive? We haven't broken the language barrier yet."

"No." Jordan made a sound of frustration. "Why would anyone go through the trouble of plotting and executing a hijacking without bothering to learn basic English? It doesn't make sense! Look at him—he's clean cut and well fed. He had to have picked up at least one major language during his education."

An Indian man with a heavy accent spoke up. "He has seen American TV and movies. I know. Your shows play all over the world, even where they are banned."

"And don't forget the Internet," said Dillon.

Ben nodded his agreement. "I bet he's lying, and he *does* understand us."

"But how would that help?" Jordan argued. "It's only slowed things down."

The pediatrician, who had been checking the unconscious man's vitals, beckoned to Jordan. "Check this out."

Jordan crouched next to her. Carefully the doctor rotated the man's head so Jordan could see behind his right ear. A row of unfamiliar letters or numbers was etched permanently into his flesh. Six symbols, crisp-edged with no distortion.

Jordan cringed, shuddering involuntarily. Whatever had carved those symbols into his skin must have cut through to the tendons. "What is that?" she asked.

"Barbaric," the doctor said with disgust. "It's a brand. One made with an extremely high temperature. And behind his ear! The things people will do to decorate themselves."

Jordan had Ben summon the passengers, a few at a time, to read the markings. Though some understood languages as diverse as Hebrew, Cantonese, and Greek, no one could identify the runes.

But to Jordan, the markings looked less like tattooing than like identification. Unexpectedly, she felt a twist of sympathy for the man. Who knew what kind of background he'd come from? It couldn't have been good, if he'd ended up in this line of work, terrorizing innocent people. And history had proven that atrocious childhoods could leech every ounce of compassion out of a person. For the sake of them all, Jordan prayed that this man's heart was still human.

The doctor put the medical equipment she'd used back into the emergency medical kit. "Well, for what it's worth, I also find it hard to believe that he doesn't speak English. He looks as American as the Marlboro man."

Natalie snorted. "The Marlboro man crossed with Attila the Hun."

At first that struck Jordan as a strange observation. But the more she studied their hostage, the more she saw that his appearance was one of contrasts. Stark contrasts. He was indeed long and lanky, like a well-built cowboy. But there was nothing laid-back about him. His body was taut, tense, like a coiled spring, even in unconsciousness. His good looks weren't classic; they were brutal. Nicely formed lips didn't quite soften a severe, unforgiving mouth, and all he needed was a monocle to go with the pale, needle-thin scar that crossed his right eyebrow and ran all the way to his jaw. His skin was bronze-toned, yet fair enough to show the shadow where he'd shaved, medium brown stubble, matching his neatly trimmed hair.

He was well groomed; that should make her feel better. But she remembered those black eyes behind his closed lids and shivered involuntarily.

She sat back on her heels. "Check him for concealed weapons, identification. Anything. Ben, help me out."

Garrett aimed the Taser while Jordan and Ben bent to the task of frisking the hostage. Dillon gripped the overhauled, supercharged AED, and Natalie appeared poised to rip out the guy's throat with her lacquered fingernails.

Jordan pulled a hard, hand-size black oblong case from the man's right chest pocket. It looked like a fancy holder for eyeglasses. The light pressure of her fingers caused the lid to open, revealing the contents. "Glasses." It was comforting to learn she'd been right, she thought, and handed the case to Ann to examine more closely.

"Here's more," Rich, another flight attendant, said as he walked toward the group huddled on the floor. "This was the pair he was wearing when we zapped him."

Ann stored both pairs of glasses in the case. Ben stopped his search at the man's left forearm. "There's something here." He pushed the sleeve higher. "Whoa. Look at this."

Jordan leaned closer. "I think it's a watch. Or a computer. Or both." The device fit like a cuff on the man's lower forearm. Riddled with optic fibers and minuscule blinking lights, it was labeled with letters she recognized from the items he'd worn on his belt. "Technology like this costs money. A lot of money."

"All the more reason to question why the guy doesn't speak English, German, French, or any other widely known language," Natalie pointed out.

Ben muttered, "Look at the face of that watch. If it is a watch."

Jordan's attention shifted to a round dial in the center of the cuff. It had *nine* digits on its circular face, not twelve. Gingerly, Jordan reached for it. There was a low-pitched beep. She jerked backward as the digits floated off the face, fluid and featureless, as if they were made of liquid mercury.

"What the hell is that?" Natalie blurted.

"Tell me it's not a timer for a bomb," Ben muttered drearily.

"Pow! Pow! Die, spaceman!"

They whirled around. A very serious little boy was aiming a plastic *Star Wars* pistol at the out-cold hijacker.

His mother swept him up in her arms. "He's not a spaceman, Christopher," she said as she hurried him away to a safer distance. "He's a bad man."

"Yeah! He's Darth Vader! P-pow!" Christopher continued shooting over his mother's shoulder.

As the woman hauled her son to the rear of the plane, it grew quiet in the first-class cabin. Very quiet. Everyone gaped at the unconscious man's wrist computer with new understanding and dawning fear. The three-dimensional digits twirled in place just above the flat circular surface like nine miniature silver ballerinas. Jordan had never seen anything like it. On Earth.

Her heart rate doubled. Instinctively her fingers flew to the photo she'd stowed in her shirt pocket. Drawing on an inner reserve of strength that came from her overwhelming desire to see her child again, she tried to appear calm for the sake of those around her. But slowly, inexorably, her mind opened to a new and terrifying possible scenario like eyes adjusting to a darkened room: United Flight 58 had been abducted by aliens.

Chapter Seven

Kào was a boy again, a small boy, sitting astride a huge, muscular horse. The rhythm of its gait rippled through his body, and they rode as one. Where the sun should have risen, odd, greenish lightning erupted, sending rainbow-colored waves rolling across the sky like ripples on a soap bubble. Painful surges echoed in Kào's ears as the horse pitched recklessly forward. Clouds the color of an ugly bruise boiled closer; the stench of ozone was so thick that he could taste it. The heavens were about to rain down upon them all.

But he and the horse were trapped, imprisoned by a fence, tall and rough-hewn. The vast corral was a staple of this fearsome place, a barrier as enduring and ever-present as the wind and the sky. Lightning flashed again, closer now. Kào's eardrums pinched painfully. The horse reared up, front hooves pedaling. Kào clutched leather reins, pressed skinny, sinewy legs to the saddle. "Jump," he cried out.

But no one could help them; no one could hear.

The image distorted. He was running now. The ground burned the soles of his shoes. Half blinded by light that seared his skin, he couldn't find his mother or father. Then a bird appeared before him, a bird of prey whose wings were made of flame, turning the sky into an inferno. He thought it had come to save him, but fire exploded in his head.

The dream split in two, then split again, until he faced a mosaic of nightmares, darker images, of unrepentant cruelty, of torture never-ending. He was older, and a pink-skinned, fine-boned hand gripped a blade. The blade sliced his face, temple to chin. Poison seeped into the cut, molten agony. They wanted him to talk, but he had nothing to tell them. They wanted to break him, but he was no longer whole. At first, they couldn't make him scream. Later, they could make him utter any sound they liked.

Images whirled and shattered. He was the boy on the horse once more, powerless, both of them. The horse raced toward the mighty fence. It would try to jump, to shatter the barrier with powerful hind legs. Kào's heartbeat thumped with dread, and with hope. The horse whinnied, rearing high. Instinctively Kào clamped down with his legs until his thighs trembled, but he slipped backward.

The scene shifted, splintering into a montage of impotence and pain. The screams, he could never tell who made them, but they ricocheted in his mind. Laser burns. Body stretched to the breaking point. Water poured down his throat. No air! He fought to free his limbs. His arms were paralyzed; his legs, too. . . .

"Can't breathe!" Kào sucked in a mighty breath and jerked awake. His heart hammered. His skull ached. Tipping his head back, he stifled a groan.

Blast it all. The dream. Always the same. A powerful horse trapped in a corral. And Kào, a small boy, on its back. If not for the terror of trying to keep from sliding off the creature's back, and the snatches of horror left from his time as a POW, the sensation of riding would have been one of utter exhilaration. His ancestors were horsemen, fierce, in-

71

dependent folk. Riding was in his blood, or so he'd been told. But as far as he knew, he'd never sat upon one of the beasts in his life.

He heard a voice, female and foreign-tongued. Blinking, he tried to clear his vision, while his mind remained muzzy from the vivid dream. A woman appeared in his narrow circle of sight. The Earth leader. She leaned over him, her expression a mix of anger, sympathy, and fear.

He struggled to move. Razor-sharp pain bit at his wrists and ankles. He was bound. And he must have thrashed about in his dream, causing the restraints to cut into his skin.

Other refugees gathered around. The air was warm, stagnant. It smelled of rotting food, of human waste, and more strongly of fear. He was familiar with the scent of fear, and he forced back the memories that acrid scent raised in him.

His attention shifted back to the blond commando, whose face paled when she saw the blood seeping from where the binding had cut into his right wrist. Vivid blue eyes scrutinized him, her jaw flexing as she gritted her teeth. It was evident that she felt guilty. And she deserved to.

Incorrigible troublemaker, he thought irritably. She was the bane of his existence. And now she'd taken him hostage. It seemed he'd escaped his nightmare for a reality just as maddening. He could only imagine what Trist was going to say about this.

"Impetuous fools," he scolded the refugees, though he knew they didn't understand. "Do you have any idea how you've complicated matters? Is civilized behavior not possible for you? If not, it's going to prove a very long journey to your relocation point—for all of us." *Particularly for me.*

His exasperation made little impact on the leader. She regarded him strangely. Repelled and engrossed. Fearful and fascinated. Her face gave away so much of her inner

72

emotions that he stored away the discovery to use in the time to come.

"My glasses," he told her. "We need them in order to communicate. Bring them to me." He tried to gesture with his bound hands, but everyone tensed. A man, flame-haired and sharp-featured, held a device that Kào assumed was a weapon, and his expression reflected a disconcerting eagerness to do him bodily harm.

Again he tried to communicate what he needed. This time he was more insistent, and waited until he had the Earth leader's full attention before he gestured to his eyes.

To his relief, she understood. A shorter female crew member gave the glasses to the leader, who then turned to Kào and offered them to him.

He fumbled trying to put them on with bound hands. The leader saw his difficulty and helped him. Her warm hands slid over his cheeks. Soft skin. Firm fingers.

A frisson of awareness shot along his spine.

He held himself very still, avoided meeting her gaze. How could an accidental caress spark desire in a body and soul he'd left for dead? He didn't know what to think of that, or of the women whose touch had affected him so. But now was not the time or place for further reflection. "The other conversion-glasses," he said, and gestured. "Put them on now."

As she donned the glasses, an array of primitive weapons remained aimed distressingly at various parts of his anatomy. He pretended to ignore them, just as he habitually disregarded the stares aimed at him by his father's crew. The latter were to be expected, he supposed—the stares. Not only was he the commodore's son, he was an infamous ex-soldier with a spectacular military failure in his file. Which of the two conjured more speculation? Who knew? He wasn't motivated to figure it out.

Frowning, he gathered his thoughts and focused on his

task. The first lines of dialogue would set the tone for the rest of their conversation. "We gathered a vast amount of data during the brief time we orbited Earth," he began.

The Earth leader's hands shot up, presumably to tear off the conversion-glasses. But she must have recognized the translation of his words scrolling across the inside of the lenses, for her arms froze in midair.

"What is it, Jordan?" the male crew member demanded, and Kào read the words as they were translated. "It's too dangerous. Take them off—"

She waved her hand. "Shush!"

Kào continued slowly, enunciating each word. "Using that database," he explained, "and what was collected in recording your conversations within your vessel, the ship's linguist was able to translate much of your language into ours, Key. Do you see the words I speak in my language presented as captions in yours?"

Streams of data flickered behind the leader's lenses. Her lips parted slightly as she took in information that he hoped she'd comprehend. "Yes . . ."

"What's happening?" her people asked her. "What's going on?"

"The glasses are translating his words. I see them floating in front of me." She tried to reach for them, but of course her fingers closed over nothing but air. "It's incredible. The technology . . ."

Her explanation launched intense muttered discussion among the refugees. Some of what Kào heard was translated by the conversion-glasses. Much was lost.

She gave her people a halting summary of what he'd said. Mayhem followed. Not all of what they said translated properly. He watched their body language and guessed that they were arguing about his origins.

One of the females dressed similarly to the leader made a panicky sound of dismay. She tucked her arms to her chest and blurted, "Heaven help us. He's an *alien!*"

"Oh, puhleeze," another uniformed woman said. She was taller, darker-skinned, and sported long, curved claws on the ends of her fingers. "He looks too human to be an alien."

"Well, he doesn't look like a terrorist, either."

"What exactly does a terrorist look like, Ann, if you don't mind my asking?"

The shorter, rounder female's gaze settled on him. "I don't know," she said softly. "He just doesn't look . . . evil."

Her companion snorted. "Right. Ted Bundy's dates said that about him, too."

The Earth leader made a sound of exasperation. With her forearm she wiped damp hair away from her forehead and exchanged a glance with her male co-worker that revealed her impatience with her crew. She appeared to have control of these people, but on the fringes disorder simmered. Babies cried and older children whined; the air was thick with odors; adult voices combined in hushed conversation and shouts. Body odor was rife. So many people of so many ages and backgrounds, drawn together by fate. Yet their animated humanity attracted him.

It occurred to Kào how sterile his shipboard life had been since his release. Orderly, predictable. Not at all like this chaos, this assault on his senses. To his shock, he couldn't deny that he found the experience fascinating, almost pleasurable, in a way he couldn't quite grasp. It stirred something deep within him, that much was certain. It was clear that he shared something in common with these people, something that no one else onboard the *Savior* did.

They were orphans of destroyed worlds, he and these refugees. Survivors, who could never return home. At the time Moray had rescued him, Kào had been too young to comprehend his loss. But as an adult, he felt it as a deficit in his soul, an intuitive grief that was an integral part of him. Only now, among these Earth survivors, did he have a hunch as to what it was that he'd lost.

Kào exhaled, laid his aching head back as the noise of the arguing refugees blended with the buzzing in his skull. True, he'd taken on this task because his father had asked. But in doing so, he could assist these displaced people, as Moray had helped him all those years ago.

"Quiet!" the leader's male partner shouted. "She can't concentrate, and he can't hear her."

The noise subsided somewhat. The leader leaned over Kào. "Do you understand me?" she asked.

He waited for her words to be displayed in Key. "Yes, I do," he replied.

She read the translated caption. Then her words came forth in a rush. "Where—? Where are you—?"

Too fast. He couldn't understand half the questions. They translated as gibberish. "Speak slower."

That appeared to be an effort for her. "Where are we? Where are you taking us? Why are we here?" she asked.

The crowd of refugees pressing in all around them quieted. *Where are we? Where are you taking us?* The questions he most dreaded answering were those they most wanted answered, of course.

"We are aboard the Perimeter Patrol ship *Savior*, commanded by Commodore-elite Ilya Moray. We came upon your world, Earth, quite by accident. Our normal duty is to range along the Perimeter, the border between the farthest reaches of explored space and the central Alliance worlds."

The Earth leader gave a quick, anguished laugh. "That can't be right." Her eyes beseeched him to agree.

"Do not be afraid. You're safe now. All of you."

She sat back on her haunches, her knuckles pressed to her stomach.

"Jordan, what is it?" her shorter female colleague asked her. "What's wrong?"

Her voice held the slightest of trembles, barely discernable, but it was there nonetheless. "He insists that we're up in space."

Several people screamed.

"Quiet, please," her cohorts shouted.

But the leader—Jordan?—didn't answer. She continued to stare at him over her conversion-glasses. Her cordial demeanor was gone, replaced by shock, fear, and heart-piercing resentment. "You abducted us. You took us on your starship."

At that, some cried out; others wept. More voices, louder voices, made it difficult to tell whose words he read.

"Be quiet!" he shouted. The uproar ceased immediately. His tone they could interpret, if not his words. "You were not abducted. You were *rescued*."

The leader pressed the side of her index finger to her upper lip. Kào's frankness seemed to have mollified her somewhat, although even after she'd read the translation, he wasn't certain she believed him. "Explain how you rescued us when there was nothing wrong with our airplane."

"*Kào—where are you! Report!*" A voice emanated from Kào's wrist comm: loud, demanding. Nasal.

Blast it all. It was Trist. And she suspected, rightly, that something had gone wrong. He had little doubt that she'd react badly, too. He had to prevent that. "Trist!" he called out, sitting up. The pull of his abdominals was hell on his bruised ribs.

"I am safe—"

The flame-haired man with the strange weapon shoved his heel into Kào's chest and pushed him backward.

Kào's head hit the carpeted floor with a thud. The ceiling spun above him. Black spots flooded his vision. But he managed to stay conscious—a talent he'd often cursed during Talagarian torture sessions.

A scuffle dragged his attention upward. He squinted, try-

Susan Grant

ing to focus. Jordan jumped to her feet. "What the hell are you doing, Dillon!" she shouted, shoving Kào's attacker backward. Her male co-worker stepped between them and took over. Kào adjusted his conversion-glasses and tried to follow the conversation. Too many voices. And the cadence was too swift. But he caught enough of the discussion to follow along—barely.

"You are *not* a member of my crew," Jordan scolded as her co-worker held on to the man's arm. "Do you understand, Mr. Dillon? You do nothing unless my flight attendants or I order it. Or I swear—I'll use that AED on your head."

The man was clearly surprised by her vehemence. "I thought we didn't want him talking to his comrades."

Jordan pulled off the glasses. "You've heard only my half of the conversation. He told his partner that he's okay— *okay*? I would have stopped him myself if it had been anything I deemed dangerous. No more interference in my negotiations. *None*." Sliding on the glasses, she stalked back to Kào, muttering to herself. "Everyone's a vigilante."

"I would advise your overeager friend not to try another stunt like that," Kào told her. He was an expert in unarmed combat, and although he hadn't practiced his skills lately, he was certain they'd be more than sufficient to knock this nuisance onto his rear.

After an awkward pause that characterized their caption-guided dialogue, the Earth leader threw a disgusted glance at the flame-haired man. "I've dealt with the problem."

"Good." Kào's ribcage creaked ominously, sending streaks of fire across his chest and abdominals as he sat up. His ribs had gotten worse. Perhaps they were broken after all.

"*Kào!*" It was Trist calling again. "*Show me your face. I want proof that you're all right, or I'm calling security to storm the ship.*"

78

Blast her impatience! It seemed he, too, was caught dealing with crew members eager to take matters into their own hands. "Stand by, Ensign! Do not send security up here."

"Security?" Jordan asked, alarmed. "Do you mean police? Soldiers?"

"I asked her not to send them," he said. "In return I ask that you trust me."

Kào placed his hand over her forearm in a gesture meant to convey sincerity. The damp heat of her skin raced up his arm. They jerked away from each other—Jordan regarding him as she touched her fingers to the place where he'd laid his hand, and he confounded by the awareness that had sparked between them. But now was not the time or place to reflect on the matter.

He cleared his throat. "I'm going to go to the doorway now and show myself, so that my people see that I am safe. But you'll need to release me."

She conferred with her crew. Then a male co-worker broke off from the group and freed Kào's ankles from the binding.

"Ensign Pren!" Kào called out. "I'm coming to the exit now. Do not take any action. I repeat, do *not* take any action." As he climbed to his feet, his extremities tingling and sore, the interior of the Earth vessel plunged into darkness.

Chaos erupted all over again.

Fury and betrayal blazed in Jordan's eyes. "What the hell is happening?"

But darkness had strangled their ability to communicate with the glasses. Fortunately, his comm still worked. He bellowed, "Trist! I said hold off! That's an order—*hold off!*"

Too late. Kào felt as if he were floating. And not from hitting his head. A feeling of lightness, of well-being, often accompanied the use of sedative gas.

By the Seeders—who had given Trist the right to make such a decision? Her hasty actions would destroy the fragile bridge of trust formed between him and the refugees.

In the midst of the confusion, he heard the Earth leader pleading for composure. "Everyone, keep calm! Panic is not going to help . . ." Her voice slurred and trailed off. The screams quieted. Even the babies' cries ceased. The drug was taking hold.

"Lie down." Kào fumbled for and caught the leg of Jordan's trousers, tugging her to the floor. It was better that she went down while she still had the wherewithal to break her fall than to pass out and risk injury.

Her struggle to regain her feet was fleeting. An objecting sigh escaped her, and she sagged to the floor next to him. Kào had only a moment to ponder the dozens of possible ways he envisioned throttling Trist before he, too, spun into unconsciousness.

Chapter Eight

An entire third of a shipboard day later, Kào stormed toward Commodore Moray's main meeting room adjacent to and within sight of the bridge. *Stormed* was an optimistic description of his gait, however, as his legs were wobbly as göhta fronds.

A few men and women who Kào recognized as key members of his father's smallish crew filed out past him. Clearly, there had been a meeting in his absence. He wondered if the refugee situation had been handed over to someone more appropriate to the task. A few thirds ago, he would have hoped for such a development. But now he was determined to see the matter to its successful conclusion. Stubborn pride or masochism? Only time would tell.

Halting outside the entry as the room emptied, he massaged the back of his neck and cast an impatient glance at the doctor who had trailed him from medical. Even though Kào had walked under his own power, the physician had insisted on accompanying him. Everyone was prone to coddling the commander's son, he supposed, even one who was a failure. The situation was reminiscent of his boyhood, and one reason he had been so eager to strike out on his own, joining the Alliance Space Defense Force at the minimum age to become a weapons officer.

"Please, Mr. Vantaar-Moray, sit down. You've only just woken."

"I have duties that cannot wait," Kào told the physician without the impatience he felt. The man was only doing his job. True, his ribs ached, his head throbbed, and his back was stiff, but that was as much from having to deal with exasperating, irrational, and unpredictable people all blasted day with no respite as it was from the aftereffects of the gas. Once he got in a full sleep cycle—true sleep, not drugged unconsciousness—and some blessed hours of solitude, he'd recover. But for now, sleep would have to be put off.

"You are dismissed," he told the doctor in as kindly a tone as he could manage. "I no longer need your assistance."

The man's hesitation was evident. "But—"

"If I need you I will call," Kào assured him and strode into the meeting room.

Only his father, Trist, and two aides—one of them also of Talagar ancestry, Kào noted cheerlessly—remained inside. His father and the aides were in deep discussion at the far end of the room and didn't notice his entry. Trist sat at a large rectangular table made from rare, naturally phosphorescent wood that was the showpiece of a conference room that was infinitely serene in its understated luxury. Moray's quarters, as well as Kào's and those of the senior members of the crew, were similarly equipped. No one could ever accuse his father of not traveling in style.

As Kào neared the ensign, he saw that she studied a

primitive computer taken from the Earth vessel. To her left sat a pile of discarded devices, stacked one on top of another. Something told Kào that the machines were no longer functional. And he wondered what the former owners would think of that fact once they learned of it. "It's time for us to have a little talk, Ensign Pren."

She straightened so quickly he feared she'd fall off the chair. "You startled me."

"Apparently," he said dryly. He walked to the table and leaned back against it, arms folded over his stomach. Trist's slitted red eyes watched him warily. He couldn't look at her without thinking of the Talagars who had tortured him and killed his friends. "Your use of sedative gas was disruptive. You're a scientist, not a soldier."

"We had reason to believe you were in danger."

"I responded on the comm. I asked you not to use the gas."

"Your father thought otherwise."

Kào's lecture faltered. "My father . . ."

"Yes." Her chin lifted a notch.

So that's who had given the order. An odd feeling of betrayal replaced Kào's anger. But it was unfair to blame the man for wanting to preserve what was precious to him.

His only heir.

Long before Moray had adopted Kào, he'd lost his wife and two children in a Talagarian slaver raid. For Moray, rearing Kào had been an unexpected second chance at being a father. As such, the commodore was fiercely protective. It made sense that he'd do all he could to assure his adopted son's safety.

On the other hand, Trist knew that. In true Talagarian fashion, she had likely taken advantage of that to resolve the standoff as she wanted.

He swerved his attention back to her. "What is the status of the refugees?"

Trist appeared to consider her words before answering. "I just now gave the order to have them removed from their vessel."

"*You* gave the order?"

"You were unconscious—"

"Thanks to you."

"If I'd known you'd be up so soon . . ." She cleared her throat. "Not being clear on your status, I took action, as I felt that continued sedation was not in the best interests of the refugees' health."

"Ah. At least there is one decision you have made—all on your own—that I agree with." He walked away from the table. "And the leader is with them?"

"Yes. I didn't ask for her to be separated out. The refugees haven't been revived yet."

"You're moving them as they *sleep?*"

"It's perfectly safe," she protested.

"If you don't mind being treated like a box of freight."

Her silence only exacerbated his burgeoning irritation. "I'm going down there to oversee the operation. And to find the leader. We need to involve her in the process. Blast it, Trist. They're her people."

He took a step and then stopped. "I came here intending to take you off the assignment."

Alarm tightened her features.

"But I need you," he explained bluntly. "Or, more precisely, I need the language instruction program you're developing. So I'll keep you on the project. For now. The refugees must begin learning Key immediately. But the situation, unstable as it is, gives me no choice but to bar you from unsupervised contact with them. Is that understood?"

Her lavender-tinted lips thinned. "Yes." Her hands flattened on the table. She sat there, staring at her fingers.

Poor, misguided female, he thought. Didn't she know that he wasn't able to conjure the emotion required to feel sorry for her? His time in Talagar custody had assured that. "Contact me on the comm the moment the language instructional is ready." He forced himself to add, "I do appreciate your expertise in the matter."

He felt her eyes on him as he walked to where his father stood with his aides. The room was so expansive that the man didn't hear Kào's approach until he was nearly at his side.

Moray's face lit up. "Ah—he returns to life!" The commodore's booming voice sounded jolly but his eyes reflected his concern. "I didn't expect you to be up and about so soon. You had two cracked ribs."

Kào took a deep breath. "They fused successfully. I don't feel a thing."

Moray gave him a skeptical look.

"Incoming call for you, Commodore," called someone from the hatchway.

"I'll take it on the bridge, Rono." His father rolled his eyes at Kào. "It's been like this all day. Come. Walk with me."

Kào fell into step beside his father. Hunched over her confiscated computer equipment, Trist did not glance up as they walked past.

"I need a moment of your time, sir," Kào said as they entered the hallway outside.

"Of course."

It was not his place to criticize his father's decision to use the sedative gas, but neither did he care for the consequences of that choice. Tactfully he began, "It may not have been the best course, using the sedative to subdue the refugees. I fear that aggressive measures will destroy the understanding begun between us."

"I worried for your safety, Kào. When Trist recommended that the sedative be used, I gave her full authority to do so."

85

"Understood, sir. However, I was in contact with her at the time. I informed her that I was safe. Yet she defied me. And now she has removed the refugees from their vessel without my consent—or theirs. It will worsen the situation, I'm afraid. Therefore I have removed her from any further unsupervised interaction with the Earth people."

Moray glanced at him sharply. "You have?"

Kào nodded. "But I realize I need her expertise in language development and instruction. I've decided to keep her on the job, but in a supervised capacity only."

Moray's personal communicator began beeping. "Almost there," he growled into his wrist gauntlet computer. Then he confided to Kào out the corner of his mouth, "Crazy today, just crazy. I thought we'd caught up with that Talagar vessel we're after. But all we caught in our nets was a motley flotilla of independent traders who haven't seen anything, either. But Headquarters won't let it go. Apparently, we're the only Perimeter Patrol vessel presumed to be near where they were last spotted. Every blasted time we call off the search, they reinstate it."

Kào cursed himself for adding yet another concern to his father's full share. Patrolling the Perimeter for stray Talagars who resented the Alliance victory was a thorny and complicated undertaking; yet it was one Moray handled with aplomb. Kào, in contrast, seemed unable to even cope with a couple of hundred displaced primitives.

On the bridge, the aide Rono handed the commodore a blinking handheld communicator. Moray opened the message, but his remarks were directed to his son. "As you well know, this is not the first time I have come upon a people in need of rescue. But these are the first to turn against me. The Earth leader managed quite the enviable coup. He caught us all off guard—"

"She."

Contact

"—making for a bit of a rough start, yes, but . . . He's a *she*?"

Indeed. Just wait until Moray saw whom he was battling in his efforts to settle the refugees. "That's correct, sir."

"Interesting." Moray thought for a moment. "Well. No matter. A face-to-face explanation of her situation ought to quell any further thoughts of rebellion."

"I plan to give one, sir. I'll speak with her as soon as she wakes."

Moray shook his head. "No need. I'll talk to her. Call me when she's on the way." He gave Kào's shoulder a squeeze. "And don't tell me how busy I am. I'm glad to be of help."

Moray strode to a waiting knot of aides, who enveloped him, all vying for his attention, while Kào stood at the edge of the circle, feeling once more like an outsider. Exacerbating the familiar sensation was Moray's flip-flop on the refugee debacle. He'd given Kào full authority over the refugees, only to take over the most sensitive task of all: informing the Earth leader of her home world's destruction.

He subdued the urge to argue Moray's decision; the very ship his father commanded was named after the man and his heroic past. The *Savior*. Moray had earned the label through his good deeds and judgment in dealing with victims of tragedies. It was his renowned area of expertise. Who was Kào to disagree if the man wanted to wrest from him the reins of the initial briefing? And yet, he did.

But it was futile, wasting another thought on the matter. He had a refugee leader to wake up.

Cold air whooshed across Jordan's mouth. She'd left her bedroom window open again.

No. She wasn't home. She was at work, napping in the drafty cockpit bunkroom.

Another blast of frigid air hit her face. She batted at the sensation with her hand, but her arm felt as if it weighed a

87

thousand pounds. She hadn't slept this deeply on the airplane in ages.

Wait. On flights with only two pilots there were no scheduled breaks.

Her heart lurched. The events of the past day rushed back in full force: the black object that had captured the plane, Brian's death, the people who might be aliens. . . .

Cold air hit her again. She forced her eyes open. Shadowy forms loomed over her, speaking in a language that sounded like that of the man she'd taken hostage.

Squinting through drug-blurred eyes, she saw that the two forms had brown hair and were dressed in smart uniforms. Colorful patches, black leather piping, and crafted metallic-silver fittings spruced up the outfits. The men tugged her to her feet. Her legs weren't working right, but that didn't seem to bother them. Her body was so lethargic that they had to drag her along.

"What are you doing? Hands off," she mumbled. Her tongue was stuck to the roof of her mouth. Not merely stuck, but plastered. When she worked enough saliva into her mouth to free her tongue, it made an awful sound, like Velcro being undone. It meant she was dehydrated. How long had she been out? If her dulled senses, aching head, and stiff limbs were any indication, it had been hours.

They hauled her from First Class to Business, through Economy, and toward the rear of the airplane. All the exit doors were wide open. Which meant that security was hopelessly breached.

Seesawing between lucid consciousness and a nausea-laced dream state, she was too disoriented to put up a decent fight. As if it would do any good. How would she be able to help the others if she acted like a hothead and got herself killed?

Her father once described how the POWs in Vietnam tried not to chastise themselves over every little concession made to their captors. Better to save your strongest resistance for the biggest battles. She'd cooperate. For now.

Jordan stumbled. Only the two sets of hands clamped around her upper arms kept her from falling. A solid but giving lump had tripped her. As her vision cleared, she saw that the objects they were steering her around weren't bumps at all but the bodies of the passengers and crew.

Everyone appeared to be sleeping, but the sharp, tangy smell of urine and fresh vomit clogged her nostrils. *Good God.* They'd been drugged. All of them.

She moaned softly as nausea gripped her stomach. Ah, but she couldn't give in to it; she needed to stay alert, to be strong. For the passengers, for her crew mates.

For Boo.

In the dim light at the rear of the airplane, Jordan stumbled over yet another inert body. The man holding her left arm yanked her upright. Then someone, another man, rebuked her handlers in an authoritative tone. She guessed he'd warned them against hurting her. Although Jordan didn't understand the language, she recognized the source: the scarred man, whose dark eyes were black and empty of warmth—eyes that could fill unexpectedly with penetrating compassion, she'd discovered to her shock. Her former hostage. Now she was his captive. *What goes around comes around.*

Hands clasped behind his back, he waited for her on the platform outside exit 5-L, the rearmost left exit. His features were as ruthless and hard as his body, a tall, broad-shouldered frame that was menacing in the way it blocked the light pouring into the airplane.

She refused to be afraid. Her father would have told her, *Courage is mustering the strength to stand up when it's easier to fall down.*

That's right. Her hands weren't trembling, she told herself. Her stomach wasn't doing somersaults, either. And she didn't feel like she wanted to pee in her pants. Nope. No way. Who cared if the guy looked like Attila the Hun on a bad, bad day? He'd said he wanted to help. She had to conjure some semblance of trust in that promise, or she'd lose it, right here, right now.

Attila stepped to the right, allowing the guards to lower her to the platform. Her pupils couldn't contract enough to compensate for the bright artificial light. Pain stabbed her eyes and made them water. That damned drug, she thought, squinting. It had mucked up her nervous system and God knew what else. Attila said something, and the guards released her.

Her legs were too wobbly to support her weight. The tall man steadied her with strong hands and pulled her to his side, almost knocking the breath from her. Her hand flattened atop an abdomen as unyielding as his utility belt, which ground into her ribs and hip. His hard thigh pressed against hers. Too close—all of him was. But if she could have stood on her own, she would have. Wooziness made her head spin all over again.

She must have blacked out. She woke to find herself sitting on a white molded bench seat. Blinking, she stared blankly at four black boots. Two were hers, she decided after a bit, familiar black-leather ankle boots. But the other pair . . .

Her gaze swung upward. Dark eyes. A hard-jawed face. The tall man stood in front of her. With one hand he clutched a strap hanging from a curved ceiling that held rows of similar straps. And he was wearing the magic glasses.

So was she, she discovered, her fingers touching the smooth frames. He'd put them on her when she'd been out cold. It meant they could communicate. "Where is my crew?" she demanded. "Where are the passengers? I'll do what you want. Don't hurt them." Desperate to find the glimmer of compassion she'd glimpsed earlier, she searched his face. "Please."

He recoiled at that. "I will not hurt them. Or you."

She would have expected to find him gloating, having turned the tables on her so expertly. But the cold strength radiating from this brutally handsome man contrasted with the apparent genuineness of his concern, a poker-faced empathy that just as unexpectedly burrowed into her soul. Without knowing anything about him, she suddenly felt that this was the kind of guy who'd walk between you and puddles in the street, who'd open car doors and put his coat over your shoulders if he thought you were cold—

Holy crap. What was she thinking? Squaring her shoulders, she wrenched her gaze away from his black, penetrating eyes.

She was delirious, she told herself. Doped up by the gas. She had to be. Why else would she be acting like Miss Wishful Thinking, putting Earth characteristics, chivalrous Earth characteristics, on a man who was a stranger in the truest sense of the word? He might appear concerned for her welfare, but the fact remained that he had captured her and her airplane.

Squinting upward, she tried in her disoriented state to make sense of him, of who—or what—he was. Impassive, he regarded her with equal scrutiny. Holding on to a ceiling strap, he swayed slightly, as if the molded white tube that enclosed them was moving.

Her attention swung outside. A blur of color and light whizzed past the small, circular windows. The tube *was* moving! It was a shuttle of some kind, reminding her of the monorail at Disney World. Were they flying or speeding along on a track? She wasn't sure if she wanted to know. "Where are we? Where are you taking me?"

"You are safe now. You and your people." His eyes asked her to believe him. But she mustn't forget that the people he worked with had rendered them unconscious. And yet . . . the last thing she'd heard before passing out was his command of inaction. Maybe he did intend to help.

Or maybe it was only a trick. She didn't know what to think.

He pulled a small device from his utility belt. A tiny but very clear screen showed passengers and crew being laid down on beds in what looked to be a clean and spacious bunk area. "See? They are safe. We want to help you."

She read the caption in his lenses. "Help us? Why? You make it sound like something bad has happened."

He began to answer, stopped himself. She had the feeling that he wasn't going to explain until they got to wherever they were going.

They lapsed into awkward silence, and she sagged back in her seat. Oh, to be lost in drugged sleep with everyone else, while some other poor slob bore the responsibility of negotiating for food, water, and freedom. A fresh spurt of adrenaline made her hands shake. Was she up to the task of negotiating for her life and those of the passengers and crew?

In the corner of her vision, she caught the man studying her. When he realized she'd noticed, he averted his eyes, his jaw flexing. Strange that he was curious about her yet so uncomfortable in her presence. Was it because of his plans for her? She forced away the thought. *Stay positive.*

She grasped for normalcy, for civility. "Jordan is my name. Jordan Cady." She poked one finger to her chest.

His expression softened. Well, maybe *softened* wasn't the right word, but he regarded her with a certain leniency. She found herself wondering how he'd look when he smiled. *If he ever smiled.* She remembered the symbols branded on his neck. It was doubtful that a man with marks like that had much to smile about.

"Jor-dahn," he repeated.

Contact

"Yes." She decided that she liked the way he said her name, the J soft, more like "zh" or "sh."

He spread his hand over his chest. "Kào. It is my given name."

"Kay-oh." He had a mother. A father. Someone had named him. For some reason the idea reassured her.

The shuttle—subway—whatever it was—glided to a halt. Doors opened with a hiss. As she followed Kào outside, she heard an airflow noise just below the level of her hearing, but the air itself was still, devoid of any scents. Like the bay that housed the 747, the walls and floor here were molded and white, and all the inscriptions were foreign to her. It was like when she'd traveled in mainland China; she'd found it impossible to orient herself when there were no recognizable words or letters. Then she looked to the right, and her breath caught.

The hallway swept up and away from her, and seemed to have no end. She jerked her gaze to the left. It wasn't an illusion—the walkway did bow very distinctly upward. She followed it with her eyes to where it disappeared on a somewhat hazy horizon high above. A few people, mere specks, moved along the path near the "ceiling." They were on a ship—one that dwarfed anything she'd ever seen.

The sight threw off her already shaky equilibrium. Her hands shot out, searching for balance, clawing for something to hold on to. Kào's sleeve. In that protective, masculine way of his, he steadied her. But she couldn't look at him. Couldn't breathe. That kid on the 747 was right: Kào *was* Darth Vader. An alien. And she was on his spacecraft.

A huge spacecraft. The truth hit her with the raw violence of a fist in the gut. *Oh, God.* But she was going to find a way home; she swore it. She had a daughter waiting there, a little girl who needed her, and a family who loved them both.

Tears pricked her eyes, but she'd be damned if she'd

93

break down. She had to be tough, to perform a role she never dreamed of playing, in a place she never imagined being. Strength would get her home. And get there she would.

Chapter Nine

Kào led Jordan into Commodore Moray's meeting room. Moray and his staff had not arrived yet. At one end of the gathering table, Kào pulled out a chair and offered Jordan a seat.

Her gaze dropped to his wrist where his sleeves didn't completely cover the thin dermal regeneration strip placed over a laceration there. "From when you tied me up," he said dryly. "Have I done the same to you? Why, no, of course. It seems I'm a far better host than you were a hostess."

Her lips compressed. Over the glasses, he saw her wide blue eyes flick to his. He'd baited her, and wasn't sure exactly why. He wasn't the teasing sort. Was it an attempt to ease her apprehension before his father's briefing? The bad news she was about to receive would be a blow.

"If you find gas preferable to handcuffs," she returned drolly after a moment. He felt oddly rewarded that her expression had eased somewhat; she'd recognized his banter for what it was.

Sitting in the chair, she clutched its armrests as if she feared she'd fall. The chair bobbed only a few standard feet off the floor, but likely she hadn't possessed the technology for floating furniture on her primitive world. Buoyant engineering was only a few hundred standard years old. Of course, since its inception the technology had brought improvements to almost every aspect of Alliance life, making it hard to imagine life before its discovery.

"Sorry to keep you waiting, Kào." His father strode into the room trailed by his staff and a bevy of aides. The *Savior*'s crew was small but every other person seemed to be either an aide or a staff member. His father had not needed such a large contingent in the past. Now everywhere he went, his assistants went, too. Among them, trying hard to evade Kào's glare, was Trist, clutching an armload of computer equipment to her chest.

Moray dismissed all but the linguist, then indicated that the two of them plus Kào and Jordan should sit around the table. He then donned a pair of conversion-glasses. Trist followed suit.

"Ah," Moray said. One broad hand over his chest, thick fingers spread, he nodded warmly. "I am Commodore-elite Ilya Moray."

Jordan offered what appeared to be a wary, reserved greeting in her language. "Jordan Cady, captain of United Fifty-eight."

"Ah. Captain Cady. Is that the correct title? Welcome."

Jordan nodded, then frowned at her floating chair, taking great pains to steady it. Posture erect, she sat with her fists knotted in her lap. Her uniform needed cleaning, but she'd freshened up considerably when Kào had offered her the chance just before arriving here. She'd dampened her hair and combed it, but loose strands around her forehead had already re-formed into tight ringlets. He'd never seen hair like hers before, curly but pale Talagarian blond. As if she sensed his gaze, Jordan locked eyes with him. Kào cleared his throat and forcibly diverted his attention from her.

"Have you met Ensign Pren?" Moray asked Jordan.

"She did," Kào interjected. "Indirectly."

Jordan's uneasy gaze settled on the ensign, specifically on the almost-clear support strip gracing the bridge of the woman's nose. Both women's faces reflected what appeared to be forced neutrality.

Kào contemplated his folded hands as Moray began to describe the *Savior* and its mission. "We are a military warship tasked with providing protection for vessels traversing the border between the settled areas and uncharted space. Secondary to that is exploration and the charting of undiscovered worlds, such as your Earth."

Jordan regarded him stonily. "State your reason for detaining my ship."

Moray seemed caught off balance; no one spoke to him in that tone. Kào winced even as he found himself secretly admiring Jordan's grit.

"Shall I explain?" Kào offered when Moray didn't immediately reply.

Moray held up one hand. "I'm afraid I have bad news," he said at last.

Jordan sat as still as a statue as she read the translation: "Earth, as you knew it, is gone."

Seconds ticked by. Then she recoiled, as though struck.

Kào's jaw knotted. He'd always been a fan of bluntness, of not mincing words. Humans and computers, he dealt with them the same way: in a straightforward and consistent manner. Yet, this time, he felt an overwhelming urge to soften the blow dealt by his father.

"What ... happened?" Jordan's voice was hoarse but steady.

"At times, and thankfully not often, an inhabited planet will cross paths with a comet or asteroid. That is what happened to your home."

"It's a mistake," Jordan protested. "The astronomers always watch the sky. We would have seen it coming. We would have had warnings."

The commodore hefted his large frame off of his chair and walked to the window, where there wasn't much to view other than a distorted starscape. "That is not always the case with what is known as a comet shower," he argued. Behind him, Jordan looked lonely and lost in her small chair at the enormous conference table. "They are less dense than asteroids, made of dust and ice as opposed to rock and iron. If they fragment before coming into viewing range, there would be no warning at all, unless your civilization utilized long-range space buoys for early detection, which you did not. It was just such a comet shower that struck your Earth." Sorrow deepened the creases between Kào's father's bushy brows. "I wish I could have saved more of you."

Excruciating minutes ticked past while Jordan deciphered all Moray had told her. After experiencing the conversion-glasses, Kào knew that not all of what was said translated properly. But enough would be displayed as captions for Jordan to discern Kào's father's meaning. "But there'll be survivors," she insisted. "There always are."

The futile hope that infused her voice made Kào's chest ache.

"There are so many places to hide," she maintained. "Underground shelters, buildings—"

"No, Captain. These relatively small and less-dense objects, the remains of a comet, are actually the most dangerous of the hazards from space. They break up into pieces that explode just above the ground, a mile or so, no more."

The optimum altitude for maximum devastation, Kào knew from his years as a weapons officer for the Alliance.

"There were nine major impacts, Captain Cady, and hundreds of smaller ones. They left behind a wasteland of flattened, charred buildings and blackened corpses. The oceans vaporized, infernos raged. Within a short time, what was left of the atmosphere was so thickly laden with particles that sunlight couldn't reach the surface. And it won't, I'm afraid, for centuries."

Jordan absorbed Moray's bleak assessment. Kào's watch chimed the third-hour, a cheerful sound at odds with the miserable mood in the room.

The Earth leader's mouth trembled. Then she lifted her glasses to swipe her knuckles across her cheek.

Moray appeared to be at a loss for words, as well. Even Trist acted uncomfortable.

Enough. Kào may have handed over the reins of this meeting to his father, but Jordan's suffering compelled him to take them back. She'd learned of her home world's fate; why prolong the misery? "I think we have accomplished most of what we set out to do, Commodore," he said tactfully. "Now it is time for me to return Captain Cady to her people."

But Moray held up his hand, stopping Kào. "How many people were on your vessel, Captain Cady?"

Jordan turned her eyes to Kào before she answered. She'd seen the interchange; she understood what he'd tried to do. "Two hundred and ninety-one," she said tightly. "But that includes the captain—the original captain. He's dead."

"I am sorry," Moray murmured. "There are two hundred and ninety total, then." After translating the figures and typing the information into his handheld computer, Moray continued with more questions: numbers of infants, children, ages, and the general health of Jordan's people.

Kào found it odd that Moray was so concerned with these details when a staff member could have passed the information along to him later. His father took too much onto his shoulders. He always had. By the Seeders, the least Kào could do for the man was lighten the load.

This time he stood. "Sir, you have duties that demand your attention. I can pass along the rest of this information later. I thank you for participating in the briefing, and for sharing your expertise in these matters. And you, Ensign Pren, for the conversion-glasses that made this briefing possible. Any questions? No? Good."

As Moray sat back in his chair, clearly surprised by the abruptness with which Kào ended the meeting, Trist removed the glasses covering her crimson eyes and gaped at him. Kào told her, "I want to keep two pair of glasses for Captain Cady and myself. I'll have them returned to you later. I expect you'll want to download additional data for your language program."

Her voice was still nasal. "The instructional program is by no means perfected as yet. I've had some trouble with the phonics. But it will suffice. For now."

"I'm sure it will more than suffice," Kào assured her.

The woman appeared all at once baffled, pleased, and troubled by his compliment. With a furtive glance at Moray, she gathered her items and left the room.

Kào spoke to Jordan next. "If you'll excuse us for a moment, Captain. Commodore Moray and I must confer privately."

Moray pushed himself out of the floating chair, slowly, as big men do. He did a reasonable job of hiding his displeasure at his son's curtailing of the briefing. "Please accept my deepest condolences, Captain Cady. Mr. Vantaar-Moray is the primary intercessor between your people and my crew. I hope you will cooperate with him. It is ultimately the best option for your people."

She took longer than usual to read the translation. "I understand."

Moray raised his brows at Kào. *Ensure that she does,* his eyes said.

Kào followed the commodore to just outside the hatch. Moray's aides converged on them, but Moray waved them off when they tried to crowd around him. He tore off his glasses. "You cut short the briefing. Why?"

Kào removed his own conversion-glasses. "I'm sorry, sir," he said, though he wasn't, really. "She's endured about all she can. I need her in reasonable condition to brief her own people. If we went on much longer, she wouldn't be."

"A valid point." Moray rubbed one hand over his face and released a sigh. "Ah, Kào. I'm weary and in need of sleep."

"Ah, and who isn't?"

They regarded each other with warmth. Then Moray turned serious. "I've ordered a lockdown, you know."

It meant the refugees would be confined to their quarters—for an unknown length of time. There had been no word yet on where or when the Earthers would be dropped off at a resettlement port. "Is that necessary?"

"Your job will be much easier because of it, Kào," his father insisted. "With the Talagar situation the way it is here in the Perimeter, I can't afford unrest on my own ship. Should there be any unrest, you are authorized to use force to subdue it. Use as many of my security team as you require."

"Yes, sir." But he was shocked by the strain he saw in his father's face.

"If you need me I'll be on the bridge." Moray's troubled gray eyes sharpened with worry. "Be careful, Kào."

"Don't worry, sir."

I'm *an ex-prisoner made jailer,* he thought as Moray strode away into a huddle of waiting aides. Not only unpalatable, the concept bordered on ludicrous.

He slid his glasses back over his eyes and returned to the

101

meeting room. "Door—close," he commanded. The door whooshed shut.

Aware that Jordan followed him with her gaze, Kào filled a tumbler with water from the dispenser in the wall and set it in front of her. Then he returned to his chair. "Drink," he commanded.

Her fingers curved around the opaque white glass, but not before he saw them quiver. It took all he had not to cover her hands with his. She'd lost everything. Just as he had. He was a stranger to offering comfort, but something about this particular woman, and what they shared, drove him to try.

"You have someone on Earth—*had* someone," he amended. Her shoulders went rigid. He searched for a generic word to use to accommodate the religious and cultural differences between their societies. "You had a . . . mate."

Jordan read his words and flinched. Kào longed to pull the glasses off her face and see what was in her eyes. "No, no mate. A daughter . . . a six-year-old child," she whispered. She took a breath, and then another. "Oh, God. I loved her so much. . . ." A choked sob escaped her. She pressed one hand to her mouth.

He stared at her, unable to fathom the depth of her grief, to grasp what it might be like to be so close to someone that losing them tore you apart. He and Moray shared a loving father-son relationship; yet somehow, if Moray were to die, Kào doubted he was capable of feeling what Jordan so clearly did now. There was no question that'd he'd do whatever his father asked—blast, he'd give his life for the man—but he feared that that stemmed more from intense loyalty and obligation than from deep emotion; it was less a symptom of Moray's parenting than it was Kào's inability to conjure intense feelings. Even before the war and his imprisonment, Kào had felt oddly hollow, as if something once there was gone. Fondness for his birth family, and theirs for him, he imagined privately. But he'd admitted that notion to no one; it was illogical to mourn something of which you had no recollection.

"I'm sorry for your loss," he offered awkwardly. Her nostrils flared, and she pressed her fist into her stomach. Blast, he was mucking this up.

"It should have been me." Her knuckles turned white. "Not her."

It should have been me. Dark memories clotted Kào's mind, memories of Talagar prison. He'd been the only one of his captured squadron-mates to survive it. Why? Why had he lived when others were more deserving? The question had haunted him since his release, stealing his sleep and, when he did sleep, invading his dreams.

He studied the patchwork of faint scars on the back of his right hand. "Some say that it's worse to be the one left alive."

Her head lifted. Had she recognized the pain behind that statement? His neck muscles bunched. "Drink," he ordered.

She sipped some water and clumsily set the tumbler back on the table. The clatter was overly loud in the heavy silence. She stared at her hands until she'd composed herself. He knew she would. She was in charge; she couldn't give in to personal pain, no matter what the cost. Kào knew all about that.

One of his father's Talagarian aides—or, more correctly, an aide of Talagar ancestry—peeked inside the meeting room. He blurted an apology and ducked out of sight.

Kào returned his attention to Jordan. "Shall we go to your people now?"

Her distaste at breaking the news to them drew her lips into a tight grimace. With equal dislike, she pushed out of the buoyant chair, leaving it bobbing gently as she followed Kào from the meeting room.

"They are being brought to supplementary crew quarters

103

on deck Sublevel Three," he explained as they walked. "There you will be confined until further notice."

After reading the translation, she glanced sideways at him, her accusing gaze as stinging as a slap. "I thought we weren't captives."

"You are not!"

"But if we can't leave where you're putting us, then what else are we? And why don't you look happy about it?"

It seemed that he couldn't mask his expressions any more than she could hers.

He tried to determine the best way to explain that the lockdown wasn't his idea without revealing his aversion to the order itself. He was serving his father. This wasn't war, but the outcome was just as important to his father's future. As in battle, to achieve victory, it was imperative that they all present a united front, regardless of personal opinion. "It's in your best interests to stay within the safety of your quarters. It would be easy to be injured, wandering around a strange ship—"

"Tell me the truth."

His head jerked around. Her eyes blazed, challenging him. He exhaled, turning his gaze to the far side of the ship, focusing somewhere she couldn't see. "You know nothing of the Talagars. Or the war."

Her tone wasn't as steady. "No."

What innocence. He envied it. And then he ended it.

He told her of the Talagar Empire and the war, though not his role in it. By the time he'd finished explaining what the *Savior* was doing in the Perimeter, she'd paled. Her gaze darted around the corridor, as if she were certain an attack was imminent.

Let her feel that fear, he reasoned. It might save her life someday.

Then he shored up her apprehension, feeling no guilt as he did so. "The Talagars would think you and your people the perfect prey, Jordan. Dependent, unaware of galactic politics, and possessed of no identification records in the universal database. This is a hazardous zone we traverse. None of us dreamed we'd be transporting refugees through it." *Particularly me.* "I hope that Headquarters makes a swift decision as to where you're to be relocated."

"So do I," she murmured, appearing downright ill. Her mourning threatened to break through her façade.

As they made their way down to Sublevel Three through largely deserted corridors—the small size of the crew was noticeable on a ship this size—he sought to reassure her. "But we'll meet daily. Your meals will be delivered; clothing will be provided; all your needs will be met. And as your primary intercessor, I'll be able to provision anything else you might need."

But it was clear by her deepening scowl that the prospect of captivity while onboard the ship didn't please her. He hadn't anticipated otherwise. But what he hadn't expected was her refusal to pass on that information to her people. "They're scared enough as it is. I can't tell them that they're prisoners, too."

"Not prisoners. Confined for their own protection."

She made a face. "Protection against a slave-owning empire of sore losers bent on fighting until the end? Hmm. It'll be tough enough dealing with what I'm going to tell them now. If I heap on any more, they'll panic." Her face contorted in concentration. Then she brightened, as much as shock and fatigue would allow. "We'll be in quarantine."

"Quarantine? You needn't worry about protecting the crew of the *Savior* from unknown diseases."

"Actually, I had in mind that my people needed to be protected from yours."

Kào thought he sensed a hint of haughtiness in that comment. Or was she goading him, as he'd done to her in his father's meeting room? But it was her sly dodging of his request to tell her people of the lockdown that bemused him. "Just so you're aware, our medical staff can accommodate any differences in our physiology," he explained.

"Swapping diseases is still a risk. We're different species." Her eyes slid sideways. "Though you look so . . . human."

"I *am* human." He covered his incredulity that this basic fact was news to her, that Earth didn't know of their common heritage.

"I thought because you were from another planet that you'd be . . . something else."

"No. There are many different races, displaying many different characteristics, but all are human. We are the Progeny—you, me, and the rest, even the Talagars. All are descendants of the Original Ones. The Seeders, we call them. Several hundred thousand years ago, they sowed their DNA across the galaxy. It was their legacy. *Human* DNA. We are the same people, Jordan, the same species. That you don't know this explains your initial fear of me. And it corroborates the commodore's theory that your world was separated from the Alliance long ago, before your recorded history." He watched as she absorbed the translation. "I don't know how Earth became separated," he admitted. "Or why. I have my theories, but that discussion is best saved for another day."

I agree, her overwhelmed expression told him. "When everything's more stable, I'll brief them on the truth, Kào. That we're in danger flying through this area." She paused, and then said, "And there's something else, too."

Something had told him there'd be more. This day would never end. "What is it?"

"Part of why my people were scared on the airplane was because they were scared . . . of *you*."

He opened his mouth to argue, then reconsidered. He'd been told that his looks could be rather, ah, intimidating.

That had served him well in the arena of war, but this was a situation that required diplomacy and patience, neither of which were his strong points. "So you think that calling your confinement 'quarantine' as opposed to a lockdown will make them more inclined to trust me."

"And that will make them more inclined to cooperate."

With some amusement, he noted her sly manipulation of his father's words. Although he had no intention of disobeying the commodore, he stared hard at the floor to keep his admiration for Jordan's cleverness from appearing on his face. "It does not matter what you call it, Jordan, as long as your people stay where they are put."

And stay put they would. As much he shared in common with Jordan and her people, his loyalty remained with Moray, and his duty was to ensure that the refugees didn't interfere with shipboard security in the risky days ahead.

In grudging agreement, they stopped outside the hatch to the refugee quarters. Jordan smoothed her hands over her hair as if she could conquer the matted mass of curls. "They must be worried about me by now."

"If only in their dreams. They're asleep. I asked that the antidote not be administered until you arrived. I assumed you'd want to be with them when they woke."

Surprise and gratitude were apparent in her voice. "Yes. I did." But when he opened the hatch, she didn't step through it. Her fists, tight at her sides, opened and closed.

"You may enter the room," he prompted.

She took a couple of deep breaths. "I know." She rubbed her hands on her trousers. "The original captain is dead. I've taken his place, and I've accepted that. But . . . damn it . . . it doesn't mean I'm ready for it."

She swallowed the rest of her words, as if mortified that she'd divulged so much. "It doesn't make a difference if I'm ready or not," she muttered. "Let's do it."

"You are correct, Jordan. It does not make a difference.

Susan Grant

I've seen many types of leaders, good and bad, in the best and the worst of circumstances. I was in the war before this assignment, you see."

Assignment? A laughable description of the current state of affairs, he thought. He was here on the *Savior* only because of his father's charity, his celebrated benevolence now extended to his son.

Regardless of the scornful discourse in his head, Kào continued, "The best leaders' skills are instinctive and not necessarily learned. This perhaps is the case with you, Jordan. Go with your gut. Tell your people what you think you must, and I believe you will have nothing to worry about."

She tipped her head so that she could study him over her glasses, her searching stare intense as she studied his face. He felt her penetrating gaze as if it were a physical thing. Likely it was only for seconds that he lost himself in those sea-blue eyes, but it felt like an eternity. "Thank you," she whispered, jolting him back to rationality.

By the Seeders! She unbalanced him, this woman. He opened the hatch. "No need to thank me," he replied in a crisp tone.

Appearing somewhat flustered—had she sensed how she affected him?—she preceded him through the door. Her rigid shoulders reflected her renewed discipline. Clearly, she, too, knew that any interaction between them that was less than strictly professional was unbecoming.

Inside, four armed security guards waited, reminding him quite clearly of the promise he'd made to Moray: Handle this situation so that the commodore didn't have to. Refocused on his duty, he followed Jordan into her temporary new home.

Chapter Ten

In the newly assigned refugee quarters, Jordan stopped at the last of the beds, all of them full. It had taken an eternity to count all the sleeping bodies. Fighting bleariness, she added up the slashes representing passengers and crew that she'd made with a light pen on a scroll that was really a computer screen. Not including Brian, whose body was supposedly being kept safe until she arranged for his funeral, and not counting the infants who, because their parents hadn't purchased seats for them, weren't logged on the passenger manifest, she was three people short.

She whirled on Kào, her escort, a man who was unintentionally charming in his aloofness and frighteningly on-target with his understanding. "Not everyone's here. Where are they?"

The guards, instantly alert, swung their attention her way. To her relief, these men had normal pigmentation. It wasn't that she cared about skin color; but something about the albinos unsettled her, something in their eyes—though she couldn't define what it was. "Did we count wrong?" she asked Kào in a more civil tone. She didn't want to get shot by security for no other reason than reaching the end of her emotional rope.

Kào dropped his gaze to his handheld computer. "I logged two hundred and eighty-six."

She waited until the numbers translated to English. "We're supposed to have two hundred and eighty-nine, not including me." She knew her tone was terse, but she couldn't help it. When it came to priorities, courtesy was running a distant last place. She was gut tired, nauseated, and cold deep, deep inside. All she wanted to do was collapse into a tight little ball. But her personal problems were last in line to far more important considerations. "I have a missing crew member." *Ann.* Her partner in crime, the level-headed flight attendant who'd helped her make the escape slide into a defensive weapon. "And two passengers."

Kào lifted his arm and barked an order in his computer that also served as his communicator, or "comm," as he called it.

"I've put someone on the task," he told her. "They'll recheck the vessel. And the morgue."

"The morgue?" Her heart sank. Had her glasses translated correctly?

"What happened to your captain could have happened to others, as well."

Anger boiled up unexpectedly. "Death from fright, you mean."

His mouth hardened into its usual grim slash. He could go from bleak to unintentionally charming to bleak again so quickly that she couldn't figure out which was his true self. And she wasn't sure if she wanted to know. "Couldn't you have thought of a less terrifying way to accomplish a rescue?"

"Had we paused to think on it, we would have lost all of you."

God. She wiped her hand over her face. He and his shipmates had saved her from certain death, and she was attacking him for it. "I'm sorry," she said. "Let's do a recount."

Kào agreed. "Perhaps we miscalculated."

They headed back across the huge common area, a triangular-shaped room from where three passageways housing individual bunkrooms sprouted. Kào's people had a thing with threes. Even their day was divided into thirds. What resembled very ordinary cots were grouped in nines and twenty-sevens, separated by molded privacy walls, soundproofed and glowing incandescently from within, lighting Jordan's way as she passed by her sleeping passengers and crew.

They finished the second head count and exchanged notes. Ann and the two passengers were still missing. A call came in over Kào's communicator. He answered it, pacing in front of her as he argued in his language. Then, his expression bleak, he lowered his comm.

She tightened her abdominals, knowing she was about to receive another kick in the gut emotionally. "What happened?"

"Two of your adult males died from encephalitic shock. A severe allergic reaction to the sedative gas."

Jordan's heart raced. Her churning stomach made her throat burn. "And the third?"

It appeared to be an effort for him to form a translation she could understand. "Your crew member hemorrhaged from the loss of an unborn child. They discovered the bleeding too late to revive her."

Ann. She'd been pregnant, lost her baby. And then bled to death in her sleep. Instinctively, Jordan placed her hand over her womb.

111

Kào followed the gesture with his eyes. Then he glanced away, his jaw flexing.

"Apparently, the gas caused spontaneous abortions in all the pregnant females."

"Sweet Jesus," she whispered. There had been three pregnant women—that she'd known about. How many others had lost babies as a result of the gas? Impotent fury and horror clogged her throat.

"Trust me when I say that I'm as revolted as you are by the consequences of the gas. But that is of little comfort to you now, I imagine."

She answered with a sound that was a cross between an enraged huff and a sarcastic snort. Then she squeezed her eyes shut and shuddered.

"Jordan. . . ."

She cringed. Kào's voice was almost tender. She didn't want tenderness. Not from him. Not from anyone. Anything soft would seep into the hairline cracks in her armor and shatter it.

Hugging her arms to her ribs, she marched away. Kào didn't follow. But his face remained imprinted in her mind like the afterimage of bright lights behind closed eyes. She "saw" the wall's glow illuminating the harsh hollows of his face, and the glasses that hid his eyes. His expression hid his feelings just as well. But he'd seen his share of suffering; instinct told her that. And now, that same gut feeling screamed at her to trust him, to take his remorse at face value. The problem was that she didn't *want* to trust him.

She wanted to pummel him with her fists, scream at him for treating the people on her airplane like animals. It made her so goddamned angry. And she had the feeling that she was going to be angry for a long time, maybe forever. Angry for not being with her daughter in the darkest possible moment, angry for being alive when everyone she'd cared about was dead. Angry for being in charge when it was the very last thing she wanted.

Some say it's worse to be the one left alive, Kào had said.

A choked moan escaped her. *I'd give anything to change places with you, Boo.* She forced away the image of her daughter cowering as the sky fell, her mother not there to hold her, and she pressed her fists into her ribcage, as if that could somehow blot out the other, unspeakable pain slashing at her broken heart.

It's not about you, Jordan.

That's right. She couldn't let her own pain take over when nearly three hundred people depended on her. And already she'd lost three of them—on *her* watch. Self-pity wasn't going to be an option.

Slowly she turned around and faced Kào, who waited. Silent. Enigmatic. She wished she could appear the same way; it might prove useful someday when the passengers' shock wore off and they started questioning her decisions, but she didn't have an enigmatic bone in her body, unfortunately. "Waking them up isn't going to kill anyone, is it?" she asked.

"I should hope not."

Hope. What was hope when your life had turned into its antithesis?

She gave her head a curt shake. Straightened her spine. Cleared her throat. "Okay, then let's do it. Let's wake them up." The people of United Flight 58 had a right to know what she'd learned. All she could do now was pray she was up to the task of telling them.

Not everyone roused immediately from the sedative. Even after she'd gathered her crew and passengers in one place, the central section of their quarters, a vast triangular area designed for meetings with large numbers of people, the effects of the gas lingered. Nausea and cold sweats; uncon-

113

trollable shaking and mental confusion. A whopper of a dose they'd been given.

Jordan fought the urge to put the blame on Trist Pren, the albino woman whose nose they'd broken. Had she been in Trist's shoes, she might have been tempted to crank up the dosage, too. Nothing beat a little revenge.

Though if it had been "a little revenge," three people and a still unknown number of unborn babies died because of it. That was unforgivable, if that was how it had gone down.

For a few hours, fury overcame her grief, and she welcomed it, but by morning—the *Savior*'s version of morning—numbness had cloaked her like a cocoon. Just as well. It was time to brief Flight 58 on what had transpired. And so she did, repeating what the commodore and Kào Vantaar-Moray had told her.

"The comet broke up before it came close enough to detect," she explained. "And no one was prepared for what happened. Maybe it was a blessing. I don't think there was anything anyone could have done to stop it." Her voice grew hoarser, and she swayed on her feet. But she barely felt her exhaustion, let alone anything else. Only a persistent coldness that erupted in periodic shivers reminded her that she was still alive.

At last she reached the end of what she had to say. Although most were strangers, the people of Flight 58 huddled together as if they were one family. Wan and shocked, they drew on the elemental need for human companionship in the face of unimaginable tragedy.

"I asked about survivors," Jordan told them. "They told me that no one could have lived through it. I wanted us to go back, to make sure. But they can't—or won't—do it."

Outraged grumbles broke out. Her own bitterness on that particular point must have been more apparent than she'd intended. Kào was monitoring the briefing from near the door leading outside to the disorienting curved hallway and the rest of the ship's hallways. She felt his intense regard shift to her. The back of her neck tingled as those black eyes burned into her. She bit back her personal opinion on the no-return-to-Earth policy, because she knew what he was thinking: If she couldn't keep her people calm, his people would take over.

No way would she let that happen. She might be new at this game, feeling her way using training, not experience, as her guide; but she knew enough not to give away what little power she had. Once you abdicated command, you never got it back. She'd better keep the peace. "As soon as we're settled wherever we're going to be settled, we'll work on going home to Earth. If not to live, then to see what's"— she swallowed—"left."

She cleared her throat and checked the notes she'd scrawled on her notepad. There were many issues to cover, and she didn't want to miss any.

She was flanked by her flight attendants with the conspicuous and heartbreaking absence of Ann. Natalie stood on her left side, and Ben, ironically on her right. The chief purser was being anything but her right-hand man; he'd been a mess ever since she'd informed him of the situation. She found herself hoping he'd transform into one of those quiet, dependable guys who were there when you needed them. Men like her father and brother. But if he didn't, she had Natalie to appoint in his place, a smart-talking kickboxer whose guts had impressed her.

She turned to Ben and asked encouragingly, "Is there anything I missed? Anything you wanted to say before I wrap it up?"

He whispered in her ear, "I wish he'd get lost."

She blinked. "Who?"

"Scarface." The purser hunched his shoulders. "He gives me the creeps. Look at the way he's staring at us."

Jordan's gaze tracked down the front row of passengers and she caught a good number of them sneaking dread-filled looks at Kào. Good Lord. They were terrified of him.

But she saw that Kào was too engrossed in the gathering to notice. He seemed to observe them with an intensity that bordered on fascination, just as he'd done on the airplane. She tried to see the scene as if through his eyes: several hundred grieving people hunched together, sobs and whispers, children squealing or whining, a baby crying irritably. Coughs and occasional sneezes added to the commotion. Jordan hadn't seen much of the *Savior*, but what she had seen left her with the impression that the ship was run precisely, efficiently, and with discipline. Yet here was Kào, gazing at the people of Flight 58 with such hunger that it left her with the indelible impression that he was lonely onboard this ship.

A heartbeat later, her sympathetic thoughts were shattered by the sight of a guard passing by on his rounds behind him. An armed guard. It reminded her that Kào's people were dealing with the sloppy aftermath of war; that their enemy consisted of a bunch of psychos who got off keeping slaves and worse, practicing their perversions on them. An enemy that, apparently, hadn't been completely defeated, making the prospect of a real abduction a horrifying possibility for Jordan and her charges.

Her chest constricted with apprehension. Kào wasn't their problem, she wanted to say. The Talagars were. But few were ready to hear the news that Kào and his people were all that stood between getting to a resettlement port safely and capture by aliens who'd make them slaves.

She prayed that Kào was right about leading by gut instinct, because that was what she was doing.

"I can't ask him to leave," she whispered back to Ben. "He's the only intermediary between his crew and us. If he goes away, who's going to take his place? Frankly, I don't want anyone else."

Ben's breath brushed her ear. "So you trust him already?"

"Not completely. But he hasn't done anything to make me suspicious, either." As for Kào's kindness . . . well, Ben had no proof of that, only what she'd told him and the rest of the crew. "I agree that he's not exactly Mr. Cheerful. But that's no reason to make him a scapegoat. What happened to us isn't his fault."

"How do we know?"

In truth, they didn't. At that thought, her stomach plummeted. The passengers were straining to hear what she and Ben were saying. She lowered her voice further. "Look at them—do you want mass panic? It's a miracle everyone's as calm as they are. Don't screw with it, Ben. Don't scare them." She clenched her teeth together. "Or me."

Ben raked his jet-black hair away from his forehead. "Didn't mean to. I'm not myself right now," he said under his breath.

I hope not, she wanted to say, but somehow she dug deep and acted civil. That's what leaders did, right—acted civil? They didn't strangle their second-in-command.

She returned her attention to the others. "Sorry," she called loudly, for the room was large and her voice was growing hoarse. "The purser and I wanted to compare notes. We want to make sure we cover everything."

"Take your time, Captain," a Good Samaritan shouted to her from the middle of the crowd.

She smiled, appreciative, and inspiration seemed to come out of nowhere. "For now, though, we'll postpone the rest. Our main concern is just to survive. All of us. No giving up. We have to force ourselves to face tomorrow, and the next day, and all the days after that, even though many of us feel like we'd rather have died with our loved ones. I know it's going to be a difficult path, but we'll endure. We have to. We owe it to those we lost at home and here on this ship to keep their memory alive." The faces of her family flashed in her mind, and her throat constricted as the passengers hung on her words with teary eyes and sympathetic nods.

Go numb. She brought the pad closer to her face in the guise of scrutinizing her messy handwriting. Who was she to think she could give a pep talk when she so desperately needed one herself? Who boosted the *captain's* spirits, for crying out loud?

Courage is mustering the strength to stand up when it's easier to fall down.

She could almost hear her father's voice as his advice came to her, boosting her. "Are there any questions?" she asked gruffly.

"When will our stuff get here?" someone called out. "I have medication in my suitcase."

Ah, the grassroots concerns—those she could handle in the state she was in. "The luggage is on its way to us. Plus anything they find in the cabin. The shipboard medical staff is synthesizing medicine for those they determine need it. But keep taking what you have with you until you hear otherwise."

Natalie asked her, "Do you want me to go around and see what other immediate needs there are? I've got a spare pen and paper. I can find out the details of everyone's medication. What they take and how much."

Jordan nearly fainted with gratitude. "Yes. Do that."

Another passenger raised her hand. A middle-aged woman. "We're sleeping in dorm rooms."

"That's right." Jordan was the only one with a private room, small as it was.

"My sister's not in my area. I want to sleep near my sister."

More people called out with their personal preferences for sleeping arrangements.

"Tell me this is a good thing," Jordan muttered to Natalie. "That they are more concerned about roommates than Earth being vaporized by a comet."

"I think this is only the tip of the iceberg."

An iceberg sank the *Titanic*. Jordan sighed through clenched teeth. "We'll work everything out tomorrow," she assured the crowd.

"Our food, too?" a man wearing a skullcap queried in a Middle-Eastern accent. "I have special dietary requirements."

"Tomorrow." She lifted her hands, fingers spread, as if she were calming a room full of Boo's play-pals. "Your flight crew is working overtime. Everything will be solved soon." To the rest of her flight attendants, she said, "We'll meet later, after we all have some time to recover."

Natalie stayed behind after the rest walked away. "How are you doing, hon?" she asked.

Jordan was afraid to admit how upset she was. "It's too surreal to grasp . . . that we're here and Earth's gone. It doesn't seem possible."

"Because it's nothing we could ever imagine," Natalie said, sounding a bit husky herself. "Like when the World Trade Center towers collapsed . . . only a million times worse."

Jordan took the translation glasses out of her pocket. Staring at them, she didn't really see them. "Yep."

Natalie's dark eyes radiated sympathy. "And you had a kid, too."

Jordan's laugh was clipped and false. "Now I have two hundred and eighty-six kids."

But the flight attendant saw her joke for what it was: an attempt to cover up the pain. She rubbed Jordan's arm in a caring caress. Then her chin jerked up.

119

"You've got company coming, and I'm outta here. Call if you need me." With her braided ponytail bouncing behind her, Natalie strode off on her assigned mission.

Jordan shoved on her glasses and turned around. Kào's own glasses glinted in the soft overhead light. So did the nubs of his beard on his chin and above his upper lip, but not where the scar sliced across his face. She tried not to think too hard about what Ben had asked: *How do we know?*

"It is time for me to take my leave," Kào informed her in a careful tone, the way he'd sounded in the commodore's briefing room. His voice took on a certain husky quality when it deepened like that. She swallowed. How much had he heard, and understood, of her conversation with Natalie? She hoped little. As it was, he saw too much of what she tried to keep hidden.

Suddenly her voice was tight from too much talking and a throat thick with the unrelenting need to bawl her eyes out. She didn't like the way the guy was able to get under her skin like this. Ben was right—Kào *was* dangerous. But in a way that the purser never imagined. "I'll see you at our meeting tomorrow," she responded crisply.

"Only after you take your much-needed rest."

She tempered her tone. "You look like you could use some oblivion yourself."

For a moment, he looked as if he bore the weight of the world on his shoulders. "Oblivion," he agreed bleakly. "One of the few things in life that is not overrated. If the chance presents itself today, in any form, take it."

Leaving that uncomfortably true statement echoing in Jordan's head, Kào turned on his heel and left.

Later, alone in her quarters, Jordan took his advice. But oblivion turned out to be elusive. And the sobbing session she'd expected never came. The next day and the ones afterward were a blur of shock and mourning for everyone on Flight 58. The crew and passengers asked little of her, respecting her sorrow as they nursed their own. If ever there was a time to fall apart in the privacy of her room, those first days were it. But the pain never broke her.

She couldn't decide if that was a good thing or bad.

After that, she busied herself keeping up with everyone's requests, complaints, and questions. Kào returned every day, once a day, as they'd decided. He declined to enter the refugee quarters unescorted, and she'd overheard him instruct Commodore Moray's aides, Rono and Poul, to adhere to the same code. Now, when those red-eyed assistants came around with their administrative questions—"Is anyone ill? Do you have enough bedding?"—they waited until Jordan met them at the door and spoke to her there.

She wanted to believe that it was Kào's way of respecting Flight 58's sovereignty over this small area. But he might only be using caution. Despite her efforts to create a climate of understanding, many, including Ben, the chief purser, inexplicably focused their bitterness on the aliens for what had happened to Earth—and shot Kào the dirty looks to prove it.

On the afternoon of the fourth day, Kào showed up with two handheld computers. "Hi-tech, palm-sized language converters made from an improved database that transforms speech to text," he began without preamble. "Handheld translators, we call them. There are too few pairs of conversion-glasses onboard, so we will use these now."

He thrust out his hand. She removed her glasses and dropped them into his huge palm. In exchange, he gave her the new translator. It fit perfectly in the hollows of her cupped hands. "How does it work?"

"Read the text scrolling across the screen."

Like before. Only now all the letters were correct, whereas some had been mirror images or upside down when using the glasses. "I thought I'd miss the glasses. But this is better. Much better."

"You can thank Ensign Pren. She programmed three hundred of these devices, enough for all of your people, with leftovers to spare."

Jordan sensed a tensing in his demeanor whenever he mentioned the ensign's name. He didn't like her, she guessed. But there was something else, too, hidden from her, hidden by this man whose face revealed little. Her eyes searched for and found the terrible brand on his neck, the puckered tip of which peeked above his collar. When it came to secrets, she'd bet that his issues with Trist were only the tip of the iceberg.

"Contained in the translator is an educational database, as well," he explained. "Alliance history, language, science—it is all there. Study it. The more you know, the better off you will be. Extensive information can also be obtained at the workstation we provided."

"Yeah. Dillon's new best friend," she said wryly.

Even as she spoke with Kào, the charming Irishman was struggling to learn the ropes of the new computer mounted in the wall. He'd lunged at the machine as soon as it was installed, his hunger to see what it contained comparable to a starving dog's. "When are we going to get our own computers back? People are asking for them." While the luggage had been returned, there had been no sign of the laptops and walkmans, or of any of the electronics.

"Now that the language database is complete, I see no reason why you can't have the items returned," he said to Jordan.

The crew and passengers straggled back from the dining area, where meals were dropped off three times a day. The chatter was louder today. Some were beginning to feel more like themselves, she guessed. The children certainly were, weaving between the adults in a rowdy taglike game, the rules of which only the kids could understand.

Kào watched them with curiosity and longing. "Your people remind me of a large, noisy family."

His wistfulness told her that he was homesick. She imagined that life on a starship was similar to a navy man's life, being at sea more than at home. "You must come from a big family. Or have one."

He appeared taken aback by both observations. "I've no life-partner, or mate—*wife*, in your language." To her shock, he'd used the English word. "As for being from a large family . . . if I am, I have no memory of it. I was orphaned when I was not quite three Earth years of age."

Jordan's hands clenched. For a moment, she forgot her own sorrow. Kào hadn't been much more than a toddler when he'd lost his parents.

"My situation wasn't the tragedy it might seem, Jordan." He had the strangest way of answering questions she hadn't asked. "I had a solid upbringing, although not a conventional one, by any means. I was adopted by a widowed but well-to-do military officer, and I grew up aboard starships, a series of them. They were Perimeter vessels, like this one, tasked with patrolling the border areas. At times, it was treacherous duty, and no families were allowed aboard. Thus, I found myself the only child among hundreds of adults: one father, who was busy for three thirds of the day—and then some—and more self-appointed parents than I could count. I never had to learn what it was like to compete for attention as one of many siblings." His eyes unfocused, as if he were searching for memories. A flicker of deep sorrow brought clarity back to his gaze and his attention back to her.

"Do you want to sit down?" she offered quickly. Everyone she'd encountered all day had desired direction, or had complained, or had been needy of support. Kào asked nothing of her. Suddenly she found she longed for a few moments of quiet conversation, of simple, undemanding companionship. "I constructed a briefing room today. Would you like to see it? We can meet there from now on, instead of here in the middle of Town Square."

"Town . . . Square?" He scrutinized his translator.

"We've dubbed it that, yes. It means a central place. And while we're at it, I might as well welcome you to New Earth."

He nodded, his eyes dark, unreadable. If his mouth hadn't softened, she wouldn't have known he approved. "New Earth it is, then."

With soldierly formality, Kào followed her to a corner she'd blocked off from the rest of the expansive room by a movable divider. There she'd dragged a table and enough chairs for all the flight attendants. Office supplies had been gathered from those who had them, and stored. The activity had given her an hour or so of distraction. "It's working out well," she said with satisfaction. "Less noise, and much more private."

He gazed at her efforts in that peculiar, careful way that males do when you call their attention to something you want them to admire. "It is quieter," he agreed, peering between the divider and the wall, looking almost disappointed that he'd lost his full view of New Earth. From what he had just told her, he probably was.

With deference, he pulled out her chair. "Please, sit." His formality was endearing, the way he acted like such a gentleman around her. Chivalry had become a dying art on Earth.

Then, holding his own floating chair in place, he sat, releasing a breath when he was finally settled. He was strong, athletic, but today he moved like an old man.

"What happened? Were you hurt?" she asked.

"I spent the day in medical. My ribs had to be broken and reset."

Uh, yeah. "Thanks to me."

He read the translator. His expression didn't change. But then, it rarely did. "A hazard of the job," he said. She couldn't tell if he was goading her or not. "No need to worry, however. It was a minor procedure. Just time-consuming." He pointed to his abdomen. The gray-blue fabric stretched across his chest. It wasn't hard to imagine the hard body he kept hidden beneath his uniform. "The medics forced me to lie prone for two full thirds of the shipboard day to make sure the bones fused to their liking." He took a deep breath as if to prove he was fit for duty. He didn't need to prove anything to her; the evidence was clear.

She swiped her Earth-made clipboard and pen off the table, trying to focus on the list she'd made. It was tough to decide what made her more uncomfortable, knowing that she was responsible for his injuries, or that she'd bothered to admire his male attributes in the depths of grief. "Okay. Next item on the list," she said a little too sharply. "The people who are eating enough to care have complained about the food. It's bland. Tasteless." She put down the clipboard. "I understand if you're worried about allergic reactions after what happened with the sedative gas, and I'm grateful, but this food—some of it tastes almost synthetic." She remembered trying the white patties mixed with rubbery purple flecks that had stuck to the roof of her mouth like sunflower seeds mixed with peanut butter, only without the flavor—*any* flavor.

He sat back, not seeming to care that his chair bobbed like a duck on water. "Odd. We don't switch over to synthetics until near the end of a voyage, and only if it's a particularly long one." He typed something into his computer. "I'll look into it."

Kào's comm beeped. He exhaled impatiently and answered the call. Trist Pren, Jordan wagered. The woman had perfect timing—ten, fifteen minutes into their appointments, she always interrupted Kào. Jordan hadn't seen her in person since that first day, but found it interesting how she'd managed to disrupt all four of their meetings. On purpose, or not? To thwart Jordan's efforts as leader, or coincidence? Either way, Jordan hoped to set things right between them eventually. She'd acted in self-defense the day when she'd injured Trist with the escape slide, not out of spite. She wanted Trist to know that, if the woman didn't already.

Sure enough, the ensign appeared in the tiny, high-resolution, three-dimensional screen on Kào's computer. If Jordan hadn't recognized Trist by her pink skin, white hair, and unsettling red eyes, she would have by her bright lavender lips.

Jordan flipped over her translator to keep from eavesdropping on Kào's conversation. His clipped tone said it all: Whatever he heard, he didn't like.

Kào closed his comm and looked at her. "The rest will have to wait until tomorrow," he said, standing with some effort. "I've been called away."

He was even more reserved than usual as she walked with him to the exit, which was good—he didn't notice the dozens of wary looks following him across Town Square.

At the doorway, he stopped and frowned down at her. "Have you informed your people of the risks of traversing the Perimeter?"

"So far only my crew. As a group we'll brief the passengers."

"Good," he said sharply.

Her heart skipped a beat. "Why?"

"The vessel the commodore has been tracking reappeared. It may be independent merchants thinking they can operate without clearance—that is not uncommon. Or it may be Talagar." He said the word with such revulsion that it made the hairs stand up on the back of Jordan's neck. "Likely it is a false alarm. Every ship we have encountered so far and cleared has been of Alliance registry. But I thought you should know of the development, nonetheless." With a curt bow, he left.

She stared after him, again feeling as if she'd been dragged into someone else's war.

Chapter Eleven

It was springtime. Birdsong and the sound of laughter, Boo's laughter, floated in the crisp, clean air. Jordan climbed down from her mount and raced her daughter across the meadow. Hands clasped, the two whirled around, making circles of trampled grass. It cushioned their fall. Above was a dome of perfect blue. The clouds floated past. Boo's sun-warmed head was tucked between her mother's breasts. Then there was a deep voice. Big gentle hands. This was Jordan's lover . . . the love of her life. She threw open her arms and embraced him, too. A scratchy cheek and soft lips, warm against her neck, moving playfully lower . . .

A giggle woke Jordan. Her own giggle, she realized belatedly and with a good deal of private mortification. "Crap." Her head fell back on the pillow, and she stared into the twilight of her quarters on the *Savior*. She was on a starship, untold miles from home. Yet she could still smell the flowers and green grass, and the clods of moist dirt the horses' hooves kicked up. And the sounds—she could hear

128

them, too: Boo's delighted shrieks of laughter, and another voice, a man's voice, in a quiet, sexy, loving tone she knew instinctively he used only with her.

In her dreams, he was her lover. By day, he was Kào Vantaar-Moray, the grim mediator between her people and his.

He'd kissed her, Kào had. In the dream. And her pulse still raced from the fireworks he set off inside her. *Ay-yi-yi.* As for the psychological implications—well, she didn't want to go there. The man was off-limits, she reminded herself. He was an officer on this ship, and she was a refugee on it.

Why, then, had he started showing up in her dreams?

She groaned, dropping her arm over her eyes. A muffled chorus seeped into her private quarters from the common area. Singing. The multidenominational prayer service had begun. Jews, Muslims, Christians, and members of a few smaller religions gathered together every morning now. Three weeks into their odyssey, they needed all the routine they could get. Pastor Earl said that routine led to ritual, and ritual comforted. Sooner or later, comfort would heal.

For her, healing still seemed a long way off.

She swung her legs over the edge of the bed and sat up. The handheld computer she'd stayed up too late studying slid off her stomach. She was determined to learn to read and speak Key without it. Maybe it was just her dogged sense of responsibility kicking in, driving her to stay up late cramming a new language into a mind scrambled with shock and grief. She'd soaked up Alliance history, too, until her head ached with it. But she didn't see that she had a choice. She was in charge of this ragtag group; she had to be smart enough, aware enough, and fluent enough to communicate their needs to their rescuers, here and wherever they'd end up.

Her bare feet hit the climate-controlled floor. Warmth

worked its way up her legs. Automatically she reached for her little black date book and crossed off another day. Here on the *Savior*, there was a mind-boggling variety of technology available to tell time, but Jordan preferred the ritual of checking her Earth wristwatch and marking off the days in her pocket calendar with her ordinary Earth pen. And she'd keep doing so until one or the other failed. It was her own little ritual, using personal and familiar items from home. Somehow it had helped her to keep it together. Captains didn't have the luxury of falling apart.

A fresh round of singing reminded her that she'd overslept. She never overslept. Hunched over, she rubbed her eyes. She was surprised that no one had come looking for her this morning.

Or likely someone had, like Natalie or Ben, and decided not to wake her. The past two weeks had been hell for her, and they knew it. Jordan had been inundated with questions, requests, demands, complaints, confessions, and hugs. Even dirty looks. The full spectrum of human need. What a change from the first week. During that horrible period, they'd asked little of her, and she'd passed on to Kào only a fraction of what information she had for him now. But in the past few days, the passengers' veneer of shock had melted like ice cubes in hot tea. The minute Jordan stepped outside her quarters this morning she'd have to deal with it all over again. Today, tomorrow, and for as long as they were on this ship. And most likely beyond, when they settled in their new home, wherever that would be.

Her father would have told her: *Courage is accepting the challenge though it's easier to give up.*

She got ready with the detached efficiency of a robot and stepped inside her tiny "cleansing booth." A vaguely applescented wheeze signaled the start of the sterilization that passed for a shower. A waterless mist enveloped her. It was

130

safe to breathe, Kāo had assured her, but she tried not to. If sedative gas could cause spontaneous abortions, who knew what sanitizing mist might do?

As soon as the timed application of mist cut off, she picked through the contents of her suitcase, a small black Travelpro Rollaboard that held two days' worth of clothing, a pair of shoes, a hair dryer that was useless now, a paperback, and a makeup bag—routinely packed items that had transformed suddenly into treasured heirlooms: Wear them out and they were gone forever. No Earth-made items would replace them. Ever. And that was still so freaking hard to imagine. . . .

Go numb, she told herself. It worked. And it was getting easier all the time. Sometimes she wondered if forcing yourself not to feel was like crossing your eyes: You could become stuck that way. But who was to say that permanent numbness was a bad thing? Who said she had to *feel* to fulfill her responsibilities as leader?

She chose her usual outfit of jeans and a T-shirt, eternally clean from being run through a clothes sterilizer every evening. The aliens had provided all their guests with melon-colored jumpsuits, but no one wore them; they looked too much like prison outfits. Dry-brushing her hair turned it to frizz, but the vanity that caught her finger-combing gel through her blond curls seemed out of place, considering her circumstances—but she did it nonetheless. "You can't stop treating yourself," Natalie insisted. "Or you stop living."

Wrestling her unruly mop into a ponytail, Jordan took a deep breath to ready herself for the onslaught of demands. She shoved her feet into white Nike slip-ons and walked from her sleeping area into the chaos of Town Square.

She found Ben sitting in the back row of floating seats at the prayer service. Her seat bounced gently as she sat, and she frowned, planting her feet on the ground. "I hate these chairs," she grumbled to herself. They weren't anchored to the floor. It was an odd reason not to like a piece of furniture, but she was afraid of heights, too. Yeah. Her. Scared of heights. A pilot. She'd spent the greater part of her life explaining that one to people. She didn't understand why everyone was so surprised to hear that. There was a difference between flying and falling. When you sat strapped into an airplane seat behind a closed window, it was nothing like peering over the edge of a tall building or climbing up, up, up the rungs of a high diving board. Her stomach turned to ice and her legs to rubber just thinking about it. Her older brother John, in his relentless teasing, told everyone that her desire to fly had been downloaded into her body by mistake, because it didn't match anything else in her personality. He swore that somewhere there was a kindergarten teacher who looked like Chuck Yeager and hated airplanes.

John. . . . Her heart turned over, and she stared harder at her clipboard. She had no doubt that her fire-chief brother had spent his last moments rescuing everyone he could. The thought conjured the familiar ache in her throat. Quickly she willed herself into numbness.

Awkwardly she adjusted her fanny on her chair and scooted closer to Ben. "Hi," she whispered.

"Hi." He didn't glance up from his meditation.

She closed her eyes, seeking her own. But her weak concentration was too-easily shattered by a clicking noise.

She opened an eye. Natalie was striding toward her on high-heel sandals, her multi-braided ponytail bouncing behind her. A sheaf of paper was wedged under one arm, and she'd stuck a pen behind one ear. She meant business. And there was nowhere for Jordan to run.

The flight attendant hopped onto an empty chair and glided over. In a gesture of futility, Jordan shut her eyes.

"It won't work, hon," Natalie said under her breath so as

not to interrupt either Father Sugimoto, the soft-spoken Hawaiian Catholic priest, or the effusive black minister they called Pastor Earl. "I saw you look at me."

A Post-it note held delicately between two red-lacquered fingernails landed in Jordan's lap. "I added more names," Natalie said. "Karen Hoskins says she's missing a gold chain. Let's see—ah, Katherine Schlem, she wants the airplane searched for a lost earring. And Janice Bennett had a tote bag of paperbacks with her and can't find it—says she needs to read to stay sane."

"We all need something," Jordan grumbled, fighting both inadequacy and irritation as she scanned the list of personal needs, all of them critical to the originators. Fifteen new requests. Yesterday's list had thirty. And there'd be more as people came out of their shock to discover that they'd lost possessions onboard the airplane or couldn't find items that should have been brought to New Earth when Kào's helpers retrieved luggage from the cargo compartments.

Search airplane—PERSONALLY! She scribbled the note into her date book. She hadn't seen the 747 since that first day. She had no idea of its condition. Of course, an airliner was useless to them now, but she had a proprietary interest in the craft all the same. "Everything else is from yesterday, right, Nat?"

"Yeah. I just thought you'd like them written down."

"My brain's a trampoline." Jordan agreed. "If it's not written down, it bounces off."

Natalie rubbed her arm in a caring caress. "You got that right," she said softly. "Hey, I'm giving pedicures later. Stop by and treat yourself." Wearing her no-arguments expression, she gathered her paperwork and moved on to her other duties.

The woman never sat still. Maybe her defense mechanism was staying busy so she wouldn't have time to think. Jordan's gaze slid to the chair next to her. Ben sat hunched over, his face cradled in his hands, his lips moving as he muttered fervent prayers. Now, *there* was a guy who thought *too* much.

A movement in the corner of her eye pulled her attention from Ben. Ian Dillon, the redheaded Irishman. It was obvious that he was waiting for her, and she used it as an excuse to sneak away from the prayer service before it ended, moving her a few steps closer to her secluded corner briefing room before everyone was released.

As she approached, Dillon gave her a concerned perusal. "You look tired."

"Find me one person who doesn't."

"I don't think I could."

"I'm not sleeping well," she confessed. Dillon was the least needy of everyone onboard, and the least likely to panic at any perceived weakness on her part. If life had stayed normal and she'd met him on Earth, she might have thought about dating him. But life wasn't normal anymore, and starting up a relationship was the furthest thing from her mind.

"Nightmares?" he commiserated.

"No. Dreams." Of Boo. Of horses, meadows, and sunlit glades in the Rockies. Of all the things lost to her forever. She forced a smile. "So, what's up, Dillon?"

"I need your blessing."

"I'm afraid you'll have to ask Father for that." Jordan glanced over her shoulder. Father Sugimoto caught her eye and cocked a brow. Guiltily she crossed herself, to his obvious satisfaction. What did she expect after admitting to the priest that she was raised Catholic and then sneaking away from Mass?

Dillon chuckled and beckoned for her to follow. "Not for this I won't. I've embarked on an exploration venture of sorts. I want to show you what I've found before I proceed any further."

Before they could move, the prayer services ended, sending throngs of passengers in search of Jordan.

"Captain," a woman called out as she rose and limped toward them, a fifty-pound hitchhiker attached to her leg. A little girl, a year or so younger than Boo, clung to the woman's thigh. "Hi, Lydia Funneman here. And that's Katie." She smiled indulgently at her child and ruffled her hair. "The kids are going to hate me for asking, but have you found out anything more about us getting fresh fruit and vegetables?"

"I'm working on it. The medics were worried about food allergies." Jordan took out her date book and to her growing list she added, *Ask about diet!* "I'll be following up on it later today, Lydia," she assured the woman, who smiled and moved on.

Next a group of five women crowded in Jordan's direction. She was overwhelmed with a desire to flee, to tell everyone to fend for themselves. But it wasn't that she didn't want to help; she just needed a break. Inspiration hit. "Did I see you ladies at yesterday's two-mile speed walk?" she asked. "No?"

That stopped them. Jordan flexed her biceps. She had begun bullying everyone to get in shape. Who knew what conditions awaited them wherever they were going? " 'Stay strong and survive,' right? Oh, look. Over there, at the far wall. Another walking group is forming. Give me a few minutes, and I'll join you."

The women looked less than enthusiastic and turned away from her. Jordan grabbed Dillon's elbow. "Let's go." A businessman in a flowered shirt waved at her. She pretended not to see him. "Dillon, help. Start talking to me nonstop, as if whatever you're telling me is the most important thing to our survival."

"It may very well be." He took her by the arm and swept

135

her forward at high speed. It worked: everyone let them pass by.

He led her to the community computer, sleek and inset into the molded wall. A floater chair bobbed next to it. Empty food containers and sanitizer wipes indicated that Dillon was spending a lot of time here. "I'm in," he said, bouncing onto the chair.

She squinted at the screen. The alien workstation was linked to the shipboard computer. The letters and numbers still looked like gibberish to her when taken in all at once. "What do you mean, you're in?"

"In the computer."

"But they gave us the computer. We're *supposed* to use the language program and the educational database."

"The educational database looks quite fine, actually. But look. I just accessed a schematic of the ship."

"How?" She leaned over his shoulder. Like every computer she'd seen so far, this one had a screen that could be bent to fit any surface, even rolled up and shoved in a pocket. "Their stuff is nothing like we have on Earth."

"Ah, that is where you're wrong. Their computer programs rely on the same small set of standard modules— forms to accept data to a program, files to keep the data in, calculations to transform that data, techniques to sort the data, forms to present the data to the user upon demand, the ability to present results in various graphics, and so on."

His freckled fingers smoothed over the flexible screen and found the keyboard, or what she guessed was the keyboard. He began typing, using the alien runes. "They're on what's similar to a network in Earth terms. It allowed me to get into the main computer."

"The main *ship* computer?"

He nodded.

"Good Lord," she mumbled. She glanced nervously over

her shoulder. What was the punishment for breaking and entering?

"As expected, when I got there, the mainframe, I was located in an applications program. Just like on Earth, it's all that's needed to call up a veritable buffet of other applications. Which I have. I've been dining quite nicely all day."

"Yeah?" She leaned over his shoulder. "On what?"

"Shipboard schematics," Dillon said. "This is one of the decks. I'm not sure which, though." His fingertips tapped away. The image changed. "And this—I think it's a maintenance status page for that deck."

She was speechless. Dillon was a bloody genius, in his words, if he'd learned enough Key and was computer-adept enough to log on and wander into places that might not be intended for their viewing.

"These are life-support readouts." He frowned, typing faster. "Temperature . . . moisture content in the air. I'm better at reading Key than speaking it. And I've got my numbers down pat," he added proudly.

All around them, the chaos of a couple of hundred people in relatively close quarters simmered. But Jordan's attention was riveted by Dillon's fingers pitter-pattering over the glowing runes. Each keystroke brought up new images on the computer screen. Despite an obvious language and technology handicap here on the starship, Dillon was working the computer like a pro. She'd bet he was one of those lucky folks who tackled computers instinctively. "You said you worked for a high-tech company," she prompted.

"Network Global Technologies. In Dublin." Regret he didn't need to explain washed over his face. "Beautiful city, it was, Jordan." He resumed typing.

"Were you . . . a hacker?"

"Hackers have an undeserved bad name," he replied in an obvious non-answer. "Easily ninety percent of the infor-

137

mation anyone wants is available for the taking. The difficult part is recognizing and analyzing it. Of the remaining ten percent, half can usually be inferred from the material you already have. There's no greater fun than developing an understanding of a system and finally producing the skills and tools to defeat it."

"And you're having the time of your life figuring it all out." In a way, she envied him the distraction.

His blue eyes sparkled. "For me, the process of 'getting in' is always more exhilarating than what I discover in protected files."

His excitement was contagious, a much-needed dose of optimism. "What was your job title at Global?"

"Senior VP."

"Yeah, but what were you really?"

He barely glanced up. "A spy."

"Get out of here." All she could think of was 007. Ian Dillon didn't look like James Bond. But he'd transformed a heart-starting device into a weapon and had hacked into a computer built by a civilization capable of light-speed space travel. One didn't learn such skills in prep school. "Who'd you work for? The UK? Scotland Yard? The Russian Mafia?" she threw in for good measure.

"Nothing that tedious, no. My chessboard of intrigue was industry—the computer industry. I checked up on the bad guys. And when the bad guys hired me, well, I'd get them information on the good guys."

"You spied for both sides?" She wasn't sure if she liked that.

"Money has a way of erasing borders and loyalties." He said it as if the concept was one she'd relate to or understand. "It cost a pretty pence, though, for what we could do."

"I'm sure it did." Jordan tapped her chin with her index finger. Dillon reminded her of her two pet cats, loyal because they *wanted* to be, not because they *had* to be. "While you're exploring, see if you can find out anything about our resettlement plans. It's been over two weeks, and I know nothing. Kào says that's because his government hasn't decided where to put us. But sometimes I think he's as in the dark about things as we are. But unlike him, we've got to understand what our future involves, even if it means digging for the facts ourselves. I think you may have just made that possible."

Dillon went back to work. His mouth remained in a smile. Obviously, he was pleased with her encouragement. "Ah, look," he murmured in his leprechaun-like brogue. "More deck diagrams. Next I'll figure out where our rooms are in relation to the rest of the ship. We could use a map."

"We sure could. Be careful, that's all I ask. I don't want us getting into trouble before we know what 'trouble' means to these people."

"Darth Vader's here!" It was Christopher's usual delighted warning cry. He sang it out every time his "spaceman" showed up at the door.

"Speaking of trouble." Dillon jerked his hands away from the computer, and the flexible monitor snapped into its container like a window shade on a roller. Folding his hands on his lap, he began whistling an innocuous, I'm-so-innocent little tune.

With that proverbial hand-caught-in-the-cookie-jar feeling, Jordan turned around. At the far end of the common room, Kào Vantaar-Moray stood in the doorway, his hands clasped behind his back.

Chapter Twelve

The epitome of chilly composure, Kào appeared unaware that he was the target of Jordan's attention; he was too mesmerized by the bustle of Town Square. "He's early, way early. I hope we didn't trip an alarm by hacking into the computer."

"Oh, he's come around in the morning before," Ben said, appearing out of nowhere and joining Jordan and Dillon at the computer station.

"I never see him," she said.

"You're too busy to notice. He doesn't ask for you; he stays in the doorway, watching us, like he's doing now."

Their eyes shifted to Kào.

"Check out those eyes," Ben muttered. "It's like he's sizing us up to sell on the market."

Dillon stopped typing. "What market?"

"The human market. I don't know."

"Come on, guys," Jordan complained. Ben was scaring himself.

But Dillon took the ball and ran with it. "Would they intend to sell us individually or as a package deal? It would depend on the going galactic rate, I suppose. And what we'd be sold as, too. Food or slaves."

"Stop it," Jordan hissed. "The last thing we need is a rumor like that turning dormant fear into panic." Ben already looked like he was about to be sick.

Dillon's fingers returned to the community computer keyboard. "Is there a way to check the futures market for humans, I wonder?"

Jordan groaned. Grabbing Ben by the arm, she tugged him toward the conference room. "You haven't been to a single one of the meetings between Kào and me. It's time you started attending."

"Right now?"

"Now."

He resisted at first. Then he gave in and walked with her.

"You'll change your attitude once you talk to him," she encouraged. "He's not as intimidating as he looks."

"Well, forced to choose, I'd rather hang out with ol' Attila than those two red-eyed aides. They know something that we don't, I swear it. Those albinos . . . Something's up, but I can't tell what."

His apprehension was contagious. She girded herself against it. Unless she kept a clear head, she wouldn't be able to sift the facts from the unfounded fears that bombarded her daily. "I respect your opinion," she said, more softly. "Just tell me the minute you figure out what it is that's bothering you, okay?" Or maybe Dillon would find out first.

They passed a group of people performing Tai Chi. Others lifted makeshift weights. Men and women jogged

around the perimeter of the room, and four of the five ladies Jordan spoke to earlier had heeded her suggestion to
join the speed walk.

Natalie breezed past the groups and waylaid Jordan with
a new list that looked to be a mile long. "How about I
handle it?" Ben offered.

In her heart of hearts, Jordan wanted nothing to do with
the list. Ben clearly wanted nothing to do with Kào. "All
right. Why not?" she gave in with a sigh, exchanging
glances with Natalie. "I'll see you both at the staff meeting."

She turned her attention back to look at Kào. Strangely,
the weight pressing down on her shoulders lifted. Relief
filtered down through her body, bringing an almost-bounce
to her step. All of a sudden, she felt ready for anything,
even trying an unaided conversation in Key, her new
tongue.

She tucked her translator into the back pocket of her jeans
and approached him. "Good day, Kào," she said, speaking
to him in his language for the first time.

His face lit up, as much as a face as forbidding as his
could brighten. She remembered her dream and endeav-
ored not to look at his mouth. "Good day, Captain," he
responded.

They regarded each other expectantly. Jordan was
tongue-tied. Deciding what newly memorized words and
phrases to use was like trying to choose a chocolate from a
just-opened box of candy. "You are here," she stated in an
ill-fated attempt at witty conversation.

A fleeting sparkle of amusement illuminated the man's
eyes. "Yes, I am. I see that you are here, as well."

His teasing sent an airy, happy feeling floating up
through her middle. After the stomach-churning misery of
the past couple of weeks, the sensation was welcome. Particularly after the most recent scare with the sighting of yet
another wandering starship that in the end turned out not

to be Talagarian. "I not see you here," she tried to explain, "at morning." She shook her head. "*In the* morning."

"Typically, you are immersed in your duties. I don't want to interrupt you."

She waved her hand. "I will like."

His eyes gleamed. "Then I will."

She did just what she said she wouldn't: She watched his mouth form each word. Were his lips as warm and soft as they were in her dreams? Heat flared in her cheeks and warmed her lower belly. Now she was tongue-tied for a different reason.

"Captain Cady." An elderly Hawaiian couple approached. Neither was over five feet tall, but their eyes glowed with feisty strength. Jordan had assumed that Kào's presence would keep most people at bay, giving her a bit of a break. Apparently not.

"The senior citizens of United Fifty-eight would like to start an afternoon bridge club," the woman announced.

Jordan wondered if she'd be expected to approve every activity, no matter how inconsequential. "I'm all for anything to help ease stress," she said.

The couple nodded eagerly, thanking her. Behind them was yet another pair of passengers, two women, their faces drawn with irritation. Jordan recognized one of them as the lady who'd started the deluge of roommate-swapping requests the night they'd arrived. The other woman could be her twin, and perhaps was. Jordan smiled. "How are the sleeping arrangements working out?"

"Not good. *She* doesn't want Sherri in our bed group. I do."

"Sherri?" Who the heck was Sherri?

"I didn't say I wanted her to leave," the sister argued. "But she has to toe the line. She has to try to get along."

The first women rolled her eyes. "Try heeding a little of your own advice, Lee, and maybe we'll get somewhere."

The verbal jabs flew back and forth. "Hold it!" Jordan's hand flew up. The women shifted their attention to her. "Wasn't this already brought up to the flight attendant in charge of your sleeping area?" It sure sounded familiar. But Ben and the other flight attendants were charged with keeping tabs on the many squabbles. Jordan hadn't the time to keep up with them all.

Lee answered sullenly. "Yes, it was."

"Then it'll be taken care of. That's your supervisory flight attendant's job."

"Today?" Lee's twin ventured.

"Yes." Jordan tried hard to keep her voice even. Patient. Understanding. Calm.

The sisters exchanged glances, then they nodded what Jordan interpreted as their thanks and stalked away.

Jordan glanced apologetically at Kào, giving him a shrug that said: "It's not always this bad." She couldn't afford to have it get back to the commodore that her reins of command were slipping. She might not like the job of leader, but she liked the idea of a stranger in her position even less.

The Darth Vader-shooting boy named Christopher skidded past, his feet slipping on the smooth flooring.

"Come back, Christopher!" Katie, the little girl Jordan had seen earlier with her nutrition-concerned mother, chased after him. "I want to play with you!"

Kào's black eyes sparkled and, incredibly, a dimple appeared in his right cheek.

A dimple! Who would have guessed? *Steel on the outside, marshmallow on the inside.* That's how her mother would have described this man.

The children skidded and stumbled around their legs. "They're so active," Kào observed. He reached out to tousle Christopher's hair. The boy shrieked in surprised delight. "Darth Vader" had touched him.

The dent in Kào's left cheek deepened. "You like children," Jordan commented with some surprise.

"I know nothing about them. Nor have I seen many—and certainly none in years."

"Did you know that that little boy, Christopher, was the first to figure out that you were an alien?"

"An alien?" Kào pretended to be affronted. "I'm not an alien. *You* are the aliens."

"That depends on your perspective."

"Indeed."

"Extraterrestrial would have been a better word," she acknowledged.

"Too many syllables for a boy his size."

Jordan laughed softly. He'd made her laugh, actually made her laugh when she'd wondered if she ever would again. *Thank you, Kào.*

"Did you have siblings?" he asked out of the blue.

An invisible fist punched her in the stomach. One look at Kào's face told her he regretted the question as soon as he saw its effect on her, or maybe as soon as he'd asked it. She had the feeling he was not a man to whom light conversation came easily, or maybe any conversation at all. It touched her that he wanted to try with her.

"I have an older brother. John. We're very close," she almost whispered. "He's a big sweetie." She could tell by Kào's face that the colloquialism hadn't translated. "Big sweetie—it means a 'good guy.' "

"Sweetie," he tried in heavily accented English.

Her smile almost returned, but her mouth wasn't quite ready. "You and John, you're a lot alike."

At that, Kào's eyes flashed with startling pleasure. But before she could finish telling him about John, his wife and kids, his career as a fireman, his penchant for barbecues and beach volleyball, and their family traditions, hoping that some of it at least would be translatable from a cultural

145

standpoint, the boy Christopher raced past and tripped over Kào's boots.

Kào tried to keep the boy from falling. But Christopher evaded his grasp, stumbled, and took off again, the girl right on his heels. Giggling, they disappeared into the crowd without looking back.

As Jordan watched them run off, desolation unexpectedly formed a tight little ball in her chest. The children reminded her that her own baby was gone, that Boo had died in terror without her mother there to hold her. Why did there have to be kids aboard?

She found Kào studying her. In his perceptive gaze, she felt naked, her personal misery, her guilt, laid out for him to see. "They're your future, Jordan."

Again he'd answered a question she hadn't asked aloud. She was too surprised to reply with anything but the truth. "It's not that I don't want them here. It's that every time I look at them, I wish *my* child were here, too."

"That I know."

Three simple words: *That I know.* His compassion was so bluntly apparent and unadorned with ulterior motives that it was all she could do not to fall into those strong arms and cry until her tears were dried up and her voice was gone. If she wasn't careful, his kindness would seep into the cracks in her armor. It might open the floodgates, releasing all her pent-up grief. What if she drowned in the deluge?

She couldn't risk finding out. Better to keep her emotions tightly sealed. Although, around Kào, that was getting harder all the time.

His communicator rang, and she almost jumped for joy. *Saved by the bell*, she thought. Kào opened the device and—no surprise there—answered, "Go ahead, Trist."

The pair spoke rapidly in Key, too rapidly for Jordan to

understand. When Kào closed the communicator, she guessed, "You have to leave." It was with mixed feelings that she said the words. Having someone see right through you was pretty unnerving, but she didn't exactly want him to go so soon, either.

"Yes." He searched her face. "Do you remember me telling you about the observation deck?"

"It's where you go sometimes after our meetings."

His voice lowered to a private tone. "I would like to show you why."

She hesitated.

"It won't take long," he assured her. "Come with me."

Come with me. She read the words reeling across her translator. Inner alarms clanged in her mind. It would be crazy, going off with him alone. *But wasn't it you who just compared him to your brother?* Yes, but John didn't have numbers carved into the side of his neck. "We're in quarantine," she reminded him.

"That's what you call it. But the rules are in fact that your people cannot leave your quarters without an escort—a *Savior* crew member."

He was right. Not that anyone had yet been in the frame of mind to want to leave.

Her attention veered to the group of people waiting for Kào to go so they could corner her. There were thirty of them at least, their eyes shining with unmet needs. She was used to ensuring others' happiness and postponing her own. But would it be so terrible to do something for herself for once? Just for a little while?

Nodding, she stepped toward the exit. The passengers thronged forward. "I'll be right back to answer your questions," she told them. She was going to treat herself. Unknowingly, they'd made that decision for her.

Susan Grant

She spotted Ben and Natalie staring at her. *I'll be right back,* she mouthed.

Then, without waiting to see their reactions, she held her head high and left New Earth for the first time since arriving.

Chapter Thirteen

Outside New Earth, Jordan peered upward to where the walkway disappeared behind what resembled silver and white scaffolding. A mistake. Vertigo made her head spin.

"This way," Kào said.

To purge her dizziness, she trained her eyes on the path's corrugated gray surface as she tried to keep pace with a man who'd grown up on starships like this one. She, on the other hand, had spent her childhood on a series of Air Force bases, with neat little houses and tree-lined streets where neighbors got together for barbecues and it was still safe for kids to ride bikes to the convenience store. Suburbia idealized. And so very different from *this*.

The bottoms of her slip-ons felt sticky, forcing her to lift her legs higher to walk properly. The sensation had something to do with the ship's artificial gravity. Gravity that wasn't quite what she remembered from Earth.

Kào stopped at a locker and pulled out a floor-length

white jacket with a hood. The material was as light as gauze and as durable as rubber. "What's this for?" she asked.

"To keep curiosity at bay."

Fraternizing with the refugees—there must be rules against it. Or maybe the lockdown was still being taken seriously by Kào's crew, even though it had been weeks since she'd seen guards pacing outside the door to New Earth. She shoved her arms into sleeves that were gossamer thin and pulled the hood over her head. Peering at him from under the fabric, she asked, "What would one wear this for?"

"To help keep sterile when cleaning up debris."

So he'd disguised her as the janitor. She shrugged and fell in step with him.

A short distance away stood a tube that sprouted up from the floor, disappearing into the ceiling. "A vertical transport," Kào explained as they stepped inside.

In other words, an alien elevator. It was clear in front, opaque in back, and inside the passenger compartment, no more than six or eight people could have stood close together.

As the tube's door whooshed closed, Jordan's ears popped, and acceleration upward pressed her feet even more firmly to the floor. Kào looked so determined about taking her wherever he was taking her that for those few precious seconds she forgot her pressing sorrow and the headache of leadership, and found herself anticipating what might happen next.

The elevator stopped smoothly and the door opened, letting them out. "The observation deck," Kào announced.

Jordan drew off her hood. At first, she saw nothing. Darkness disoriented her after the bright lighting in the tube. The sudden silence was equally disconcerting. It was so quiet that she could hear her breaths and Kào's slower ones.

As her eyes adjusted, she realized she was in an expansive circular room bathed in starlight.

Stars . . .

Stars were above and all around her, except on the floor that was soundproofed by a thick layer of carpet. A tremor ran through her. It was as if they were in a gigantic clear bubble about to lift off the top of the ship and drift away into infinity. Only her sigh of awe interrupted the silence.

"It is where I come seeking peace," Kào said. "And to think."

"I can see why," she breathed. Although her feet were firmly planted on the carpet, she was unable to shake the sensation of floating. "It's wonderful. Amazing. *Incredible*." Better to use more than one English adjective, in case some didn't adequately convey her awe. She was rewarded when her words translated to a glimmer of happiness in Kào's eyes. He came here for comfort, and he'd wanted to share that joy with her.

As her eyes adjusted further, she noticed that the stars were smeared across the heavens like shooting stars frozen in mid-fall. "I read that the stars look like this because we're traveling in hyperspace."

"Yes. Greater-than-light speed makes the stars appear distorted."

Intellectually, the concept made her curious. Emotionally, she tried not to ponder where the ship was speeding so relentlessly: a new home about which she knew nothing. "I agree with you that this place makes you think." She made a face. "I'm not so sure about the peace part."

"Wait and see." Kào spread the fingers of his right hand and placed them against the clear barrier, all that separated them from infinity. "The farthest detectable stars are ancient. Impossibly so. They were created at the assumed birth of the known universe. Look at them and you see a snap-holo of life fifteen billion years into the past. Worlds that reached their zenith eons ago and are now extinct. One of those long-gone worlds was that of our ancestors. Yours, Jordan, and mine."

A shiver tingled up her backbone. "The Seeders."

"Yes, the Original Ones. Their purpose, their history, their triumphs are a mystery. Except for one: the sowing of their DNA across the galaxy."

"On Earth, we didn't know that. But we had many different beliefs as to the origin of life. Of human beings. The scientists say that we've evolved from earlier forms of life. Creationists believe that God made Earth and everything on it."

"And you?" Kào asked.

She sighed. "Tough question. Both, I'd say. I'm an evolutionist. But I also have faith in God. And now I see that that view may not have been as crazy as I thought." From what she'd learned in her nightly studies, the Seeders were to Kào's people what God was to her. In the past weeks, she'd prayed to, cried to, and screamed at God—*her* God. Did Kào do the same? Did having scientific evidence to prove the beginnings of life strengthen faith or weaken it? Did it demand the human need for religion or denounce it? She didn't know. But it hit home how little she grasped about the culture and history of the Alliance, and how much she had yet to learn.

"Did you know that Seeders fought to keep humanity alive in the shadow of their demise?" he asked. "They knew their time in this realm was ending, yet they never turned their backs on the future, they never stopped looking ahead, looking forward. They never gave up hope." His dark eyes bored into hers. "Don't you, either, Jordan Cady."

Her heart leaped, and her gaze jerked up from the translator.

He regarded her steadily. "I saw the way you gazed after the children, and how you speak of your brother as if he were still alive. But walk among the dead, and it will leech all the pleasure out of your existence. When you cease caring, you become callous and cold." He lifted his arm toward her, making a fist as he abruptly dropped his hand.

She almost whispered. "Is that what the stars tell you?"

"Look to the future and not the past—yes."

He'd reached out to help her without her having to ask, without him thinking her weak in some way.

"What about you, Kào?" she dared, her heart beating hard. "Do you look to the future and not the past?"

A soft, harsh laugh escaped him, though no smile accompanied the sound. His fingers came to rest briefly on the horrible brand on his neck. "What kind of man asks others to do what he himself cannot?"

For a heartbeat, she thought he might end their visit to the observatory. But he stayed, turning away from her to glower out through the clear barrier at the starscape. "The brooding routine won't work with me," she said. "I know all about you big quiet types." And their aversion to accepting comfort. Seeking out help meant you were weak— that's what they thought. She knew, having grown up surrounded by men just like him. Being like him in some ways, herself.

She walked up to him and stopped. "Are you going to tell me why you have numbers burned into your neck?" Gentler, she added, "I want to know."

His tone was flat. "It was how the Talagars told their prisoners apart."

He'd been a POW. Now, so much more about him made sense. "I couldn't imagine being in one of their prisons," she said, suppressing a shudder.

"No, you couldn't." His hand slid to the back of his neck and massaged the muscles there. She would have done that for him, soothing him with her own hands, had she known

153

him better. If anyone was in need of a little tender, loving care, it was Kào.

"Tell me about the scar," she persisted.

He scrubbed his face with one hand. "I was in the Alliance Space Force, a weapons officer, though my father had high hopes that I'd advance into visible, influential leadership positions, once I'd made a name for myself as a celebrated war hero," he said with a certain irony.

"What does a weapons officer do exactly, besides blow up things?"

"Very simply put, that summed up the job. My area of expertise was weapons of mass destruction." He stated it so easily that she could only stare at him in fascinated horror. "There were many different types of weapons from which to choose, and that required much interaction with the battleship's onboard computer. I enjoyed that, and every aspect of my duty. I wanted to purge the Talagars from the galaxy, because they killed my father's family, his first family, in a long-ago raid. That nearly broke him, losing his wife and daughters." He stared outside at the stars. She couldn't help thinking about Trist and the others aboard the *Savior* who looked Talagarian. Jordan liked to think of herself as tolerant and unbiased, but it must be difficult for the Alliance crew members to work with descendants of Talagars, knowing how bestial their ancestors were.

Kào's fingers dragged over the numbers etched in his flesh. "But you wanted to know how I got this, so I will tell you. The Alliance declared war against the Talagars. As soon as I was of the minimum age, I enlisted. Now I could finally avenge my father's family, and do something for *him*," he said with such loyalty-driven passion that it tempered his shocking declaration that his job had once entailed producing as many casualties as possible. "My father is a great and honorable man. He saved my life and gave

154

me a new one. I owe him everything. And I've given him *nothing*." His voice was thick, revealing the intense emotions his face could not.

"Kào. . . ." She stepped toward him, not sure what she intended to do when she got there.

But his hand shot up, a barrier between them. "A year into my service, my warship and the six others traveling with us were to join the rest of our squadron, which was massing in preparation for a major offensive to free the Daldénne system. It was a strategically critical area comprised of many populated worlds that were being ravaged by the Talagars. It was one of my duties to decipher and verify the encoded targeting messages that came in from intelligence scouts posted throughout the galaxy. That day, my message stated that a large Talagarian weapons and ship-building facility had been left virtually undefended because of other clashes draining what was becoming our over-extended Space Force. It was a crucial target, Jordan. If we could destroy it, it would cripple the Talagar force in that vital area. We'd be heroes. Such honors meant little to most of us, though. All we wanted was to bring down the Talagars."

His eyes unfocused, as if he were living the day all over again. "But we needed more than just one battleship if we were to take out that facility. The commanders met. All six heeded my recommendation. We went after the target expecting an easy victory."

He squinted, and his mouth stretched thin. "But the facility wasn't undefended. The message was wrong, or had been a ploy. A Talagar battle force five times our size was waiting for us when we arrived. Since I hadn't expected significant resistance, I led the ships in closer than I would have deemed prudent otherwise. And indeed, it wasn't prudent." He looked to be in physical pain, but she sensed it was emotional agony that gripped him. "The fighting was intense. But all who weren't killed outright in the battle met a fate far worse."

"Talagarian prison," she whispered.

His jaw pulsed. "Yes. As you've probably noticed, our technology is superior to what you knew on Earth. The Talagars have taken that technology and used it to perfect ways to induce human suffering and obedience. There was no way to resist them, if they wanted something from you." He stiffened, fists at his sides, and swallowed forcefully.

They broke you. Oh, Kào, she cried silently. It explained so much, why he was so bleak and reserved.

"To this day I don't know who told them," he went on. "It could have been me. I don't remember. Or it could have been another. Either way, the interrogators learned of the plans for the Daldénne offensive, and used the information to bring about the biggest Alliance defeat of the war."

If Kào's expression was any indication, he carried the weight of that entire catastrophe on his shoulders to this day. She wanted to remove some of it. She said: "That's right. Anyone may have given up that information. Maybe all of you were drugged, beaten, and tortured into talking. You're the only one left alive for your people to blame though. A 'scapegoat' we call it in my language."

"It translates," he informed her with an expression that told her placing a label on his shame brought little consolation. That same expression told her that he truly wished he'd died along with his comrades.

Her chest tightened. What a nightmare he'd lived, and lived still. But how could she, a woman who hadn't been able to help her own husband, a man whose troubles paled in comparison to Kào's, possibly be able to offer solace? Surely, anything she said would be totally lacking. But she tried anyway. "When I was a girl, my father taught me what he called the three laws of courage. Whenever I'm afraid, or I don't know if I can take the next step, I pick the law that fits and repeat it in my head." She took a breath. "Courage is doing the right thing even though you are scared. Courage is accepting the challenge though it's easier to give up. And courage is mustering the strength to stand up when it's easier to fall down."

After a pause, Kào said: "A wise man, your father."

"He had so much wisdom to offer. He was a fighter pilot; he'd fought in a war—the Vietnam War, we called it. Some of his friends were shot down and taken prisoner, brave and honorable soldiers. Like you, Kào."

He grimaced at that, but she continued. "But you wouldn't know it from talking to some of them. Like you, they didn't see themselves as brave and honorable. One man never forgave himself for what he perceived as cracking under the pressure of torture, starvation, and drugs. Impossible odds for anyone." She rubbed her hands up and down her arms. "My father wanted me to know this. He sat me down on the day of my husband's funeral and made sure I listened."

"Your husband died before Earth's destruction, then. That is what you meant when you said that you had no mate."

"Yes. He was killed in a car wreck when my daughter was an infant." She couldn't believe she was telling a man she hardly knew her most personal secrets, her deepest insecurities. But she was. She filled in the details as best she could, taking into account language, planetary, and cultural differences, explaining Craig's difficulties with her success, how the happy-go-lucky part of him shriveled into resentment. And how he'd died, drunk and despondent.

"My father said he couldn't bear to see me take the blame for what was out of my control. 'You did the best you could,' he told me. You did, too, Kào. You did the best you could. You can't ask more of yourself than that. No one can. You've lived through so much. It probably doesn't mean

157

much, but I admire you for all you've done, all you've been through. I truly do."

He read her words on his translator. Then he swallowed thickly and stared out at the stars, seeking out the streaks of light as if they were old friends. "It does mean something, Jordan." He turned around.

"I'm glad," she whispered back.

A glimmer of awareness passed between them. She'd felt it before, this attraction, but here on the observation deck they were alone. It gave their rapport, their developing friendship, a dangerous edge. Dangerous because her developing feelings for him were unexpected. And dangerous because it felt too damned good.

She swallowed hard, finding sudden interest in the toes of her white Nikes. Kào moved closer. His scent was definitively male: a mix of musk, clean, hot skin, and the work-worn leather fittings of his uniform, ludicrously softened by a hint of apples from his shower.

Her heart thumped harder as she dragged her gaze upward, past the thick belt around his waist, up to his broad chest, and finally to the scarred and unconventionally handsome face she'd come to see nightly in her dreams.

His eyes turned darker than midnight as he dropped his gaze to her mouth. Her breath caught.

He wanted to kiss her.

Desire coursed through her in a heated rush. Unbelievably, she *wanted* him to kiss her, hard and hot, taking her to another place, a place where she could forget, where she only had to think of *now*—she and a man she hardly knew, but who somehow no longer felt like a stranger.

Her awareness of him flared hotter, throbbing like her pulse, burning like her skin.

Lord. She wrenched away her eyes, breaking the crackling tension. But the heat between them still sizzled. Jordan had never felt anything like it in her life.

She took a moment to catch her breath, grateful for the starlight so Kào wouldn't see as starkly how flustered she was. "I didn't tell you about the fourth law of courage," she whispered. "My mother's law. 'Courage is feeling happy and alive when it's easier to feel sorry for yourself.' "

Kào read the translation. His jaw muscles flexed.

"It always sounded overly simplistic to me, but now I think I finally get it." She gazed into infinity. "Look to the future and not the past."

His eyes blazed. "If I try, will you?"

The question, spoken with such directness, took her completely aback.

Her hand flattened at the base of her throat. There, her skin was damp with perspiration. Only then did she realize how affected she was by their rollercoaster conversation. *If I try, will you?*

Could she? Could she focus on the future without forsaking Boo? Her heart, her *life.*

"You still have not given me your answer, Jordan."

She clutched her computer until the blood left her fingers. What drove Kào to work so hard to draw her out? Having someone so intent on dismantling her defenses was exhilarating. Exhilaration in the throes of grief; it made no sense. But what did make sense anymore?

Courage is feeling happy and alive when it's easier to feel sorry for yourself.

"I will," she said. Two words, sealing their pact.

Satisfaction warmed his harsh face as he lowered his translator. "I had better return you to your people." His tone was low, intimate, reflecting the fact they'd shared their darkest secrets—and almost a kiss. "They'll be wondering what happened to you."

They'd come here in silence, and they now departed in silence. A long and exhausting afternoon loomed, but afterward Kào would be back for his usual visit. She didn't care how many lists Natalie had given her by then, or how many times she'd had to give Ben a pep talk. She'd have Kào's company for a while. For now, it was all that mattered.

Barb Jensen joined her son John on a tree-shaded redwood deck in the backyard of his ranch-style suburban home. The fall day was crisp and sunny, and the sound of children's laughter rippled from the play area, a sound she used to savor. But now it only reminded her of how much things had changed.

A lump in her throat, she watched her granddaughter Roberta, playing by herself only a few yards from where her cousins clambered on a jungle gym and swings. The boys would soon be her brothers, two older, one younger, when the paperwork was completed, allowing John and his wife to adopt Roberta as their own. Jordan would be happy, knowing that her child was so loved in her absence. But being a close-knit family had its down-side, too. Jordan would have hated the gaping hole her death had left in their lives.

John propped one hip on the railing and folded his muscular arms over his chest. "Look at the kid, those toy horses. That's all she does, Mom. All day, all the time, lost in a fantasy world. It's not normal." He sighed deeply. "She needs closure."

"Closure," Barb muttered. Her fireman son, using psychobabble—she never thought she'd see the day. But then they'd all changed since Jordan's death. "Closure is a myth. People who use the word haven't been through something like this."

"Whatever you call it, Mom, as long as that airplane remains missing, we're not going to have it."

"It's been three weeks and not one piece of scrap metal has washed up." Or had been dredged up, or even found floating. "The flight's vanished. An entire 747—how can you lose something that big?"

John made a sound of frustration in the back of his throat. "God, if I only knew. If any of us knew . . ."

Barb sipped from a glass of iced tea. Despite the mystery surrounding the accident, she'd finally accepted that Jordan was dead. Everyone had: the family, the rescuers, and the news people. Only Roberta refused to give in, refused to believe that her mother's body lay under miles of dark, cold water.

In a way, Barb envied the naïveté that allowed her to do so. The child's therapist might not approve, but that childish optimism was exactly what Roberta needed.

Barb left her glass on the deck and walked across the lawn. A herd of plastic horses was nestled in the grass where her granddaughter's skinny bare legs formed a V. Two knobby, scabbed knees provided the perfect corral.

Roberta held one of the plastic toys with slender fingers. Chipped glittery purple nail polish decorated her nails. "Hi, Grandma," she said without looking up.

Barb crouched next to her. Her knees made popping noises. Roberta's smile showed off a gap where two front teeth used to be. "The grass isn't wet," she assured her.

Barb chuckled. "All right, I'll sit down." She arranged herself on the grass and watched Roberta maneuver a plastic pony around the pen she'd made with her legs. A few leaves that had evaded the lawnmower went tumbling past in a gust of wind. "So, how are we doing, sweetie pie?"

"I dreamed of Mommy last night. She was talking to a man." Roberta's blond curls fell forward, hiding her profile. "Not Daddy."

Not Daddy. Barb's breath caught in her throat. Roberta knew her father was in heaven. If Jordan wasn't "talking" to Craig, then to whom? Was the child psychic? Did she "see" a place—an island perhaps—where Jordan and the others were stranded? *Daughter's Dreams Lead to Mother's Rescue!* It sounded like a feature in the *National Enquirer*, but so did airliners disappearing without a trace. Eagerly, Barb replaced an image of a watery grave with that of a tropical paradise. "Where, Roberta?"

"In the sky."

Barb's wild hopes fizzled. "Ah. In the sky."

Her skeptical tone didn't escape the girl. Shame flitted in those wide-set blue eyes. Even at six years old, the child must understand that her claims were ridiculous. But she clung to them all the same. In a thin, scratchy voice she said, "I dreamed that the man likes horses. And Mommy, too."

Barb twiddled a piece of grass between her fingers. Dreams, that's all they were. Roberta had told the therapist she'd been having them nightly. But Barb was too morbidly fascinated by Roberta's frank answers to let the thing drop.

"Is Mommy happy . . . in the sky?" she couldn't help asking. Craig had never been the man her daughter needed. No matter how strong a woman was, she deserved a strong man. If a good relationship had eluded Jordan in life, then at least she could have one in her little girl's imagination.

But Roberta shook her head. "She wants to come home."

The cold, dense ball of sorrow in Barb's chest expanded. *God help you, baby.* "Maybe this man is an angel sent to help your mother's soul find peace."

The child pursed her lips, and a determined little valley formed between her brows. "No, Grandma. Mommy's not dead. And the man is not an angel."

Chapter Fourteen

Kào strode onto the bridge with a decided spring in his step. On his way past a row of mission techs manning their monitors, he spied a familiar white head. "Greetings, Trist," he called out. "The language program you created for the refugees is working quite well."

The woman almost dropped her handheld.

He walked onward, whistling an old soldier's ditty, until he noticed that the entire row of mission techs stared at him. He paused a moment, then continued. Heads turning and whispering behind hands wasn't new; they all did it when they thought he wasn't looking. Frankly, he didn't care. He rarely socialized with the crew.

The psych-medic had suggested that Kào's self-imposed isolation was a consequence of the length of time he'd spent in solitary confinement in the Talagar prison, but Kào knew better. He simply lacked the urge to form acquaintances.

As a child, he hadn't any playmates, but that was a mat-

Susan Grant

ter of circumstance more than preference. Moray's weren't family ships. As a soldier, he'd finally experienced friendship, camaraderie forged by hardships and fear. But those men were dead now, killed in the war. There had been the occasional longer-term lover over the years, when circumstances permitted such liaisons, but friendship had never been involved or expected. The relationships had been based on sex, an arrangement that had suited the women as much as it had him.

If he looked at his social history objectively, as it was his inclination to be analytical, it didn't make sense that he was so drawn to Jordan. Ah, but he was.

"Kào, my boy!" His father's jubilant voice called to him from across the bridge. Then the man stopped, gaping at him.

Kào cast an uneasy glance down the front of his uniform. "Don't tell me I brushed up against the wet paint in the corridor."

"Your hair is damp."

"Ah, that." He smoothed the fingers of one hand through the cropped wet strands. "I took a water shower." Water was used for cleansing only rarely. Medical insisted on the waterless hygiene showers for health reasons. "I had a particularly long workout, and treated myself."

"Well." His father grinned. "I don't know which pleases me more, that you're working out again or that you treated yourself."

"It was only a water shower, Father," Kào said wryly. "You act as if I wallowed in luxury."

"It's your duty with the refugees." His father waggled a thick finger at him. "Did I not tell you that it would yank you from your doldrums?"

"Actually, Father, you didn't." Kào's mouth quirked. "But I long suspected it was the reason you handed me the chore."

"You know me too well, son." Moray pounded him on the back. "I'm glad it's been a positive experience for you. I admit that I had my doubts after the start."

He wasn't the only one. Jordan Cady had caused them much trouble that first day. But now she caused Kào turmoil of a different sort. His feelings in the wake of their intense and intimate conversation on the observation deck had left him spinning like a lost observation buoy. "She's really something," he mumbled to himself.

"Who is, Kào?"

Instantly Kào regretted letting the remark slip. "Jordan Cady, the refugee leader."

"You're quite taken with her, I see." Even as his father made the statement, the man's narrowed eyes searched Kào's face for confirmation. "Don't lose sight of the fact that she's a refugee, Kào, and you're a ship's officer."

"I understand that, sir."

"I consider you the best man for the job—I still do—but if the refugee woman is complicating matters for you—"

"Nothing is becoming complicated, sir." *Or was it?*

"Good." Moray took a blinking handheld from a passing aide. "Have you given more thought to marrying?"

Kào gave a quick, disbelieving laugh. "No."

"Well, I have. A well-placed mate, that's what you need. As I predicted, the recent elections on Sofu have presented us with many opportunities. Ones I would imagine that you will be as anxious as I to snap up."

Ah, so it was back to this battle again. But today Kào didn't feel like arguing. He felt like . . . whistling.

Moray noticed. "Kào, are you not feeling well?"

"I'm feeling fine." Kào walked to the viewing window where he could see the stars. He stretched, inhaling deeply. "As a matter of fact, I'm feeling more than fine. The best in years." And it was almost the truth. He didn't think he'd ever purge the guilt and the pain, or fully escape the dreams of Talagarian torture that shattered his sleep like broken glass, but the shadows had been pushed farther from his consciousness than ever before.

He turned around to find his father wearing a disconcerted expression on his florid face. "As I said, Kào, I'm glad to hear you've taken to working out again. Weights? Running?"

"Both. Your officers-only holo-arena is an impressive facility." He'd been on the ship for months, but he'd just made his first visit after his observation-deck rendezvous with Jordan. The arena was immense, the three-dimensional, digital holographics vividly real. His father had spared no expense.

"But physical conditioning isn't all I've worked on of late," he continued. "To make sure you receive full credit for your efforts, I had to forward Earth's coordinates to the Ministry of Planetary Registration on Sofu. I thought we already had, but apparently, in the confusion afterward, no one had gotten around to it."

Moray's eyes widened. "Did you first verify the coordinates with my science staff?"

"Yes. And a good thing I did. Apparently, there was a glitch in the data that would have placed the planet in an entirely different zone. But that's been corrected now."

Moray's entire body deflated with his exhalation. It proved to Kào that his father shared his belief that the Earther rescue was critical to restoring his former standing in the Alliance.

"The Ministry is quite taken with the possibilities of your discovery," Kào said proudly. "I'll admit that I, too, am fascinated with the theory that the planet had become separated from the rest of the Alliance in prehistory. I made sure that the Ministry was well aware that you'd made the initial discovery as well as first contact. *And* orchestrated the entire rescue operation."

Moray puffed himself up. "You flatter me," he said with the barest trace of humbleness.

"I want this for you, father," Kào said with quiet conviction. "I want to make up for what happened in the war. Before I leave this ship, I promise you your name will be respected and praised once more throughout the Alliance."

Moray's smile faltered. "What is this talk of leaving the ship?"

If the commodore had his way, he'd keep Kào by his side forever. The man had lost his first family. Kào knew he was loath to lose a second. It was with patience that he replied, "We act as if my recuperative stay here is an open-ended visit, but we both know better. I hold no official position here. Sooner or later I'm going to have to find my own way, my own life."

An aide tiptoed up to them. "Commodore Moray, here is the report on the rogue vessel," he said meekly.

"Thank you, Jinn." Moray made a sound in his throat and took the handheld. "Join me for dinner, Kào. We have much to talk about. And not enough time in each other's company lately to do it."

"Very good, Father. I look forward to it." And normally he would have, Kào thought. But the commodore took his evening meal at the bottom of the second third, cutting into the time Kào had set aside for Jordan and refugee affairs. Dinner with Moray meant that he'd miss their meeting. But such was a son's obligation to his father.

Moray turned away, then stopped. "A thought just occurred to me. Ensign Pren mentioned that her team is finished with the refugees' computers. Perhaps you'd like to give them back. It would be seen as a nice gesture." He smiled and walked off.

Kào rubbed his chin. He'd taken to visiting Jordan in the mornings. Their official meetings remained in the early evenings. Now today he'd be able to show up at midday, too, if he were to use the computers as an excuse.

He returned to Trist's station. "Ensign, the commodore has told me you're done with the refugees' computers. Please arrange for immediate return of the items."

Trist's mouth thinned. "That will not be a good idea."

"Why not? They've lost everything. If we can give them something back, even the smallest link to their lost world, then I want it done."

"But many of the devices were damaged in the data collection process. Not intentionally, Kào, but that was the end result." She tucked wispy strands of colorless hair behind one pink ear. "My advice to you is not to give any back, not knowing which are functional. The refugees will be angry, and blame it all on you. I recommend you schedule the whole lot for destruction—the computers, that is," she said, her red eyes glittering in what appeared to be a smirk. "Not the refugees."

She'd made a joke, one at which only a Talagar would have laughed. Kào frowned. "If you can't save all the computers, then destroy them all? Is that your thinking?"

She shrugged, unrepentant.

Trist had been born and raised under Alliance rule, but her behavior was pure Talagar. He knew, having met enough of the creatures in the past three years to last a lifetime. *Ten* lifetimes. But even Trist couldn't spoil his mood. He was on his way to New Earth, bearing gifts—a brilliant suggestion on his father's part. If decorum prevented him from bringing Jordan flowers, then, by the Seeders, he'd bring her computers instead.

He smoothed his uniform and ran his fingers through his damp hair. "The computers will be returned to their rightful owners, Trist. End of discussion. I thank you for your assistance in the matter. Good day."

Contact

Humming the old ditty that was stuck in his head, Kào fought the unsettling sensation of more than one pair of disapproving red eyes following him as he walked off the bridge.

Chapter Fifteen

The afternoon staff meeting with the flight attendants had just broken up when Christopher galloped up to Jordan, his blue eyes sparkling with excitement. "Darth Vader's here!"

Her gaze swung to where the child pointed, and her heart did a flip. Hands clasped behind his back with that soldierly stiffness that endeared him to her, Kào stood in the hatch, observing the bustle of Town Square. Aloof, self-assured, he looked every inch the cold military man he once was. But Jordan knew that on the inside, he was anything but chilly and detached.

All in one movement, she hopped off her floating chair and shoved her feet into her shoes. "He's early," she said to the others sitting with her. It wasn't easy to keep her pleasure at Kào's unexpected appearance from showing on her face as she gathered her handheld and to-do lists. She could hear the flight attendants' murmurs behind her as she hurried across Town Square. Tough. Let them speculate.

The way she saw it, in a life gone suddenly dark there was one bright spot. And he'd just shown up at the front door.

Kào spied her hurrying toward him and lifted his hand in the Alliance greeting. For a fraction of a second, his gaze dipped to her mouth, sending a frisson of desire racing through her belly.

"Greetings, Kào," she said, a little too breathlessly.

Luckily, he didn't seem to notice. His eyes sparkled, though, and he looked . . . well, he looked great. Happier. The thought that she had something to do with his transformation over the past few weeks warmed her even more. "I have an appointment that will keep me from meeting you at our usual time," he informed her. "I came now, so I could return these."

He disappeared into the corridor, returning with a three-foot-long black pole in one hand and the handlebar of a floating pallet loaded with electronics in the other. He looked like a cross between Santa Claus and a futuristic shepherd as he pulled the cart into the room.

Jordan immediately turned around and called out, "The computers are here!" A cheer went up. All the laptops, CD players, cell phones, and electric shavers had been confiscated the day they'd arrived. She'd assumed it was for security reasons. Now it looked as if they were getting them back.

Near the top of the pile was a scratched and battered, aqua-blue Walkman with a heart-shaped *Black Beauty* sticker on its face. Jordan winced. Just when she thought she had it all under control, one of the shards of her shattered life would slice across her heart. But she put on her "official" face and expressed her gratitude. "Thank you for returning our things." Her appreciation was echoed by many of the others. Kào acknowledged the thanks with a pleased nod.

Ben and Natalie pulled the pallet farther into the com-

Susan Grant

mon area, and the passengers surged toward them.

"Stand back," Natalie ordered in her no-nonsense flight-attendant voice.

"Set them on the floor," Jordan instructed the woman. "And supervise who takes what. Log each transaction, too, in case we have a dispute later."

Kào took the pole he'd brought with him and stood it on the floor. "This is the power stick. If your items don't work for lack of power, touch them here." From the pallet, he chose a mini DVD player and brushed it across the pole's smooth matte-black surface. One stroke and the batteries were recharged. Applause and cries of astonishment rang out. One by one, people brought their electronics to the power stick, reverently, like worshipers laying offerings at an altar. Cheers accompanied each success. It was an impressive piece of tech, answering Jordan's question as to how they were going to charge appliances, since it was doubtful the *Savior* operated on electricity as they knew it.

Kào was scoring big points with everyone, she thought. Unlike her, the others didn't know him. Most remained wary, and she couldn't blame them. But this gesture of goodwill would go a long way toward gaining their trust.

Ben couldn't pass out electronics fast enough. If Kào was Santa, then Ben Kathwari was his industrious elf. He even smiled at Kào for the first time. "This is good, real good," he told Kào as he helped a woman sort through the pile. "Thanks."

Kào appeared quite pleased.

"This baby's mine," the woman Ben had helped said as she found her laptop. "My kids are stored in here." Her lips trembled. "My husband, too. God bless that digital camera he made us buy." She touched the laptop to the power stick. With sharp anticipation, she hurried to a floating chair and opened the case.

Jordan smiled. It was a real boost, seeing Ben and the

others animated after so much ashen-faced gloom.

Then an anguished cry silenced the happy chatter. It was the woman. "There's nothing here! The hard drive was wiped clean!"

"Mine, too," someone else yelled.

Jordan's heart sank. There was a problem with the computers.

"You bastards! You goddamn bastards!" Ben cried.

Kào whipped his arms up in a protective block as Ben plowed into him, throwing them both to the floor.

"Ben! Kào! Hey—break it up." But the two men were too preoccupied to hear her. "Garrett, Rich! Over here—*now*!"

The men pushed their way through the cheering, jeering crowd. Jordan wrung her hands and began to pace in short, jerky steps. She couldn't believe it. Ben and Kào were brawling to the whoops of what sounded like half the population of New Earth. This was exciting to them? This was *fun*? Were the people letting off steam, or were they honestly happy about one of them taking down a ship's officer?

Kào was an expert in hand-to-hand combat—that was obvious. In seconds, he'd used his body with the unemotional efficiency of a top-notch weapon, immobilizing Ben with deadly grace. Flipping Ben beneath him, he pinned him with an armlock to keep the purser from throwing any more punches.

Garrett the Marine grabbed Kào, and Rich Stein, one of her other male flight attendants, took hold of Ben, and they jerked the men apart.

Pulled to his feet, Kào stood with his boots planted wide. His heaving chest was the only sign that the fight had taken anything out of him. His hands were held behind his back by Garrett, but he didn't resist. Ben, to Jordan's dismay, seethed, straining against Rich's hold.

"Return the translator," Jordan ordered. Kào's handheld computer had skittered across the room. It would be his only way of discerning what was said, since everyone had reverted to English. One of the passengers retrieved it and handed it to Kào. "Now let him go," Jordan told Garrett. It wasn't Kào she was worried about, it was Ben.

Jordan turned toward the purser. "What the hell is wrong with you?"

Ben gasped, "He destroyed our laptops!"

Kào's voice was cool, unemotional. "It was a mistake. It wasn't done intentionally."

Jordan translated for Ben. The purser's brown eyes blazed with hatred. "Bullshit! His lips curled back, and he spat. A glob of saliva splattered on the floor near Kào's boots.

Jordan stormed over to Ben. He was shaking from head to toe. "I don't know what's gotten into you," she said under her breath, "but one more move like that and I'll lock you in the brig." Brig? They didn't have a brig. But today's events indicated that they'd eventually have to make one.

But to her appalled shock, Ben shouted past her to Kào. "To you we're animals in a zoo. Have some fun with the monkeys. Get us all worked up over a banana and then take them away. Those laptops were ruined and you knew it—"

"Mr. Kathwari!" Jordan shouted. "Enough." She glared at him until he finally capitulated, sullenly and reluctantly.

"Believe me when I say that I did not know the condition of your computers." Kào enunciated slowly, allowing the few who had studied Key to follow along if they didn't have their translators. "We needed data to build a language database for you," he explained. "Unfortunately, the data-collection process must have erased the hard drives. But we have functional translators now, yes?" He raised his handheld. "And many of your languages from Earth are now stored permanently in the galactic database, never to be forgotten. Your world, in this way, will live forever. I hope

Contact

you'll see that your sacrifice was for the greater good." He
glanced at the sobbing woman who had lost the photos of
her family. "But know that I truly regret the loss of your
personal data. I can collect the affected electronics and see
if there is anything that can be recovered."

After Jordan showed Ben the translation, he spat out,
"Data? It wasn't data. It was their *lives*. Family and friends.
Pictures. E-mails." His voice cracked. "It was all they had
left." Jordan's heart twisted as Ben's eyes filled with the
tears he'd fought. "And now it's gone," he whispered.
"Damn you. Damn all of you."

Ben broke down. Awkwardly she slipped her arms over
the purser's quivering shoulders. She was grateful that the
expectation of imminent death had finally left Ben's eyes,
replaced by garden-variety resentment, which was a lot less
awkward to deal with. Not because soothing Ben had reminded her of trying to cheer Craig when he'd drunk too
much and felt depressed, but because she envied the purser
his ability to cry. Since the day she'd arrived here, her own
grief had throbbed inside her, trapped like a river behind
a dam. She longed to release it.

"It's going to be okay," she whispered, rubbing Ben's
back. "It's going to be okay."

Natalie, bless her heart, took over. "Have you heard
about my famous neck massages?" she crooned as she
steered Ben away. "I bet you could use one. . . ."

As the two crew members ambled off, Pastor Earl walked
up to Jordan. "Grief seeks focus," he confided, an explanation that obviously meant something to him as a coun-
selor and a man of God.

"If grief seeks focus, then Ben's begs redirection. He
blames Kào for everything, and that's wrong." On the other
hand, his outburst on behalf of the passengers had knocked
him out of his zombie state. Maybe now he'd resume his
duties as her right-hand man. She was glad he could cry,

175

but he needed to pitch in and accept his share of the responsibility that had been thrust upon them. She was tired of doing it alone.

Jordan searched for Kào and glimpsed him standing outside the hatch, arms folded over his chest. There was no mistaking his we-need-to-talk look. Her stomach twisted. After he left here, what would he tell his crew? That the Earth survivors had traded stun guns for fists? What if he brought armed guards along the next time he came to visit? Ben might have blown it for all of them.

Several other flight attendants hovered around her, plus a gaggle of worried-looking passengers, waiting for her to say or do something, she guessed. Jordan glowered at them, wondering who'd cheered for Ben. Only her own stubborn professionalism kept her from asking those responsible to step forward. *Courage is doing the right thing even though you are scared.*

Or angry.

It gave her the strength to ignore the fact that many of them had acted like children. Instead, she'd use the fistfight to drive home something that had been on her mind.

"I'm embarrassed," she told the group. "Kào's been nothing less than professional from the very beginning. I wish I could say the same for my crew. He didn't have to give us back our electronics. He's on our side, damn it. Why don't you see that?"

Some people coughed. A few nodded, murmuring their support.

"This incident proves we have a language and culture barrier. We can't rely on our fists to communicate any more than we can those translators. We need to become fluent in Key before we get to wherever they're dropping us off. Or we're going to make mistakes there, too. Maybe fatal ones."

Gasps and grumbles. "How?" she asked for them. "No more dillydallying. We're going to try language immersion, and that means periods where no English is allowed. Maybe not today, or even tomorrow, but as soon as my crew and I work out the details. And expect a similar emphasis on galactic politics and history, too." She gentled her tone. "I know we're still hurting. But ignorance isn't bliss, folks. It's dangerous."

Chin jutting high, she grabbed her translator and ducked out the hatch before they could bury her in complaints and requests. She half expected someone to chase after her to complain again about the showers or the beds—or the prospect of longer hours in school—but no one did. Maybe she was finally getting the hang of this leadership thing. Feeling a certain affinity with Napoleon, or maybe Stalin, she stopped in front of Kào. "I'm sorry. Are you okay? Did he hurt you?"

His mouth curved. "No."

"This shouldn't have happened. I—"

"The fault is mine," he cut in. "I should have prepared your people for the possibility that their computers might no longer work, instead of letting them find out for themselves, with hopes held high." He grimaced. "As I was warned they might, more or less." He sighed tiredly.

So did she. "Ben's usually not like that. Ever since it happened . . . Earth . . . he's been very quiet, very depressed. Maybe this was what he needed, losing his temper, getting his anger off his chest." Her voice softened. "He hasn't been there for me. Maybe he will be now."

"I hope that will be the case," Kào said.

Awkward silence followed. He didn't seem to want to leave.

If she was honest with herself, she didn't want him to go. She thought of him all the time. Even when she slept, he was there, in her dreams . . . dreams of Colorado that engaged all her senses, leaving her bereft and sharpening her sense of loss when she woke from them. She'd never have that life: the horses and the ranch; Boo, and the man who loved them both. But something about Kào soothed her, made her feel as if everything was going to be okay.

She sighed. "I'd invite you in, but—"

He shook his head. "My presence will make some uncomfortable, in light of what happened." She followed his gaze through the hatch. Inside Town Square, things were getting back to normal. A reading group gathered in the makeshift library. A few men Jordan recognized from the business-class roster were preparing to jog on the flexible track—the super-rat treadmill, Dillon called it. Pastor Earl was holding a Bible study, while Father Sugimoto sat hunched over in a chair, listening to a forlorn-looking woman recount her sins. When Natalie was done calming Ben, she'd meet her kickboxing devotees for an hour of Tae Bo kicks. All the children were in "school." Jordan had worked hard to organize the activities, and she'd planned to make appearances at most of them after the staff meeting. But here she was, standing in the corridor with Kào.

"Your duties call you," he guessed.

Her gaze whipped around to his scarred face. He had that uncanny way of reading her mind. "Your people aren't telepathic, are they?"

He lifted a brow. "As in being able to read a person's thoughts? I'm afraid not."

"Well, you do a pretty good job of reading mine." A fleeting expression of satisfaction crossed his face. "So, yes, duty calls. But, no, I don't feel like answering." She glanced up. "That's awful, huh?"

"Not awful, Jordan. Human." He brought his hand to his chin and studied her. "Would you like to see the arena?"

"The arena?" Yep, she'd read her translator right. He said "arena." In the wake of Ben's outburst, maybe he was going to feed her to the lions, then follow with the rest of her balky crew.

"It's where I exercise every day. Since you mentioned that you enjoy working out, I thought you might like to view the facility. There's exercise clothing stored on site for your use, should you decide to lift weights or run." A mischievous twinkle shone in his eyes. "Or simply escape your duties for a short time."

That giddy nervous feeling swept over her all over again. It still seemed surreal that she and this tall, forbidding man had spilled their deepest secrets on the observation deck. "I'm out of shape."

"So am I."

"Really out of shape." He had no idea. She was so far out of practice with guys that just talking to one she was interested in tied her insides into knots.

But just as he'd patiently drawn her out that day on the observation deck, he wasn't deterred by her foot-dragging. "When out of shape, it's recommended that you work out with a partner."

He tipped his head, waiting for her answer. He'd accept a genuine "no," she thought, but he wasn't going to fall for a weak excuse.

She smiled. "Okay. I'll go. But I'll have to find a baby-sitter . . . maybe a couple of baby-sitters." She remembered the white janitor's jacket he'd used to disguise her and asked, "Do you want me to change into a jumpsuit?"

He shook his head. "The jackets have a hood."

He was serious in not wanting anyone to know that he kept company with her—off duty. "Wait here," she told him. "I'll be right back."

Moments later, after briefing her crew on her plans, she was leaving New Earth and her needy charges behind. Natalie and Ben had been nice enough not to voice the disapproval she saw in their eyes.

Near the shuttle tube, Kào stopped at a locker and pulled out a long white jacket with a hood. She donned the disguise as she walked along. Refugee to janitor in 10.5 seconds flat, she thought wryly.

Kào was taciturn, as usual. She didn't mind. It allowed her to take in as many details of the ship as she could. One of these days, the knowledge might prove helpful. It made her excursion seem less of a jaunt if she used the opportunity to collect information.

But some of what she learned, she didn't like. When he'd taken her to the observation deck, they hadn't seen any other people. The ship had a smaller than usual crew, he'd told her, but here, in the main part of the ship, some were out and about. Those who crossed paths with them did so with uneasy greetings and humbly averted eyes. Jordan frowned. Were they afraid of Kào or repelled by him? Either way, he had to live with these people. No wonder he seemed lonely.

But Kào didn't appear to notice the way the crew acted. Or maybe he didn't care. He walked with his head held high, his body always wedged protectively between her and anyone who veered too close.

A pair of burly male albinos swept by, nodding respectfully at Kào. By now, Jordan was used to seeing the few Talagars onboard, with their snow-white hair and red eyes, but she'd stayed up too late last night reading about Talagarian atrocities, and curiosity pulled her gaze over her shoulder just as one of the muscular Talagar men looked back over his.

Their gazes met. Heest. A choking sensation rose up in her throat. He was the guard she'd knocked out with the escape slide.

Heest's eyes narrowed. Surprise flickered in their crimson depths, followed by a disdain so pointed that it made her blood curdle. He'd recognized her. But he didn't stop, continuing on with his buddy.

Jordan's heart pounded against her ribs. So much for

Kào's efforts to disguise her. Nervously she glanced at him, but he hadn't noticed the exchange and carried on as detached as before, aiming his wrist computer at a panel mounted in the wall. An elevator appeared in the adjacent tube, and they climbed aboard. Kào selected their destination and tipped his head for a retina scan. Wherever he was taking her to work out had higher security requirements than the observation deck.

Jordan's heart rate slowed, and she tried to put the red-eyed security guard out of her mind. A brief elevator ride took them down to another deck. The door slid open to a vast, featureless room. "The officers-only holo-arena," Kào announced.

She whistled softly. The far wall of the arena was so distant that she could barely make out the details. To her right were computers and what she guessed was exercise equipment: a spiderweb of laser-light-connected graceful mechanical parts and buoyant add-ons. The entire setup gave the impression of wealth, with its muted colors, thick padding, and elegance of design.

"I've been on the ship for months," Kào said. "But I've only recently resumed working out."

He appeared so genuinely excited to be sharing this with her that she hated to have to break eye contact to reference her translator. "Are all Alliance ships this well furnished?" she asked.

He made a sound in his throat. "It's acceptable for captains in the Alliance fleet to draw on their own funds to furnish their ships. Let me simply say that Commodore Moray is a man of means. This arena is impressive, even by his standards. The arena is equipped with voice-control. I registered my voice print yesterday. Let's see if it recognizes me." He spoke louder. "Computer. Holo-run—show options."

The beige walls pixilated into a forest, lovely and alien.

Head tipped back, Jordan turned in a circle. The scene was so real that she expected to fill her nostrils with the fragrance of mossy dirt. Tree trunks were covered with velvety nut-brown scales and topped with drooping fronds. High above, the giants leaned into each other, their leaves laced together to form a canopy that muted the sunshine, tinting it blue-green. Birds that looked more like moths with split wings and featherlike antennae flitted and collided near the higher branches. Amazing. The entire room had transformed, just like that.

Boo, you would have loved this. She braced herself for a stab of sorrow, but the unbidden thought of her daughter added to her pleasure in the moment. In a way, they were sharing it, she thought with a lump forming in her throat. "This is beautiful . . ."

"That's the running trail over there." Kào pointed to a sun-dappled dirt path that disappeared into a grove of gently swaying trees. She would have missed it if he hadn't shown it to her. "Or we can run here. Computer. Holo-run—show next option."

The scene splintered into tiny squares and re-formed. Now they stood in the center of a field that swept away from them on all sides. Yellow-green grass billowed in a stiff breeze that she couldn't feel, undulating to the distant horizon, tinted ochre by dust.

"Computer," Kào commanded. "Wind, level four."

A gust pushed her backward. "Ah!"

Kào caught her. "Computer—level two!" he shouted above the roar of the wind and her laughter. The gale had reduced to a gentle breeze. "I'm still getting used to the various enhancements," he admitted.

She grinned as she shoved tangled hair out of her eyes. "I like this one, too. But"—she wrinkled her nose—"dust is hell on my allergies, simulated or not."

"Computer," he said. "Holo-run. Show next option"—his

GET UP TO 5 FREE BOOKS!

Sign up for one of our book clubs today, and we'll send you
FREE* BOOKS
just for trying it out...**with no obligation to buy, ever!**

HISTORICAL ROMANCE BOOK CLUB

Travel from the Scottish Highlands to the American West, the decadent ballrooms of Regency England to Viking ships. Your shipments will include authors such as CONNIE MASON, CASSIE EDWARDS, LYNSAY SANDS, LEIGH GREENWOOD, and many, many more.

LOVE SPELL BOOK CLUB

Bring a little magic into your life with the romances of Love Spell—fun contemporaries, paranormals, time-travels, futuristics, and more. Your shipments will include authors such as KATIE MACALISTER, SUSAN GRANT, NINA BANGS, SANDRA HILL, and more.

As a book club member you also receive the following special benefits:

- **30% OFF all orders through our website & telecenter!**
  (Plus, you still get 1 book FREE for every 5 books you buy!)
- **Exclusive access to special discounts!**
- **Convenient home delivery and 10 days to return any books you don't want to keep.**

There is **no minimum number of books to buy**, and you may cancel membership at any time. See back to sign up!

*Please include $2.00 for shipping and handling.

YES! ☐

Sign me up for the **Historical Romance Book Club** and send my THREE FREE BOOKS! If I choose to stay in the club, I will pay only $13.50* each month, a savings of $6.47!

YES! ☐

Sign me up for the **Love Spell Book Club** and send my TWO FREE BOOKS! If I choose to stay in the club, I will pay only $8.50* each month, a savings of $5.48!

NAME: _____

ADDRESS: _____

_____

TELEPHONE: _____

E-MAIL: _____

☐ **I WANT TO PAY BY CREDIT CARD.**

☐ VISA   ☐ MasterCard.   ☐ DISCOVER

ACCOUNT #: _____

EXPIRATION DATE: _____

SIGNATURE: _____

Send this card along with $2.00 shipping & handling for each club you wish to join, to:

**Romance Book Clubs
20 Academy Street
Norwalk, CT 06850-4032**

Or fax (must include credit card information!) to: 610.995.9274.
You can also sign up online at www.dorchesterpub.com.

*Plus $2.00 for shipping. Offer open to residents of the U.S. and Canada only.
Canadian residents please call 1.800.481.9191 for pricing information.

If under 18, a parent or guardian must sign. Terms, prices and conditions subject to change. Subscription subject
to acceptance. Dorchester Publishing reserves the right to reject any order or cancel any subscription.

JOIN NOW!

dark eyes twinkled—"no dust, no dirt, no wind."

She began to laugh, but the room shattered like a car windshield and fell away from them. *Literally* fell away. She saw sky, pale blue and dotted with white puffy clouds, on three sides. And below . . . she couldn't force herself to look.

She threw herself backward to where her survival instinct told her there was a wall. Only after her back was pressed to the solid surface did she work up the courage to look down. Her feet were rooted on the only part of the floor that still appeared solid. But the black strip was barely wide enough to hold her feet. Her toes hung over the edge, below which a valley floor spread out before her. Indistinguishable from the real thing, the basin was dotted with vegetation and sliced through by a meandering river.

Her stomach plummeted, and she fought the almost overwhelming urge to pee. They had to be twenty-five thousand feet in the air at least, and here she was, an admitted acrophobic, clinging to the edge of a cliff.

Chapter Sixteen

"Kào," she squeaked, her hands clawing for something to hold. But he'd already walked away, gazing all around him, clearly fascinated.

She tipped her head back against the wall and gulped. This was worse than the time she visited the top of the Eiffel Tower, a view she'd found impossible to enjoy because it couldn't be viewed safely from behind glass.

"Jordan!"

Kào called to her. She was too petrified to reach for her translator. Panting, she felt a cold sweat prickling her skin. She pressed herself so firmly to the wall that she was sure her molecules and those of the surface fused.

"Come, Jordan. You can't get the full effect from there." He faced her as he walked backward. "The view is astounding."

The view. He'd said something about the view. She didn't care about the view. All she wanted was to see solid ground beneath her feet. "Computer—next option," she croaked.

The computer didn't respond. And Kào didn't hear her. He stopped, searching the scene around him. "Perhaps we ought to ask for wind. Level one? What do you think?"

"No wind," she almost shrieked. A cold sweat prickled her skin. Her knees were shaking. She would have gladly slid to the floor, but she was terrified that the itty-bitty cliff wouldn't accommodate her butt.

Finally it hit Kào that something was wrong. "What is it? You don't look well."

She brought the translator around to her eyes and chanced another downward glance. Big mistake. A flock of birds flew past, thousands of feet below. She crammed her eyelids closed.

"Are you afraid of heights?"

"Yes," she gasped.

"But you're a pilot."

"So?"

His eyes glowed. "Airplanes go up into the atmosphere. Rather high, in fact."

"It's not the same thing. You're strapped in a seat, behind glass. You can't fall out. And don't bring up the four laws of courage, either, because none of them applies. I know. I've tried them all. Let's go to the next option. Is there a beach? I like running on the sand. Or what about that forest—that was nice. Yes. I like the forest."

He regarded her from where he stood in the center of the sky, looking like a vengeful god from ancient mythology.

"So I'm afraid of heights," she blurted defensively. "Nothing else bothers me. Don't look at me like that, Kào. I'm telling the truth. I've landed airplanes in typhoons, pulled a dog from a burning house, killed a rattlesnake . . . with my bare hands." Actually, she'd whacked it with a broom, but that wasn't important now. "I ate a grasshopper,

185

a *whole* grasshopper, in survival school, and that's not all." She stopped to catch her breath, which was proving all but impossible.

Kào read his translator for long moments before he finally returned his midnight eyes to her. His dimple had returned. "The six-legged green insect, was it alive or dead?"

"Damn you, Kào, it's not funny! Change the scene."

"Exactly. It's a scene, a simulation." He stomped on the floor to prove it. "See? It's not real."

"This is an irrational fear. Reality has nothing to do with it."

He started walking toward her and didn't stop until he stood only inches away.

He towered over her. She could hear his slow, even breaths, could smell the sterilized fabric of his uniform and his skin—warmly scented with the apple fragrance of a recent shower and mingled with his own scent, one that was undeniably male.

She gulped.

"Jordan." He said her name in that sexy, meant-for-her-ears-only voice, the way he sounded in her dreams. She shuddered, this time not from fear of heights but from fear of losing her heart, of giving in to her inexplicable attraction to a stranger of strangers, a man with a past so dark that the worst of her nightmares wouldn't do it justice. But no man had ever touched her heart as he had.

"I'm not going to ask you to pretend your fear is not there," Kào said in his deep, resonant voice.

"Good."

"And I'm not going to force you to leave the wall."

"Ah. Even better."

"*You're* going to do it."

A thousand butterflies took flight in her stomach, and she chanced another downward glance. Her feet were planted firmly on the "cliff." But Kào's floated in the "sky." Simply looking at the sight made her queasy. But it also confirmed what common sense told her: The scene was a simulation.

It wasn't real. If she stepped off the cliff, she wouldn't plunge to her death. The only thing holding her back was her mind. Stepping away from the wall would have to be a choice, a conscious choice of which she had complete control.

"But if you would like me to change the scene, Jordan—"

"No. Wait." She cast her gaze across the expanse of valley and sky. In a way, her reluctance to walk across the arena was symbolic of everything that her life had become. If she could take a step forward, just one, the next one would be easier as well as the one after that, a challenge no different from waking each morning and getting out of bed despite her sorrow. Maybe that was what Kào already knew, and why he insisted on her making her own choice. "It's like looking to the future, isn't it?"

He paused, then smiling with his eyes he nodded.

"You know it won't kill you to do it, but you're scared to death to try." She swallowed. "Or at least *I* am."

Kào held out his hand, palm up, beckoning. *You can do it,* his eyes said. He was forcing her to do something that scared her, just as she'd forced him to examine his own fears on the observation deck. If he could face his horrific past, then she could face . . . *this.*

Bracing herself mentally, she grasped his hand and walked off the cliff. Her stomach wobbled like a bowl of Jell-O, and convulsively her fingers closed over Kào's fingers.

Her reward was a brilliant, heart-stopping grin, and the first true smile she'd seen on him. It transformed his face. "It's like flying," he said.

"Yes," she breathed. "Flying."

"You can't fall."

"No. . . ." Her spirit sang. Her heart beat wildly as she

Susan Grant

took another step, and then another, tugging Kào to the center of the arena. Not daring to let go of his hand, she gave a loud whoop and whirled around to face him. "Look at us, Kào! *Look!*"

Impulsively she threw her arms around him. He looked startled for the briefest second before she felt his arms slide around her waist.

His smiled faded as he gazed down at her. The silvery light didn't flatter his stark features, but to her he'd never looked more handsome. Easily, she could have attributed her attraction to the honesty in his eyes, his broad shoulders, or his large, wide hands with those long, blunt-tipped fingers. But it was more than that, and it always had been: Life had not been kind to Kào, and yet he didn't let that stop him from being kind to others. To *her*. His encased-in-armor compassion touched her to the depths of her soul, stirring unexpected feelings at the absolute, most dismal, rock-bottom point in her life.

"Thank you," she whispered in Key, stroking one hand over his cheek. His mouth was so close to hers that she could see the tiny nubs above his upper lip where he needed to shave. She wanted to pull him close, to feel the roughness of that skin against hers.

As if on its own, her thumb moved in a tender and curious exploration of his cheekbone and jaw. His skin was warm, golden, and smooth where his beard didn't grow and raspy where it did. His scar, pale and needle-thin, ran in a raised ridge from eyebrow to jaw, a scar that cut far deeper than what was apparent at first glance. The aliens had plastic surgery; he could have had the scar erased. But he chose to keep it—in protest? In memory of his comrades who hadn't made it out alive? Or because he, too, had trouble letting go of the past? Her hand shook as she traced the scar's length with her fingertip.

Kào grabbed her hand, stopping her. His eyes bored into

her, dark and intense. "You took a chance, Jordan."

"Yes . . ."

Dry fingertips skimmed lightly down her cheek to her throat. Parted slightly, his lips grazed over hers, his breath warm and soft. She shivered from his caress. "So will I, Jordan," he whispered. "So will I."

With one big hand cupping the back of her head, he slanted his firm mouth so that it fit perfectly against hers. A surge of heat coursed through her, a sigh parting her lips. Kào might appear harsh and cold, but that was not the way he kissed: When his tongue swept into her mouth, it was with such sensuality and tenderness that her knees went weak.

She ran her hands over his back, savoring the movement of hard muscle beneath the fabric of his uniform. His arms folded around her, molding her to his body. Passion scorched her, igniting her every nerve ending. His mouth muffled her sigh, and his tongue penetrated hungrily, passionate and demanding. The kiss deepened with mutual urgency, and he slid his hands upward, stopping just under the swell of her breasts before he started another downward slide.

Frustration swelled; her taut, sensitive breasts rubbed the inside of her T-shirt. She wanted to feel his hands on her bare skin, his hot mouth on her body. Thoughts of making love with him exacerbated the sweet-hot ache between her legs that said her body was ready for more—even if she wasn't.

Look to the future, he'd said. But their relationship had no future. He must know it, too, or he wouldn't be holding back from touching her more intimately. She should be happy that he respected her enough to keep the whole thing platonic. If it was recreational sex she wanted, she could get it in New Earth—a passenger or even one of the male flight attendants, any number of them might have filled the bill.

But she was hopelessly old-fashioned. Emotional closeness and trust put the "love" in lovemaking, in her opinion. That was probably why she'd gone so many years doing without. She'd dated occasionally, but her focus had always been on her daughter and she hadn't looked to deepen the relationships. Maybe she hadn't wanted someone else to take care of, like Craig. Maybe she'd wanted a guy who'd be there for *her*, for once. A man like Kào.

But she was a refugee on her way to a relocation port and he was stationed aboard this ship. He couldn't follow her, and she couldn't by any stretch of the imagination stay with him and abandon her people.

She jerked her mouth from his and buried her face against his chest, breathing hard as she listened to the powerful thumping of his heart. Kào's fingers played tenderly in her tousled curls. Desire flared. She almost groaned aloud from the temptation of lifting her mouth to his and starting all over again.

She lost track of how long they stayed there, holding each other close. There had been so much pain lately; she hungered for something that didn't hurt, something that made her feel good about herself and gave her something to look forward to. Kào was all those things.

Floating in the afterglow of the kiss, she had no desire to open her eyes. It was like waking from one of her dreams; she wanted to hold on to the happiness for as long as possible, knowing full well it would disappear.

"As much as I don't want to," he said low into her hair, "I have to bring you back to New Earth. It's growing late."

"I know," she whispered, understanding and speaking in Key.

He kissed her forehead so tenderly that her belly contracted. "But we can come back."

"I would like that."

"Computer," he called. "End program."

Contact

The arena returned to normal, beige walls and all. She took Kào's hand and walked with him to the exit. In so many ways, her developing relationship with Kào reminded her of the stories her grandfather used to tell her about being stationed in Europe during World War II. The ones she'd liked best were those of the star-crossed lovers of that era, the wartime romances of local women and GIs.

That was how it was with her and Kào: two people from different worlds who were never supposed to meet, thrown together by cataclysmic events and destined to part when real life caught up to them. And catch up to them it would. Of that, she had no doubt.

Spring fever was the closest Jordan could come to describing how she felt in the wake of Kào's kiss. Inhaling deeply, she let out her breath in a sigh and walked through the hatch into New Earth. All she wanted to do was lie on her back in bed and daydream about Kào for an hour or so. Fat chance. With one glance at the displeased faces upon her return, Jordan's euphoria fizzled.

"You were gone a long time," Natalie said as she glided up. Her white teeth were clamped together. "I was worried. We all were."

More than a few passengers cast curious looks over their shoulders. Jordan's lips still tingled, and she hoped no one guessed why. "I didn't realize I'd been gone that long. What's happened? Let's take a seat and you can brief me."

Natalie spread her manicured hand firmly on the small of Jordan's back. "Nothing's happened, but I'd like to chat," she agreed. She steered her to a group of floating chairs in a quiet corner.

The flight attendant plopped into one and waited patiently for Jordan to get comfortable in the other. Natalie's brown eyes were soft as she leaned forward and rested her

191

folded hands on her knees. "Have you heard of Stockholm Syndrome?"

"Stockholm Syndrome? I've heard of it. It's a psychological condition. I think they named it after a Swedish bank robbery. The hostages developed positive feelings for their captors." Jordan shrugged. "Why?"

"I think you might have it."

"What?"

Natalie pressed her hand to Jordan's knee. "You and the alien, Kào. You've gone off with him alone. Twice, that I know of." Natalie searched Jordan's face with knowing eyes. "There's definitely an attraction there. A spark ... *something.*"

"For crying out loud, Natalie. Ben attacked him. I had to go patch things up."

Natalie raised a brow. "Did you?"

"I think so." Warmth fluttered inside Jordan as her thoughts swung back to Kào's kiss. "But Stockholm Syndrome? Come on, Nat. Who put this in your head? Ben?"

Natalie pulled a folded piece of notepaper out of her pocket. With her Versace reading glasses balanced on the edge of her nose, she read: "Stockholm Syndrome results from sensory deprivation, from being forcibly removed from your daily life and put in a strange place from where you can't escape." The flight attendant waved at the expanse of Town Square. "Bingo. Our whole world revolves around our captors."

"Rescuers," Jordan corrected.

"That's what they say. But we're pretty much stuck here."

"We're confined for our own safety. They just ended a war. This ship is looking for enemy ships trying to sneak past the border. Those enemies take human slaves, Natalie. I don't think you want to be one of them. If we wander around this ship, we might muck up their security. Or worse, get hurt."

Natalie looked unconvinced.

Jordan threw her hands in the air. "So I'm overprotective. That means I have Stockholm Syndrome? What do you find lacking about my leadership? Maybe I wasn't so smooth in the beginning, but I think I'm doing a pretty decent job as captain now."

"Of course you are. Hey, hon. I'm not saying I believe you have the syndrome. I want you to be aware of it, that's all." Her voice dipped to a private tone. "The reason I brought it up at all—besides the fact I care about you—is because of the rumors going around. The word on the street is that you seemed more concerned about Kào than Ben. And you seem kind of fed up sometimes. It's got some people worried that if push comes to shove, you'd take the aliens' side and not ours."

Jordan's voice shook with indignation. "Everything I do is for us. You guys come before anything I want."

"I know . . . I know."

Jordan shoved her hands through her hair and glowered at the floor. She'd be the first to admit that she was vulnerable right now. Kào's affection and empathy filled the gaping hole left from the loss of her family, and she knew it might be giving her the sensation of falling in love when in fact she wasn't. But she was self-aware enough to know that her attraction to Kào wasn't Stockholm Syndrome. Wasn't she?

Groaning, she cradled her head in her hands. "Shit."

"Come on, girl, give me a hug."

Jordan submitted to the squeeze. But her mind spun with self-doubt as her blood boiled with anger. Natalie had ruined the sweetness of her developing relationship with Kào. Never again would she be able to feel her heart leap when he walked into the room without thinking it was some dumb captive syndrome. It wasn't, but the gloss had been rubbed off their relationship all the same. Maybe it was better this way. Maybe she wouldn't be as distracted and could concentrate on what was ahead. The relocation port. A new life. A life she wouldn't have been able to share with Kào anyway.

The two women moved apart. "You okay?" Natalie asked.

"Yeah, Nat, fine. You've given me a lot to think about." Jordan stood. "Now, I've got stuff to do."

"Me, too. I'll catch you later. Dinner?"

"Sure," Jordan replied tiredly. "I'll see you at dinner."

Feeling as if someone had anesthetized her brain, she tromped toward her quarters, hoping to disappear for a while before the evening meal was delivered. But when she was halfway there Dillon sidled up to her, hands in his pockets. He was one of the few who'd taken to wearing the pale orange jumpsuits.

"So you're back," he said.

"Yes, I'm back." Silently she dared him to say something about Stockholm Syndrome.

"I've been thinking," he said in his lilting voice. "The deal with the hard drives. Kào said it was a mistake."

She sighed. It must be bash-Kào day. "Don't you believe him?"

"Currently, I have no data to the contrary so, yes, I suppose I do." He scratched the orange stubble on his chin. "It begs the question, though. How prone are his people to errors? We know that their technology is fantastic. Couldn't they have extracted the data from the laptops without destroying them? Couldn't they have recovered what data they lost? But they made an error, so they say. What about Earth? Could the finding that no one survived the comets be an error, too?"

Jordan's heart flipped over. Survivors! There could be people left *alive*. Suddenly she couldn't breathe. Roberta, the rest of her family, they might be among them.

Unexpectedly, tears burned her eyes. She'd told her daughter she would come home. She'd never dreamed she wouldn't. What if now she could?

Dillon searched her face. "It changes everything, doesn't it?"

"Yes, everything," she whispered. Her entire outlook had changed in the space of five minutes. Dillon had planted the seed of doubt and it had blossomed into hope, sending her roller-coaster existence crawling up another steep hill. "What Kào told us might be a mistake."

"Or worse," he said. "A lie."

Ah, Kào. Would you lie to me? To my face? After what they'd shared, she couldn't fathom it. Unless that, too, had been a lie. A sharp sense of betrayal shredded her insides. "Why would he lie? What would be the point—except to exert control? And he already has that. *Total* control."

Wringing her hands, that nasty habit she'd picked up, she began pacing, another addition to her repertoire. "Kào told me that they recorded the disaster. He even invited me to watch it, but at the time I said no." she glanced at Dillon. "Maybe he hoped I'd say that."

Unease slithered up her spine, and she clutched her knotted hands to her chest. "If there are people left, we have to go back, no matter what the aliens' official flight plan says." Her mind percolated with hatching plans. She hadn't realized how disheartened she'd been by the lack of hope until it came flooding back. "Do you know where we are in relation to Earth?" She pressed her hands together. Her palms were damp. "Can you access the ship's navigation system?"

"I'm trying."

"Don't get caught, or the only door we have into their activities will slam shut in our faces."

"I know. It might take a while before I can get in. How much time do we have? When are we due to arrive at the relocation port?"

195

"I don't know. I need to, though. And I will, Dillon. I'll find out." When she next saw Kào.

Damn it. She should have been asking him those questions today and not kissing him. What was wrong with her? Stockholm Syndrome or not, where was her common sense?

She'd call a staff meeting right away, her key flight attendants only. She'd brief them not to say anything to the passengers until they knew more; she didn't want to incite panic. She scrubbed her face with her hand. "I've got to go. And what we talked about stays between us, okay?"

"Mum's the word. I'll be at the computer if you need me."

With a nagging sense of foreboding, she watched him go. Then she turned back toward the epicenter of chaos better known as Town Square. Two hundred and eighty-six people expected her to guide them through this mess. She might not have wanted the job but, by God, she intended to see it through.

Chapter Seventeen

"And when she finally gave the goblet back to me, it was filled with rocks and not wine!" Commander Moray's laughter was rich and deep. And as always, contagious.

"Rocks?" Chuckling, Kào stretched his legs out in front of the sinfully plush chair he occupied in the commodore's quarters. "I fear you might have deserved it."

"Deserved it?" His father roared with laughter. "I'll tell you who deserved what—*she* did, and she got it, too."

His father rarely spoke of his encounters with women, and when he did, Kào reacted with the mix of revulsion and disbelief he suspected all offspring experienced when envisioning a parent's sexual activity. Yet his father's bluntness meant he was in fine form tonight and that more stories would follow. Sure enough, they did.

As the commodore's melodious voice filled the chamber, Kào sank deeper into his chair, sipping an after-dinner liqueur made from a piquant berry also used to spice stewed meat. It had been a long time since he'd been able to enjoy an evening with his father. But he'd have enjoyed it more had not Jordan's second-in-command expressed his grief with his fists. Here he was, relaxing with his father, while Jordan struggled with the fears and demands of her people, aggravated by the turmoil Kào had caused. Trist had warned him, hadn't she? And blast it all, she'd been right; he shouldn't have returned the computers without an adequate briefing to curb high expectations.

Kào half listened to his father while he pondered whether he ought to check back with Jordan after dinner. Jordan—by the Seeders, he'd *kissed* her. Recklessness, spontaneity—those characteristics were not what he'd use to describe himself, but that's what he'd shown today in the arena.

But she'd been so sweet, so willing, so right. . . .

"Your mind is not on my tales, Kào."

Kào dropped his hand. Then he exhaled. "I won't bother fabricating an excuse because you'll see right through it."

Moray tipped his head back and laughed. Wiping the back of his hand across his eyes, he smiled broadly. "Thank you, Kào. I get more than my share of fabricated excuses from my staff."

They regarded each other warmly. "I was thinking of the refugees," Kào admitted. That wasn't quite a fabrication.

"Ah, Captain Cady," Moray commented coolly. He fingered his goblet. "She distracts you," he accused.

She enchants me, Kào wanted to say. But something held him back from being so forthcoming with his father. "She's . . . a very capable woman."

"I knew when I first met her that she wasn't the type to shrink from a challenge. I wonder, though, to what extent she'd go to help her situation."

Kào tried to place his father's remark within the context of logic . . . and failed. "Sorry, sir. I don't understand."

"Would she behave in a manner to cull favors from our

officers? From you, specifically? There's not much more we can give the refugees, or do for them, in this particular situation, but she may not understand that."

"There has been no favor culling," Kào replied crisply. Or had there been? It was true, he didn't know Jordan well. She might think that trading sexual favors for—for what? No, this was just Moray's doing; making him question, making him doubt. "There has been no untoward behavior, sir."

On Jordan's part. His, on the other hand, deserved closer scrutiny, he acknowledged as his thoughts returned to the holo-arena.

"Be careful, Kào. That's all I wanted to say."

"You have no reason to worry."

Moray pondered that. Then he leaned forward in his chair. His smile didn't quite reach his eyes. "Do you know what I missed the most when you were gone? This. Our talks. How I treasured them over the years. You were always so frank with me, always told me what was on your mind. You never kept secrets, and I know that won't change." His hands tightened around his goblet. "Will it, Kào?"

Kào tried to keep his tone light. "Is that a compliment or a warning?"

"Neither. Only a statement." Moray smiled a soothing smile. "What, then, holds your thoughts, Kào? The refugees, you said?"

"Like you, I'd hoped that returning the computers to the refugees would facilitate future dealings. It did quite the opposite. Their second-in-command tried to take a piece out of me."

Moray's face showed a mix of emotions. "He hurt you?"

"He tried."

The man's furry white brows disappeared into his hairline. "I hadn't heard this."

Susan Grant

"That's because no one knows."

"You should have told me—told security. These are the people who broke your ribs and shattered Trist's nose!"

"Weeks ago, sir. And under far different circumstances. We have to remember that incidents like this will arise anytime people are contained in close quarters. Recall, if you will, Ensign Laravar and that brawl he started in The Black Hole."

"Don't remind me," Moray growled. The ship's bar was the source of periodic trouble on an otherwise disciplined ship. "That put four mission techs in medical and cost us fifty thousand Alliance credits in damage." Frowning, he tugged up his sleeve and began typing on his wrist computer. "I'll assign you protection. An armed security squad. You shouldn't be going there alone."

"An entire squad? Father, you must be spending too much time with Trist."

His father's hand stilled. "Trist?"

"The Talagarian linguist."

"I well know who she is, Kào."

Moray's snappish reply aside, the proprietary glint in his eyes stopped Kào cold. It was the look a man might give if you insulted his mother. Or wife. But Trist was a minor member of the ship's crew. Skilled linguist or not, she was low in rank, and would normally be all but expendable to her commodore. But she'd stirred such a passionate defense that it gave Kào cause to wonder if she was more to Moray than a favored staff member. Was she his lover?

Kào couldn't imagine it—his strapping, enthusiastic father in bed with that slim, slight, cold and cunning Talagarian. But it didn't matter what he thought. Whom Moray bedded was his business, not Kào's.

He resumed cautiously, "My feeling on the matter is this: The refugees are skeptical, independent-minded, and quick to balk at minor administrative foul-ups. They've lost everything, sir. A show of force will only aggravate their feelings of vulnerability and resentment. If my safety is your concern, rest assured that when you taught me to use my body as a weapon, you taught me well." Kào flexed his right arm, sore from subduing Ben. "*Very* well. I consider the situation settled, sir."

Moray heaved a huge sigh and downed his drink in a single gulp. "Then I will, as well." The man plunked his empty goblet on a table fashioned from a delicate alloy made to look like petals of a flower, inset with chips of blue stained glass.

Sea blue, like Jordan's eyes, Kào thought. Her fair coloring belonged to a frigid climate, but her skin was burnished by sunlight. He'd like to kiss every freckle on her nose and wherever else she had them. He covered a smile by sipping from his glass of liqueur.

Then he saw that Moray regarded him with worry. "I'll pay a visit to New Earth after dinner," Kào reassured him. "Just to make sure all is settled."

"New Earth, is it?"

"It's what the refugees call their quarters."

"I see you spend a lot of time there."

Trist must have passed along that information, Kào thought. He decided that if his father wanted frankness, then, blast it all, he'd give it to him. "Not because I have to, but because I want to. The noise, the crowds, the smells . . . when I'm there, something imprinted deeply in my mind resonates—memories, I believe, of my origins. Memories I can't recall. I keep returning in hopes that something will be revealed."

"I see . . ." Moray said.

"I know this has caught you unawares, sir, but I know so little of the world I came from." Or the family who'd birthed and raised him for almost three years. The desire to know more burned in him. As an adopted child, Kào

201

certainly had the curiosity. But worries that too many questions would hurt or insult the man he called "Father" had always held him back from asking. Now they were both adults. Moray well knew Kào's feelings for him, his gratitude and loyalty. What would be the harm in seeing what the commodore knew about the lost years before Kào came to live with him?

That he even dared to broach the subject tonight was indicative of the myriad changes in him since the *Savior* had taken the Earth refugees aboard. Or, more specifically, since he'd come to know Jordan.

"I must have been from a large family," he resumed cautiously. "It makes sense, I suppose, my ancestors being rural horsemen." Who had, according to what little Moray had told him, lived an unsophisticated, outmoded life, by galactic standards, on the windswept grasslands of Vantaar. "Lacking high-tech amusements, I suspect that after dark with nothing else to do they'd gather around a communal meal and share stories. I can imagine myself as a toddler in a houseful of older siblings and likely extended family, too: cousins, aunts, uncles. . . ." A memory flickered. Kào tried to grasp it, but it was gone in the next instant. The fleeting impression evoked a sensation so primal in its pleasantness that he shuddered.

Startled, he glanced up from his drink to see Moray staring at hands he'd folded in his lap. Drained of his usual vitality and good cheer, the commodore looked weary and old. "I could never give you that . . . brothers and sisters, a mother."

Guilt coiled in Kào's belly, even though he imagined it was precisely what Moray wanted him to feel, punishment for broaching what had always been tacitly forbidden: questions about his life prior to his adoption. "I don't bring this up to cast doubt on my loyalty to you, sir. I would hope my devotion to you is beyond question. You're my father. You raised me." Not the faceless, nameless figure that sired him. "Brothers, sisters, a large family . . . it's speculation on my part, nothing more. I mentioned it only in hopes that you might have remembered more. My apologies. Should I call for the meal? I'm hungry. How about you?"

"You recall nothing of that day, the day you came to me." Moray searched his face. "Do you?"

"No, sir. Nothing."

"Ah, you were far too young. But I . . . I have never forgotten it." Moray's eyes took on a faraway look as if his thoughts had slipped into the past. "It was your swift feet that saved you that day," he murmured. "Your spirit, your will to survive, glowed so brightly that it touched me in a way you cannot imagine."

Kào froze. This he had never heard.

"I was a bitter and disillusioned man, had been for years—having lost Jenneh and the twins—but when I took you home it all changed. I was a man without a family. And you, Kào, a little boy who needed one."

Moray's eyes glinted moistly. "Always I've tried to do the right thing by you. If that hasn't always seemed the case, if my actions haven't made you happy, or harmed you in any way, know that I've had your best interests at heart." He turned his hands over in a rare gesture of supplication. "I still do."

"I know that, sir." The man's heartfelt admission indebted Kào more than ever.

"Ah, Kào. Don't despair. We will live to see the day when your records are cleansed of that incident in the war."

"The 'incident,' Father?" Kào stifled a bitter laugh. "That *incident* nearly lost the war for the Alliance."

"It was not your fault. Those responsible will be punished. If it's the last thing I do in this life, I will make it happen. With you by my side, nothing can stop me. Our

future is bright, my boy. Wait and see. Keep an open mind;
that's all I ask of you."

Kào felt suddenly heavy in his chair. He wanted a life of
his own choosing, and had even revealed as much to
Moray. But with the man so intent on masterminding his
future, Kào began to wonder how far his father was willing
to go to keep him by his side.

The door chime rang. "Enter," Moray called. Two young
men guided a buoyant cart through the hatch. A savory
scent filled the chamber as the aides set out the meal: a
platter of meat, crisp-bread for sopping up gravy, and a
bowl of nutrient-rich but synthesized vegetables.

"Synthetics, Father?" Kào couldn't help asking after the
aides departed. His father usually insisted on fresh produce, switching over to fabricated produce only near the
end of an overlong mission. The galley crew must have
started the refugees on the synthetics before everyone else.
No wonder Jordan had brought him complaints on that list
of hers. "Are we conserving? Or is there a problem with
the greenhouse?"

"Conserving," Moray replied as he painstakingly
trimmed excess fat from his meat. Kào's own piece was so
tender that it fell into bite-sized pieces. "I've been tasked to
make a perimeter run along the Rim to sniff out that reported Talagar ship."

The Rim was the farthest reaches of civilized space. Beyond even the system where they'd found Earth; beyond
anything Kào had ever visited.

"You're going home, Kào," Moray said, chewing. "Home
to the region of your birth."

Kào almost came out of his chair. "I was born in the fron-
tier?"

"The most backwater stretch, my boy. As you know, your
people shunned technology except for medical purposes
and the most basic conveniences. They shunned the Alli-

204

ance, too, kept out of politics and conflicts, content to farm, or whatever it was they called taming the land and their beasts." He shook his head. "It was their downfall."

Kào's head jerked up. *Downfall?* He wasn't sure he understood what Moray meant by that. But another, more pressing question begged to be asked. "You say we're going after that Talagar ship. According to Perimeter procedure, that calls for you to disable the craft by removing its crew and replacing it with our own. I don't know if I care for the idea with the refugees onboard."

"They won't be onboard."

"Where will they be?"

"We're taking them with us to the Rim, because they're to be settled there," Moray declared. "Be proud of your role in this great undertaking, Kào, for the Alliance has chosen to settle the Rim at long last, and your refugees have won the honor of being the first colonists."

Chapter Eighteen

Survivors—on Earth! Pure terror alternated with giddy hope in Jordan's mind. The resulting turmoil wouldn't let her sleep, but she was exhausted enough to try. She couldn't afford insomnia; she had so much on her mind, so many people to take care of, so many things to get done, to organize, to fix, to consider. She couldn't be groggy or forgetful. Or careless. But the minutes crawled by in the dimness of her quarters, and sleep didn't come.

Jordan's eyes found the clock. Bottom of the second third in Alliance time, which meant it was late evening. The crew of the *Savior* worked around the clock in three shifts, their duty divided like their day. From now through the end of the next third was what she'd come to consider "night."

Groaning, she rolled from her stomach to her back. She was wired. The prospect of going home, of reuniting with her family, had grabbed hold of her and wouldn't let go. But lurking in the recesses of her mind were the terrifying what-ifs. What if Earth still existed? What if Kào had lied? And if he had lied, why? And where was he taking them?

He didn't kiss you like a lying man. No, he hadn't. And that made it so tough to accept that he'd deceived her, if he'd deceived her. Why bother with affection, with tenderness, if he meant to hurt her? He could have just taken his kiss, or more, and not cared about what she felt. But that hadn't been the case. He'd given all he had, and she'd soaked it all in. She hoped it meant that Dillon was wrong, that his hypothesis had no basis in fact at all. Facts—she needed them. And she wasn't going to find them by tossing and turning in bed.

She pushed herself off the mattress, pulled her jeans over her panties. Shoving her head of blond frizz through the neck of her T-shirt, she went in search of distraction. Town Square. It was late. She doubted anyone would be up. But she didn't care as long as she wasn't alone in her room with her worries and memories for company.

As she passed through the hive of bedrooms, she could hear soft voices coming from behind closed doors and the sounds of one couple clearly enjoying themselves having sex. Her thoughts immediately swung to Kào. *What kind of lover was he?*

She could almost feel her fingers combing through his hair as she kissed him, the cropped, silky strands damp with sweat, his long, lean body covering hers as he moved inside her, hot and wild, making her forget everything but his taste, his scent, his touch—

"God." Jordan blushed hard, rubbing her hands over her face. Her future was more uncertain than ever and here she was, fantasizing about sleeping with the one man who held all the answers. Maybe Natalie was right about her.

"Hey, girl." The husky voice came from the shadows.

Jordan's steps faltered. Speak of the devil. Natalie was sitting on the floor cushions. Someone else was there, too, a head silhouetted in the dim light. Jordan said, "Hey, Nat. I'm not interrupting anything, am I?"

Natalie laughed. "I don't think so."

A man spoke up. "It's me, Jordan—Ben."

Squinting, Jordan bent forward as she walked over. "It is you." She made a face. "And why shouldn't I suspect anything was going on with you two, hmm?"

Natalie snorted. "Because I'd bust his ass, that's why."

"Right," Ben shot back. "Why don't you try me sometime and see."

"Maybe I will. And I'll bust your ass."

Jordan laughed softly. They probably had no idea how much their banter helped take the edge off her anxiety.

Natalie tapped the cushion with manicured nails. "Join us."

Jordan sank onto the cushion. "I can't sleep. What are you guys up to?"

"We're just philosophizing about life and death," Ben explained. "Nothing too heavy."

Jordan sniffed the air. "And nipping at the cooking brandy, too, I see."

"Cooking brandy, hell," Natalie said. "Cognac from First Class." She lifted her small glass to the overhead light. "Courvoisier. VSOP Exclusif. But pick your poison." As graceful as a cat, she unlocked the cabinet below the entertainment area where she and Jordan had stored the remaining miniature bottles of airline liquor. Only the two of them knew the digital combination.

Making herself comfortable, Jordan cracked a can of tonic water and poured the contents into an opaque white cup. "Remember limes?" she murmured wistfully as she stirred in the contents of a tiny bottle of Tanqueray.

"Yeah, limes." Ben gazed at his drink cupped in his hands. Jordan noticed that his nails were bitten to the quick. "Beer is what I miss most, I think."

Natalie sighed. "No, chocolate. Godiva chocolate."

As Ben and Natalie lost themselves in memories of lost pleasures, Jordan made her mind go blank. Soon her drink imparted its numbing warmth. There was nothing better than alcohol to sand away the sharp edges of anxiety. It was a good thing that they were hoarding the last of the liquor, or she might have been tempted to develop a drinking problem.

Ben broke the amiable silence. "You look like hell, Jordan."

"Yeah. Well. I feel like hell."

They lapsed into silence. This time the atmosphere was tense, reflecting their unease.

"Maybe Kào doesn't know the whole story about Earth," Ben said out of the blue. "And maybe those red-eyed assistants do. They know something we don't. I can see it in their smug little eyes."

Jordan shuddered. That Talagar Heest, the guard she'd passed in the corridor—she wouldn't soon forget the look he'd given her.

Ben yanked on his cuffs. "I don't know. I just don't feel good about this, Jordan. About us. Call it a hunch . . . a bad hunch. I've had them before." His eyes took on that fearful look that had characterized his first days on the *Savior*. "And they're usually right."

Jordan lurched to her feet. "That's it. No more waiting. It's killing me. Kào had an appointment tonight, but he's got to be done by now. Dillon's mapped out the ship—in glorious detail. Why waste all that work? Let's track down Mr. Vantaar-Moray and find out what the hell is going on. I want to see that flick they made of Earth. Then we'll know what they know, and we can go from there. Right now we know nothing." She wriggled her feet into her slip-ons. "Who's game?"

Ben stared up at her. "You mean . . . now?"

"Yes, now."

Ben's eyes shifted to the exit, sealed shut during the night hours—from the inside, thankfully. "Are we allowed? To leave, I mean? We're in quarantine."

"No, we're not. We're restricted to quarters, remember?"

"That's the same thing."

"Sorry, Ben. I don't care what the rules say. I've been out twice now and haven't seen anyone guarding this area. I'm going. I promised my little girl I was coming home. And when I make a promise, I keep it. It's only a promise to one person, my word to a single individual, a child, but it's everything to me." Her throat closed, and she turned away quickly to hide the emotion she knew flared in her face. Then she started walking across Town Square.

"Uh-uh. No way. You're not going alone." Natalie wedged her feet into her spiky sandals, her fuchsia toenails glittering in the overhead lights. "I'm coming with you," she said and sashayed after Jordan.

Ben jogged after them. "No, that's my job. I'm the purser, the second-in-command. Nat, you need to stay here and watch the store." His eyes shifted to Jordan. "If that's okay with you, Captain."

Jordan was so startled that Ben had volunteered to come along, she could barely speak. Then her brain snapped into gear. "We'll bring our translators and the maps." She dispatched Natalie in search of both. Then she told Ben, "Let's change into the jumpsuits they gave us. We're going to stand out in the crowd, but we'll stand out more dressed this way."

A storage shelf contained hundreds of the pale orange outfits. Ben and Jordan tugged clean, pressed jumpsuits over their clothing.

Natalie rejoined them near the exit hatch. Jordan pressed a glowing red rectangle on the door control panel. The rectangle changed from red to green and the door slid up into the ceiling. Then she stepped into the corridor.

Cool, dry air slapped her in the face, but it didn't alleviate her usual vertigo from seeing the floor bowing upward to the ceiling. She squinted, working on her balance.

Ben caught her by the elbow. "You okay?"

"I'm still not used to it." She pointed at the walkway. "That doesn't bother you?" That Ben wasn't bothered by the interior of the immense starship was a good sign. Maybe taking him along might be less of a liability than she thought. As she'd hoped, after his laptop outburst he seemed to be coming around. Mentally she crossed her fingers. She'd need him tonight.

"Nope. Doesn't bother me." He peered up the bowed path, then at her. "But you're a pilot."

She groaned. "One has nothing to do with the other." She'd spent the day explaining that, it seemed. She faced Natalie. "While we're gone, you're in charge."

"Aye-aye, Captain." Natalie gave Jordan a mock salute. "Everything will be under control."

Jordan smiled. "I have no doubt. Listen, I don't know how long this will take."

"I'll wait up for you guys," Natalie assured her.

Jordan squeezed her hand. The woman's fingers were icy. Then she turned to Ben. "You ready?"

His throat bobbed. "Ready."

"Let's roll." Maps in hand, they took off into unknown territory.

Their first stop was the storage locker Kào had opened on the way to the arena. "Jackpot!" More than one white jacket was stored inside. She pulled two folded garments from the compartment. "Their janitors wear these."

They shrugged on the jackets. "Alien windbreakers," Ben said.

"Exactly." His sense of humor was a good sign. In fact,

he seemed a bit giddy. From adrenaline or booze, she wasn't sure, but at least he wasn't weeping.

"Where to now?" he asked from under his hood.

She read the map, then peered down the corridor. "We're on Sublevel Three. The officer's quarters are on Upper Level One. We can take the shuttle. I remember how to get there."

With purpose, they resumed their walk. It was late, but there were a few others out and about. Ben refused to make eye contact, keeping his gaze trained on the floor. She, on the other hand, had no choice but to be observant. Not only was she in charge of getting them from one place to another, if she were to bump into any Talagar types, she wanted advance warning.

Silent, they waited for the shuttle. A man ambled up beside them. "Greetings," he said.

"Greetings." Jordan could hear her heart beating. Hell, she could hear Ben's heart beating. Ben nodded, and the man turned his attention back to the shuttle station.

After a few moments, he frowned. Jordan's stomach twisted in knots. She hoped he didn't try talking to them; they'd hidden their translators in their pockets. "It should have arrived already," he grumbled. Impatiently he yanked up his sleeve and aimed his wrist computer at a flat, featureless panel that Jordan thought was part of the wall. In seconds, the shuttle glided up.

Jordan exchanged a sheepish glance with Ben. "It's a good thing he walked up," she whispered in his ear when they'd boarded, sitting out of earshot of the man. "Or we'd still be standing there."

The shuttle ride was uncomfortably long. At a few stops, someone got on or someone got off. She and Ben sat, heads lowered, taking in the scene from under their white hoods. A curious rider glanced at their orange pants, but didn't appear troubled by the outfits. The white jackets worked well at hiding who they really were.

She was pretty good at reading Key, but worked hard at discerning the symbols flashing on viewers overhead. When "Level One" appeared, she took Ben by the arm and left the shuttle behind.

She stopped to consult the map. Ben peered over her shoulder. "Where to next?"

"We take a right and keep going. We're still pretty far away. I'd guess a ten- or fifteen-minute walk before we get to the crew quarters, and then a little farther after that to the officers' rooms. They're grouped at the bow of the ship."

More confident now, they headed in that direction. Jordan wondered what Kào would say—or do—when she showed up at his doorstep, unexpected. The vulnerable feminine side of her that was starting to like him a little too much hoped he was alone.

As they neared the crew quarters, they heard noise and voices coming from around a bend in the corridor. There was music, too, faint with an undertone of a pulsing beat. "Someone's stereo?" Jordan wondered aloud. "Or do these people even have stereos as we know them?"

"Whatever it is, it must be an incredible sound system."

"It is even better up close," a husky feminine voice said. In accented English.

Jordan spun around. Standing behind them was a woman whose flesh was so pale that Jordan imagined she could see right through it. The sleeveless, short, skin-tight black dress she wore on her slender body only emphasized the lack of pigment in her hair and skin. But the amused red eyes were what Jordan remembered and wouldn't forget. The officer smiling at them was none other than Trist.

Chapter Nineteen

Automatically Jordan's eyes focused on Ensign Pren's small
nose. It gave no hint that it had been broken, which would
have marred what was really a very pretty face. Trist owed
her exotic, elfin look to eyes that tipped up at the outer
ends. All the Talagars had that appearance, but Trist's was
more pronounced.

"You need an escort, yes?" She sounded breathless, as if
she'd run hard to catch them. Her English was accented but
fluent enough to make Jordan wish she could speak Key
this well. "I am glad I heard of your departure. I did not
know if I would intercept you in time, but here you are."
Her lavender lips curved into a smug, self-congratulatory
smile.

Jordan shot Ben an irritated glance. They'd been caught
less than fifteen minutes after setting out. And Trist
sounded positively gleeful about it.

"Good to think of wearing protectors," Trist went on. "I

214

makes you look not like a refugee, but eager to clean the ship." Her red eyes settled on Ben. "Ah. Ben Kathwari. *He* will not clean ship." With that, she laughed, husky and deep. "I have heard of you."

"So the rumors have gotten around," Ben said with an arrogance Jordan wasn't sure he intended.

"Not 'around.' But I hear." She winked at them. "Trist hears all. And I must see all, too." She waved a hand at them. "Because I find you, yes?"

Jordan's chin edged up. "Let's not prolong the suffering. If you have to take us back, just do it already."

"Do you want to go back?"

That was not the response Jordan had expected. "No."

"Then I won't."

The conversation was going every which way other than what Jordan expected. But she'd been given the chance to flee, and she was going to take it. "We're late for an appointment. Places to go, people to see, you know the drill. Goodbye, Trist."

"Not goodbye yet." Trist reached behind Jordan's neck and fumbled with the collar of her orange jumpsuit. Her smooth, warm skin was a shock; she'd expected corpselike cold. There was a sharp tug, and Trist pulled back her hand. In her palm was a tiny square silver-colored rectangle. It resembled a computer chip. "Your locator. If you wear this, everyone will know where you go."

"We have homing devices in our clothes?" Jordan asked.

"Yes." Trist acted as if tracking devices in clothing were just another functional accessory, like belts or gloves. Next, Trist reached for Ben's collar and jerked the locator loose. "It is how I found you."

The aliens had sedative gas that killed unborn babies, showers that eradicated bacteria, so why not clothes that told everyone who wanted to know where you were going?

Thank God she hadn't worn a jumpsuit on her excursions with Kào.

Trist took the locators to an elevator station. Nonchalantly she tossed the chips down the empty shaft. "There," she said, wiping her delicate hands. "Now we can go."

"We?" Jordan asked. She still hadn't decided if this was a good-twin-bad-twin mixup, and she didn't want the evil twin tagging along. "Kào Vantaar-Moray summoned us to his quarters," she lied, and badly, too.

"I don't think so. He is not there. But I will bring you to where you can await him. Come. I am your official escort. You will follow, yes?"

Trist took the lead, her pointed black shoes click-clacking purposefully over the floor. The fabric of her dress was encrusted with beads or tiny pieces of glass that glowed—literally glowed—some coming on as others winked off, giving a mesmerizing three-dimensional effect. And her dress was so short that it barely covered her buttocks. Jordan hated to think of what would happen if the woman bent over to pick something up. Ben must have been contemplating the same thing, but with a different attitude, if the male interest she saw in his face was any indication. Apparently, his aversion to the Talagars extended only to the males of the species.

Jordan lifted her hands. "I have no idea what's going on. Do you?"

"No." Ben took her by the elbow and urged her along, his eyes fixed on Trist's rear end. "But if we'd walked around with those locators, security would have found us and brought us right back. She helped us."

"Did she? Or is this just the part where the cat plays with the mouse? What does your hunch meter say?"

"That the cat definitely wants to play," he acknowledged. "But we're not the mouse."

"Who is? Kào?"

216

He shook his head. "Don't know."

Trist stopped in front of a doorway. From inside, Jordan could hear music throbbing, the same music she'd noticed earlier. "Welcome to The Black Hole," Trist said and waved at the open door.

At second glance, the entrance wasn't open exactly, but covered with a film. It wavered, transparent and rainbow-colored, like a soap bubble.

Trist answered Jordan's unspoken question. "Nano-computers in liquid." She put her thumb and index finger close together to indicate something tiny. "Computers too small to see. They talk to our personal computers." Trist pointed to her wrist and the belt around her waist. "And read the data. Then it is recorded how many times we come and how long we stay."

Ben grimaced. "Orwellian to the max."

His comment bewildered Trist. Still, her grasp of English was amazing. But she was a linguist, after all.

"Do not worry," Trist said. "By the time they notice you come through with no computers, you will be gone. Ready to go inside? Good." She lowered her voice. "Say nothing and look at nothing. Keep head down and follow me."

She pressed through the film. It molded around her body like a sheet of lamination. Then, with a barely audible pop, the membrane snapped closed behind her.

"After you?" Ben asked.

Jordan gave him a thanks-a-lot frown. Then she took a breath, held it, and pushed through the film. It clung damply to her skin for a fraction of a second. On the other side, she felt as if nothing had touched her at all.

Ben walked through next. "Pretty cool," he said.

The Black Hole was a bar, a luxurious bar. The crew was a small one, and only a few people sat in plush floating chairs and couches. Music played, sounding Indian to her ears, with a pulsing, sexual beat. But no one danced. Maybe it was due to a difference between Alliance culture and hers, or ship's rules, she didn't know. But fun wasn't lacking. Some were engaged in conversation; others watched walls that showed scenes—a beach with two suns, a forest like the one in the holo-arena. As her eyes adjusted, she noticed that the wall-watchers were wearing soft helmets and gloves that were attached to computers. Virtual reality suits?

As she and Ben followed Trist deeper into the bar, from under the lip of her hood Jordan searched the crowd for Kào. According to Trist, he came here, but she'd have never guessed it. Warm and sensual—somewhere he'd learned to kiss that way. Maybe it was here. It hit her how much she didn't know about him, whom he hung out with after hours, whom he saw, or slept with. . . .

She clenched her jaw. That wasn't important now. Getting home to Boo was. Kào had told her to look to the future and not the past, but if there was a chance her past still existed, then she wanted it back.

Trist took them to a table surrounded by six buoyant chairs. Ben's hand closed around her bicep and squeezed. Jordan's gaze flew in the direction that Ben jerked his chin. Talagars!

There weren't many crew members of Talagar descent on the *Savior*, but of the ones that were, it seemed to Jordan that all except Trist were in attendance at a drink-and-food-laden table for six. Her heart beat harder. She saw their red eyes, thought of the atrocities she'd read about, and what their kin had done to Kào. Not kin, she reminded herself; these men were Alliance citizens. Yet the prejudice remained. She hated it in herself; she'd never before judged people by their race. Yet something about these men made her skin crawl. Maybe it wasn't their race at all, but the evil she sensed within them as individuals. Curiously, she didn't exactly feel that way with Trist.

Jordan dipped her head as she passed them so that her hood covered her face. But the men saw her, recognized her. They had to. Why else would they be watching like a pack of jackals, their eyes glittering with speculation, making her feel as if she were an exotic and expensive item for sale?

Maybe it was genetics at work. Eons of slave ownership made them appear that way. But if not, then something else was at work on this immense starship, and it was time to get worried.

"The refugees are to be settled in the Rim?" Kào thrust his hands in the air. "Why, there's nothing there."

"There will be, my boy," Moray said. "The Alliance plans a mass transfer of population to the Rim with military support. As it stands now, with a sparse population, it remains vulnerable to settlement by fugitives of the Talagar Empire."

The Talagars—or what was left of them—were on the run. Settling and fortifying the Rim would keep them from gaining a foothold in an isolated area and rebuilding their empire. The strategy made sense. But the idea of the refugees, of Jordan, as experimental and possibly expendable colonists in the most desolate area of the galaxy pricked every protective instinct he had. "Why wasn't I told of these plans?"

"I have only today received the orders."

Kào put down his utensil. He'd lost his appetite. "It infuriates me that the Alliance would make such a decision about a band of homeless people. It borders on inhumane." His fist balled on the tabletop. He dared not say more, as he didn't trust his temper to remain in check.

"These are unstable times, Kào. Unstable times require bold measures."

"I understand. But why these people?" *Why Jordan?*

"I wondered that myself. Clearly, it was our proximity to the Perimeter that drove the decision. And that the refugees have no home and are in need of being resettled."

Kào couldn't argue the need for the measures the Alliance had taken. Nor could he refuse to participate in the mission, for he'd vowed to help strengthen his father's name, and that meant ensuring that the refugees got to the Rim in the name of galactic peace.

Go with her.

How? By blood and patriotism, he was morally obligated to help his father carry out his orders. His personal feelings on the refugees' unwitting role in the plan had little bearing.

His gut clenched. Hated images flashed behind his eyes: the tall fence in his dreams over which he could never jump; his treatment at the hands of the Talagars, drug-induced confessions that spilled from him at their whim. In neither situation had he the ability to exert control over his destiny. It was no different now.

A call came in on Kào's comm. He opened his wrist computer and read the message that flashed there. "Security, sir," said the man in the tiny screen.

"Go," Kào prompted him.

"There's been a breach in the refugee area. Two of them left without clearance. We tracked them to the shuttle. They de-boarded on the central axis, Level One, where they headed toward the officers' living area." The man frowned. "But then they very rapidly descended in a vertical transport to Sublevel Five. We lost them."

"Sublevel Five. That's the cargo bay." Where their aircraft was stored.

"Yes, sir. But they're not there. We sent a team down and came up with nothing."

"I'm on my way." Kào closed the comm. He draped his

hand cloth over his unfinished meal and pushed away from the table. "I've got refugees on the loose."

"Find them," Moray said.

"Yes, sir. I'll report back when I do."

Trist had ordered the drinks because of the trouble Jordan and Ben had reading the menu. *Zakuu* it was called. Colorless and carbonated, the liquid filled three glittering flutes that were a foot tall and only about a half-inch in diameter.

Trist was totally at ease, while Jordan sat tensely. Her goal tonight was to find Kào and see what she could find out about Earth's destruction . . . or lack thereof. But worry made it tough to sit still. Her eyes kept flicking back and forth between the Talagarian men, Trist, and the main entrance to the bar. She liked it better when she and Ben had been proactive, hunting for Kào rather than sitting, waiting for him to come to them.

"Try the drink," Trist said. She took a delicate sip. Jordan and Ben barely touched their lips to the tart beverage. Trist folded her slender arms on the table and leaned forward. "You are nervous, yes?"

"We have a lot on our minds."

"I can see why. You have developed some interesting extracurricular activities."

Had Trist somehow found out about her trip to the holo-arena with Kào? She'd die if their kiss was common knowledge. But she gathered her wits and replied with equal aplomb. "And which extracurricular activities might those be?"

Trist's fingertip rapped her data-input panel. "Your spying."

"Spying?" Jordan threw a startled glance in Ben's direction.

"Well, snooping," Trist hedged. "I think that is your

221

word for the lesser form of spying. Spying on the computer."

She meant hacking—Dillon's hacking. Her heart in her mouth, Jordan tried to get a fix on Trist's purpose. But she didn't sense animosity or anger. Nothing in the woman's body language indicated that she was tense, while she and Ben were wound up tight enough to shatter. "The computer was given to us. We're using the educational program to educate ourselves."

"I did not know the ship's maintenance files were part of the program."

Ben looked as if he were going to faint. Jordan worked at keeping her panic from appearing in her face. So far, all Dillon had gotten her were the maps, which had served her well tonight. But the goal was to find out their current location in space with respect to Earth, so they could find their way back home, if they had to. If survivors remained. *Don't lose heart, not yet. Keep quiet and hear out what she has to say.*

Trist appeared mildly surprised when Jordan didn't offer a defense. She glanced around to see if anyone was listening in. Then she checked her wrist computer and belt comm, as if to make sure they were turned off, and her voice dipped to a private tone. "*I* created your education database. I know how you found your access and what you look at, because you used *my* files and codes."

Once more Trist glanced at the bar's entrance, as if she expected someone to arrive at any minute. Jordan prayed it wasn't the ship's security team, and that spying wasn't punishable by death.

"Relax." Trist spread her hands on the table. She wore tiny silver bands on all her fingers. "I have known what you see and do for a long time. I not worry. You stumble onto those records while using the education program, yes? You did not do on purpose."

Jordan took the hint. "That's right."

Trist shook a finger at them. "Bad refugees," she scolded with a hint of dark humor. "Always causing trouble. I will have to keep watch for now on. As if I do not have enough to do. In fact I have so much to do"—her sly red eyes shifted from Ben to Jordan and back again—"I will not notice if your snooping continues."

"You're not going to stop us?" Jordan couldn't help asking. "Why? Why help us?"

"Not help. A favor." Her smile epitomized the word *inscrutable*. "I do you a favor, then someday you do one for me, yes?"

"What can we possibly give you? Or do for you? We have nothing."

Trist's red eyes glinted. "You have more than you know, Jordan."

Jordan sagged in her chair, her thoughts spinning. What had just transpired here? Trist told them that she'd look the other way with regard to their hacking, and Jordan had agreed to the terms—a favor for a favor; a future one, but what? She was just beginning to wonder if she'd sold her soul to the devil when the devil himself stormed into The Black Hole.

Kào was out of uniform. Long-sleeved, his dark blue shirt stretched across his broad shoulders and reached to his waist. If he raised his arms over his head, she suspected he'd expose his navel and some nice abs. The pants fit snug, making it easier to imagine the long, lean legs underneath.

It took him a moment to search the crowd, but when his eyes met Jordan's, he pushed his way through. When he saw that she shared a table with Trist, astonishment and disapproval hardened his cold features.

"Security," he said into his comm as he walked up to their table. "Call off the search. Targets found." Then he lowered his comm and narrowed his eyes at Trist. "You called me on my private channel."

"Yes. Otherwise the entire security squad would have stormed over here," the linguist explained glibly. "I suspected you wanted to find them first."

"I did. But I didn't expect to do it here."

Jordan couldn't tell if he was angry or hurt. Or both. "You look . . . different," she said. *Different? Lame, really lame, Jordan.* Blame it on sleep deprivation and her lack of fluency in Key.

He smoothed one wide hand over what Jordan decided looked like dark blue hi-tech, up-scale sweats. "It is not my usual attire," he admitted in a curt tone. He glared at Ben, who looked as if he wanted to sink into the floor, and then at Jordan. "Perhaps we should start with the simplest question first. What are you doing here?"

"Easy question? I have easy answer," she retorted in his language, crossing her arms over her chest. "I was waiting for *you*."

Chapter Twenty

"You were waiting for me?" Kào wouldn't have conjured this scene in a thousand standard years: Trist sharing a table with Jordan and her second-in-command...in The Black Hole.

"Yes," Jordan replied in accented Key. "Trist tell us you come here."

"Trist," he growled warningly. A waitress glided up to the table to take his order.

"Sit down, Kào," Trist said.

Everyone stared at him expectantly. He exhaled and sat down. "Water," he said. The waitress shrugged disapprovingly and walked off.

He folded his arms across his chest. He noticed that Jordan hadn't fished out her translator. It meant that Trist must have been speaking in English. He envied the linguist her skill, for he found the translators bothersome but necessary.

Jordan cleared her throat. "I need to talk to you, Kào."

At the sound of his name on her lips, his chest felt strangely tight. The unaccountably intimate tone of her voice made him think of moonlight and kisses. "It wasn't necessary to go to these lengths to do it," he snapped. "It could have waited until the morning."

She appeared stung by his terse manner. He shouldn't take out on her what he'd learned from his father, but he wasn't the even-tempered, logical man he once was, it seemed. She fumbled for her translator and dug it out. "Sorry, but what I have to say I can't yet in Key." She took a deep breath. "When I first came on this ship, you offered me the chance to watch a recording of my planet's destruction. I didn't want to then. I don't want to now. But I have to. Tonight." Her voice shook, and her partner stared at his hands.

Kào couldn't fathom why they'd want to view the holo-recording when their discomfort at the idea was so obvious.

Trist watched the unfolding scene, her red-eyed gaze speculative.

Jordan focused on Kào. "You told us that the entire population of Earth was wiped out. Gone. But what if there was an error in your assumption? What if your readings of that comet were faulty? What if it didn't happen at all? All we have to go on is what the commodore told us."

"Do you think he lied to you?"

"I don't know. Would he?"

Kào read the translation. It was not an error; her insinuation was just as appalling the second time around. "You're new to the Alliance, new to its heroes. You don't understand who Moray is." It was difficult to imagine anyone not knowing. But her world had been an isolated one, well outside the confines of civilized space, an unusual circumstance in its own right. "This ship, the *Savior*, is named for him and his heroic efforts. The commodore is a great humanitarian. It's an insult to imply otherwise."

Ben shifted in his seat, his jaw muscles flexing. Jordan, wan and silent, observed him uneasily.

"You see, the commodore is a man of integrity. Of honor and courage." He did not pull his gaze from Jordan's. "He is also my father."

She made a sound of surprise. Or was it dismay? "He's your *father*? The commodore?"

"Yes. But his deeds transcend any relationship we might share. The evacuation of the Ceris Six space colony, for instance. It happened years ago, but it remains the event most associated with the Moray name. As fate would have it, he was nearby on patrol when the Ceris distress call went out. Of the thirty thousand inhabitants, more than half were lost in a massive explosion. But he coordinated the rescue of the rest, on his ship, and on others. He was credited with saving twelve thousand lives. Twelve *thousand*! I believe that powers beyond our comprehension see his strength and generosity and place him where he's needed. Like it was with your Earth, Jordan."

"There's no denying that he's a hero, Kào." Her expression made it clear that she was still recovering from the bombshell of Moray being his father. But her words proved her desire to find out what had happened to her world. "Still, if there's a chance Earth wasn't completely destroyed, we want to go back to rescue survivors. I have to see it, the recording. I have to know."

She sought the eyes of her second-in-command. "Ben and I, we both do—so it's not just one person's word, one person's opinion, on what happened to Earth."

She'd gotten her hopes up for nothing. The recording would simply cause her pain. But he couldn't deny her the request. Viewing the holo was her right. He rose, suddenly weary. "Are you coming along?" he asked Trist.

The linguist appeared surprised that he hadn't excluded

her. But she'd kept Jordan and the purser out of trouble. Inviting her to join them was the least he could do. Only he never imagined she'd accept.

"I will come," she said in her husky voice.

Filled with misgivings, Kào led the group from the bar.

"This is the viewing room," Kào said as they followed him into a plush, dark, chamber. "Lights." Lighting embedded in the walls came on slowly, a rich, soothing glow.

"The system is set up much the same as the holo-arena," he explained. Jordan's gaze flicked to his, a blush tinting her cheeks. He felt the answering heat in his loins. He'd been thinking of her incessantly. Her eyes told him she'd done the same. But they couldn't have more things conspiring to keep them apart.

"Let's get it over with," Jordan said and joined Ben on the couch.

"Lights off," he commanded. "Show holo nine-alpha, four-two-one. Earth."

The walls fell away. They floated in simulated space, stars all around them. In the dim light, Kào could see Jordan reach for something to hold. It was Ben's hand she found. It should have been his.

Earth showed up in the center of the forward viewing screen. "Look," he heard Jordan murmur. Taking out his translator, Kào read her words. "It's beautiful." Her voice was hushed, poised on the edge of pain.

"It looks whiter than I expected," Ben commented.

"Cloud cover. I thought it'd be bluer, too, though."

"We're not used to seeing it from space."

"True."

They spoke to cover their apprehension, Kào knew. As they remarked nervously upon their home-world's appearance, he paced behind the couch for the very same reason. It was worse for him, for he knew what was coming. He'd seen the textual description if not the event itself. He knew she'd be watching the nearly simultaneous destruction of billions of people, one of them her child.

But if this was what it took to put her past permanently behind her, so she could move on, then watch it she must. Jordan's steadiness had been an anchor for him, allowing him to dwell less on the dark memories and more on the here and now. Tonight it was his turn to be there for her.

Kào stole a glance at the time counter on the bottom left area of the forward screen. Any moment now. He tightened his abdomen. *Three, two, one. . . .*

A white-hot streak plunged into Earth's atmosphere. There was nothing at first, then a blinding flash from the surface, near the equator. A massive shock wave rolled outward, across the equator, to the poles, bringing unimaginable destruction.

"Oh, my God." Jordan muffled a cry. Kào fought the almost overwhelming call to go to her. But she had made it clear she wanted her distance from him. He respected her enough to give it to her.

Ripples of devastation spread outward from that first, enormous impact, one that would have challenged the planet's survival on its own. But the attack from the cosmos wasn't over. If there was ever a doubt in Jordan's mind that those on the *Savior* had deceived her, or that survivors had been left behind mistakenly, what followed would end those false hopes as brutally as the comet had ended life on her planet.

There was another bright streak, and then another. The comet had broken up, and now the fiery tail of debris came in fast and hard. Fragments of rock and ice glanced off the atmosphere, blood-red slashes.

Lashes.

Lashes from a whip. Jaw tight, stomach knotted, Kào paced faster, his hands fisted behind his back. He felt the paralyzing sting of every one of those impacts, as he'd felt them once across his back, chained naked on a cold, filth-stained floor, kneeling in his own waste.

He glanced up, his breaths ragged. Jordan sat as still as a statue, watching the aftereffects of the collisions. The planet's cloud cover glowed incandescent orange-red now, reflecting the massive firestorm far below on the surface.

Running, terrified, the ground burning the soles of his shoes; he couldn't find his mother, his father, couldn't see, blinded by light that was as hot as fire and seared his eyes, his skin—

A guttural sob yanked Kào from the flashback. Not Jordan's, but Ben's.

In the darkness, the man stumbled from the couch. "Sink . . . where's a sink?"

Trist pushed Ben to the sterilizer basin. He bent over, retching.

Kào strode to the front of the couch where Jordan sat, wan and still. "Well?" he demanded gruffly. "Have you seen enough?"

Her voice was quiet. Controlled. "Yes."

He exhaled. Thank the Seeders. He wanted no more of this. "Lights. Computer—holo off."

The walls went dark and the room's lights came up slowly, like dawn over a battlefield. Ben hunched over the basin, the back of his hand pressed to his open mouth. Trist stood to his left, contemplating him. Was that concern in her cold eyes? Were Talagars capable of compassion? A shocking notion, to say the least, and one he'd have to consider further. But not now.

Jordan sat as still as a corpse. Kào leaned over her, hands on his knees. "Are you still in doubt?" he asked gently. The rings under her eyes were so pronounced that she looked bruised. "Would you like to see further proof? I can show the recording again." He had to ask the question—if he didn't eradicate her skepticism, it would continue to sour their relationship like a festering sore.

"No." Her voice was rough. "Thank you." Her hands clutched the couch at either side of her hips. She was calm. Too calm. Her eyes were reddened, but he saw no tears.

He went to the food-and-drink dispenser, crouched on his knees to access a special decanter deep within the bowels of the storage chamber. Ah, there was still some Rig's Burner left in the decanter. The clear blue liquid was vile, bitter, and powerfully alcoholic. The only times he ever bothered with the stuff was to dampen the nightmares that plagued him in the early weeks aboard the ship.

Trist helped distribute four tiny, fingertip-sized glasses of the drink. "Down all of it," Kào ordered them.

He tossed back the contents of his glass only after he saw the others do the same. His head spun for a moment; then his vision cleared. Following the alcohol's initial punch was the expected feeling of well-being, faint, false, and temporary.

Ben set his glass on an antique buoyant table of dark synthetic wood. With the fractional added weight of the empty glass, the table whispered the characteristic pulsating hiss of the early years of the technology. After a startled second glance assured him that the table would do him no harm, Ben shoved his fingers through his black hair. "Jordan, we'd better go back now."

Jordan began to rise and then stopped, balancing her elbows on her thighs. She stared at her feet. Her face contorted in what was obviously an outward sign that she struggled with something. "I have something to say to Kào first. I don't want to make you stay. Go. I'll meet you back there."

Ben appeared reluctant to leave Jordan alone with Kào. "That's okay. I can stay."

"You're tired."

Susan Grant

"Not that tired."

"Ben, don't worry. I'll be fine."

Ben's mouth thinned. Unspoken communication passed between the pair, and a hint of red tinted Jordan's cheeks. "You can tell Natalie not to worry," she added crisply.

"Trist, escort Mr. Kathwari back to New Earth." Everyone's attention jerked to Kào after he issued his curt command. The linguist's pink-white hand closed over Ben's upper arm, and the purser regarded the gesture with surprise. But not, Kào noted, with distaste. Trist's expression, on the other hand, was Talagarian-neutral as she escorted Ben from the viewing room, leaving Kào alone with Jordan.

Comfort, particularly the emotion-rich comfort that females often required, was far from being his strong suit. He felt wholly inadequate to help her, but, blast it all, he was going to try.

Chapter Twenty-one

Jordan pushed herself off the couch and walked back and forth in front of it. Movement in the corner of her vision caught her attention.

The couch . . . it was moving.

No, it was an illusion given by the holo-fabric. The rich, earth-tone cloth wasn't a single pattern, she saw for the first time, but two, changing from tiny bronze spheres on a dark background to spinning gold-and-brown cubes, depending on her position in relation to it. But none of the modern wonders of Kào's world could distract her from her embarrassment.

"Kào," she said. She turned her hands palms up. Kào sought eye contact with her and waited for her to speak, giving her his tacit respect, but making no move to push her into conversation.

"I stayed because I wanted to apologize in private," she said in English, forcing him to use his translator. But with the words she was about to say, she couldn't afford the message to be garbled. "About Earth. About your father. We—I hadn't seen proof about the comet. Maybe someone got the facts wrong. Maybe there were survivors left—one or a billion—we didn't know. That's what I started to think. I couldn't let it go. I know you told me otherwise, but deep down I wanted you to be wrong. I wanted my daughter, my family, to be alive." Agony bubbled up inside her. She held it back somehow. Her voice shredded to a whisper. "A mistake gave me hope. Even a lie would have given me the chance to go home."

But that chance had been taken—*stolen*, as was her daughter's life and billions of others' in a travesty of cosmic justice she'd never hope to understand as long as she lived or as hard as she prayed.

She threw down her translator and switched from English to halting Key. English was done. Finished. She had no need for the language anymore. "But instead I insulted your father. I insulted *you*."

"Jordan, you didn't know. And I responded harshly, a defensive reaction, and I was wrong in doing so. For that, you have *my* apology. I am sorry."

"Too many 'sorries,'" she rasped. Her chest ached. She was tired of saying "sorry," of hearing "sorry," of *being* "sorry." She sat heavily on the couch and with an even heavier sigh fell backward, letting herself drown in the plush cushions of a piece of furniture that by some miracle didn't float. She scrubbed her fingers through her corkscrew curls. Her hair was wild, falling over her face, half hiding the big, quiet man standing in front of her, so achingly sincere in his awkward and obvious desire to comfort her.

She shrugged off the white windbreaker and unfastened the jumpsuit to her waist, reaching inside to the T-shirt under it. The photo she withdrew from the pocket over her right breast felt cool against the pads of her fingers. It was

234

a picture of Roberta dressed in a bright yellow and blue soccer uniform. She'd so loved playing soccer. When her mother had to miss a game due to work, her grandparents and Uncle John were always there to cheer her on, as they were on the day the photo was taken. A giant smile revealed Boo's missing front teeth. Accentuating her heart-shaped face were her long, tight curls, gelled heavily so they'd stay scraped back into a ponytail wrapped in a sparkly blue scrunchie. Jordan dragged her fingertip across the face she could no longer kiss, the hair she could no longer tousle. There'd be no more laughter to hear, either, or whining, or runny noses to wipe, or fears of the dark to soothe. Jordan's throat closed.

"Your child?" he asked.

"Yes."

Kào swallowed thickly. "May I see?"

She extended her arm, the photo held between two fingers. He took the picture, studying it for long moments. His dark eyes lifted, fraught with longing, wonder, and a thousand emotions she couldn't name. "She looks just like you."

Misery welled up inside her. "She was part of me," she whispered. "My heart breaks a little more every day I think of her. I feel indescribable guilt because I couldn't and didn't protect her on that day." She turned her hands over. "I promised her I'd come home. I promised . . ." Her hands shook. Then a guttural cry tore from the depths of her.

Kào caught her before she sagged to the plush floor. The anguish she'd held inside her for so long gushed out in harsh, wrenching sobs. Kào's arms closed around her, holding her hard to his chest. Cradled in his lap, she wept uncontrollably. Her chest and lungs felt as if they were turning inside out. Contractions squeezed her stomach muscles. Her nose ran; the tears flowed. Inconsolable, she cried for what seemed like hours, until she was almost too drained to draw another breath.

Certainly, her heart was too battered to keep beating. Yet somehow it did. Distantly, she was amazed by that fact: that she'd come out the other side alive.

Through a haze of emotional exhaustion, she heard a deep voice murmuring to her, tender, loving words in an alien, exotic language that had become mournfully familiar. A hand stroked her hair, and strong arms held her. "Kào," she rasped. Her eyes were too puffy to open fully. Blindly she reached for him. Her fingers bumped into warm, soft lips, a bristly chin. With a fistful of silky hair, she pulled him down to her. "Need you," she whispered.

His calming hands soothed her arms, her back, her neck and hair. Warm breath teased her skin as his mouth found all the tender hollows of her face. The rhythm of his breathing picked up, matching hers. Then their lips met, and her quiet hiccups melted into soft, sipping kisses.

She didn't resist when he rolled her onto her back. What she needed from him, he seemed to need from her. The kiss deepened. Their passion was pent-up and frenzied. Her fingers closed greedily around his thick wrist and guided his hand under her unfastened jumpsuit to where her T-shirt clung damply to her breasts.

His thumb grazed over her hardened nipple. The feel of his cool hand was a shock to her overheated skin. She shivered as she burned for him, disparate sensations that dizzied her. Her whimper brought her breast a gentle squeeze and a circling of his thumb over its exquisitely sensitive tip. Thick, liquid heat pooled in her lower abdomen. His fingers found her other breast, plucking the tip gently, coaxing it to a tight peak. Then his weight shifted, and his mouth, hot and wet, suckled her. She arched her back, her mouth falling open in a soundless moan.

Before long, he came back for more kissing. Neither of them could get enough of that, it seemed. His mouth covered hers, hard and demanding, but his strong fingers were somehow gentle as they skimmed over her taut, sensitive breasts. The embrace heated. His male scent filled her nostrils. He grew almost forceful in his need, before his touch gentled abruptly, as if he'd fought and won a battle to restrain a much more powerful urge.

But she wanted that power. She wanted all he could give. "Kào," she pleaded, her voice hoarse. "I need you." To take her pain and push it to the farthest recesses of her mind, where it could no longer stop her from feeling, from *living*. "Now," she whispered, lifting her eyes to the striking dark depths of his.

He fitted himself between her thighs. Rigid, aroused, he rested himself against her. "Do you know what you're asking, Jordan?"

Her laugh was husky, hungry, and sorrowful, all at the same time. "I hope so."

His warm hand rested for a brief moment against her cheek. "Then we share the same desire," he said gruffly. His gaze was so steeped in carnal promise that it made her toes curl. It brought reality crashing down all around her.

"Kào, pregnancy—I am not safe . . ." How to say in Key that she wasn't protected?

"The shower mist keeps the crew infertile."

Her revolted expression was reflected in his eyes, dark and searching. "We are protected, Jordan. That's what you wanted to know." He bent his head and tasted her lips with each word. "The method—is it so important?"

"No," she breathed. It was proof she was in a foreign place with far different customs: enforced sterilization, as if they were animals. It was an impersonal, manipulative way to guarantee birth control. But she couldn't argue with its efficiency.

Kào's hands curved around her jaw, holding her steady, demanding her full attention with a deep and hungry kiss. Only when she was rendered breathless did he leave her.

Crossing his arms, he pulled his blue shirt over his head. The lack of body fat on his upper body sculpted every muscle, every tendon, every vein, making his scars that much more noticeable. He wadded the shirt, tossed it aside. Well-toned stomach muscles flexed below a broad chest lightly and evenly coated with dark brown hair. But ribs showed under that golden skin. Evidence of a body starved, she thought, a body that was still healing, still gaining its strength.

Slowly it sank in, in vivid detail—the abuse his body had endured from the Talagars. Thin scars that looked like marks from a whip disfigured his left shoulder and most likely his back, too. Indentations over his right breast looked as if they were made with a sunburst-shaped cookie cutter pressed into his skin repeatedly.

To her, he was beautiful. The evidence of his suffering made him even more so. It proved how much he'd endured. Getting on with his life was a triumph all its own, yet he was willing to give so much of himself to her. She lifted her upper body off the floor and kissed the horrible brand on the side of his neck. The skin felt puckered under her lips. But she lingered there, her lips caressing the evidence of his ultimate humiliation.

She heard a harsh exhalation. "Ah, Jordan . . ." His mouth slanted over hers in a fierce kiss, forcing her backward onto the plush, carpeted floor.

The mood between them intensified. His increasing ardor magnified her own wildness, and she reveled in their out-of-control passion, losing herself in the pleasure. Urgency made her fingers clumsy as she unfastened the upper closure on his pants and wrenched the waistband down his thighs. Her hands were all over his body, impatient, demanding. This wasn't like her, not like her at all. All thoughts of propriety had fallen away, and desire, raw and carnal, annihilated her qualms. She wanted him; she wanted more. And he did, too.

He forced her arms up and over her head. Deftly he removed her jumpsuit and, underneath, her T-shirt and jeans. She didn't want to think about where he'd learned to get a girl out of her uniform so quickly, and so well. But the feel of his cool fingers sliding between her bare thighs sent her spinning into a place where the doubts couldn't reach.

His breath was hot against her ear as he slipped a finger inside her, a sensual invasion that set every nerve ending in her body on fire. Kào knew a woman's body, and knew it well. With little trial and error, he found where she was the most sensitive. Wet from her excitement, his fingertip glided through her soft folds and uncovered her tiny, sensitive nub. She gasped, her hips jerking. "Not yet," she whispered harshly. "Not without you." She pushed hard on his shoulders, rolling him onto his back.

He pulled her with him, and she landed astride his hips. Gripping him with one hand, she rose up on her knees and took him inside her. The penetration was instantaneous and deep. Her thighs trembled as he filled her completely.

She squeezed her eyes shut. Gulped air. Her desire for him was nearly as overpowering as her grief had been. She knew without a doubt that the second he moved inside her, she'd lose any hold she had on rational thought. With one innocent shift of her hips, Kào's breath caught. He clutched her thighs, holding her still. Inside her, his shaft gave a sharp spasm, and a soft groan escaped his locked jaw.

He was teetering on the edge, as she was.

At last, he gained control, incredible control.

Lifting her hips, she rocked against him, slowly at first, moaning as she moved faster. He encouraged her, his hands hard on her hips. Unreservedly he allowed her to take her pleasure, asking nothing of her and giving all, his face taut with the enjoyment she was grateful she could somehow bring him. She rode him hard, her head tossed back, her hair tangled and wild, whipping around her shoulders and over his chest. She'd never felt anything like it, this frantic hunger. She needed him to fill the void, to assuage her grief, to make her believe he'd be there and would catch her if she fell. And he did—God, how he did.

Her inner muscles clamped around him, and she cried out, poised on the exquisite threshold of pleasure-pain. She imagined that her heart stopped in that fraction of a second before she came apart, clutching at him, clawing at him, not knowing how to direct the wild passion exploding inside her.

Distantly, she heard him groan. He pulled her down to his chest as he thrust into her. His powerful body went rigid; his mouth opened against her damp and tousled hair. Then his hands convulsed over her shoulders, all gentleness forgotten as he exploded deep inside her in a prolonged, white-hot rush of heat.

His body went slack, but his arms curled around her and she sagged, boneless, across his sweating body.

They must have dozed, for when awareness returned, Jordan saw that they were sprawled on the carpeted floor. They lay side by side, she with one tired, aching thigh hooked over his legs, Kào with his fingers tangled in her hair.

Guilt pushed at the edges of her mind. *Roberta*. Her daughter was dead. How could she justify making love with wild abandon? Using joy to blot out the sorrow? Even if temporary, it seemed an insult to Boo's memory. Maybe others felt this way after the loss of a child. Maybe over time the guilt would fade, just as she imagined her grief would become easier to bear.

Look to the future and not the past.

Try.

Contact

Drained emotionally and physically, she kept her eyes closed and floated in semi-aroused bliss. Kào woke, smoothing his hands over her body. Sighing, she snuggled into his warmth. His hand slid down her thigh. He found where she still ached in the wake of their violently passionate lovemaking, and her body gave an involuntary start.

"You're sore, Jordan," he stated worriedly.

She lowered her head to his chest. "It was worth it."

A darkly amused, male chuckle rumbled beneath her ear. Speaking Key was getting easier with each passing hour. Spicy banter was still a ways off, but at least Kào understood her jokes.

She raised herself on one elbow and looked down at him. The muted overhead light played across his chest, blurring the scars there and shadowing his flat·stomach. "It was a long time for me." She traced her fingertip across his lips. "You are first . . . since my husband."

His surprise—and gladness—at that remark was tangible. "How long, Jordan?"

"Six years. In Earth time."

Kào's brows drew together as he calculated the converted number. "For me, it has been somewhat less than half that."

"Before prison?"

"Yes. And none since. I hadn't the interest, physically." His hand slid behind her head, cradling her skull. "Until you." He pulled her down to his mouth and kissed her. Her eyes closed and her lips opened under the soft, warm pressure.

Lovingly his tongue stroked hers. Kào's embrace reassured her in the most primal of ways, muting the pain of the gaping wound torn in her heart.

Other than her father and brother, he was the only man who hadn't run when she'd needed him, the only man who had the balls to admit his weaknesses and the strength of will to override them. In only weeks, Kào had become her rock, her anchor, a man who was there for *her*. It was a new experience, one she sensed she'd waited for all her life. Exist independently, she could. But she didn't want to lose Kào, not now; not ever.

She willed her lips to remember this moment, and for his to remember it, too. She wasn't naïve; there would come a day—soon, in fact—when they'd have to say goodbye. But for now, she'd try not to think about it.

When they finally moved apart, she smiled down at him, her fingers playing in his damp hair. "Since we speak of years, how is your age?"

"How old am I? Twenty-seven."

"In Earth years."

"That *is* in Earth years."

"You are not twenty-seven."

"Why, do I look younger?" He lifted a dark brow. "Or older?"

"Older," she blurted out. "Much older." She covered her eyes. "I did not know I rob cradle."

"Cradle? In which babies sleep?"

"Yes!" She dropped her hand, poking her finger into his chest. "I have five years older. Almost six!"

"You *are* five years older," he corrected patiently. "Then you are thirty-two, almost thirty-three."

She laughed. "Yes. See? I rob cradle."

He flipped her onto her back. Holding her in place, he fitted himself between her thighs. Already he was hard. "Do I feel like a boy?"

She gave a husky laugh and shook her head. Then she frowned. "Do I look like old woman?"

As he shook his head, he pulled back to gaze at her. He took in every feature of her face and then the rest of her body before returning his eyes to hers. His hand shook as he smoothed her hair away from her forehead. He placed a kiss there and at each temple before pulling back. "You are beautiful, Jordan," he whispered huskily. "A beautiful woman."

She couldn't help sighing. No one had ever said those words as he'd said them, or looked at her the way he looked at her now. She was a freckle-nosed tomboy, not the type of woman who ignited men's passions. Exposed to his frank appraisal, she felt her body responding—tightening, warming. Her thighs opened, and his rigid shaft glided over her moist folds. She inhaled sharply at the sudden heat, and her pelvis tipped up. She was so wet that he entered her. Groaning, he jerked his hips and thrust into her the rest of the way.

He was buried inside her, but he didn't move. "Does it hurt?" he asked low in her ear.

"No," she whispered on a sigh.

His strong arms tightened around her, molding her to his warm body. He began to rock his hips slowly, moving inside her easy and deep, rekindling the heat that had subsided to a slow burn.

She murmured to him, caressed him, slow and cherishing. Everywhere she could reach, she placed tender, loving kisses. Eyes shut, he let his head fall forward, soaking in her affection thirstily, as if he'd craved this all his life. She could almost feel his harsher edges melting away.

From within his chest came a deep sound of contentment as she dragged her mouth to his chin, his eyelids, his jaw. There the stubble pricked her tender lips, before their mouths came together again.

Their first time together had been a Class-Five hurricane. This was morning mist. The first time, she took and took; this time, she gave it all back, caressing his battered, beautiful body, doing everything in her power to convey what she felt for him, how she treasured him, savored him, admired him.

It was clear that he'd needed this, needed *her*, as much

as she did him. Maybe even more. Two halves of the same whole, brought together by the most horrible tragedy imaginable.

His hips rolled, slow and sure, the thrusts deepening. "Jordan . . . my Jordan . . ." he whispered over and over. She wrapped her legs high over his back to take him in as far as he would go, until she imagined he'd become part of her and she of him. She held him tight, unwilling to let him go, until he at last found his release. If only for now, she thought, she'd found her peace.

Morning was coming fast. But they had some time left together before the first third began and the corridors would fill with the day shift. As Kào lay sleeping, Jordan smiled at the ceiling, her arms flung over her head, her body sated, lethargic. *My Jordan.* That's what he'd called her. "My" Jordan. Without hesitation, she'd be this man's anything.

Little aftershocks of pleasure still rocked her; every nerve ending sang with heightened sensitivity. She snuggled into Kào's warmth, and the movement woke him. "You're smiling," he said in a sleepy voice.

"Of course I smile." She winked at him. His sweat-dampened hair had dried spiky. She mussed it with her fingers. "Why should I not?"

Disquiet flickered in his face before he managed to hide it. "Ah, Jordan. Everything has changed."

"Yes, make love and everything changes," she said dryly, wishing she had the ability to formulate a properly sarcastic comeback in Key. "It always does."

He came up on one elbow and gave her a withering look. "You should know me better than to think I would regret,"—he lowered his voice a fraction—"making love to you." His cool gaze returned to the viewing room's hatch, as if he expected it to open at any minute. "There are other matters on my mind. Last evening at dinner, the commodore informed me that your people are to be settled in the Rim."

In her gut a wave of unease matched what she'd seen in his eyes only a few seconds before. "No one lives there," she said.

"A few do. But mostly the region's habitable planets consist of wild, unsettled worlds."

She rolled away from him and dug through the pile of discarded clothing until she found her translator and Kào's. This wasn't love talk; she couldn't risk misunderstanding anything that had to do with the people for whom she was responsible. "Why there? Why not a city?"

He sat up and let out a tired sigh. "In the aftermath of the war, our government fears that the Talagars might seek to rebuild their empire. The Rim would be the perfect place to do it. What few people live there have little protection. They are spread among many worlds, in isolated pockets, most living rural lives with minimum, if any, technology to assist them. It would be easy for the Talagars to absorb them into their society as slaves. They would need slaves . . . to re-form their empire. It is how their society is structured. They know no other way."

"This is not reassuring news, Kào." Her head started aching, and the tight knot of stress that had lived in her stomach for weeks now returned. "It sounds like we're going to be left as slave bait on some isolated planet."

"You won't be without protection."

"What kind of protection? An army? Or a cache of ray guns we don't know how to use?"

In profile, his frown deepened as he read her question on his translator. "You won't be alone, your people. You're to be joined by a massive wave of new immigrants from the more populated regions."

"Volunteers?" Unlike Flight 58.

He glared straight ahead. Obviously, the subject was a

sore point with him. "It is not what I thought would happen to you and your people, or I would have protested the decision. But now it's too late. The plan has been approved by the seat of the Alliance government on the planet Sofu, our capital world."

He swallowed thickly. Eyes narrowed, he stared across the room. Seeing what? Thinking what?

She rose to her knees and positioned herself behind him. Unlike when they were on the observation deck, this time she knew him well enough to comfort him physically. Her hands worked the tension out of his knotted shoulders, and she pressed her lips to the flexing sinews on the side of his neck and jaw. "We'll be fine. You don't have to worry. So the relocation port isn't going to be paradise; no one ever said it would be. None of us really thought it, either."

She pressed her fingers into his muscles. He tipped his head back, leaning into her kneading hands. "It'd be selfish to complain," she reasoned. "How can we, any of us? We're *alive*. I know about five billion other people who'd like to be in our place."

At that, he glanced over his shoulder, his eyes soulful. She knew she'd reminded him of her inconsolable weeping for Boo. "Thanks for giving me a heads up, though," she said with a lightness she didn't feel. "Now I can brief the passengers and crew to expect less-than-ideal conditions. It'll be the best thing for them. Everyone's been getting soft lately—three square meals a day, comfy beds. Now maybe they'll do more exercise and be better about practicing their Key without me having to bully them all the time."

After he read the translation, his face looked bleaker than ever. He was only twenty-seven. He looked sixty.

She plopped down next to him. Her small breasts bounced as she drew her knees to her chest. Curving an arm around her bare calves, she flexed her toes, studying the tendons on the tops of her bare feet and the frosted pink nail polish Natalie had used to paint her toenails. *Even captains need pedicures*, the woman had insisted.

"If it's the remoteness of the Rim that bothers you, don't let it." Jordan forced a can-do smile. She refused to let a minor item like this little detour shake her resolve to face the future head on. "I don't mind isolation. In fact, I prefer it." *Sunny pastures, mountain pines, a sweeping blue sky.*

Her mind filled with a hundred memories of happier times. How much more she would have appreciated them if she'd only known they'd never be repeated. "My family owned land in a place called Colorado. Now, *that* was paradise." She told him about her plans, how she'd wanted to move there with Roberta. "We'd build a home and raise horses."

"Horses." His brows drew together, and he peered into her eyes, into her soul.

The unwavering scrutiny sent a shiver careening down her spine. "What is it, Kào?" she asked worriedly, scrolling back to see what she'd said to so unbalance him.

He let out a breath and shook his head. "Sometimes I think there were higher forces at work when they brought you to me."

"What do you mean?"

"My ancestors were equestrians."

"Horsemen? That's what you would have been if you hadn't lost your family?"

"I believe so. They were rural people, proud and hardworking. I'd have lived my life outdoors, as you wished to, Jordan, working the land, raising food, toiling long hours, and riding. Riding horses."

No wonder he resembled the Marlboro Man, she thought.

"Swift, four-legged creatures," he went on. "With long, tufted coats."

"Long and tufted? Ours were short and glossy!"

"Making them swifter animals, I imagine. Perhaps the

Seeders had perfected the species by the time they reached your planet."

She couldn't resist the opportunity his remark presented. "They perfected the humans there, too."

His mouth quirked. "Did they?"

"They did." She struck a pose. "Can't you tell?"

Amusement warmed his harsh features as he read the translation. "A superior race? Perhaps that explains my attraction to you." He drew her close and rested his chin on her head.

Jordan sagged against his chest. Her crew and passengers were being forced by fate to spend the rest of their lives in the wild and woolly far reaches of the galaxy, possibly as a human barricade against a new Talagar Empire, people whose lifestyle made the marauding Huns look like nuns. But in Kào's strong arms, she felt snug, protected. The sensation reassured her, as his presence always did.

His lips found the side of her throat. "I love when you do that," she whispered with a shudder. He gathered her closer, nibbling her ear, his hand cupping her breast. He captured its tip between his fingers, kneading gently. "And that, too. . . ."

Desire stretched in a taut hot string from her breast to the inner places that were still tender from lovemaking. And he was ready to repeat the act a third time. Quick recharges were one benefit of having a younger lover, she supposed, although she had a feeling it was more than physical craving that drove him to initiate sex. His news of the relocation was worrisome, and he wanted to distract them both.

But the world outside the doors of the holo-viewing room had different ideas. Kào's wrist comm beeped, and they jumped apart. "Kào here," he said and turned away from her to take the call. It was a private message. Those always came over the wrist-viewers in text format.

It occurred to her that Trist hadn't interrupted a single time during their long night together. That was a first. Up until now, it seemed that the woman had done everything she could to keep them from growing closer, only to practically throw them together last night. Jordan's thoughts swerved to Ben. He'd left with Trist. And his eyes had been plastered to her half-exposed rear end. With the anxiousness of a protective mom, Jordan hoped to heaven that Ben was sleeping peacefully and alone in his own bed.

Kào closed the screen. "I must go. I've been summoned to the bridge."

"Is there a problem?" she asked.

"No. My father wishes my presence."

They hastily dressed and tidied the area on which they'd lain. Kào's mood seemed to darken considerably the closer they got to New Earth.

Outside the still-closed hatch, they stopped, turning to each other. The passion they'd shared served as a powerful connection, drawing them closer despite many unanswered questions. She glanced around to see if anyone was looking, then rested her hand on his bicep. His skin was hot under the soft blue fabric. Awareness tingled between them. "Good luck with your father," she said.

"This morning I think I will need it." His smile made her heart twist. "However, I won't let it concern me. For now, all I want to do is enjoy you."

"I won't argue," she said on a breath. For now, it was all she wanted to do, as well. She'd never lived this intensely, this recklessly. But she'd learned hard lessons about the fragility of life, about loss. She knew how quickly life could be taken away. "Live in the moment. That's what we have to do. People think they're going to live forever. They don't."

"No, they don't. More than ever before, I see that." He cast his dark and sorrowful gaze around the deserted corridor before placing a tender kiss on her lips. His fingers curled around her jaw and into her hair, bringing the heat of desire. His expression warmed fractionally, as if he'd felt what she had. "Later I will return for you," he said, his deep voice husky with sexual promise.

Arms hanging limply at her sides, she watched him go. Every cell in her body cried out for her to run after him, to hold him prisoner in her bed all day, to kiss, to talk, to share food, to dream next to him. Feeling as if half of her were missing, she opened the hatch leading into New Earth and walked inside. She wasn't sure if it was a miracle or a curse, but her body had come back to life on the very night her old life died.

Chapter Twenty-two

Showered and changed, Kào met his father in the private meeting room off the bridge. No one sat at the glowing table, only Moray, his face softly shadowed. "Sit, Kào," he said without taking his attention from his handheld computer.

Kào slid a buoyant chair under himself and eased into it. The seat bobbed gently. The drowse-inducing rocking motion reminded him that he hadn't slept last night. Ah, what he wouldn't do for a long nap . . . with Jordan asleep next to him. The thought of her warm body held protectively in his arms brought a stirring to his loins. Tonight, he thought. He'd bring her to his quarters. There, privacy would be guaranteed. No one would know if she stayed with him all night.

Moray began reading from his handheld, jarring Kào from his trance. "Had Earth survived, it certainly would have gained scientific notice, as all humans, even red-eyed

Susan Grant

Talagarian bastards"—his father raised a sardonic brow—
"are progeny of the Original Ones, who seeded the galaxy
eons ago with their DNA."

Kào propped his elbows on the conference table and
leaned forward. "Those are my words." His *exact* words. It
was a text version of the holo-message he'd sent to the Alliance Academy of Science on Sofu in a long-shot effort separate from the official missive he'd directed to Alliance
Headquarters. Kào's goal was to ensure that the Alliance
understood the significance of finding Earth, and that his
father received full credit for the discovery. Gaining the
support of the scientific community would help tremen-
dously in achieving those goals.

But unlike his formal communication with Headquarters,
Kào had routed this private appeal through a doctor he'd
met but a few times, the only medic who'd examined him
inside and out after his release from prison who had treated
him as a fellow professional despite having every reason
not to. And now here was Moray, reading what he'd assumed was a personal and unofficial request.

"Where did you find this, sir?" Kào asked. "Surely not
from the Academy. I'd have thought it would have been
tossed out with the trash weeks ago."

Moray held up one finger, silencing him. Kào's mouth
twisted in a resigned smirk. He felt nine years old again.

"How a world like Earth became separated from the rest
is a great mystery," Moray read. "If Earth exists, then it
follows that other lost worlds do, too. It is my wish that
this possibility will spawn a new era of exploration, and a
galaxy of thanks for Commodore-elite Ilya Moray, a selfless
hero, a true visionary, and"—Moray lowered the handheld—"my father." The commodore's eyes were moist.
"Thank you, Kào."

"I said nothing more than the truth." The men regarded
each other silently. "I haven't heard anything from Head-

252

Contact

quarters. I hope it means they're giving the matter proper consideration."

Moray spread his meaty hands on the table. The excitement in his gray eyes was unmistakable. "We've done it, my boy. Never did I think it would happen this quickly. We're on our way. Before you know it, we'll have you installed in the Grand Forum." He gazed somewhere far off. "Perhaps a senate seat. It's well within your abilities, you know." He brought his attention back to Kào in sharp focus. "We've always known that. Soon they will see your potential, too. Ah, yes, this is but the start."

"What is, Father? I'm afraid you've lost me."

"Your war records, of course! They've agreed to review them. Headquarters has. You'll be vindicated; your name will be cleared, just as I told you. Wait and see."

"My records are to be reviewed?" Kào shook his head. "My correspondence with the Academy led to this?"

"Yes, son. Your efforts on my behalf spurred Sofu to reopen the case. Just as you'd hoped."

"My hope was to clear *your* name, not mine. My actions brought about the biggest defeat of the war—"

"Lies, Kào! All of it." The crimson tinting Moray's neck rose to his jowls and cheeks. "I've forwarded them the additional information I've gathered over the years. It will clarify what we already know, that you made your decision that day based on the best intelligence available to you. You were doing your duty as a loyal Alliance soldier. No more," he growled, "and *no less*. You were made a scapegoat."

Kào stared at his scarred hands. If what Moray told him was true—and he had no reason to believe otherwise—there was a real possibility that his record could be wiped clear of all blame for the mistaken attack, because he'd acted on faulty intelligence. As for the information he had let loose in the prison camp, there was no proof; and all the other suspects were dead.

253

Kào drew a deep breath. This turn of events he would never have imagined. This was more than all he'd ever wanted: the chance to clear his father's name. But the victory was a hollow one. Jordan would leave for the relocation port with her people, and he'd be obligated to remain on the *Savior*. An open and active investigation would take an unknown period of time. There would be data requested, interviews, and likely a holo-appearance before a military tribunal.

Moray watched him, clearly awaiting a response of some kind. With conviction he didn't feel, Kào said, "This is good news, good news indeed."

"It certainly is." His father's eyes narrowed. "You look tired, Kào."

"I am, sir." *Of being more a puppet than the master of my destiny; of not being the man Jordan needs me to be.* And he was tired of his overwhelming sense of debt to his father, which blinded him to what choices were the right ones.

Kào thanked the heavens that Moray didn't know that his relationship with Jordan had turned intimate. He needed breathing room in which to give the entire dilemma the deliberation it required. Pricking his father's misplaced protective instincts would only make matters worse.

"Perhaps today I will exchange my workout for a nap," Kào said lightly and pushed himself to his feet. "Is their anything else you require of me?"

"No. Go rest. You well deserve it."

Kào returned the man's warm smile and trudged to the exit.

"Oh. One more thing, Kào."

He turned around. The man dug something out of his chest pocket. It was a two-dimensional image of a pretty little girl with blond hair and eyes of blue. Kào couldn't name what swept through him upon spying the familiar reproduction of Jordan's beloved daughter, but if one were to take outrage and defeat and mix them together, it'd be pretty blasted close to what he felt gazing at the picture of Jordan's child in Moray's hand.

By the Seeders! Had he and Jordan been so distracted that they'd left this behind? Apparently so.

"This was found in the viewing room," the commodore said and placed it on the table.

"It belongs to one of the refugees." His back straight, his shoulders squared, Kào returned to the table and collected the image. "Thank you."

The picture burned a hole in his hand as he strode to the hatch. The image of Jordan's child had led to an encounter so moving and so life-affirming that the presence of the photo in this environment and under these circumstances conspired to sour that experience. But he steeled himself against the temptation to give in, to let something so valued be stolen from him. As a man with a dearth of beloved memories, he wasn't apt to part easily with what few he'd gained.

Something made him stop in the hatchway. A sixth sense. Gut instinct. He didn't know what to call it, but the impulse had often served him well. "By the way, sir," he said, turning around. "Who found this?"

Moray made a show of gathering his handheld and other items. "Trist did."

"Trist," Kào repeated flatly. *Trist!* Blast it all. What goal had she in mind, taking the picture to Moray and not directly to him?

"Yes. Trist," Moray replied, as casual as could be. Kào couldn't fathom his father not pondering the implications behind the appearance of the picture in the viewing room shortly after dawn. He must know now that Kào had brought Jordan there, though not, he hoped, that they'd ended up making love on the viewing room floor.

"Trist knew that I'd called you to the bridge, Kào. I suppose she thought to save time by giving the image to me to pass along instead of returning it in person. She's been rather busy of late with her duties."

"Yes, she certainly has." Busier than Moray knew, what with escorting refugees to the ship's bar.

The two incidents were related, Kào decided: Trist giving the picture to his father and her involvement with the refugees last night. But Kào couldn't discern the connection. It was like trying to string together two matching beads with a too-short cord. Fortunately for him and perhaps not for Trist, he enjoyed puzzles. His mind was already working on solutions as he gave his father a curt nod, backed up two steps, and left the room.

"Carte blanche," Jordan repeated to Dillon's surprise as she peered over his shoulder, watching him probe deeper into the *Savior*'s computer. "Trist said we can poke around the computer and she won't say a thing."

"A green light," he said, his fingers tapping atop the keyboard. "Look. The files that were protected aren't anymore." Periodically he'd stop and study something. Then he'd be off again. "What do we owe her for the privilege?" he wondered aloud as he typed.

"I asked that, too. She'll want an eye for an eye, apparently." She pulled over a pair of ottoman-type chairs that Dillon had grounded for her by disabling the buoyancy. But to be at the same height as someone sitting on a floating chair, she'd have to stack them. She lifted the second and balanced it on the first. Atop the double chair, she scooted backward until she felt secure on the cushion. A momentary twinge between her legs reminded her of what she'd been doing most of the night before.

Ah, Kào. She missed him already. Their time together would be too short. They should be spending every last moment together, but they had responsibilities, both of them. She worked at keeping her feelings for Kào, or anything that might hint at her extracurricular activities with him, from appearing in her face.

Dillon watched her with some skepticism. "Piling the chairs one atop the other." He shook his head. "I thought that's why I fixed them for you, because you didn't care for the height."

"Height I don't mind exactly. It's a perceived lack of control that I can't stand. I'm a pilot, remember?"

"Yeah." He cracked a smile and returned his attention to the computer. "So . . . an eye for an eye, is it?"

"Yup. We owe Trist a future favor. God knows what we'll be able to do for her. I say we got the better end of the deal."

"Ah . . . here we go."

"What, what?" Her heart rate picked up, and she leaned forward.

"I plugged in Earth's coordinates, and there's our star map."

The image was three-dimensional, reminding her uncomfortably of the holo-recording. "Now all we need is our present position and we'll know where we are in relation to home."

"Home," Dillon murmured. "It'll always be that, even burned to a crisp, eh?" He bent his head to his task again.

Ben sauntered up to where they sat. "He found Earth's coordinates," Jordan told him.

Ben peered at the numbers scrawled on Dillon's scratchpad. "That's not right. The fourth symbol . . . it's their number four. The half C with the squiggle on the top. You've got a seven."

"How the hell would you know?" Dillon asked.

Ben tapped the side of his head. "I have a photographic memory, remember? You said it would come in handy someday, and it did. In the holo-vid last night I saw a string

257

of numbers, bottom right-hand side, like they'd labeled the flick. It was the same format as what you've got there—almost the same number, too, except for the seven. If it wasn't the coordinates, then what was it? Especially with the numbers being so close to the ones you've got there."

Dillon traced his index finger across the flexible screen, distorting the image under the light pressure. "There are twenty-six numbers in galactic coordinates. That's a lot of figures to remember. You sure about that four you saw?"

"Yeah, I'm sure."

Dillon swore under his breath, grumbling as he went back to work.

"What's his problem?" Ben asked Jordan under his breath. "It's probably just a typo."

"But which one has the typo?" Jordan murmured back. "Dillon's been working on this day and night, trying to pinpoint our present position."

"Why not just ask where we are?"

"I did," she said. "It's classified. No one but the senior staff knows our position at any given time. If they haven't told Kào, they're not going to tell us."

"And Earth's coordinates?" Ben whispered back. "Can't you ask about those?"

Dillon interjected, "Those I had to find myself. Or at least I thought I had. Now you tell me they're wrong."

"Hey, man, I'm sure what I saw was a misprint." Ben tried to appease him with a smile.

But Dillon was already hunched over the computer, so deep in concentration that he hadn't heard him.

"I'll let you work, Dillon," Jordan said quietly. "Good luck with it."

Ben offered her a hand. She grabbed it for balance and hopped off the double chair. "It seems to me he's going through a lot of trouble for nothing," Ben remarked as they walked away. "What's the point of knowing where we are in space now? Maybe it was a big deal once, when we didn't know where they were taking us, but now we know. Kào told you. The Rim."

"Dillon wants to know. He won't give up. And frankly, I hope he doesn't. I think it's safer to question, to confirm things on our own. Thank God Trist is letting us. Or we'd be totally in the dark."

"Like we are now."

Jordan shrugged and sighed. "We're in the dark and searching, Ben. That's better than the alternative. I guarantee that if Dillon were to throw in the towel—and he won't—I'd jump right in and take over. And, no, I wouldn't know what the heck I was doing, any more than he'd be able to fly that nice jet we've got parked downstairs, but I'd feel like I was doing something." She rolled her hands into fists. "I have to feel like I'm doing something. Going forward. In control."

Ben rubbed her back. "Ah, Jordan. This whole thing sucks."

She sighed. "Yeah. But it's getting better." *Thanks to Kào.*

They stopped by the water dispenser, where it was blessedly deserted. They filled glasses and drank. Ben refilled his cup. "Last night must have been pretty intense for you," he said under his breath.

She choked on her swallow of water. *He doesn't mean Kào.* She cleared her throat. "It's going to be a while before I stop seeing the explosions every time I close my eyes."

He sipped pensively. "Trist helped me put things in perspective."

Jordan lowered her glass. "You've got to be kidding."

"No. She's a lot different than we thought. She's . . ." His eyes unfocused, and then his mouth curved smugly as his attention came back to Jordan. "Really *nice*."

"That's . . . great." Jordan didn't know what else to say. She'd had a very different first impression of Trist than

what the woman was turning out to be. If she made Ben
happy, then the least she could do was try to like her.

Ben chuckled. "I called her 'snow angel.' She didn't know
what to say."

"I can imagine."

"She looks like one, you know, with that skin and white
hair. And she's so tiny. Really delicate."

"Size is deceptive. I wouldn't underestimate her strength."

He gave a very male-sounding laugh. "I won't anymore.
Not after last night."

It was all Jordan could do to keep her jaw from dropping.
Had he slept with Trist? Had there been time? When Jordan
had walked through the front door, Ben was already sitting
on the couch with Natalie, waiting for her. But if he and
Trist had made love only once, one quickie instead of . . . A
hot blush flooded her face, and she tried to hide it by taking
a deep drink of water. "Snow angel, huh?" she prompted,
swallowing.

"Yeah . . . last night was pretty incredible. But she's in a
relationship." He shrugged. "She didn't tell me until after,
though."

Whoa. After? After *what*?

Ben regarded her thoughtfully. "So, did you and Kào . . .
you know?"

This time she managed to swallow without choking. She
thought of fibbing. But what was the point in denying her
involvement with Kào? Ben and Natalie would figure it out
soon enough, especially if her plans to sneak away to Kào's
quarters became a nightly thing. They'd already seen the
official Alliance uniform she planned to use as a disguise,
courtesy of Kào, that just happened to be folded neatly inside a large box delivered that afternoon along with a surprise ration of rare, fresh, ready-to-eat produce for everyone
on Flight 58. On Earth, he would have sent roses. "He's a

really good guy, Ben," she replied as enigmatically as possible.

"You need a good guy."

"For however long I have him around. He can't leave the ship. And we have to." She wished she could feel as casual and unconcerned about the prospect as she sounded. The bittersweet feeling of "doomed romance" settled over her once more. Two people destined to cross paths and never see each other again. God, she was depressing herself all over again. *Buck up, Jordan.*

She forced a smile. "So, why the sudden change in heart about Kào? Only yesterday you had him at the center of a conspiracy to keep us all as prisoners."

"Let's just say that I learned a few things." He rubbed his shadowed cheek. "People aren't always what they seem. And you can't judge a book by its cover."

"Meaning the Talagars."

"Yeah."

If Trist had wanted an ally among the refugees, she'd found one. "Well, I'm happy for you, Ben." She was. Really. Everyone needed someone in difficult times, and who was she to judge? "So, are you ready to get to work? Let's finish that inventory we started. I want listed everything we want to take with us when we leave the ship. Including what's left on the airplane, *and* the airplane itself, if they let us take it. We're not going to have the chance to come back and look for anything we left behind."

Broken hearts included.

Chapter Twenty-three

Kào's quarters were bathed in a romantic amber glow, and the air was scented with something fresh—simulated outdoors, Jordan guessed, since it smelled like a forest after a soaking rain, clean and fresh. Luxury settled all around her like a downy comforter. Languidly she glanced at the time. It was the middle of the last third. When it ended, Kào would have to sneak her back to New Earth. But for now, they were together.

The bedding was twisted around her ankles. Her lips tingled, abraded by the roughness of his beard. The tender skin of her inner thighs tingled for the exact same reason. And more, much more. They'd made love impatiently as soon as the hatch had sealed behind them. It was always like that: first the hunger and then the tenderness.

Kào lay with his back toward her. She snuggled closer, bumping into Kào's translator. She longed for the day when they wouldn't have to sleep with their computers. Though she'd be gone by then, she thought sadly. "You were pretty wonderful," she murmured in his ear.

He answered with a grunt. She propped herself on one elbow and forced his shoulder down to the mattress, shifting him onto his back. His mouth was hard; his scar stood out starkly. And his eyes burned as dark and ominous as a late afternoon thunderstorm in the Rockies.

She pursed her lips. While she'd been lying in bliss, he'd been brooding. She should have figured as much; he seemed to have a tough time assimilating happiness. "Someone is wearing the world on his shoulders again."

He picked up his translator and gave it a funny look. "I don't understand the phrase."

"It's vernacular for putting pressure on yourself, taking everyone else's problems and making them your own. Because how bad can your problems be"—she traced her finger over his shaven jaw—"after tonight?"

He sat up and swung his legs over the edge of the bed. The blanket, wadded between them, was made of a holo-fabric. Tiny spruce-colored leaves danced atop a matte background of black-ticked gold. Absently she waved her palm above the pattern. Her hand didn't pass through the leaves but above them, destroying the illusion. "You're shutting me out, Kào."

The muscles in his back bunched under the brutal lash marks defacing his smooth golden skin. His voice was gruff and hushed. "Jordan, I share something with you and your people that no one else onboard the *Savior* does. We're orphans of destroyed worlds. We can never return home. At the time Moray rescued me, I was too young to comprehend my loss. But as an adult, I carry the emptiness here"—he pressed his fist to the center of his chest—"the place that pride in my land, my heritage, would have filled. The very least I can do is ease your people's transition to your new world."

Susan Grant

"Meaning?" She tried but failed to keep the yearning out of her voice.

A look of profound pain crossed his face. He hooked her with one arm and flung her to the mattress, deftly pinning her with one hard thigh. His skin was hot and his hands were thorough. Before she knew what was happening, he was kissing her with the same, dizzying attention.

"Wait," she mumbled, pushing against his bristly jaw. "We weren't done talking."

"Talking." He groaned in wry, male exasperation. He was aroused; she felt the hot, rock-hard length of him sagging heavily on her belly. The minute she took him inside her, she wouldn't get another coherent word in edgewise. Kào knew it, too.

"Yes, talking." She twisted out of his embrace and sat up, sweeping her tangled mane off her face. She gave him a sideways glance through her curtain of hair. "You're not used to sharing, are you?"

"The night is nearly over," he snapped irritably. He climbed off the bed and stalked to where he'd discarded his clothes. He was magnificent, a provoked, fully aroused male. "Since we are done here, we'd better gather our things and go."

"Oh, so we're done, are we?" She grabbed the T-shirt and jeans he held out to her. "You big, quiet types always brood when you're worried, to the point of shutting out the very people you're worried about." She noticed that he was left holding her panties and she snatched those, too. "Don't deny it. I know all about guys like you, thanks to my father and John, my brother."

He pulled on his pants, his back to her. "And this is what you think I'm doing—shutting you out?"

"Yes." She lowered her translator. "Something happened today, and it's bothering you. I guess we could spend the rest of the trip pretending otherwise. Or doing *this*, making

264

love, *having sex*, but I can't. I don't want to, Kào. For what little time I have with you," her voice caught, "I want *all* of you."

That took the wind out of him. His shirt hung from one tightly fisted hand and his translator from the other. He pointedly kept his broad, scarred back toward her.

"I'm your friend, Kào. Confiding in me is okay."

He turned around, scowling. "You're more than a friend. We turned that corner last night. And that is the crux of it."

"The crux of what?" she persisted.

His jaw tightened, and his gaze bored into her. But as their eyes met and held, his anger dissolved into something she didn't understand. He walked slowly to where she sat perched on the edge of the mattress and reached for one of her long blond curls.

With his thumb and forefinger he moved her hair away from her cheek, gazing at her for the longest time. When he finally spoke, his voice was gruff. "When I first saw your eyes, I thought of the sea. . . ."

Her heart wrenched with the profundity of the simple statement. His lashes shielding his gaze, he tucked the strands behind her ear with such poignant regret that she thought she'd die on the spot. Time stood still as they regarded each other, more passing between them in those moments than any words could ever convey. The sense of good-things-never-lasting swamped her. She averted her eyes, her nostrils flaring. Her hands trembled as they clutched her translator. "What did you mean when you said you wanted to help our transition to our new home?"

He sat on the bed, his hands flat on the sheet. "I want to leave with you and your people, to assist as you settle there. I'd pondered doing this well before we"—he lowered his voice in that adorable way of his—"made love. Then, weeks ago, I thought you'd wonder why I'd want to come along.

Now," he said quietly, "I hope you might not wonder at that."

She shook her head. "I wouldn't wonder." She cleared her thickening throat. "How long would you be able to stay?" If more heartache was in her future, she wanted to gird against it now.

He curved his big hand over her cheek, moving his thumb back and forth over her lips. "Does forever frighten you?"

She couldn't breathe as she shook her head.

"I will stay by your side if you choose to spend the rest of your life with your people. I suspect, though, that over time, many will seek their own lives, and you might feel free to leave with me then. There are other worlds on which to settle, where we could have land and freedom, technology if we wanted . . . or not. And someday, if you were willing, and you wanted me in that way, I would like to make a family with you, a new family. Children, as many as you were willing to bear."

Jordan bit her lower lip. Her eyes ached with sudden, pent-up emotion. After crying for Boo, she was sure she wouldn't have a tear left. She'd been wrong.

Hastily he put in, "It would not make the memory of Roberta any less important to us. We would honor her, Jordan. Our children would know her name."

Our children would know her name.

A sigh slipped from her. That was it; she was a goner. If she'd wondered before if she was falling in love with him, she didn't have to wonder anymore. He'd won her heart, fair and square.

"I'm not good with men, you know," she warned him.

He shrugged. "You never met the right one."

She sighed again. For a big, brooding, silent type, the guy was good, really good. He had all the right answers. And better yet, he meant every one.

His expression darkened. "But there is the problem with my father. Honor binds me to this ship, but my heart binds me to you."

"You're not obligated to me." It pained her to say it, but it was the truth.

"Obligation." The way he said the word told her that it embodied a concept with which he struggled. "If it comes from commitment—of the heart, of the spirit—then it is as pure a concept as love and loyalty. But if used as an instrument of compliance . . ." He shook his head. "Such is my relationship with my father, Jordan. When he returned the picture we left behind in the viewing room, the message was clear: He wouldn't take kindly to me spending time with you."

"But you are."

He gave a bitter bark of laughter. "Of course I am. I may be obligated to the man, but I'm not enslaved by him. Yet he appointed himself the architect of my life. My successes are his. As are my failures, unfortunately. He once saw me pursuing a seat in the Grand Forum, a senate seat, and despite my war record, he dreams of it still. Power and prestige, channeled through me to him. Currently he's busy trying to arrange a marriage. All the front-runners are daughters of powerful politicians."

"I see."

Kào's smile was soft, self-deprecating, and frank. "No, Jordan. You have no worries. Such a union would never happen, even if I hadn't met you. Glorious ambitions don't flow in my blood as they do his."

"Why didn't he pursue for himself what he wants for you?"

He shook his head and pondered that. "I don't know."

"Just the other day you were telling me how much you owed him, how much he means to you." She lifted her hands. "I don't want to come between you two."

267

"I have much to smooth over with him," Kào acknowledged. His face reflected his indecision and the pain it brought him.

"Just be sure, Kào, before you leave. Or you'll come to resent me. You'll blame me for the divorce from your father. I experienced that with my first husband—his resentment. It was pointless, and it hurt. I won't go through it again." Her voice turned husky. "Not with a man I care for as much as you. I don't want to find out later that you made a mistake, after it's eaten you alive." *He's not Craig; don't compare the two.* Fighting to compose herself, she turned away,

Kào said nothing as he stood. Silently, he lowered his pants. Jordan knew that he hadn't reached any decision regarding his father though he threw the pants aside and came back to bed—and to her. With one look in his midnight eyes, she knew that he remained torn between obligation and personal desire, even as he reached for her, drawing her into a kiss.

"Be sure," she whispered against his mouth.

His kiss told her that he was sure about her. A future together looked full of difficulties, but at least they had now, the present, time stolen from those who didn't want them to have it.

Seeking completion, Kào rolled her onto her back. She welcomed him with a feverish moan as he thrust inside her. They made love with silent heat, their hands clasped together. When she climaxed, he held her close, reaching his own release soon after with the same soundless intensity.

Kào had fallen into a deep sleep. As Jordan caressed his back, combing her fingers through his hair, she couldn't help thinking that his mind had instinctively sought escape from the burdens he carried, and the decisions he felt he soon had to make. In that respect, she was grateful for her sudden freedom, however unwanted. She was duty-bound

to serve the people of Flight 58, but she was otherwise
unattached. For the first time, what she did with her life
and whom she chose to be with was up to her. She wanted
Kào . . . if he was hers to have.

Kào's body twitched and he whimpered. His legs
swished under the sheets, as if he were trying to run. Then
a groan rumbled up from deep in his throat.

He was dreaming. Instinctively she soothed him by rubbing her hand over his chest. His breath hissed furiously.
His head rolled from side to side. Then his entire body went
rigid, his back arching. The sudden move bounced her head
off his shoulder. The muscles in his arms bunched. She
rolled away from him.

He let out a harsh, guttural yell, swinging his fists. She
barely dodged the flailing arms as she struggled free of the
tangled bed sheets. She crouched naked at the far edge of
the mattress, her heart in her throat. "Kào! Wake up!"

She could feel the horror radiating off his sweating, convulsing body. It slammed into her in violent waves, making
her cringe. A nightmare, a gruesome nightmare; he was re-
living against his will an atrocious past that she knew kept
its claws buried tenaciously in his psyche.

He'd been like this once before, although not as violently
so, that day they'd zapped him with the stun gun on the
747.

He gasped, as if suffocating. His big hands opened and
closed, grasping the bed sheets. Jordan half stumbled, half
crawled back across the bed. Grabbing his shoulders, she
shook him hard. "Kào! It's Jordan. You're in your quarters
and it's okay." *Damn.* In her urgency, she'd spoken English.
"Open eyes," she urged him in Key. "Kào, please. Is okay."

He cried out, a hissing, hideous bellow of pure anguish.
His body convulsed brutally, and he lunged up to a sitting
position, his neck tendons corded, his eyes open and wild
and unseeing.

She watched helplessly as every muscle in his body went rigid. Then, as if he were released from some horrible bond, he jerked awake.

"By the Seeders. . . ." he breathed, falling backward onto the mattress.

"Kào?"

He lifted a shaking hand to wipe the sweat from his brow. He focused on her, blinking. An expression of startled amazement glowed in his face, a face that only seconds ago had been contorted in mental agony. "I broke free," he rasped. "I escaped."

"What? What did you escape?"

"The fence!" A laugh of disbelief shook him, and she wondered fleetingly if he'd gone crazy. "Always in my dreams for my entire life, there's been the fence. I'm on a horse—I'm a boy again, and we're trapped. As I grew older, the dream mixed with flashbacks from the war. A bird made of fire." His throat bobbed and he shook his head. "The fence, it was always there. But just now, I escaped. *Escaped.*"

He choked out another laugh, and she tried to understand the sharp resolve that glowed suddenly in his face. "The horse found a weak spot and kicked apart the timbers. The entire stockade thundered down behind us. I can still hear it, Jordan. I can feel it, crashing all around me."

His dark eyes glinted with sudden emotion, and she crawled into his arms, snuggling close, breathing his scent, tasting his wet, salty skin. He gripped her to him, and she could hear his heart thumping fiercely in his chest.

"That blasted fence. It symbolized my life! My not having a say in my fate: the destruction of my birth planet Vantaar, the circumstances of my rescue, grateful as I am for the outcome. Then there was the war. And prison."

And the torture, she thought. The insult done to his body.

270

The damning, damaging words wrenched from him through drugs and beatings.

But Kào's thoughts were on none of that now. His left hand closed, grasping the sheets as he had during his nightmare. "It's a message, Jordan. A sign. I respect Moray, and I honor him as a man and as my father. But I'll no longer be controlled by him."

Chapter Twenty-four

Kào expected Jordan to react to his soul-shaking declaration with joy. Instead, when she tipped her head to look into his eyes, her gaze was anxious and sad.

She was worried. Because she cared for him, he thought. She'd said so to his face. He was a hardened, battle-scarred warrior with a disgraceful past who was more comfortable with weapons of mass destruction than he was with the ways of women, and yet she wanted him, faults and all. He hadn't felt this lighthearted since the day he left to join the Alliance Space Force at eighteen years of age.

"It won't be easy," she warned him.

"Jordan, my Jordan. Just because the heavens spoke to me in the form of a dream doesn't mean I'll lurch into this unprepared. I have a plan."

"Be sure," she whispered.

Wasn't he? Never had he gone against his father before. In small ways, yes, but never like this.

But he'd made his decision. He was going to be the man Jordan needed—he was going to be *his own* man—starting now.

"Moray told me that my war records are about to come under review," he told her. "That means there's a chance I will be cleared."

"Kào," she breathed. "That would be wonderful."

"I don't want it for me," he argued. "I want it for him, for Moray. I want his name to shine again as it deserves. But why must I be on this ship to assist in the process? I can communicate with Headquarters from anywhere."

"Even the Rim?"

"Yes. Even the Rim."

"That's wonderful! It's perfect!" She laughed joyfully.

He loved hearing the sound, one so rare. He vowed that someday he'd hear her laugh daily.

Smiling, she cuddled next to him. As he absently smoothed his hand over the warm, silky curves of her bare back, he considered the mechanics of his plan. Moray didn't like surprises; he liked to think he had control of a situation. It was obvious that Kào would have to proceed as if his father were the most volatile explosive on the market.

His attention returned to Jordan. Her breathing had lengthened and deepened, and she hadn't said anything in a long while. Kào smiled. Instead of rousing her, he was afraid his gentle massage had done quite the opposite. Two nights in a row of little sleep had caught up to her.

He lifted the long hair that clung damply to the nape of her neck, breathing in her scent that was mixed now with his. "Jordan," he whispered in her ear. "Are you awake?"

He saw her smile into the pillow. "No."

His teeth found her tender earlobe and tugged. "Then this is a dream."

"Mm. I like this dream." Her rounded buttocks brushed

273

against his swelling member. The jolt of heat made his loins ache with wanting her.

Groaning, he pressed his lips to the back of her neck, where tiny white hairs made a downy fringe under her hairline, and kissed her. Tiny bumps pebbled her skin. "You don't wish me to wake you?"

"No," she said on a sigh. "I want to see how this dream ends."

He chuckled low and deep and raised her appealing little rump to his belly. He'd longed to bury himself inside her while holding her this way. "So do I." He tilted his hips and—

His wake-up chime beeped shrilly from where it sat on a thick clear table carved to look like glacial ice. He swore under his breath.

Jordan reacted to his curse and the alarm. Flying off the bed, she threw him off balance as she yanked the bed sheet from under his knees and took it with her on a mad dash across the bedchamber. Just before she disappeared through the closest door, she whirled around, her blue eyes wide as she clutched the sheet to her breasts. "You answer the door. I'll hide in the bathroom."

The hatch swished closed behind her.

When he gathered his wits, he began to laugh. "Off," he said to silence the alarm. Still chuckling, he launched himself off the bed and walked to the door through which Jordan had fled. He slipped inside the small compartment and closed the door behind him. In the dim light, Jordan's sheet-wrapped form was hardly visible among the folded towels, blankets, and sheets.

"This is a closet," she said in Key. She hadn't brought her translator.

"Yes, it is."

"I thought it was the bathroom."

He fought a smile. Like a heat-seeking missile, he honed

in on her. He grabbed hold of the bed sheet and tugged. It was nice to discover that his targeting abilities had not deteriorated over the years, particularly with such a tempting objective.

She let the sheet fall away from her body. Her pale curves glowed in the dusky light. He knew how warm and supple her skin would be under his palms. He knew how she'd taste. And where she'd be silky smooth—and slippery and wet. For him. His loins ached powerfully. But the darkness must have hidden the naked hunger in his eyes.

"Who was at the door?" she asked.

"No one."

"I heard the chime and thought it was your father, coming to drag me to security for defying the lockdown."

"My father! It was my wake-up chime."

She made what sounded like an Earth swear word. Then she laughed. "I feel like idiot!"

"No." He slid his hands behind her waist and laced his fingers at the small of her back. "You feel incredible."

Her laugh was softer, huskier this time. "You not so bad yourself." Her eyes sparkled impishly in the darkness.

He laughed and buried his face in the crook of her neck, pressing smiling lips to her pulse. The oddest sensation took hold of him, as if he were standing apart from his body and watching his interaction with Jordan. This teasing, this love-play, he had never done before. It was as if he'd become a stranger to himself, a good stranger. Or perhaps he was seeing the man he'd been all along. He saw the promise of a future with Jordan: laughter, warmth, and affection. That was what he'd experienced with his birth family; he knew it as surely as he breathed.

He arranged her untamed hair behind her shoulders so that he could gaze at her body. "Why did you think my father would come knocking at my door?" he asked, unable to confine his touch to her hair.

"Because of what we talk about," she tried to explain as he smoothed his palms over her body, gliding them up her ribcage to mold his hands to her breasts. "We plan a new future. One he does not know."

"He *will* know it." He turned her around to face a low shelf of soft, folded towels. "And by the time I'm done with him, he'll be happy for us." His mouth found the side of her throat. He inhaled her scent, and his, and the sweet fragrance of clean sheets.

"If he does not already," she breathed. "Parents have a special sense. They know when you plot to go against their wishes."

He bent her forward over the shelf. Her buttocks jutted into his thighs, and he pulled her tight against him. "Like now?"

She let out a throaty moan. "Like now."

He gripped her hips, spreading her thighs. Bracing himself for the rush of pleasure, he pushed inside her. She gasped, coming up on her toes. He reached around to where her breasts hung loose and free. Gently he twirled her tight nipples between his fingertips and he felt the answering clamp of her inner muscles. She liked being touched that way. And here, too, he thought, moving his right hand lower as he moved inside her.

Pushing back the shielding flesh, he opened her to the circling caress of his fingertips. A cry exploded from her, and her hips writhed. He looped one arm under her belly to bring her hard into each of his thrusts as his hand paid intimate attention to her body, rubbing, circling, a never-ending rhythm that came to him instinctively, as if he'd lived his life, gained his experience, so that he could bring pleasure to this one woman. The realization nearly pushed him over the edge.

Not yet.

His breath hissed past his locked jaw. Perspiration tingled on his body and on his brow. His belly tightened as desire dragged him toward completion, but he held back to ensure her peak before he took his own.

He stroked her between her legs, exploring, caressing, until she writhed, pushing her bottom against his thighs, rhythmically, deepening their contact. The closet was snug and dark, taking sight and heightening all the other senses: smell and taste, touch and sounds. Jordan's sighs, her soft groans of delight. He groaned, shuddering as he drove upward in steady strokes. He could hardly believe he was the same man who not too long ago mourned the loss of his strength following his years in prison. And now, with Jordan, he had nary a worry about his stamina. It proved how much power the mind had over the body. Or how desperation ruled the spirit, he thought. He wanted Jordan, a future with her, a desire that went against the obligations that had ruled him since his earliest memories.

He brought her upper body off the folded linens, his upward strokes steady. She arched her back, standing on her toes, her bottom jutting into his abdomen. "Yes," she gasped, her hands closing convulsively atop the linens. "Oh, Kào, yes."

She sheathed him, slick, tight, possessively. His teeth pressed into the flesh of her shoulder. He fed on her mounting pleasure. He filled her. She filled him. Her spirit burned in him, giving him life. He was alive.

Alive!

After so long, too long existing as a dead man, he'd been wrenched into life. He felt it now, making love to Jordan—his rebirth. The lovemaking was a celebration, affirming life, for both of them. "Ah, Jordan," he gasped. "My woman, my love."

His love.

Saying it aloud made it so. He thrust into her with renewed vigor, claiming her. She jerked, shuddering in his arms. "Kào!" Her legs went rigid, and a rhythmic, pulsing inner squeeze began deep inside her body.

She gasped—English words. His hands molded over her heaving breasts. Thrusting deep, he rocked faster until her cries, her climax, pulled him over the edge.

Her head fell forward, exposing her slender neck, and together they sagged forward onto the plush towels. He cushioned her fall with one arm, while catching his weight with his other.

Never would she fall in life without him there to catch her, he vowed. And when he next saw his father, he would take the first step toward making good on that promise.

Ian Dillon dashed across Town Square. He wove through the crowd as if he were back in downtown Dublin stuck in Friday afternoon traffic. He careened into an elderly Hawaiian woman, apologizing as he stumbled past and left her cursing in his wake, and arrived breathless at the small portion of the common area that was designated CREW ONLY. "Jordan!"

Jordan was asleep on the small couch. Hands raised, Natalie intercepted him like an outraged mother bear before he could get to her. "Be quiet," she whispered loudly as she pushed him backward. "Can't you see she's sleeping?"

"I surely can, miss. You've got to wake her up." He paused to catch his breath. "I found something."

"Yeah?" the tall black woman said archly. "What is it?"

"I'll tell her first, and then she can tell you."

"She's exhausted. I don't think she meant to fall asleep, but since she has, come back in a half hour."

Their attention shifted to Jordan, curled on her side, her hands pressed together and wedged under her cheek. She looked different. Happy. At peace. But there were rings under her eyes, attesting to a lack of sleep. Dillon peered at her. "Why, she has a hickey. Two of them." He pointed to his neck. "There and there," he said and grinned.

Natalie frowned. "Are you the one who gave them to her?"

"Me? Hell no." He blushed hard.

"Then why do you care?"

"I didn't expect . . . I just thought . . ."

Jordan rubbed the back of her hand over her eyes. "Hey, who's talking about my hickeys?" she mumbled sleepily.

Dillon shuffled his feet. Natalie glared at him. "You woke her."

Jordan opened one eye. "Dillon?" She groaned and sat up, her hand going to her neck. "I told you I was going to need that makeup, Nat."

"I'll get you that camouflage as soon as I send Mr. Dillon on his way. Mine's too dark, but Karen has some."

Dillon held his ground. Jordan pushed herself upright, sweeping her hair away from her face. "No, Dillon can stay. We're working on a . . . project. What's up?" she asked him.

"I know where we are."

All sleepiness fled Jordan's eyes. She fixed him with a sharp gaze, penetrating and fully alert. "You figured out the coordinates?"

"That's right. I know where Earth is, Captain. And it ain't where they told us."

Chapter Twenty-five

Kào didn't have to make an appointment to see his father; Moray summoned him.

As he had on the previous day, Moray waited for him in his private meeting room, his computer in his hands. "You're late," the man said with formal pleasantness.

"I had to shower," Kào replied.

"I imagine so."

He peered at his father, trying to read the emotions playing on the man's ruddy face. "What's happened? Was there bad news?" Perhaps Headquarters had changed their minds about reviewing his war records. He hoped not. The review could be done from the Rim, bolstering his father's name and at the same time allowing him to be with Jordan. His plan was so ideal, he was sure something would happen to sabotage it. And sure enough, it did.

"You slept with the refugee woman last night," Moray said.

It felt as if the floor dropped away from under Kào's boots.

"You did even after I told you not to, even after we discussed our plans for your future," Moray accused.

Kào squared his shoulders. "Yes, sir."

"Ah, so you don't deny it."

"Is my integrity in question, or only my choice of lovers?"

Moray bristled. "I did not mean to imply that you would stoop to lying. I—I—" The man rubbed his hands over his face. The glowing table did not flatter it.

Kào wondered how his father had found out. The corridors had been deserted when he'd come for Jordan and brought her back. She had been disguised as an officer, and they'd taken the service hallways and hand ladders, keeping off the shuttles and lifts. The only way his father would have found out was if someone had been assigned to spy on him—though Kào doubted he'd have missed the signs. Listening devices might have been installed in his quarters, but he doubted that, too. His security panel showed no evidence of tampering or intruders. Someone had told Moray, then. But who?

"I'm taking you off this assignment, Kào. Because of the continued fraternization. You are too close to these refugees. You've lost your ability to be objective."

Kào didn't argue. He was anything but objective when it came to Jordan and her people.

"I want your head clear and your charm out in full force when you speak to Senator Felleni's daughter."

Kao leaned forward. "What?"

"Kyrie is a marvelous marriage prospect. The senator and I are arranging the meeting. It will be via long-distance comm, but it's a start."

Kao squeezed his eyes shut. A distraction. That's what this was. He mustn't let Moray throw him off course. "Who have you appointed in my place as primary intercessor, sir?"

"Trist."

His world fell out from under him. Kào gripped the table, seething. *Blast it all.* He wouldn't be surprised to learn that Trist had masterminded this entire fiasco to put herself in control.

"I know you two have had your disagreements in the past, but she's proven herself to be a fine officer. Responsible." Moray's eyes warmed. "And compliant."

Kào frowned. His father's relationship with the Talagar linguist was a concept that puzzled him. There was a bond between them that Kào believed went beyond professional boundaries. But if she had told Moray that Jordan spent the night in his quarters, where would *she* have learned of it?

Someone told her.

But who? She didn't keep company with the refugees. Or did she? She'd brought Ben and Jordan to The Black Hole, after all, before she'd summoned Kào. With that, he had the eerie sensation of another puzzle piece falling into place, but the entire picture remained elusive.

Moray cleared his throat. "With the refugees about to be relocated to another ship, I need an officer in charge who is unbiased with regard to the transfer."

Kào's head was spinning, but he'd be damned if he'd let it show. "Transfer? To what ship? I didn't know of this."

"We're needed here in the Perimeter on our normal patrol. A round trip to the Rim will keep us out too long. I've decided to put that rogue Talagar ship we've been trailing to use. I found it this morning and have been in communication with the crew. They recognize they're outgunned. They won't be putting up a fight, thank the Seeders, and we'll be able to board peaceably. Once their crew is removed and our own people are installed, they'll deliver the refugees to the Rim."

Using captured ships as freighters wasn't unusual, and it made logistical sense for a ship such as the *Savior* with other, more pressing duties. Kào might have been removed from his position as primary intercessor for the refugees, but that might be good; it would allow him more time to pack his bags.

His father might not know it yet, but Kào intended to be part of the replacement crew. Then he'd be able to escort the Earthers all the way to their destination.

Yet he'd hold off on telling Moray until the man cooled off. Better to work on his father in stages than to throw too much at him and make him feel defensive. A controlling, overprotective father was one thing; a *defensive* controlling, overprotective father, Kào knew from experience, was not a pleasant encounter.

He took a breath. "I'd better go brief Trist on the details she'll need to know. As a matter of fact, we have much to talk about."

"Indeed you do." Moray shook his head, clearly torn between reprimanding Kào and soothing him. "By the Seeders, boy! I'm angry with you."

"I gathered that. I don't know what to say other than that the woman, Jordan, has come to mean much to me. I have rarely gone against your wishes in the past. But I won't agree to any order that will keep me from seeing her. Take me off the assignment, but don't keep me from seeing her. I'm a man, Father, a grown man. Such decisions are mine to make."

"Not if you are to ruin your life!" he roared, red-faced. "Not if you can't think past your cock! You can't waste your life with her. She's beneath you, Kào. You're of a higher class. She has nothing, *nothing* to bring you. You need to make a good marriage, like with the Felleni girl. That is what men of our class do. Think of the Moray name. Don't

283

we want it to stand above all the others? Don't you respect
the name I gave you at all?"

Kào sighed silently. His father knew all the right buttons
to push. "When are we due to rendezvous with the Talagar
vessel?"

Moray sat back in his chair. It bobbed heavily under his
weight. "Rendezvous is imminent. As soon as we dock,
we'll begin the transfer of personnel right away."

Kào swallowed against a throat gone suddenly dry.
Think. It used to be something he was good at: processing
information analytically and objectively. But with so much
at stake, he struggled with a mind that was all but paralyzed.

"The arrangement is a good one for us, Kào. It allows me
to return to the Perimeter in the shortest possible time,
where the Alliance needs us. If there was one rogue Talagar
vessel, there'll be others. We need to be there to intercept
them." Moray smiled beseechingly. "Just think, without
having to go to the Rim, we'll be able to serve fresh vegetables again."

"Vegetables . . . ?" Kào wasn't sure if he wanted to laugh
or swear at the man. The commodore was so assured of
Kào's compliance in all matters that he assumed he could
distract him with the temptation of fresh produce.

Moray read his deep frown accurately. "Ah, my boy.
Don't let all this trouble you. You have a future, a glorious
one. With your records under review, we're halfway there.
I have people in places . . . they'll ensure that your records
receive the attention they deserve. And they'll make sure
the board is manned with individuals sympathetic to our
plight."

Kào glanced up sharply. So the review might not have
been Moray's doing at all, but an action instigated by
Moray's "friends." The man had been busy while Kào was

locked away. "I didn't realize that you were so well-connected, Father."

"Bah! I'm not there yet. And it's taken years to come this far. Government. Politicians. You have to know how they work, and I do. I also know how to call upon favors owed. And they do owe us, Kào. They never could win your release from that prison, despite promises to the contrary. It was a travesty of justice." Moray's face turned red as his eyes glinted moistly, a sure indication that the memory of not having been able to negotiate for Kào's freedom disturbed him to this day. "You shouldn't have been incarcerated at all; instead you remained there until the war ended. Blast, how they mishandled it all!"

Kào exhaled in a quiet sigh. "I know you were involved with trying to win my freedom from the beginning, and I hope you understand how grateful I am for it."

"Involved? I lived it. Breathed it! And now your path back to respectability has been cleared. All we have to do is fill the squares as they are presented to us. Use your time away from the refugees to rest and prepare yourself." Moray's tone gentled. "I did it for you, Kào. For your own good. It is the same with the refugee woman—"

"Captain Cady. Jordan Cady."

"I have no doubt you'll be over her as soon as you're away from her bed. We'll get you help. Medical has drugs to deal with a man's baser urges."

Kào's mouth twisted. "I know all about what drugs can do to a body . . . or not. Or do to a man's organ . . . or not. You have not experienced true agony until you have sustained, against your will, an erection for an entire week. How delightfully such a condition contributes to the effectiveness of interrogation."

The commodore's throat bobbed convulsively. "They did that to you?" he rasped.

An embittered laugh escaped Kào.

Moray's comm beeped. He took the call, a private message. As he read the text, the tension went out of him and his facial coloring returned to normal. "Ah, excellent news," he said as he signed off. "Despite your loss of duties, it seems you'll be busy, after all." His gray eyes glinted with genuine fatherly devotion. "I'm proud of you, Kào. So very proud."

Kào lifted a brow. "Why is that, sir?"

"Pack your bags," the commodore boomed cheerfully. "A ship is on the way. You've been summoned to Sofu."

Jordan grabbed Natalie by the arm and drew her close. "About what Dillon just said, you know nothing. Say nothing. And hold all my calls until I can get back to you and the rest of the flight attendants and let you know what's going on."

Natalie gave her a thumbs-up, and Jordan hurried off with Dillon. Everyone from Flight 58 was used to seeing her and the Irishman rush back and forth to the computer, and they didn't give them a second glance. They had something else working in their favor. It was "Key Thursday," one of the two days of the week Jordan forced everyone to speak their new language. People would think twice before troubling her with banal requests or chitchat, since it would have to be done in their new tongue. On Key days, English was punishable with a variety of penalties ranging from no dessert—which was often a questionable substance as it was—to an additional three extra hours studying Alliance history. Jordan was sure they grumbled behind her back, but it was for their own good.

Of course, she was breaking all the rules in her excitement at Dillon's news. "The string of numbers Ben saw on the holo were altered," he'd told her. "So were the ones sent off the ship by Kào to their government, along with news of the discovery."

She remembered Dillon trying to explain in basic terms that when things were changed on a computer after the fact, footprints remained. Well, he hadn't used the term *footprints*, exactly, but it was how she'd understood what he told her.

Dillon jumped onto his floating chair and went to work on the computer. She was too hyper to sit and paced behind him. "The real location of Earth isn't what's on record," he said as he typed. "The coordinates the aliens made public put Earth thousands of light-years from where it really is."

She paced. Frowned. Swore. Tried not to revert to her old habit of wringing her hands. "Why do that unless they wanted to keep Earth secret?"

"I don't know. Those are the facts."

"How long is it going to take those science academy folks to figure out that the doctored coordinates correspond to empty space? This is an advanced civilization; they'll see the bait-and-switch sooner or later."

"Someone on this ship already thought of that."

She swallowed. "What do you mean?"

"The coordinates don't correspond to empty space." He tugged on his ear, a mannerism he took on only when he was stymied in his work. Or scared, an emotion Dillon rarely displayed.

"Dillon, where are they saying Earth is?"

"Kerils-1008, a planet about the size of our Mars. It took me a while to figure it out because the planet wasn't listed in the galactic database. But it is in the ship's log. The *Savior* crew discovered it a while back and didn't tell anyone."

She thought of the movie that showed Earth's destruction, and how the planet's cloud cover hadn't looked quite right. Unfamiliar somehow. Fear, cold and glutinous, oozed into her limbs. "Kerils-1008 didn't happen to be hit by a comet, did it?"

He gazed up at her. "One that fragmented before it hit."

"The bastards," Jordan hissed. "They lied to us. When we asked for proof, Kerils was the planet they showed us. Not Earth."

"I personally think the only thing that's changed at home is that our families think we disappeared in a plane crash."

"Honest to God, Dillon, if we're wrong again . . ." She brought her hand to her mouth, biting her finger to keep from howling in outrage. She couldn't go up the roller coaster incline again only to fall.

"It's there. Earth. The more I learn, the more I suspect it. It's why I've lived at this terminal, day and night." A muscle in his jaw pulsed. "I swear, before my dying day I'll be back in Mulligan's, a pint of Guinness in my hand."

His blue eyes watered, and hers burned in response.

"It's a sickness," she whispered. "Finding ways to keep our hopes alive. We can't keep doing this to ourselves without suffering real psychological damage."

"We weren't wrong. We were right. And we're right now. That's the way we have to think of it."

Courage is accepting the challenge though it's easier to give up.

"Anyway, this is what I won for my work." Dillon typed some more. Then he sat back in his seat as a three-dimensional digital holographic image filled the screen in front of him. "Here's where the real Earth sits in relation to the rest of the galaxy." He pointed to a glowing speck. "That depicts our sun."

She nodded. "The astronomers have always said we're out on the galaxy's arm, like that. Far from the center."

"The boonies, as you Americans say."

"The Rim, as the aliens say."

"And we haven't wandered too far from where we started."

"You're kidding? After all these weeks? And at light

288

speed? What the hell have we been doing, traveling in circles?"

"Just about," he confirmed.

Something was wrong. Dead wrong. Earth's true location was being covered up and now they were wandering aimlessly in the back reaches of the galaxy. She thought of Kào, and the news he'd gotten from his father. "The Alliance is desperate to settle the Rim. And the reasoning behind it makes sense. But are they desperate enough to take a couple of hundred people against their will? Are they planning to drop us off and go back for more?"

Dillon winced. "Sounds like *Invasion of the Body Snatchers* crossed with *Star Wars*. Alien abductions for the sake of galactic peace."

Jordan groaned. "I've got to get the crew together and brief them. Don't tell the other passengers anything until I gather my thoughts and make a plan. I can't afford panic." *Not even my own*, she thought. "But everyone needs to understand that we were lied to."

"Someone's lying to us," Dillon agreed.

"Kào?" She hated the flicker of uncertainty she felt upon blurting that out.

Dillon remained poker-faced. Tactful guy, he was; he knew full well who'd given her the hickey on her neck. "Here's the log of his computer activity. He's been corresponding with the Science Academy. No one else."

As she read the text in Key as best she could—she wasn't nearly as adept at translating as Dillon—the possibility of losing Kào over everything that was unfolding became sharply apparent. She couldn't bear the thought of it, but she'd made a promise to her kid. She'd told Roberta that she'd come home. She'd clung to that promise, until all hope was gone. Only when she believed it was gone had she finally given up. And now the hope was back.

She had a promise to fulfill. Keeping her word was her

Susan Grant

own brand of honor, honor on a much smaller and more personal scale than that of the military heroes she'd known, including her father, brother, and Kào, but to her it was just as important. If there was a way, she was going home. If she had one other wish, it would be that Kào would want to come with her.

"Kào asked for Earth's coordinates via the terminal in his quarters," Dillon explained. "And sent what the science staff gave him."

The science staff. "Trist. . . ."

"That's right. And it's what makes me think Kào's okay. He wouldn't know anything of Kerils, because he doesn't have access to those records."

"How the hell did *you* manage it?"

He exhaled. "Trist again. She opened the door and looked the other way. Remember?"

This was like playing chess without knowing the color of the game pieces. "Whose side is she on?"

"I hope it's ours," he said. "If not, I think we're screwed."

Jordan would waste no time making sure everyone in the crew knew about what Dillon had found. "Ben," she called. In an instant, the purser was at her side. With one glance at her face he knew something was up. "We have an emergency. Get all the flight attendants to the briefing room. Quickly."

Ben departed to round up the crew. Jordan wiped her damp palms on her jeans and stood. "Dillon, that means you, too."

The hacker's mouth tipped up. "A battlefield promotion?"

In spite of her anxiety, she smiled. "Yeah. You can call it that."

They gathered in the crew-only area of Town Square, the makeshift meeting room hidden behind movable dividers. Ben departed to do as she'd requested. She motioned to another flight attendant, Rich. "Make sure no one eaves-drops." She didn't want half-heard and misunderstood remarks inciting panic. Arms folded over his 'Forty-niners sweatshirt, Rich stood guard until she was through briefing the crew.

At last, she gathered and brought the passengers up to date. Then, her throat raw from answering questions, she rejoined Dillon at the computer to see what they could find that might shed light on why the aliens wanted Earth's location kept a secret.

The sight of Trist at the front hatch stopped her cold. With rumors of subterfuge in the air, the passengers gave the Talagar a wide berth. The linguist's startling crimson eyes and tense lavender mouth added to everyone's discomfort. In her tight dress, she'd been beautiful in a sleek, runway-model way. But the gray Alliance uniform hung on her gaunt frame. Her drawn face added to her spare, unforgiving appearance. "Remember that favor of which we spoke?" she asked.

"Too well," Jordan replied.

"I have come to collect it."

Chapter Twenty-six

"Did you say Sofu, sir?" Kào asked.

"Yes. You're to be picked up by an ambassadorial vessel transiting this zone and brought to the capital. Bring winter clothing. It's brutally cold there this time of year. You'll be there in time for the Ice Festival. Have a Glacial Ale in my name, would you?" Moray's comm sounded again. "Now what?" he blustered.

"Sir, the Talagars are in range," a young officer informed him, his eyes shining with unchecked innocent excitement. To Kào, the ensign looked all of fifteen. To the boy, a post-war recruit, docking with a genuine Talagar battleship would be a grand adventure.

"What is the status of their weapons systems?" Moray inquired.

"Disabled."

"The crew?"

"Complying with all instructions, sir. They're ready for us to initiate the docking sequence."

"Ah, good, Ensign. I'm on my way." Moray got halfway out of his chair when he seemed to remember that Kào was in the room with him. "Would you like to see what we've caught in our nets, Kào?" *I know how you feel about the Talagars,* his eyes said.

Kào was still reeling from the double blow: hearing about the refugees' transfer and his own impending, unbelievably ill-timed transfer to a government vessel. "I think I'll go to my quarters to pack."

Moray's relief at his acquiescence lit up his face. "I knew you'd be excited about the trip."

Not that trip, Father. But Kào let nothing in his face reveal that he intended to transfer to the Talagar vessel with the refugees, with Jordan. Anything Sofu needed, they could correspond with him there.

Withdrawn and aloof, Kào walked with Moray from the conference room. Before them was the bridge with its sweeping view of the stars. Life seemed quite a bit simpler the last time he was here, before he'd experienced the changes that Jordan had brought about in his life.

His father squeezed his arm and left his side, disappearing into a waiting knot of eager aides. Kào had intended to leave immediately for New Earth, but the sight of the Talagar battleship sitting off the bow of the *Savior* stopped him cold.

Kào's legs carried him toward the forward observation area, where he couldn't pull his gaze from the Talagar vessel. This was the craft onto which the refugees would be taken.

He clasped his hands behind his back, controlling his respiration as he watched the vessel's approach. There was a time when seeing a battleship such as this would have sent his mind racing to explore avenues of its destruction. Missiles, deadly smart-dust that detonated on impact, relativistic bomblets, ion torpedoes—so many choices. In his mind, Kào had destroyed the ship several times by the time his father shouted an order that would bring the Talagar commander's face onto the main screen.

The image of the battleship and the stars was replaced in a digital instant. A man about the age of his father came onscreen. Moray walked forward to greet him. Kào expected his father to display resentment if not open hostility; after all, the Talagars had murdered his wife and children. But, to his shock, Moray's manner was genial. "Admiral Steeg."

The Talagar nodded. "Commodore Moray." In a resonant voice mellowed by the typical Talagarian burr, he stated, "Docking may commence."

One by one, Jordan's flight attendants assembled to see what Trist wanted. The passengers gathered, too, though at a safe distance. Everyone sensed that something was wrong. The silence stretched taut. The air itself felt ready to shatter.

Trist spoke in English, allowing Jordan to keep her translator stowed. "You must do some things for me, things you may not understand. I ask that you trust me, you and your people. You owe me, yes, but this I ask to save your lives. You are a smart woman, Captain. I know you will obey my orders if I say it will bring you home."

Home. "So it's true," Jordan dared, her heart beating hard.

"No comet destroyed your planet," Trist confirmed. "Earth is as it was before."

Cheers went up all around her. Jordan wasn't sure if she wanted to whoop with joy or sob. Earth existed! Everyone was still alive. Including her family, her daughter. But her excitement only ignited her fury that they'd been lied to.

"Why did you switch the coordinates? Why weren't we told the truth?"

Trist's expression chilled. "Those questions. Answers will come in time. But now, you must trust me."

Jordan bit back her impatience. If Trist was giving them the chance to go home, they'd better take it, not scrutinize it looking for holes. "What do we have to do to make this happen?"

"Obey my instructions and you go home," Trist said cryptically. "Act rashly and you will never see your loved ones again."

Jordan set her jaw. "It's a no-brainer, then."

Trist blinked at her.

"It means we're with you," Jordan explained. "We'll do what you ask." She turned to the rest of Flight 58. "Right?"

Natalie gave her a thumbs-up. "I will."

"Me, too," Ben said, his still-astonished gaze riveted on Trist.

One by one, everyone poked a thumb in the air until all seventeen flight attendants and two hundred and sixty-nine passengers had made their support known.

Jordan's composure amazed her, frankly. And also theirs. The terror and grief over the last few months had strengthened them.

"This won't be without risk," Trist warned Jordan.

Jordan wrung her hands. Bit the inside of her lip. Tightened her stomach muscles to quell the butterflies flocking there in droves. Was this the right decision? Would she regret this day?

Courage is doing the right thing even though you are scared.

She wiped her sweaty palms on her pants. "Well, it's better than the alternative."

Trist nodded. "Ready your people, then. Time is short. You will go to your aircraft in cargo bay. You have a map.

Use back way. Hand-ladders. No lifts. No shuttles. This you must do. And quickly. No one must know."

"Two hundred and eighty-seven people traveling in a group aren't going to be easy to miss, Trist," Jordan pointed out.

The linguist gave her head a curt shake. "It can be done. Single file. Each holds clothing of one in front. It may be cold. Bring jackets, warm clothing, blankets. Be sure no one wears ship-issued jumpsuit." She pointed to the nape of her neck, reminding Jordan of the locaters. "Must not alert security."

Unease coiled around Jordan's spine and yanked tight. She wiped her sweaty palms on her jeans. "So we get to the plane. Then what?"

"You lock doors from inside and await further instructions."

"And then we'll be brought home?"

"That is the plan."

Trist's non-answer was telling. It hinted that a plan to outwit whoever on board had lied to them was under way, but that it wasn't going to be a simple or safe operation.

Jordan told her crew, "Everyone has five minutes to grab their medications, if they're assigned any. If while they're doing that they pocket some things to bring along, fine. Then get everyone into our emergency groups of twenty and form up in Town Square." Working out the emergency groups was something she'd already accomplished early in their stay, in case they ever needed to evacuate or organize quickly. The groups had become familiar to the passengers. Some had even named their teams. It had paid off: They'd be able to mobilize quickly. "Five minutes. That's all we have." Jordan didn't want to chance losing one of the kids. "Assign two people to each of the children. And make sure you do a final head count. I don't want to leave anyone behind.

"One last thing, people!" She'd better get every advantage she could in their home court. They were going to need . "Father Sugimoto and Pastor Earl—would you quickly less this endeavor, please?"

As the men led the group in a rushed but heartfelt prayer, ordan crossed herself and bowed her head, but her eyes lid to the empty hatch. It was so sudden, their move off ne ship. *Kào ... where are you?* She couldn't bear leaving rithout knowing if he'd made the decision to go with her. Ie'd said he planned to speak to his father about leaving yith her. What had happened in that conversation? Why yasn't he here with Trist?

When she saw Trist regarding her strangely, she realized nat her love for Kào burned in her face as violently as it id in her heart.

The linguist's voice was gentler. Or was it Jordan's imagnation? "Kào was taken off this assignment by the comnodore."

"Why?"

Trist's eyes were inscrutable. "Obligations."

Jordan's breath caught with a sudden wrenching in her hest. *Oh, Lord, no. Let me see him again.*

Kào wasn't happy on the *Savior*. That fact was apparent n everything he did and said. Only his fierce loyalty to his ther had kept him on the ship when he would have rather ursued his own prospects. But now it looked as if she'd ave to prepare for an alternate possibility. If he'd chosen o stay with his father until his war records were cleared, would be difficult for him to tell her that. He may have hosen to skip the step entirely.

"You must make haste, Captain. Time is short."

Jordan forced aside thoughts of Kào. "Don't worry. We'll e on the airplane." She was a professional, a leader; her uty was to keep focused on her responsibilities, not her personal heartache. Her task was to keep her people safe and get them all home.

"I will leave you to your swift preparations," Trist said.

As the flight attendants fanned out into Town Square barking orders, Jordan watched Trist go. The roller coaster of her life was crawling up another long ascent. Was there a way to end the ride without a fall? She didn't know. Loss had become such a staple of her life that it was easier to imagine a future without Kào than one with him. But the thought of a life without him broke her heart.

As the crews of both ships worked through the complicated details of the upcoming docking of two dissimilar vessels, Kào's attention remained riveted on the Talagarian admiral. With his long white hair gathered at the back of his neck in an ornate clasp, and blood-red eyes glowing in a face that looked as if it were chiseled from ice, Steeg would have been considered a handsome man among the Talagars. And his military bearing was without fault. Undoubtedly, he'd been a favorite of the once-Emperor, to have won himself his own command. Before the war, he'd probably maintained a household with hundreds of slaves, performing duties ranging from floor sweeping to fellatio. Now he'd been forced to obey the summons of an Alliance vessel where he'd be stripped of his power, his command, and eventually sent to Sofu to face trial.

But such was the ugly reality of defeat.

Buoyed by a surge of patriotism and pride, Kào stood taller. Steeg sized up the *Savior*'s bridge crew with disturbing keenness. That look, it must be genetic. The prison interrogators' eyes had glinted just as eagerly when they made the rounds, selecting fresh prisoners for their attention. But this time Kào was the victor, not the vanquished.

As Steeg considered the instructions given to him by Moray, his hand rose to cup his square chin. He wore ing. Uncannily, at the same moment the thick gold band caught the light, the *Savior* decelerated, adding a physical jolt to Kào's awareness of the crest. In its square center was a bird of prey with wings of fire. Involuntarily the word escaped Kào in a choked whisper, "Fire."

Fire. . . .

Running, terrified, the ground burning the soles of his shoes; he couldn't find his mother, his father, couldn't see, blinded by light that was as hot as fire and seared his eyes, his skin. . . .

Kào sucked in a mighty breath as a memory opened to him, a rupture in his mind torn open by the sight of Steeg's ring.

He was a small boy. His mother threw him onto a horse. Smacking its flank with the flat of her hand, she yelled, "Hai-ah!" sending the horse into a gallop. But it sickened and then fell, spilling him, forcing him to run on, half blinded by the heat and smoke.

Kào remembered how the air had seared his lungs. But the desire to survive burned hotter. He'd heard voices, and ran toward the sound.

Laughter. Gruff and deep. "What do we have here?" A hand came out of nowhere, grasping him by the collar and hoisting him off his feet. He couldn't see the man's face, but his skin was pink, like that of the white-haired soldiers who had descended from the sky and slaughtered the horses.

Kào swallowed convulsively. He remembered how he'd fought wildly, convinced that Death himself had snatched him.

"Mama! Mama!" he bellowed, spurring more laughter.

"Kill the thing," someone had said.

Whoever owned the hand that held him laughed along with the others. "I know someone who'll enjoy the task more than I. In fact, there he is now."

That was when Kào had wet his pants.

Humiliating heat streamed down his thighs. Concentrated from

Susan Grant

dehydration, his urine stank sharply. "You wet my boots!" *The hand rose up to cuff him on the side of the head, adding a new shriek to the chorus of agony that encased his body.* "I have a mind to crush your head right here." *The fist remained before his eyes, taunting him. On the middle finger was a ring. Its square crest was wet with blood, his blood, soiling a bird with wings of fire.*

Steeg's ring.

A second blow to his head nauseated him and brought about a loud humming in his ears. The man carried him swiftly away from the laughing soldiers. Kào was dropped in front of a pair of huge boots he was certain belonged to a giant.

At three years old, he'd learned the meaning of irony. Steeg had saved him only to deliver him to his executioner. He remembered staring at the toes of those boots, scarred and dust-coated with the remains of Vantaar's razed prairies, the ashes of his people's livelihood.

"It's too small. And it's not housebroken," *the ringed man added contemptuously.* "Here, put it out of our misery, Ilya."

Ilya? Kào gripped the railing. Ilya Moray?

A metallic scrape indicated a gun being withdrawn from a holster. "Stand still, little one." *But he didn't. He ran.*

He didn't know in which direction he fled; he knew only that he must escape the giant. He sprinted across the charred grasslands, zigzagging as he'd seen the rabbits run when chased by prairie-lions. His breaths scraped his throat raw, tears streamed from his burning eyes. Overhead, frightening silver ships, sleek and deadly, crisscrossed the sky like giant dragonflies. They dropped objects that erupted in greenish lightning. He felt the surges of the distant explosions in his ears. Black and orange clouds boiled on the horizon, where his village had been; the stench of dead horses was so heavy that he could taste it. But he ran, hard and fast, until the sound of thundering boots hitting the hard-packed earth caught up to him.

In his mind's eye, Kào saw that horrible hand descend,

300

snatching him off his feet. "Gotcha!" *I know someone who'll enjoy it more....*

He fought the giant until every last bit of strength bled from his thin, wiry body, until he was too exhausted to raise a fist or lift a leg. He dangled like a strangled chicken from that enormous fist, drained but not defeated. "Look at me, boy." He obeyed, half expecting the butt of the gun to come crashing down on his throbbing, bloodied skull. But the giant hadn't the red eyes of the others. His were the color of coal smoke and unexpectedly kind. "An admirable little fighter you are. I know men who could stand to take a lesson from you."

Only days ago at dinner Moray had expressed that same sentiment: "It was your swift feet that saved you that day. Your spirit, Kào, your will to survive, it glowed so brightly that it touched me in a way you cannot imagine."

And it had saved Kào from dying that day.

"What's your name, boy?" the huge man asked. "You must be old enough to know it."

It took a while to work sufficient saliva into his parched mouth to answer. "Kào."

"Kay-oh," the man had repeated, drawing out the sound. "A strong name. A name worthy of your spirit. I'll let you keep it. Your surname, however, will be mine." With that, the benevolent giant tucked Kào under a brawny arm and carried him away from Vantaar. And into a new life.

The giant had been Moray. *Moray!* A man who'd loomed larger than life to him ever since.

Kào glanced wildly about the bridge. A few aides poked up their heads from their stations. Meeting his quelling glare, they ducked quickly back to work.

Dazed, he turned back to the screen, but it displayed only the stars; the admiral's communication with Moray had ended, for now. But the image of his ring was seared into Kào's mind as brutally as the brand on his neck. On that long-ago day on Vantaar it had represented imminent death, the incarnation of a tiny boy's nightmare: *"I know someone who'll enjoy it more . . ."*

A drumbeat of disbelief thundered inside Kào as he grasped for composure. He'd been taken in and raised by an Alliance turncoat who had experienced a moment of mercy, taking a little boy off-planet instead of killing him or handing him over to the Talagars.

It was more than a moment of mercy, Kào's conscience argued. *He raised you, cared for you, taught you morals, and right from wrong.*

Kào's stomach rolled. His hands sweated. His thoughts swerved once more to the recent dinner he'd shared with Moray, when the man had confided that he'd been a bitter and disillusioned man for years after losing his wife and children. "When I took you home it all changed," he'd said. "I was a man without a family. And you, Kào, a little boy who needed one."

But how bitter was Moray? How disillusioned? Enough to betray the Alliance? He was seen by many as one of its greatest heroes. Was he in fact their greatest traitor?

"Ah," Kào said hoarsely, pressing the back of his hand to his mouth to tamp down an almost overwhelming gag reflex. Was he supposed to love Moray or hate him? Both emotions fought for dominance. Moray had saved him, a traumatized orphan, but only after participating in the destruction of Vantaar as a thug admired for his mercilessness by a Talagar who beat defenseless children.

Every deed the commodore had accomplished over the years was now tainted by treachery in Kào's mind. He'd saved thousands from certain death on the Ceris space station, but was it only so he could siphon off a countless number and hand them over to the Talagar Empire? By the Seeders, he'd been patrolling the Perimeter for years. How many Talagar ships had he allowed to pass through? And during the war, how many more? The idea of such duplicity from the man he so admired sickened Kào beyond the nausea that gripped him.

How could his father have remained such a stranger to him? How? Even the worst of the Talagarian torture sessions hadn't generated this much agony.

If he hadn't been on the bridge, he'd be ignorant still. But he wasn't unaware any longer. He knew what his father was. Memories didn't lie. Moray was a slave-broker disguised as a champion, and now he planned to hand over Jordan and her people to Steeg.

She was all he'd ever wanted, and he would lose her. She and her people would meet the same horrible fate as his family. He'd been helpless on that long-ago day on Vantaar. Was he still? Anger and anguish twisted sharply together until he could no longer separate them. History would not repeat itself, he vowed.

Find Jordan. Warn her.

A sense of urgency propelled him away from the railing.

The bridge hummed with activity as Moray, by all appearances a loyal Alliance officer, led his well-trained crew through the gauntlet of taking over the Talagar vessel. It was an elaborate ruse Moray and Steeg had concocted. Surely, Trist and the other Talagars were in on it. And who else? Kào scrutinized the faces of those who worked diligently at their stations. It was a small crew. He'd heard that many had been transferred to other ships recently. Now Kào wondered why. But those working appeared to be loyal Alliance citizens, scientists here because they wanted to explore the outer reaches of space with a famous man. Perhaps hero worship had rendered the crew blind to the traitors lurking among them.

As for the crew members of Talagarian descent, in Kào's opinion, anyone with red eyes was suspect. But what about Moray? He wasn't a Talagar, yet he acted like one. Certainly, that day on Vantaar he had been ready to kill like one.

No, an inner voice argued, *a different Ilya. Not Ilya, your loving father. Not Commodore-elite Ilya Moray, the highest-ranking officer in the Perimeter Patrol Corps. Not a humanitarian credited for saving thousands of lives over the years at the risk of his own.* But even as Kào's heart told him one thing, reason demanded that he face the facts that had eluded him for twenty-four years.

The truth about his father.

Find Jordan. Warn her. With emotions forcibly disabled, he stalked past Moray with the barest of nods. A heavy hand landed on his shoulder, bringing him to a halt. But only because Kào allowed himself to be stopped.

Moray's smile was one of fatherly concern. "What's wrong, Kào?"

He felt like that three-year-old boy again in the way the contents of his bladder screamed for release. But he had a man's control. And a man's pride. "I've spent long enough looking into the eyes of Talagars," he said truthfully. "Now that I have the freedom to decide, I don't care to spend another moment doing so. If you'll excuse me, I must go."

His father stayed in front of him, his boots planted wide. "It wasn't wise of me to allow you to view the battleship," he said. "The war is too fresh in your mind. Now I see it was too soon for you. My apologies."

Moray's tone conveyed both worry and a father's love. Kào wasn't sure if it was genuine or fabricated, but Moray had spoken loudly enough for the entire bridge crew to hear. It hit him that Moray might be using the impromptu forum to reassure those on the crew who weren't directly involved in any treachery.

Find Jordan. Warn her.

Kào shifted from boot to boot in his impatience to leave. The need to find Jordan and ensure her safety gripped him as nothing else ever had. He saw himself fully capable of murder if his father kept him from going to her. But bringing on himself death or imprisonment would defeat his plan. *Calm*. He reached deep for composure, but a tremor wobbled his hands.

With the accuracy of proton torpedoes, the commodore's eyes honed in on that reaction. "You're shaking."

"I'm tired." Now it seemed that everyone on the bridge was watching. Sympathy filled some eyes. The rest he could tell saw him as a mentally and physically wounded ex-POW who suffered post-traumatic stress syndrome. And they were probably right. "You're keeping me from my bed, Father."

"You were always frank with me," Moray persisted. "Why not now? What troubles you?"

Kào exhaled. "Steeg. I don't trust him." He waited, curious to see what Moray's reaction would be.

There was no reaction. Either the man was a sociopath or he truly with all his soul believed his cause was just. Or perhaps it was both.

Moray spread his hands. "What is the admiral going to do? His weapons are disabled. Everything in our arsenal, is aimed at his bridge. He poses no threat. Steeg will soon be on his way to the detention facility on Sofu. They're done, my boy. Through. They won't trouble us again."

"I must brief the refugees on the matter," Kào said and again tried to walk past Moray. The man stopped him with three fingers on his forearm.

"Trist will brief them."

"She hasn't been on the job long enough. I have."

"You're agitated, Kào."

"Agitated? I am not agitated!" He winced inwardly, knowing that he must sound just as Moray accused.

"Medical will give you something to help."

The crew looked on, caring and sympathetic. Why was it that when you were trying to act sane, you came across as anything but? Kào fisted his hands at his sides and swallowed hard. *Play along*, sudden instinct warned. Yes. He could put on a show as well as Moray, could he not? He'd been raised by a master of deception, he thought bitterly, and now it was time to use what he'd learned. It would buy him time, of which he had very little.

He winced and rubbed his head. "Ah. You're right. I'll see about getting myself something to help me sleep. And once I wake, I'll search out my cold-weather gear for Sofu." He forced a smile.

His father's face brightened. "You're excited about the trip." The commodore's hand landed on his back, and Kào did his best not to go rigid at the contact. He didn't want the traitor touching him. It was bad enough having to speak to him in a civil manner.

But civility would save Jordan. And her people. "About our dinner tonight, sir. I don't know if I'll be up to it. I'd better rest for the journey to Sofu."

"Ah. Just as well. I'll be debriefing the admiral this evening."

Debriefing? More like reminiscing about old raids and the latest Talagar perversions.

"And it's best I do that with my intelligence staff only in attendance."

Wise choice, Father. If I'm there, Steeg won't survive the encounter.

"Perhaps tomorrow," Moray said. As he walked with Kào to the exit, he shook his head sadly. "Soon enough you'll be gone."

"Soon enough," Kào agreed. Moray regarded him strangely. Kào couldn't care less. The commodore dropped his hand, tacit permission to leave. Kào clicked his heels together and strode away from the bastard.

Docking was imminent. He didn't know where he was going to hide two hundred and eighty-seven Earthers, but a plan would come to him. It had to.

Chapter Twenty-seven

"Darth Vader's here!"

At the sound of little Christopher's familiar call, Jordan spun around. Kào was walking toward her with the boy nestled in his muscular arms. If it weren't totally inappropriate and unprofessional, she would have thrown her arms around him. They were well into the evacuation. Three quarters of the people were gone. About seventy remained. And time was short, according to Trist.

"You came," she said, relief swelling inside her.

"Darth Vader's here," Christopher repeated, affectionately rubbing his hand up and down Kào's scarred cheek.

"I see that," Jordan whispered, her throat thick. Kào dropped the boy to his feet. As he watched the child scamper away, his eyes clouded with sadness, and he appeared exhausted to the bone.

"You look like hell, Kào," she said quietly.

Her voice seemed to call him back from somewhere far away, a painful place. "Hell?" he inquired.

"It's an Earth expression. Technically, it means the place you go after death if you've lived an evil life. Eternal damnation. In other words, you burn in horrible agony for all eternity."

Kào's dark eyes narrowed. A muscle in his cheek jumped. "May such comeuppance await the beasts on this vessel."

"The ones who lied to us, yes." Jordan grabbed him by the elbow. "Talk to me on the way. We have to hurry. Trist wants us to take shelter on the airplane. So much has happened. I'll tell you. And we're going home!"

Outrage flared in his face. "You're not going anywhere."

Some of the passengers glanced their way. "Excuse me?" Jordan hissed, then waved at the line of passengers. "Are you going to tell them that? What's happened, Kào? What's wrong?"

"I have reason to believe that the plan isn't to relocate you to a new home but to acquire you as slaves. There are slave-brokers aboard this ship that wish to make it so."

Jordan's vision dimmed as the blood left her head. "Someone wants to sell us into slavery?"

"Give us something we can *really* be scared of," cried one of the men passing by.

The passengers around him cheered. An elderly woman raised her fist at Kào. "He's right. We've heard it all. It's just another threat to keep us quiet. Another lie. Screw 'em! We're going home."

Jordan listened, open-mouthed. The passengers weren't afraid. They were angry! She could almost understand why. They'd had to absorb one shocking revelation after another for weeks now. After a while, even the most traumatizing news lost its impact.

Kào gripped her shoulder. His voice was hoarse. Urgent. She had never seen him this way, and she began to get worried, too. "Stop your people," he ordered. "Call them back. Trist is sending you to your deaths."

"No, she's helping us. The coordinates you sent to the Science Academy, the ones entered into the official database, they don't correspond to Earth. We found that out, and she confirmed it. The coordinates are for a planet named Kerils. It's not in the Alliance database, either. Someone's lying. And it's not Trist."

He read his translator with an appalled expression. "The holo-movie I showed you was Kerils?"

"That's right. Not Earth. Earth is fine. No comet hit."

He watched her intently for several heartbeats. "Treachery is indeed afoot," he said at last. Heat radiated off his lean and powerful body. He smelled like apple soap and male perspiration, his own unique scent, pheromone rich, because it aroused her in the midst of a situation in which sexual desire had no place. "And one of the traitors is Commodore Moray."

"Good God. Your father?"

He winced, as if the term "father" had become unpalatable. He quickly told her about his flashback. About Steeg. About a child's terror.

Of all the revelations, she knew it was Moray's apparent betrayal that affected him most of all. "The man who raised me, who I thought genuinely loved me and perhaps still does, embodies all I detest, Jordan. All I fought against. Now I have to stop him before he hurts anyone else. Before he hurts you." He closed his eyes for a heartbeat, but not before she'd glimpsed a flash of raw pain.

Jordan wanted to slide her arms over his stiff shoulders and soothe away his grief. She wanted to take him to bed and love him until his thoughts centered on nothing else but how much he was cherished. But in light of the unfolding conspiracy and the danger they faced, as well as their apparent opposite stance on Trist, she wondered if she'd ever have the chance to hold him like that again.

"I have a plan that will allow us to escape," he stated. "A ship is due to rendezvous with the *Savior*—an Alliance government vessel that was supposed to bring me to Sofu for the hearing on my war record. When I board, all of you will, too. I'll explain the details later."

She fought to keep calm. "Trist said if we don't follow her instructions, we'll die."

"Of course she told you that!"

"You have to trust me on this, Kào. Trist is on our side."

"Where's your proof?"

"Where's yours?"

He reared back. She snatched his hand. "I didn't mean that," she said with tenderness, and his hackles went down somewhat. They cared about each other, maybe even loved each other. Emotion was running high. She knew that his forbidding scowl and the fire in his eyes were symptoms of his fear for her. Somehow she knew and believed that. And it meant a lot. "About Trist, I know more about her than you think. That night at The Black Hole, she covered for us; she helped us evade security. And before that, too. Though we didn't realize she was helping us then. She gave us access to information on the computer that we couldn't have gotten otherwise. Without it, we wouldn't have found out about Earth, Kào. That's a fact. And she told us about the locators that were sewn into our issued clothing, so we could sneak out of New Earth without being caught. Did you know about those locators?" she asked accusingly. "We didn't."

"Tracked by locators. Like livestock." He looked appalled by the idea. "No, I did not."

She came up on her toes and reached behind his uniform collar. Under her thumbnail, she felt a tiny rectangle. Twisting the locator between her fingers, she wrenched it free of the fabric and gave it to him.

Contact

He stared at the silver object resting in his palm.

Jordan touched Kào's arm. His biceps were rock-hard under the gray fabric of his uniform. "We owe Trist an open mind, if nothing else," she said.

His focus turned inward as if he were analyzing Trist's actions over the time he'd known her, which would have been only a few months, Earth time. "By the Seeders," he whispered harshly and threw away the locator. It landed soundlessly somewhere far across the room. "Moray put her in charge because he knows about you and me. About our nights."

Her cheeks heated. "He does?"

"Trist told him. Or he guessed it with her help. Regardless, it's an excuse—the accusation of my fraternization, my lack of professionalism—whatever one might call it. It was a convenient way to get rid of me now that we're about to dock with the Talagars. He needs someone in place who's loyal to him; who'll do his bidding. And that's exactly what she's doing. They're in this together, Jordan. Moray isn't acting alone. Trist, the other Talagars—they're involved. Every last blasted one. She's worked to win your trust so she'll be assured of your cooperation."

"Your prejudice toward the Talagars is understandable. Even contagious sometimes," she admitted with shame. "But who says there can't be Alliance patriots who look like Talagars? Trist is one of them, I think. And there may be others like her onboard."

He shook his head. "Talagar and Alliance patriot—they are mutually exclusive terms."

Jordan shoved her hands through her hair. Her fingers snarled in the long strands, making her wonder briefly how disheveled she must look. A nice appearance had once meant something to her. How quickly events had taken precedence over vanity, she thought, tugging on the hem of a tie-dyed T-shirt she'd dressed in so often that she'd forgotten what it was like to wear anything else.

New Earth was now a ghost town, eerie and silent. Ben and Garrett the Marine followed the last of the passengers away toward the planes. Only Natalie and Dillon were left. Until the last minute, Dillon had been attached to the computer. Now Natalie dragged him from his chair and mouthed to Jordan: *Come on.*

"Kào, please. I'm not asking you to be friends with her; just talk to her. She might need your help."

He made a sound of disgust. Jordan wanted to scream. She teetered on the edge of losing all she'd wanted—the chance to go home and saving the man she loved—all because he couldn't see past Trist's ancestry.

A vibration shook the ship. The floor seemed to buzz under Jordan's shoes. "We've docked. We have to get to the airplane." She shook her fist at him. "Don't screw this up for us, Kào. Or I'm going to wind up on a slave freighter on a one-way trip to wherever the Talagar Empire is reforming, and you're going to end up dead—all because you can't see past your hatred of Trist."

He caught her fist. "I do not hate her."

"You hate what she is," Jordan argued. "Who her ancestors are. But the last time I checked, brutality's not limited to eye color or skin color. Ask your father."

Kào bristled. His frigid eyes made her shiver.

The silence stretched. The air itself felt ready to shatter. But he gave no hint of giving in.

"I see there's nothing more I can say to you," she whispered. "The decision is yours. I've made mine."

The words hung between them before dissipating into silence. It tore her heart, issuing that ultimatum.

Promise, Mommy? Swallowing hard, Jordan turned her back to him and strode across Town Square to catch up with the others.

"Isn't Kào coming?" Natalie asked when she did.

Jordan made a face. "He's being stubborn. Come on, let's roll."

"Are you sure?"

"I'm sure."

Natalie whistled. "When it comes to lovers' quarrels, your timing stinks."

"Shut up, Nat."

She didn't look back at Kào again; she couldn't. They clambered down a hole in the floor. It reminded Jordan of descending into a sewer but without the smell. The hand-ladders were located in narrow metallic tubes that connected the decks. Rings protruded from one side. Grasping the rings and feeling with her toes for the rungs below, Jordan led the way into the lower reaches of the ship, briefing Natalie and Dillon on Kào's revelations as they went.

The gray and blue United Airlines 747 and the hundreds of passengers climbing into it took up but a small part of the cargo bay. The jet gleamed, its familiarity tugging at Jordan's emotions, conjuring thoughts of routine flights and Hawaiian layovers, stale coffee and too-late nights.

And mysterious lights in a dark sky.

In her mind, she saw Captain Wendt struggling to breathe, his clawing hands and blue face. The day Brian died of the heart attack felt like a million years ago. She was a different person then than she was now.

She jumped down from the ladder, but remained there, holding on to the lowest rung, peering upward into the dark tube from which they'd descended. After the longest, most excruciating moments imaginable, she heard the sound of heavy footfalls from above her head. When she saw Kào's boots, joy welled up inside her. She stumbled back, allowing him to vault to the floor.

He stood there, a big, strapping, rugged man, his skin golden in the overhead light, his harsh features softened by his obvious feelings for her. "You came," she said.

In the depth of his black eyes, she saw his uncertainty, his fear. His anger. "Whether or not we agree about Trist, you will have my protection in this venture. But should it go wrong, I'm taking over, and there'll be no disobeying me."

"That's a deal," she whispered.

Dillon appeared next to them. "You coming along?" he asked.

Kào narrowed his eyes at the red-haired Irishman. "I remember you from the Earth aircraft. You were the one who kicked me in the chest when my hands were bound."

Dillon cleared his throat and looked at the bigger man. "That would be me."

Kào nodded, sizing him up. "You are brave. I will like having you on my side for once."

That was when Jordan noticed what Dillon held in his hand. "The defibrillator!" The AED might as well be a relic from ancient times, it felt so long since she'd seen it.

"It still works."

Natalie showed up next with the Taser and the crash ax. "Take your pick."

"Since you're the cardio-kickbox queen with buns of steel, I'll take the stun gun," Jordan said. "And we'd better get inside the plane."

Kào shook his head. "Inside we won't be able to view who enters the cargo bay. I'll stand guard here."

Everyone volunteered to stay with him. But no sooner than they said the words, two men walked off the main lift from the decks above: one burly Talagarian security guard named Heest, the one she'd injured badly—and had pissed off—and another man whom Jordan recognized as one of Moray's weasely red-eyed aides.

Kào went rigid. Jordan forced herself to breathe.

Heest brought his comm to his mouth. "Got 'em." Then

the two started walking forward, weapons gleaming in their belt holsters. "This area of the cargo bay is off limits. We have to take you into custody," the guard called out, to the aide's apparent glee.

Kào whispered out of the corner of his mouth, "Don't say anything about Trist."

The lift opened again, disgorging two more security guards.

And Trist.

"I spoke too soon," Kào muttered bitterly.

Trist and the two guards accompanying her wore gleaming guns in their belt holsters. "The commodore authorized deadly force to protect this area," she said, drawing her weapon. The others did the same.

Seeing the guns aimed at them, Jordan felt off balance. Vulnerable.

Stupid.

Kào had been right about Trist, after all.

Chapter Twenty-eight

Two loud "zaps" tore through the silence—like the sound of monster moths being electrocuted in a bug light. Time bogged down. Passengers screamed. Jordan lifted her arms to ward off whatever had been fired at them as Natalie ducked, pulling Dillon down with her. Kào lunged at Trist, but she fired off a shot before he reached her.

Heest flew backward at the same instant that a second security man blew away a third, leaving Trist, the aide, and the one surviving guard.

Jordan lowered her shaking arms. An awful burning smell of scorched flesh prickled her nose. Thin streamers of smoke wafted up from the twitching bodies. Her stomach rolled.

"Well," Trist said. "Not bad."

Not bad? Jordan's heart pounded erratically. She knew it'd be a moment before she got her voice back.

"That was no accident." Kào's arms were stiff at his sides,

his fists flexing. "You killed those men intentionally."

If Trist had been in a western, she'd have blown smoke from the muzzle of her pistol. "To put it mildly. It was a planned assassination. To save my mission here—and you. Just be glad we caught up to them." With both hands, she smoothed her ivory hair away from her face. "Rono, Pugmarten, hide the bodies."

Her companions dragged away the dead men and disposed of the corpses in a storage room. Then Trist closed the distance between her and Kào, her hand extended. "Tristin Pren, Colonel, Alliance Special Forces. Trist still works fine. I'm pleased to *re*-make your acquaintance, Lieutenant." Her lavender mouth tipped crookedly at Kào's obvious shock. What was he going to do know, faced with the proof of Trist's loyalty, something he obviously didn't expect from a woman of Talagarian descent?

Kào didn't take Trist's hand. He placed his weapon in it.

Jordan released a gust of air. Now that they all were on the same side, the prospect of getting home got a little bit brighter.

"That's 'mister,' Colonel," he corrected quietly. "Not lieutenant."

"Actually, it *is* lieutenant. Perhaps even a higher rank at this point, if you count time served toward promotion. Your war record is clean. We found out some things about the incident at the depot, some things I'm not at liberty to discuss. But it will lead to a pardon; that I know."

Kào paled, and Jordan's heart leaped. Leading his squadron into the ambush at the weapons depot had brought him enormous personal shame. Now with a few words, he was free of it—if completely bewildered by the information.

Kào's voice was understandably hoarse. "Tell me why you're here."

"The war is far from over. The Talagars are rebuilding on the Rim. They need human labor badly, thus Commodore Moray's eagerness to deliver these people and go back for more. They needed an uncharted world. Who knew such a world existed? But it does—and unfortunately Moray found Earth before the Alliance did."

"That's why he wants to keep us a secret," Jordan said, glancing at Dillon. "So he can return for more."

Dillon shook his head. "Slave harvests."

Jordan's esophagus gave a spasm, and for a heartbeat she was afraid she'd be sick.

Trist sought her gaze. "The Alliance will not allow that to happen. All we have to do is keep Earth's location from getting into Talagar hands."

"It already is," Jordan, argued.

Trist shook her head. "No one knows but me and Moray." She tapped her head. "I wiped everything from my hard drive once you got your peek. And I made sure nothing accurate was sent off this ship."

Kào stared at Trist as if he'd never seen her before. "There's a government ship due to pick me up and bring me to Sofu. We can transfer Jordan and her people to the vessel."

"There is no ship, Kào."

Kào dispassionately absorbed the impact of another of his father's lies.

"To be more exact, the government didn't send anyone for you. Moray did. He was transporting you to Sofu to get you off the ship. The dispatched vessel is now under Alliance control. It won't be docking with the *Savior* anytime soon."

His jaw worked. "How are you going to do it, then?"

"Save the refugees? Or destroy Steeg's battleship?"

Jordan exchanged a startled glance with Kào. "Both," he said.

"Jordan will wait with her people aboard the aircraft. No one will think to look for them there. I have some of my own in security," she explained with a glance at the surviving guard, Pugmarten. "Moray thinks the refugees are awaiting transfer in the holding room on Deck One. And of course the new primary intercessor, Trist, confirmed that." Trist grinned.

With those words, Jordan realized how much Trist herself risked in this bid to send them home. But then there was much more at stake, like galactic peace, of which Flight 58 was a very small part. "And when they figure out we're not there?"

"Pugmarten will pretend to investigate. He'll stall and confuse. By the time they find you, it'll be too late. We'll be on our way."

Pugmarten spoke up. "I'd better get back to work, or they'll be looking for me." He dipped his head and strode away.

Trist glanced at her wrist computer.

"How are you going to destroy the battleship?" Kào asked. Clearly, his military instincts had been roused.

"Remotely. The ships are docked; the computers are linked. I'm going to send a signal through the secondary airlock—the one that's located right above us, as a matter of fact. It'll cause the engines to go unstable. The warp field will collapse, and the ship will blow up."

Kào whistled. "Tactical brilliance."

"I'm an engineer and a pilot—I know something about engines," the woman replied with no lack of smugness.

Who would have known that the two former rivals would share a love of mass destruction?

"Will the event occur before or after Steeg and his crew come aboard?" A muscle in Kào's jaw jumped as he asked the question. Jordan couldn't help thinking of the little boy beaten to near-unconsciousness by the admiral.

"Steeg dies with his ship," Trist replied coldly. "It's only Moray whom Sofu wants for questioning."

319

"Excuse me," Natalie interjected in English. "If the battleship blows up . . . don't we?"

"Not if we break away and run like the wind." Again, Trist looked at her watch. "Coming here—it's delayed me. We're running out of time. I have to send the signal. But the program's on my computer—and the only other terminal I can safely use is in New Earth. I don't have time to get to either one. I'll have to try to send it from here." She peered around the cargo bay. "Where's a work station?" she muttered to herself. "I need a computer."

Dillon pointed over her shoulder. "There's one."

"He can smell the things, I swear," Natalie said under her breath.

Trist plopped into a chair and pulled down a flexible screen as Kào, Jordan, Dillon, and Natalie gathered around. Time was short. Jordan sensed it. It was all she could do not to squirm.

"You're trying to get into the operating system from an applications program," Dillon remarked in fluent Key.

Trist gave him a classic double take and banged on the keyboard, her inner anxiety revealed by brutal keystrokes. "It should have allowed me in."

"You're not at a recognized terminal." Dillon moved next to her. "Try this." He nudged aside her hands. "Sign on and send two breaks. Like this."

Trist grabbed at her hair. "That doesn't work, either. I'm going to have to run to my workstation—"

"Hold on," Dillon soothed as he tried what looked like a random combination of keys. "There we go. Two line feeds and . . . there you are."

"Ah!" Her face washed free of tension, Trist hunched forward over the terminal. She typed for a moment or two. Then her smile fell. "I got the signal off from here, but something blocked it. It can't get through."

Jordan started to wring her hands. Made fists. Crushed

them to her sides. Here they went, up the long incline, all over again. If she got home alive, she vowed never to set foot on a roller coaster for the rest of her life.

Kào, however, met the unfolding situation with stoicism. He was a soldier, a warrior. Men like him took this kind of thing a whole lot better than someone like her: a soccer mom disguised as an airline pilot masquerading as an intergalactic hero.

As if sensing her thoughts, Kào smoothed his hand over her back, his fingers spreading protectively, possessively over the curve of her spine. "You must have routed the signal through the sensor in the airlock," he surmised.

Trist pursed her lips. "I did. But for some reason, the sensor hasn't depressed. And so the computer doesn't think that the ships docked. A minor mechanical function with the worst timing you can imagine." With her fingertips, she massaged her temples. "I don't believe this. Everything's gone perfectly until now."

"Who else do you have with you to help?" Kào asked.

"There are three of us. Moray is a double agent—has been for years. The Alliance finally figured it out and put several of us on the case. Onboard the ship, he has at least six helping him that we know of. Two are now dead. The crew is ignorant of his treachery, and Moray will do everything in his power to keep them from finding out about his deeds—to the point of keeping his minions ignorant of each other's efforts. He enjoys his status as a hero. He'd never risk its ruin. His reputation is everything to him, how he's seen by others. Especially you, Kào."

"What about the rest of the crew?" Jordan interjected. "If they're loyal, they can help."

Trist answered her as she'd asked: in English. "Too dangerous. We are not certain who is who. There may be more of Moray's people among crew, not known to even us, his inner circle. We thought for a long time that you were one, Kào."

It wasn't difficult to see how much the idea repulsed him as he read her words on his translator.

"But we know now that you were ignorant of his crimes."

His scowl deepened. "Inexcusably so."

"But he worked at hiding it from you for a lifetime," Trist insisted gently. "He loves you."

A shadow passed over Kào's face. "You did your best to strain that relationship."

"It was a side project of mine. I'm sorry. I wanted to drive a wedge between you and your father. I didn't think you deserved to die along with him for no other reason than loyalty and devotion."

Jordan was certain that that wedge was her relationship with Kào. Had Trist made love with Ben so she could glean inside details? Spies did that sort of thing. She wondered if Trist had been sleeping with Moray, too, as Kào had speculated. Jordan grimaced. If that was true, the woman deserved a medal.

Again, Trist looked at her watch as if the answer to the impasse would be written there. "Blast this."

"I'll see to the sensor," Rono offered. Trist's fierce eyes veered to her companion. "No. I need you on the bridge keeping Moray happy. In fact, you'd better return there now. Everything must continue to appear normal and on schedule. The hasty docking tells me that Moray may fear he's aroused suspicion—or is in danger of doing so. He wants to speed the transfer and return to the Perimeter."

Jordan watched the man called Rono leave. The creep had been one of the commodore's aides. But Rono wasn't a creep at all; he was an intelligence agent, a spy, like Trist. And a hero.

Kào spoke up. "No one will care if I'm seen near the bridge. I'll go into the airlock."

Jordan protested.

He shook his head, his cautioning fingers brushing lightly
down her spine. He'd made his decision, and he was telling
her that. Part of her didn't blame him for wanting to take
an active role in the admiral's destruction, and part of her
wanted to give him that chance. But the rest of her wanted
someone else to do it, so she could keep him in sight, so
she could make sure nothing happened to him.

Trist accepted Kào's offer without hesitation. "Make sure
the switch depresses the sensor. Hold it down until the signal goes through. It's a large file. It may take a few minutes.
Be certain that the switch remains closed. You'll be in and
out in minutes. I've got a program ready to go that will
force us to separate from the battleship—an emergency
breakaway—so don't be surprised to hear alarms going off
when you get out." She dug in her thigh pocket. "Here's a
blade—to remove your locator."

Kào and Jordan exchanged a glance. "I already have," he
said.

Trist briefed Jordan in English. "Soon they will discover
that you do not wait on Deck One. Pugmarten will make a
report to security that you are not in the cargo bay, but we
cannot count on that—as you see, we cannot count on one
small mechanical switch. Your airplane is safest place to
hide. But there is a risk if Moray finds out you are here."
Trist pointed to the massive cargo bay doors. "Let me tell
you a story. Once, on this ship, Moray ejected a cargo-bay
full of refugees into space when he thought the Alliance
had learned about him."

Natalie's hand shot out and clutched Jordan's sleeve. The
idea of it, Jordan thought darkly, mass murder at one man's
whim, made her blood curdle. "Do you think he'd do it
again?" she asked.

"He will do anything to continue on as he has always
done."

323

"I second that," Kào growled.

"But we can prevent this one deed, at least," Trist told them. "Do you see the horizontal bar next to the doors?"

Jordan squinted. "The one with the huge hook next to it?"

"Yes. This is a manual override. When the hook is over the bar, it does not allow any command to open the cargo doors."

"Why would you even have that?" the pilot in Jordan asked. "In case of a computer malfunction?"

Trist nodded. "Today, however, we will attach it for insurance. In case someone tries to open these doors."

Jordan started walking. "Then let's put that baby where it belongs." Over her shoulder, she called, "Natalie, Dillon, you'd better get to the airplane. I'll meet you there."

Natalie and Dillon hurried away. The last of the others had long since disappeared into the aircraft. Thanks to Ben's efficiency, Jordan thought, wondering what he'd say once he heard the news about Trist.

Standing by the enormous cargo doors brought a feeling of vulnerability. On the other side of them was the vastness of space. A frigid vacuum. Infinity. It took her fear of heights and made a mockery of it.

"The hook is too heavy to lift." Trist spun a wheel that operated a hydraulically driven pump. The hook fell over the sequoia-sized bar with a resounding metallic clang.

Jordan stared at the device. "I feel a whole lot better now."

"Good," Trist said. "Now go to the airplane. Use your harnesses. It will be a bumpy ride."

Jordan turned, and Kào caught her hand. Trist tactfully stepped away, leaving them alone. For a heartbeat, Jordan was unable to say anything to Kào for fear of losing the composure she clung to by a thread. He was leaving. He was going into an airlock to unblock Trist's signal of destruction. It was a simple operation; no one would know he was there. But all she wanted to do was fall apart. And she couldn't, of course. She had to act brave, courageous, everything she'd always thought she wasn't. "Kào," she said huskily, "you damned well better come back."

He grabbed her shoulders, dragging her close. Before he crushed her to his chest, she saw something in his face that frightened her: hunger for revenge, startling and raw, anger that boiled dangerously close to the surface.

"You'll avenge your family," she mumbled against his beating heart.

His stomach muscles hardened. "I'll avenge *everything*. And then I will return for you." He tightened his arms around her, bending down so they were cheek to cheek. His breath was hot on her ear. "I'll be back for you, Jordan."

A chill drifted over her skin, bringing goose bumps. She didn't dare reply for fear of jinxing his promise. Rising up on her toes, she pressed her lips to his. His stubble pricked her chin, and his skin tasted salty. Her hand flattened on his abdomen as he drew her closer. Love and loss, hope and despair intertwined, irrevocably linked together. She closed her eyes and inhaled his scent on a shuddering breath. She took the moment and wished she could make it last forever. But grimly she girded herself for the inevitable.

Just once, she thought, she wanted to be able to love without enduring loss. But for her, maybe that was not meant to be. "I think I speak for all of us when I say we'd rather die trying for freedom than to live as slaves," she whispered. Her mouth twisted then. "My God, that sounded noble, didn't it? But the reality of it sucks."

He shook his head. "Think of the land, our life, and don't stop until you see me again. It'll be my lifeline, those hopes. It will bring me back. It will bring us home."

Home.

"And there I will make love to you in the grass." His voice was husky and deep, steeped in sexual promise. "Wearing nothing but sunshine, covered only by the sky."

The sensual image he painted with his words was so sharp that it drew out a gasp—one of desire as much as surprise. "But I never told you about my dreams of that."

"You didn't have to. I had my own."

"Ah, Kào . . ." Her hand lingered on his scarred cheek. She saw for the first time that his black-brown eyes were tinted with sherry in the middle. Or had they now finally warmed to that color? The poignancy of the discovery shook her.

Thirstily her eyes drank in the essence of his soul. When her heart couldn't hold any more, she turned and walked away.

"Commodore."

Moray glanced up from his handheld. An aide waited for permission to speak. "What is it, Jinn?"

"The refugees are not in the holding room on Deck One."

"Isn't that where they're supposed to be?"

"Yes, sir."

Moray lowered his computer. "Did you call security?" he asked with forced patience.

"Yes, sir." Jinn's smile wobbled. "It's probably all a miscommunication."

"I'm sure that's what it is. Thank you, Jinn."

Jinn smacked his heels together and strode back to his station. Moray opened his comm. "Trist."

The woman's pale heart-shaped face appeared in the viewing screen. His loins tightened with the image of her thrown over his leather bar stool, screaming as he thrust into her. Cold as ice out of bed and hot as fire in it. A good Talagar woman. "Yes, sir," she said.

"Where are your refugees?"

Her face fell. "Sir?"

"They're not in the holding room."

"They have to be. I saw them there myself."

"I'm not going to have to put Kào back on the assignment, am I?"

"No, sir!"

He smiled. She had so much pride. Her ambition would take her far.

"I'll track them down and report back."

By the tone of her voice, he had no doubt she would. "I'll be waiting," he said and closed the comm.

Chapter Twenty-nine

The aide Jinn overheard Trist's conversation with Moray.
"The refugees?"

"Pugmarten's going to track them down," she muttered.
"I can't go. Too much work." She released a breath of
feigned annoyance and sagged back in her chair. Her attention remained on the computer. Kào would be in the airlock
by now. Soon the signal would go through. Then there were
other steps she'd need to take—and fast. "We ought to have
installed a visual monitor in that holding room. Then we
wouldn't have to be bothered with false alarms."

Jinn shook his head as if she were the stupidest bitch in
the galaxy. "It isn't a false alarm. They're in their aircraft."

She flew upright, feigning surprise. "What? That's impossible. I'll have security run a check of the cargo bay."

"No need. I already called for one."

"Pugmarten. He's on duty." She swallowed. "He'd better
find them. My reputation's on the line."

Jinn's wine-colored eyes glinted. "And quite the reputation you have, too."

"You can mention that to your commodore."

Her dry retort quelled his arrogance a fraction. "I'll pass."

"Jinn, leave Moray out of this. I've got a promotion pending. This is my big break. Let me try to fix things before we get him involved."

"He already knows."

So it was Jinn who told Moray. "What'd you do that for? He's got his hands full with the docking and the transfer. If you have a question about the refugees, come to me first. I'm the intercessor."

"Trist, settle down. I see this as a good thing." He pulled up a chair and sat down. "I have a plan that might get us both promoted. We know Moray's getting paranoid, and that he plans to lie low for a while after this, to work on his son's problems, I think. Leave the refugees in their airplane."

She screwed up her face. "Why?"

He lowered his voice. "If anything happens, if the transfer goes bad, those refugees would be witnesses. A couple of hundred people testifying at a war crimes trial in an Alliance puppet court? It would be a disaster. Before you were stationed here, during the Kerils incident, we thought we had an Alliance spy onboard. Moray sent the refugees to the cargo bay, opened the bay doors and"—Jinn made a sucking noise—"no more witnesses." His mouth curved smugly. "It was my idea."

Trist formed an admiring grin. "You killed all of them?"

He preened. "Yes. Of course, the goods didn't get to where they needed to go, and that was unfortunate, but we hadn't a choice."

Trist knew that Jinn was troubled more by the aborted business transaction than he was by the loss of innocent life. It sickened her. Often she'd wondered if the compassionate

329

aspects of her nature were due to her Alliance-born great-grandmother, a onetime slave who'd escaped the Empire with her Talagar husband and settled among their own kind in the central galaxy. But her parents, Alliance loyalists themselves, were no different. Often ostracized, her mother and father never gave up trying to convince the skeptics who called themselves patriots that it was "nurture, not nature" that formed a person's character.

"It won me a promotion to third aide," Jinn boasted. "Keep that in mind before you send them back to the holding bay."

"I think I will, Jinn." Her smile was fabricated. But when he walked from her sight, her grin became genuine. Jinn could try all day if he so desired, but he wasn't going to get those cargo-bay doors open. She was well ahead of him. When it came to interrogation time after his arrest, she looked forward to seeing his expression once he learned that Captain Cady, a slavery-bound refugee, had helped accomplish the one preventative for his evil plan.

Trist shoved her hands through her hair and briefly shut her eyes. She hoped they made it, the refugees. She'd become attached to them. And Kào, too. He'd been raised by Moray, a monster if there ever was one, yet somehow he'd escaped contamination. When she'd first met Kào, all she saw was a cold, physically imposing ex-prisoner. With Jordan, he was a man who was generous and self-deprecating, and who talked openly about his life. There remained something defensive at the core of his personality, and that self-protectiveness made him seem vulnerable—as if his remoteness were meant to deflect one from noticing the sensitivity of his feelings, the hidden hurt.

Biologically he must have been programmed for goodness, she'd decided—coding that not even Moray could break. Jordan was much the same way, and Trist was grateful that the will of the Seeders had brought them together.

Nature versus nurture. It may indeed have been Kào's inherent nature that saved him, but for her, a descendant of Talagar expatriates, it was her upbringing that formed her—and she'd gladly die proving it. Possessed of much-maligned Talagar genes, she was not ruled by them; nor were the others like herself, as enlightened individuals in Alliance already knew.

Talagar culture was to blame for the evilness of their Empire, not any inborn traits. Now, in her shining moment, she'd finally have a chance to prove it.

Breaths uneven, sweat glistening on his exposed skin, Kào ducked inside the airlock and rotated the heavy hatch closed behind him. The primary airlock was used as a thoroughfare when the *Savior* was docked to another ship. It was carpeted, its rounded walls spongy with soundproofed insulating material. But this, the secondary airlock, was another story. It was a poorly illuminated tube bridging the space between two ships, no higher and no wider than a man. The walls were constructed of bare alloy, every rivet, every scar of construction as visible now as the day the vessel left the shipyard. From there, he contemplated the round hatch on the far end of the airlock. An untold number of Talagars were going about their business on the other side.

Steeg. So close.

When it came to Moray, Kào's sentiments were . . . muddled. But Steeg—Kào wanted to rip out the man's heart; he wanted to send the monster to the place the Earth people believed men like him burned in agony for all eternity. *Hell,* they called it. But it was easy to have such thoughts for a man he didn't know.

Dutifully he marched onward through the airlock, his boots clanging on the metal floor, a loyal Alliance soldier there to prove what he could not during the war: He would

331

willingly die defending the ideals his government stood for—freedom, peace, and honor. He'd gladly give his life to ensure a future with Jordan, in which she and her people, and their children, would be safe from Talagar raids. Whatever it took to stop men like Moray and Steeg, whose livelihoods fed on the human spirit, he would do it. For all those reasons and more, he'd come to this airlock ready to do battle with a recalcitrant mechanical switch that would not obey its computerized command.

The passageway in which he strode was cold and barren, serving two purposes only: as an emergency manual breakaway should the normal docking release fail, and as a backup conduit for everything from digital signals to water and air. At each end were sealed hatches—one Kào had shut behind him when he climbed inside the airlock, the other leading to the Talagar battleship. Between the vessels was a breakaway point at which a closed pressure door shielded the fragile human body from the deadly vacuum of space when the ships parted. But with one pull of the manual release handle, used to detach the *Savior* in an emergency situation, the seam would split apart. Anyone unlucky enough to be on the wrong side of the pressure door would be sucked out and sent to their almost instant death.

The docking relay switch was located in an area near the floor that required Kào to open the pressure door to access it. Instinctively he attached a safety cord to his waist belt before setting to work. He pondered that. There was a time when he was so numb and empty inside that he wouldn't have cared if he lived or died. Because of Jordan, he'd come alive, gloriously so. But with his renewed ability to feel came a blooming hatred and sharp sorrow of almost equal intensity—for Moray—along with regret which Kào suspected any man might experience if he were to sense the imminent end to a life seemingly just begun.

332

Contact

Focus, he told himself. With a harsh grunt, he yanked on the handle and opened the pressure door. His ears popped. There was always a fractional pressure differential between a pair of ships. The heavy door opened inward, toward him. With a grating scrape, it came to rest against the curved wall.

Kào crouched, setting out the tools he'd brought. Starlight and reflected illumination from the two immense vessels flanking him provided sparse light in which to work. But he knew his way around a starship better than most. Within seconds, he'd located the telltale seam in the metal wall and followed it with his fingers until they collided with a square protrusion. He saw the problem: the switch, a simple blasted switch, coated with dirt and old lubricating fluids. The congealed mess had prevented it from closing over the relay when Trist had commanded it.

He wiped his hands on his trousers, blotted the sweat of his brow. Then he gripped the handle in two hands. *For you, Jordan. For the Alliance.* "For the future," he gritted out past clenched teeth as he shoved the handle downward over the switch and closed the critical relay.

"There were several unsuccessful attempts to get onto the main computer, Commodore," an ensign reported.

"From what terminal?" Moray demanded.

"Seven-four-oh-bravo. A workstation in the cargo bay. That's all I have, sir. We're still working on it. In light of the docking-in-progress and your request to monitor the comm, I thought you'd want to know."

"Yes, yes, Ensign, thank you," he said distractedly as he began typing one-handed on the nearest terminal. "Jinn," he bellowed. In an instant, the aide was at his side. "Where is Poul?"

Jinn squinted. "He reported that the refugees were missing—or misplaced—which I passed along to you. Then he

333

left with Heest and"—his facial muscles went rigid and his eyes widened—"they never reported in."

"Traitors," Moray growled under his breath. He slammed his fist into his palm. "Check for all communication in or out of this ship."

Jinn went to work. Almost immediately, his head popped up. "A signal is being transmitted from our ship to the *Diligent*. Unorthodox code, hidden in a legitimate routine. It's being routed through the secondary airlock, sir. And whatever it is, it's big, and it's taking a while to download. Otherwise I don't think I would have seen it."

Moray's head snapped to the battleship looming outside. "Is there a chance that the signal being sent could do damage to the *Diligent*?"

Jinn's jaw moved back and forth.

"Out with it," Moray barked. "Don't give me the answer you think I want to hear as opposed to what you really believe. I didn't promote you to third aide to hear pretty-talk."

Jinn's throat bobbed. "The code could summon a larger program, once inside the *Diligent*, and put Admiral Steeg's ship in danger."

Moray swung away from the observation railing. "Get Trist to help you and abort the transfer. Purge any and all substantiation of our activities onboard this ship. I don't care how. Just do it. That signal will be stopped, if we have to tear apart the wiring in the airlock with our bare hands."

Chapter Thirty

A boom shook the 747. It came from outside the airplane. In the cockpit, Jordan jolted to full alert. Was it an explosion?

The loud bang sounded again, then stopped. For long moments. She was about to settle back in her seat when a series of thunderous reverberations rattled the airplane and her teeth. More silence followed.

Jordan threw off her seatbelt and shoulder harnesses. So much for Trist's orders; she was going to see what the heck was going on.

As she bolted down the center of the aisle in upper-deck business class, she tried to smile reassuringly at the passengers staring at her from their seats. "I have to tell whoever's doing that to hold down the noise," she quipped, although she felt anything but funny.

They merely watched in silence as she ran past. As travelers, they were an airline's dream: No one complained about atrocious conditions and lousy service.

Downstairs, Ben was straining in his harness in his flight-attendant jump seat by the forward left door. His face was pressed against the small circular window in the door, and he was looking at the cargo-bay doors. "That hook keeps lifting and banging down against the bar. Is it supposed to do that?"

She dropped to her knees and cupped her hands around her eyes to see out the window. Was the hook designed to bounce around? No. Something was wrong. One good bounce and that hook would fly off the bar as if it weighed nothing.

She fell back on her haunches. "Someone's trying the bay doors."

"Are you sure?" Ben turned white; his dark stubble stood out starkly.

"The hook moves when the command is given. Only we put it over the bar so it can't lift. In the down position, it disables a command from the bridge to open the doors."

"We'd die if those doors opened. We'd freeze to death."

"Actually, we'd suffocate first. Or would our blood boil?" She stifled a groan. "It's one of the two. And neither is how I want to go." She didn't want to "go" at all, but that was beside the point. "Every time that hook lifts, it's trying to obey a command issued by the ship's computer. It shouldn't lift at all. But maybe we didn't check to make sure it was fully in place before we came inside. I didn't back up Trist. I figured she knew what she was doing." Jordan knew how to use the hydraulic wheel to lower the hook. Lowering the hook as far as it would go would stop the bouncing. But that meant she'd have to go outside to do it.

Her stomach twisted, and a horrible feeling of vulnerability choked her. Ten seconds, she'd heard you had in space with no protective suit. Ten *seconds*. In the airplane they'd last longer if the cargo bay lost pressure—but how much longer? A minute, maybe? It might be long enough for Trist to get the doors closed from upstairs. *Might.*

Jordan grimaced. Was that reason enough to huddle in the plane when she knew how to save everyone?

She peered down the aisles, making eye contact with many of the passengers staring back at her. *We trust you, Captain. We know safety's your top priority.* Jordan bit back a sigh. That was the company line, wasn't it?

Outside, the banging started again. The hook waggled spasmodically on the bar. "Whoa," Ben said nervously. "That one got some airtime."

Jordan shot to her feet. "I've got to fix it or the next time it bounces, it falls, and we're history."

She considered calling for volunteers. Rich, Garrett, Natalie, they'd all be eager to help. While those on the airplane might survive, anyone near the doors would be sucked into space as easily as a crumb into a vacuum cleaner. No. Securing the bay doors was her duty. She couldn't escape it; she couldn't foist it onto someone else's shoulders and think she'd be able to stand herself the rest of her life.

Promise, Mommy?

"I know, sweetie," she said too softly for anyone to hear. *What can I do? I'm the leader, and this is what leaders have to do.* Leaders didn't choose another to accomplish what they themselves were too scared to do.

"Do you want me to check it out?" Ben asked. Perspiration glittered on his pale forehead. He was scared shitless. But he'd volunteered anyway.

"I need you here," she said.

A breath shuddered out of him. "To mind the store."

"Yeah. You do a great job of it."

His smile wobbled, and she reached out and ruffled his hair. "It's better that only one of us go anyway, Ben. We don't need more. Trist showed me how to lower the hook. It's a piece of cake. Really."

With both hands, Jordan took hold of the airliner's door handle and rotated it. The door swung open. *You're coming home, right, Mommy?*

Guilt bared sharp claws of regret, shredding her insides. But somehow, after all these months, she knew it would come to this: returning to her child or sacrificing herself so that the rest could survive—a terrible choice that had only one resolution she could live with.

I'm sorry, Boo. Blocking any more thoughts of her daughter, she vaulted from the airplane to the platform below.

"No! Mommy, *nooo!*"

The keening cry woke John Jensen from a deep sleep. His firefighter's senses were instantly alert. He jackknifed up in bed, gaping wide-eyed into the darkness.

His wife said sleepily, "It's Roberta. She's having a nightmare." She tossed off the blanket.

He blocked her with his hand. "I'll go," he said and hopped out of bed.

Pulling on his robe, he shoved open the door and walked into the hallway. Roberta's bedroom door was ajar. The fronds of the potted palm in the hall were still swaying. He must have missed the kid by seconds.

His gaze veered to the stairs. Then he heard the front door open. "Roberta!"

He took the stairs two or three at a time, stumbling onto the landing and almost breaking his neck. He collided with a tree fern in an effort to beat Roberta down the front porch steps. Heard the crash of the pot onto the wood floor behind him as he raced after her. He could see her now, a wraith in a pink nightgown, skinny legs pumping. "Roberta—stop! Now!"

The grass was spongy from yesterday's rain. He slipped

and fell. Righted himself and kept going. Roberta headed for the street. "No!" he cried hoarsely.

But she ran as if her life depended on it. "Mommy!" she cried out. *Or someone else's life,* he thought, his heart twisting. She'd dreamed of Jordan, but the kid had never done anything like this before.

The headlights of a car flickered to the left. Roberta dodged a fire hydrant and ran into the street. Time slowed down. He was thirty-five, he thought, but he ran with the speed of a seventy-year-old. Or it seemed that way. "Roberta!" he bellowed.

He was close, close enough to hear her bare feet slapping against the asphalt. Too far to grab for her. The car didn't slow down. No one would expect people to be running across the street in the middle of the night.

Headlights, blinding now. *Goddamn.* Roberta darted in front of the car. A horn blared. Brakes shrieked. John dove for the kid, caught her in his arms.

They rolled across the street, tumbled over the sidewalk and onto the lawn of the house across the street. John's hand shielded Roberta's head, and he managed to get their bodies to stop before crashing into a row of thorny shrubs.

Roberta tried to struggled free. "Mommy, Mommy—no!" She squirmed and pummeled him.

"Hush. You're okay now. I've got you." He crushed her close. Kissed her blond curls. She smelled like bubble bath and little girl. He'd always wanted a daughter, but he railed at the unfairness of it all that the daughter he got was his dead sister's. "Hush," he soothed, sheltering her in his arms. "You had a nightmare. It's over. You're with Uncle John now."

The kid fought him until she collapsed into a quivering mass of limp limbs. "Come back, Mommy, come back," she chanted hoarsely.

John rose with her in his arms. The driver was standing

outside the car in a pool of light from the open door, her hand pressed to her mouth. Only the chime from the interior of the car and Roberta's intermittent sobs broke the silence of the night. "I didn't see her. I'm sorry."

John shook his head. "You didn't hit her." His voice broke. "Thank you. She's all I have left of my sister," he whispered. Then he turned away and carried the child home.

Kào heard the hatch behind him open and then close, the hatch that led from the *Savior*. Kào jerked to his feet and spun around. His tools slid off his lap, falling in damning jangles to the metal floor.

Moray stood at the far end of the airlock. "Kào. . . ."

How could one word hold so much pain, so much regret? Kào felt the weight of it crushing down on his shoulders. He swallowed hard against a throat suddenly constricted, wishing that things had been different, wishing for a thousand things, all impossible now.

The moment drew out, horrible and poignant.

Finally Kào let his arms fall to his sides, palms up. "Why?" He was surprised to hear himself speak. He hadn't meant to voice the thought.

"They took Jenneh," Moray said gruffly. "My children." The words were ragged-sounding, pain-filled.

The Alliance did? "I thought they were killed in a Talagar raid."

"They were." Moray's large hands crushed into fists. "It should never have happened. The Alliance bastards left Remeraton undefended. They knew the danger to the families stationed there. I was away—on duty. Giving my soul to the Alliance!" His voice quavered. "And when I came home I found them dead. All of them."

"So you joined the Talagars? The same people who murdered your family?" Kào heard the bitterness in his own voice, and the disbelief.

"The *Alliance* killed my family. Out of irresponsibility. Out of indifference. It was then I realized I was on the wrong side. The Talagars were misunderstood—and still are. Many reasons. Their culture is a closed one. Restrictive." His gray eyes beseeched Kào. "And of course the barter of humans is misinterpreted. You would think differently of the society if you knew it as I have. Black and white. Right and wrong. No gray." Across the airlock, Kào saw a flash of pain in his father's eyes, painful in its intensity. "No *indifference*."

So. Moray had assuaged his grief by punishing those he blamed for it. Kào knew that humans weren't programmed to tackle life with the logical approach of computers—himself included—but this . . . this treason, the suffering and lives lost, the damage done to the longest-running freely elected democracy the galaxy had known, it was irrational. It was unforgivable. But after all these years, there would be no convincing Moray of it. No matter what his father's motivation, Kào knew that no one else must die for it.

Kào glanced down at the switch next to his right boot. A tiny, crisp, blinking green light indicated, he hoped, that the relay was active. Trist's file was large; it would take several more minutes to go through, minutes Kào hoped he had now that Moray had come. His father followed his gaze to the switch. Understanding dawned in his eyes. "It's going through that relay, isn't it? The signal."

"It's too late," Kào told him. "While Steeg waits for you to get the refugees, this will destroy his battleship. It's over, Father."

The man advanced on him. In that moment, Kào wished he had asked Trist for her weapon. He also hoped that his father didn't have one.

"It's not too late, Kào. We have a future. Imagine all we

can still do. I'm sorry about what happened during the war. This transfer of the refugees was supposed to correct that."

"Correct what?" Kào asked, incredulous. "You want to give these people to the Talagars to correct *what*?"

"Your career."

His *career*? A sound escaped Kào, too clipped and bitter to be a laugh.

"I want you to be a hero, Kào. To share in the credit of this rescue."

Kào jerked his chin at Steeg's ship. "For giving them to the Talagars?"

Moray swiped the back of his hand over his deeply flushed face. "You weren't supposed to know of that part. And you weren't supposed to *care*."

Kào saw the accusation in his father's face. If he hadn't gotten close to Jordan, he wouldn't have questioned—or cared about—her people's fate. The refugees would have been transferred to Steeg's supposedly apprehended ship and, in his naïveté, Kào would have allowed it to happen. "No wonder you didn't want me near her," he muttered, his eyes returning to the switch. Only a minute had passed. It felt like hours. If he could distract the commodore a short while longer . . .

He spoke with a deadly calm he didn't quite feel. It reminded him of his weapons-officer days when he planned the obliteration of populated areas: One simply disconnected one's emotions in order to perform. He needed to do that now. "You've always wanted me to have, in your words, father, a brilliant career. Power, influence. A good marriage," he added, his mouth twisting. "I wouldn't think you'd need to live vicariously through me, when you could take such power for yourself." He'd often wondered at that, his father's motives.

Shock froze Moray's features. "It wasn't to live through

Contact

you, boy! It never was. I want the best for you because . . . because you are my son."

"But you wanted me to gain the highest levels of government when I clearly didn't have that particular ambition," Kào insisted impatiently.

The two men held each other's gazes. Moray's eyes pleaded with Kào to understand, to forgive. For a second or two, Kào tried to understand. Then it became clear. He jerked backward as reason for Moray's deception hit him. "You're a Talagar sympathizer. As a man of power, I'd be a valuable conduit of information for you."

Moray nodded encouragingly. Did he still think there was a chance to bring Kào over to his side? The man was delusional! "As an innocent byproduct of our interaction. Or," Moray offered, "willingly."

Kào sneered. "Never willingly. But that wouldn't matter, would it? Because I'd assume your loyalty to the Alliance was above question—because I'd *trust* you—I'd reveal things I ought not. Or so you'd hope." He well knew the cost of exposing military secrets to the enemy. Unintentionally, involuntarily, it didn't make a difference how it happened; the consequences were the same. "At least it's finally clear to me . . . what you had in mind all these years. Why you kept a child alive when you should have killed him." He swallowed hard. "A part of me now wishes you had killed me."

Moray's face reddened with emotion. His voice was thick. "Listen to me, Kào. It's true I had plans for you, but over time—over time something unexpected happened. As the years passed, using you as a means to harm the Alliance became secondary to my desire, as your father, to see you do well."

For a moment, Kào feared the man would weep.

Moray clutched at his chest with thick fingers. "You were *my son*. My boy. I wanted the best for you. I wanted you to

343

be . . . happy. You were bright, a tenacious lad. When you went off to join the Space Force, I did everything in my power to make you a hero. I knew you would balk at my efforts, humble as you are, and so I worked behind the scenes. Got you the best assignment on the best ship that I could." Remorse crept into his tone. "And when I heard through my channels the Talagar shipbuilding facility had been left virtually unguarded, I made sure that information was passed to your squadron—*your ship*, where I knew you'd be monitoring incoming intelligence. A small price to pay for the Talagars to lose that facility. But for you it would have been the first of many steps in a glorious ascent to a brilliant career."

Kào shook his head. "Hold on—that intelligence came from *you*?" He'd received such reports daily from operatives in the field, tasked with passing up-to-the-minute information to the fleet. "The targeting message was reviewed by me," he thought out loud. "It was verified by my commander . . ." As procedure dictated, he'd passed along the intelligence and his own opinions to those responsible for making the final decisions. Regarding that particular gem, an unwary shipbuilding facility that just happened to be on their path, he'd pushed hard to go in and destroy it. But if what Moray told him was true . . .

Sweat prickled the back of Kào's neck. "The Talagars knew we were coming. They were waiting for us." It hurt to think of what happened next, so he stopped and pushed the memories away.

"They weren't supposed to be there, Kào. I swear it! Someone double-crossed me." Moray's eyes had never appeared as black to Kào as now, when the man seemed to focus inward on the past. "Someone somewhere in Talagar intelligence figured out my plans for you." Moray's scowl deepened. "They sent ships to thwart that attack. I'll find the faithless coward and kill him with my own hands, if it takes me the rest of my days."

"That little miscalculation led to my capture," Kào said humbly. "And the others'. The Talagars learned of the Dallénne offensive from one of us—or maybe all of us," he added, hearing in his mind Jordan's voice, insisting that he'd become a convenient scapegoat because he was the only one left alive to blame. "If not for that, we'd have routed them. We would have won the war years ago. We wouldn't still be fighting now."

Moray shook his head. "I don't know what went wrong. And I arranged for your release after a short time. The Talagars were never supposed to keep you there. But they did keep you alive for me. They did that, at least."

A heavy weight compressed Kào's lungs. His legs wanted to fold beneath him as Moray's traitorous face wavered in his field of vision. At last, he'd learned the answer to the question that had haunted him: why he'd survived when everyone else had died.

Sweat oozed out of his every pore. His stomach muscles were rigid. He longed to turn his back on the man he'd called father, but he couldn't afford the risk.

Focus. The commodore was the enemy, Kào reminded himself. The man was here to stop him from destroying Steeg's ship; he was desperate and using revelations quite skillfully to distract him. But Kào knew that to let his emotions take over was to fail. *Again.*

He'd die first.

Slowly, Kào lifted his gaze. His jaw clenched. "I lost my entire squadron, spent years in prison, *because of you*. And now you tell me that you intend to exchange these refugees as slaves while disguising the entire event as a humanitarian effort. With no thought of how wrong it is. It's just the first step in your plan to absolve me of my guilt. Is that

345

Susan Grant

why Sofu agreed to reopen my records? Or is that another lie?"

Moray scrubbed a shuddering hand over his perspiring face. The airlock was frigid, but both Moray and Kào were bathed in sweat. "Please, my boy. Understand. Everything I've done, I've done for you."

Fear and hatred expanded in the pit of Kào's stomach, hard and cold. "Not everything." He cleared his throat. "What happened to my family?"

Startled, Moray blinked.

"You know, *Commodore*," he said. "You were there."

"Yes . . . I was."

Kào swallowed to hide the longing in his voice. "Could they . . . be alive?"

Moray was matter-of-fact. "I know that they are not."

"What happened?" He had to know.

"They rioted during transport, hundreds of them, killing themselves along with the crew."

"By the Seeders," Kào whispered harshly. He should be grateful. They would have suffered horribly had they lived.

Moray's hands hung at his sides. He looked old, tired. "I've done everything since for you, Kào. I did it for love."

Love. The man made a mockery of the concept. Kào knew little English, but one phrase rushed out of him. *"Go to hell,"* he growled.

Moray could move swiftly for a big man, and he did so now. Kào dove for the floor, his hands cupped over the switch. Moray landed on top of him. The man was heavy, crushingly so.

Fiery pain shot up Kào's knees, which had weakened during prison. Gasping, he continued to shield the switch from Moray's clutching hands.

The green light blinked. *Not done. Not done,* it taunted. How big was Trist's program? Or had time simply ground to a halt?

346

Hold on, just a little longer.

They grappled. Gasped. Grunted. Moray's smooth, meaty hands plucked viciously at Kào's scarred ones wrapped around the handle, until he managed to grab two fingers and bend them backward.

Kào bared his teeth. The tendons stretched, began to tear. Kào panted as agony slashed ragged edges into his palms. Bolts of remembrance, of torture, tore through his brain, and his hold on the switch began to slip.

Jordan ran at full speed from the 747 to the cargo-bay doors. There came another series of sharp clangs. The hook bounced higher. Any moment it would clear the bar. With every step, every breath, Jordan prayed she would not be too late.

Halfway there, Natalie caught up to her. "Nice try, Captain. But I'm coming, too," she said, barely winded.

Jordan waved her off. "I've got it. Go back!"

"Sorry. What would Batman be without Robin, Aladdin without Genie"—her face lit up—"Ben without Jerry?"

Jordan gave a groan of surrender. "If we make it back to Earth, I'm getting you serious psychological help. How you can think of ice cream at a time like this, I have no clue."

They stumbled to a stop by the override device. The hook had gone still. For the moment. "When it starts up again, if they try one more time, Nat, that hook's going over the bar and we're history," Jordan warned.

The flight attendant's lips were coated perfectly in the MAC lipstick shade Del Rio, of which she had dreaded the day she'd eventually run out. Those lips curved. "The brave don't live forever. But the cautious never live at all."

"That works for me." Together they grabbed hold of the hydraulic-assisted handle that Trist had used. The vibration began deep within the wall. Then the hook rattled. "Faster," Jordan shouted.

Their hands were blurred. They spun the wheel until the hook had settled fully over the bar.

Jordan stumbled backward, wringing her hands. This time she didn't fight the urge. She freakin' deserved it! Triumph! "They can try all they want, but those doors aren't going anywhere."

Natalie's dark eyes were wide as they focused on the gigantic doors, large enough for a 747 to fly through, which it had. "They're trying to kill us, this means," she said quietly.

"I know." Jordan's eyes shifted to the bottom of the tube from which they'd climbed down earlier. The sensation of dread that had dogged her all along skyrocketed. *Kào's in danger.* Her heart knew it. Her instincts honed from years of motherhood screamed it. Did she ignore the warning, did she seek shelter in the airplane? "If they're trying to kill us, that means something's gone wrong with Trist's plan." She backed away from Natalie. "I've got to go."

"Go? Go where? You got to get your butt back inside, girl!"

Jordan broke into a jog. "Tell everyone on the plane to buckle in tight, to secure all their belongings in case this compartment depressurizes. Whoever wants us dead won't stop trying. They might come down here. They'll see what we did." She paused to think and catch her breath. "Brief Ben—take no longer than a minute. Then leave him in charge and go find Trist. Tell her. Whatever cover she had before must be blown. She needs to know."

Natalie shouted after her. "Hey! Where are *you* going?"

"To help Kào." Filled with a sense of rightness, of inevitability, of destiny, Jordan turned her back on the flight attendant and broke into a run.

Moray's hand gripped Kào's. Their ragged breaths hissed. Kào's neck corded. His hand burned with pain. His fingers were slipping. He cast his desperate gaze to the left. The wall. Curved. Near him.

He lurched backward, and the move caught Moray off guard. The man's hold faltered, only for a heartbeat but long enough for Kào to throw his hip to the side and his leg upward. His boots, first one and then the other, grabbed the wall. Rubbery soles provided traction, and using his momentum he ran his feet up and over the inner radius of the wall, landing heavily behind Moray.

In a heartbeat, he'd captured the commodore in an arm lock and wrenched his head back. But Moray grabbed desperately for the switch. Fingers searching, clutching, fingernails scraping over the metal floor. Inches away from the switch.

"No!" Kào grunted, yanking him backward. The man gurgled, wheezed. His hand shook as it crept toward the switch. The indicator light flashed on and off. "Finish, blast it!" Kào shouted.

And then the light stopped blinking.

Kào threw his gaze to the gleaming battleship looming silently at the opposite side of the airlock. "It went through." He let go of Moray, who sagged to the metal floor. Kào skipped backward. "Say goodbye to Steeg."

Moray regarded him strangely from where he sat sprawled on the floor.

Kào snarled, "Now get up. We have to get out of here. When that ship blows, so will we."

"I did all I could," Moray replied in a defeated voice. "But it went so wrong." Then his hand went to the breakaway handle, the docking release.

With a horrible, impotent fury, Kào knew that his father was going to pull the release handle. The airlock would open to space and they'd be sucked out of the ship like so much dust. Every cell in Kào's body screamed. "No!" he bellowed hoarsely.

Susan Grant

Moray's hand shot up. "Stay where you are." His florid coloring remained, but oddly, his facial muscles were relaxed. What could only be peace glowed in him. The realization conjured a fresh surge of urgency in Kào: The man was going to destroy himself, and take him along for the ride.

Kào focused. Analyzed the target. The man was five maybe ten paces from him. Between them was the open pressure door, useless as it was, hanging open. Moray noticed the direction of his gaze, and his hand flexed.

Kào's mouth went dry, and he backed away from that thought. If he tried to close the door, Moray would act. Kào's shoulders sagged and his arms fell to his sides. "So you've kept control of me to the end, Father," he said resignedly. "It seems you will even choose the hour and the manner of my death. You couldn't do it on Vantaar, but you'll do it now." And it was worse now that he had so much to look forward to: the promise of a future for the first time in his life. He grieved for all that would never be. But instead of weeping, he started to laugh. It was a dreadful sound, but he couldn't hold it back. All along, he'd struggled with his emotional inability to deal with the tragedies he'd endured, and now that the emotions vented, they were all the wrong ones. Yet strangely, when he recovered, wiping the back of his hand across his face, he felt purged, purified, like a prisoner who had been prepared for execution.

Moray watched the entire spectacle, his knuckles white. In silence, Kào waited for him to pull the release that would kill them both. He didn't know what else to say to this man who was both fiend and father. And he didn't know what to do when Moray's gray eyes clouded over with tears.

"Ah, Kào. Look what I have made of you." A tear made its way down his reddened cheek.

Kào stared at the droplet, half in horror and half in pity.

"To say I'm sorry is pitifully insufficient. Sometimes . . . sometimes a man's life gets away from him, you see."

"Just do it," Kào coughed out. "End it."

Suddenly Moray's gaze shifted and his mouth spread into a sad smile. Perhaps he saw the Original Ones before him; it was said that they appeared in the hour of death. "Ah, Kào. Here she is. Your refugee. She's what you want, isn't it? That life. So be it, my boy. I can give you that, at least."

Kào whipped his head around. On the far side of the airlock, he could see Jordan's blond head bent to the task of opening the outside door. His heart exploded. "No, Jordan! Go! He's going to open the airlock!"

Her eyes were wild with fear. For him, he thought. Not for her. "Can't it be closed electronically?" she screamed at someone with her.

Two heavy boots slammed into Kào's rear. The powerful shove sent him skidding over the floor and away from the manual breakaway.

There was a wrenching hiss, a shriek of wind. Vaguely, Kào was aware of Jordan and others entering the airlock, clinging to handholds themselves. She'd never make it to him in time. She'd kill herself trying.

The air turned to ice. He couldn't shout to her, to tell her to save herself. His lungs expanded to the bursting point at the same time his eardrums exploded in white-hot pain. A storm of loose detritus stung his exposed skin as he was wrenched backward.

The noise was deafening as he slid over the floor, hurtling toward space, a destination he couldn't see because the air had turned opaque with fog.

He grabbed for a handhold with frozen fingers and missed. He tried next to stop his slide away from Jordan with the rope connected to the safety harness he'd forgotten he'd donned, but it scorched his sliding hands like molten metal.

His cheeks and lips rippled with an outward rush of air from his lungs that he couldn't control. Blindly, he clutched for something, anything to stop himself.

Then, abruptly, the roaring in the airlock subsided to a shriek of wind that whistled into silence. His eardrums wrenched with a powerful reverse in pressure as the opening in the airlock shut, commanded so, he was certain, from the bridge.

The last thing Kào saw before he sank into unconsciousness, facedown on a porthole in the floor, was the body of his father, the man's swelling face triumphant in death, spinning away toward the stars.

Chapter Thirty-one

When Kào came to, he was on the floor of the bridge and Trist, Natalie, and Jordan were stripping him out of his harness. His skin tingled, and his lungs felt as if they'd been turned inside out. Awareness flooded back. Moray was dead. Trist's signal had gone through. The engines on Steeg's ship were about to go unstable. When it blew, it would take out everything within a huge radius. Kào knew; he'd seen battleships explode during the war, usually viewing each fireball with satisfaction.

"His ears are bleeding," he heard Jordan shout.

He tried to tell her that he was fine, but the words came out as an indecipherable croak. Jordan slipped her arms around him. He dragged her to his chest, pressing his hand to the side of her head, stroking her hair. Never did he think he'd hold her again.

"Get moving," he heard Trist yell. "We can't stay here."

Kào was hoisted to his feet and dragged onto the bridge,

where he was helped onto a chair and strapped in. His vision was clearing, slowly. He saw one of Moray's aides, Jinn, with blood oozing from a wound on his forehead. Bound with shock cuffs, he sat sullenly as he was searched by Pugmarten, the security guard on Trist's team.

The crew members were shocked. They hadn't known of their captain's misdeeds, nor the treachery that had gripped their ship. Kào was confident that Trist and her team had weeded out what remaining traitors were left. If not, they would in the hours to come.

The *Savior* lurched and then tipped. The vessel had undocked and was wheeling away from the *Diligent* as it accelerated. Kào caught fragments of frantic conversation, Key and English, some of which he understood and some he didn't. The voices were muffled, as if they were speaking into pillows. His strength was beginning to return, but sitting upright, he felt faint. He blinked away the sensation. Fought it. The battleship was going to blow. No weapons officer worth his weight in irradium would fall asleep before witnessing such a spectacular conclusion.

Jordan strapped herself into the seat next to him. "You need a doctor," she said, her hand on his arm.

"He'll live," Trist snapped. Acceleration pressed them all into their seats. The high speed caused buffeting and a steady vibration. "We have bigger concerns."

"Like three broken nails," Natalie complained.

"Okay, Nat, so I owe you my life *and* a manicure," Jordan shot back.

Though the women joked, Kào knew they did so to ease their trauma. "You have control of the bridge now," he ventured in a rasp that sounded barely human. "It was you who closed the breakaway."

"Pugmarten was there. He knew to do it," Jordan explained in rudimentary Key.

Kào smiled. "But it was you who sent the word to him, my resourceful captain."

He felt Jordan's cool palm slide over his. Her fingers flexed as she spoke. "Your father . . . he is dead."

"I know," he whispered. "I saw him go."

He took her hand and clasped it tightly. With vision blurred from ruptured blood vessels, he squinted at her, focused on her lovely face glowing with love. For him. The right kind of love, not the kind that took, or demanded, or used trust as leverage to cause pain.

She's what you want, isn't it? That life. So be it, Kào. I can give you that, at least.

"Yes, Father, you gave me that," Kào said under his breath, holding tight to Jordan's hand. It was her face that he watched when a distant, momentary flash of brilliant destruction bathed them both in the light of a thousand suns.

The last leg of what had to be the longest return flight from Honolulu in the history of aviation took place just after dawn, two weeks before Christmas. They'd be arriving home nearly three months after they'd left.

Trist stood in the cockpit of the 747. "So you're going to dump us out the back of the ship," Jordan confirmed, contemplating the plan they had so carefully gone over.

Trist nodded. "Is the only way. No one must know Earth's location." Steeg and his crew had known only that they were picking up slaves, not their origin. Moray had wanted Earth kept secret, a source of power. The Alliance had decided that posting guard-ships in orbit would draw attention to the planet—Talagar attention. Not revealing where Earth was located was the best way to ensure its protection . . . for as long as that lasted.

Most of the *Savior*'s crew had been transferred to another ship. The few left aboard were loyal Alliance agents. Their government was engaged in a renewed battle with the Talagar Empire, one that even Trist admitted she didn't know how it would conclude. In a quiet voice, she said, "Good prevails in the end. We can only hope it will prevail in this war, as well. But should the Alliance fall, should there be a Talagar victory, even in this one zone of space, Earth would be in danger. No one must know how to find you."

Of the two people who knew Earth's exact location, only Trist still lived. Moray would not be sending any more spaceships to fish airliners out of the sky.

"I will bring the ship into the atmosphere, open the cargo doors and then increase the body angle of the *Savior*. Your craft will fly free."

"It is not without precedent," Kào added from where he sat in the captain's seat. He was certainly not in charge, Jordan thought with an inner smile, but as a previous co-pilot, a first officer, she was most comfortable flying from the right seat. "Craft have been dropped from the rear of ships before. Not often. But it has been done in emergencies."

"Yeah, well, it still sounds crazy," Jordan said and checked the status of the auxiliary power unit, whose battery had been recharged by the *Savior*'s power sticks. It gave her the electrical energy she needed to start the engines. As for the air pressure that needed to get the huge fan blades spinning, Trist and her team had found an air hose that would work. The passengers were grateful for the cleaned toilets in the lavatories; Jordan appreciated that makeshift hose. "These engines haven't run in a while. I don't know how they'll do. What's the lowest altitude you can bring me down to, Trist?"

"Eighty thousand."

Jordan frowned. "Earth feet? I need lower. The highest flight-tested altitude for one of these babies is forty-five thousand one hundred feet."

Contact

Trist punched numbers into her handheld computer. "Sixty thousand?"

"Lower."

Trist frowned. "Fifty-three thousand is the lowest I can do without risking ship and crew."

Jordan's mouth spread in a grim line. "I'll take it." With the number-one engine running, she reached overhead for the start switch and cranked the number-two engine. Fifty-three thousand feet. About eight thousand higher than a 747 was allowed to go. It was going to be dicey, but as long as she kept the jet from stalling and kept the speed up, the engines would keep running and she'd be able to fly down to where she could better control the plane.

Trist put away her handheld and crouched by the center instrument panel, between Kào and Jordan. "At this low altitude, our arrival will make for quite an atmospheric show for Earth."

"A splashy comeback," Jordan said with a smile and impulsively pulled the albino woman into a hug. There was so much danger on the horizon for Trist. But she was a brave and noble woman who would make the military of any country, any world, proud. "I hope we get the chance to meet again."

As Trist pulled away, her lavender mouth tipped into a crooked smile. "When I next see you . . . and Kào," she said with a warm glance in his direction, "it will be to celebrate the Alliance victory."

She stood and turned to leave. Then she stopped and said over her shoulder, "No matter what happens—my death, a Talagar victory, or an Alliance one—it will only be a matter of time before your Earth is found again. If it is a long conflict, it may be years. But the day will come."

Jordan prayed it wouldn't be Talagars who made that first contact with Earth. As she searched Kào's grave face, she wondered how much time they'd have before the gal-

357

axy came knocking at their door. She didn't know. No one knew. Life was like that. Until then, she'd simply have to view every new day as a gift.

Without another word, Trist left the airplane. Kao reached across the cockpit and took Jordan's hand in his. His fingers were dry and cool-tipped. "I had never experienced love, Jordan. Romantic love. It wasn't that I was the cold-hearted sort who'd sworn off love; I simply assumed that love wouldn't ever be part of my life. And when it finally came, it was no surprise that I didn't recognize its first symptoms." He squeezed her fingers in his. "Forgive me this belated confession. Jordan, I love you."

She snapped her head back. "Oh. . . ."

"Love," he repeated. "Is it the same meaning in English?"

"Yes," she whispered. "The same."

Her fingers throbbed in his. She covered their joined hands with her other. Her voice was husky and soft and full of yearning. "I want to go home. I want the life we've planned. I want you, Kao." She tried to catch her breath. "I love you."

He tugged her hands to his mouth and kissed her knuckles.

"Don't make me cry," she squeezed out. "I've got to fly this thing in about two minutes."

His eyes twinkling, he pressed his firm lips to her hand once more and released her. "Take us home."

Jordan readied the airliner for its most turbulent flight. But when she started the number-three engine, it quit. She swore and hurried through the procedure to restart it. No dice. "It's dead, but we can fly with three," she told Kào, and started the number-four engine.

Nervousness was not in his nature. Or if he was apprehensive about the flight to come, he didn't show it. The warrior. That's what he was. But here, on the airplane, she was in *her* environment, too. She could do this. Three engines, four, it didn't matter. She was going home. *Hang in there, Boo. I'll be there soon.*

The *Savior* had to be entering the upper atmosphere. The turbulence began as a rumble and increased until Jordan was bouncing in her seat. A faint smell of something burning accompanied the rocky ride.

"Atmospheric entry," Kào confirmed. He sounded calm. But Jordan noticed that his hands gripped the armrests so tightly that the blood had left his knuckles.

"Think of all I'm going to show you, all we're going to do," she said, as much to reassure him as herself, speaking in a pidgin form of English and Key, a way of communicating that she and Kào had fallen into in the past few weeks, preparing him for his new language. "Christmas and candy canes, Disneyland and McDonald's. And snow! You'll get to see that for the first time!"

Kào's dark eyes sparkled. "Do not forget the Super Bowl," he said in his deep voice.

She grinned. "Dad and John will take good care of you." She'd longed for the day Kào would be taken into the folds of her family and, she hoped, accepted by Roberta as a father.

There was an explosive sound of rushing air. Jordan's ears popped and her sinuses prickled. "Here we go!" The cargo doors were opening.

She grabbed the PA microphone, holding tight to the steering yoke with her other hand. "Okay, ladies and gentlemen, this is it. Hang on, and I'll have you on the ground in no time."

Above the noisy roar of wind, she could hear the prolonged cheers from the back. She pulled her sunglasses out from her uniform shirt pocket and slipped them on. Then she fitted her headset over her hair. One part impatient and one part scared out of her mind, she took hold of the control yoke with sweaty hands. The second the 747 was jarred free of the ship, she'd be flying a handful of airplane. *You'll need to step on the left rudder*, she reminded herself. To counteract for the dead third engine. Other than that, she had little idea what to expect other than what Trist had briefed her.

Keep the blue side up . . . keep the blue side up. . . .

A strong hand closed over her forearm. "You'll rise to the occasion," Kào assured her. "You always do."

"Thanks," she whispered.

The bumping around smoothed for a heartbeat as the huge spaceship pulled up to a nearly vertical position. Jordan's stomach flip-flopped as the 747 started sliding backward. The scraping noise the aluminum belly of the fuselage made as it slid backward over the cargo-bay floor was worse than nails across a blackboard. There was a sharp jolt, as if they'd bumped over a curb. And then they were free.

Free falling, it felt like. The sensation of decelerating backward was disconcerting. Holding the control yoke, Jordan fought to keep the 747 level. Her boot pressed down hard on the left rudder. Ahead was the *Savior*, an awesome sight as it roared upward and away from the ocean, trailing thick plumes of white condensation. Jordan braced herself. Trist had warned her about the great craft's wake. It caught the 747, just as Jordan expected it would. Countering the vortex, she steered the opposite way. Then, without warning, the wake reversed. Between the dead engine and the overpowering outside forces, Jordan couldn't keep the airplane level.

It flipped; the sky and sea spun, changed places. *Holy shit.* She kept the roll going and made sure she didn't pull back on the yoke, which would send the nose toward the ground and into a dive from which they probably wouldn't recover. But in the next heartbeat, they were upright again and the air smoothed out.

Jordan whooped. Kào looked pale. "We did an aileron

roll," she cried, her hands shaking, her heart hammering. "In a seven-forty-seven!"

One corner of Kào's mouth tipped up as he gave her a sideways glance. "I don't quite understand your enthusiasm for the maneuver. But I do share your excitement for finishing it right side up."

Jordan didn't want to think about how that must have felt for the people in the back. And she didn't have time to ponder it. "I can't maintain our altitude." Something wasn't right. Even though they were lower now—twenty-nine thousand feet—they were losing airspeed. Instinctively her eyes went to the engines. "Number two's gone!"

"What is this?" Kào asked, not sure of her English.

She switched to Key. "We're flying on only two engines. The airplane can do it, but it's not good. Not good at all." She was beginning to wonder if she'd ever get home.

"Can you restart one or both?" he asked.

"I'll try." She did.

They didn't.

At least the losses were symmetric, the center engines instead of two on one side, which would have made flying difficult. Jordan used maximum continuous thrust on the two remaining engines and drifted down to eighteen thousand feet, where she leveled off and turned on the autopilot. Then she tipped her head back and sighed.

Promise, Mommy?

Almost there, sweetheart, Jordan thought. *Almost there.*

Her hand shook as she selected a radio frequency she hoped would work. "San Francisco radio, San Francisco radio, this is United Five-eight."

There was a telling, static-filled silence. "I bet they're busy trying to figure out what the heck the *Savior* was," she said to Kào. *Yeah, and we better pray no one shoots us down, either.* She made another transmission.

"Flight Fifty-eight?" the controller asked. "United?"

A shiver curled along Jordan's spine. "That's affirmative. United Airlines Flight Five-eight." *Believe it or not, guy.*

More silence followed during which the controllers identified them using the transponder signals sent by the airplane. Jordan was sure that more than just air traffic controllers were checking out the flight. The United States Air Force and the CIA, to name two interested parties. Would they want to harm Kào? Her heart gave a twist as she gazed at her lover's profile, eyes that had seen too much torment, known too much grief. He'd suffered enough. He deserved a run of happiness; he'd earned it. Hell, so had she. But first, she'd do everything in her power to protect him from the men-in-black folks. So would the rest of the passengers on Flight 58. If anyone wanted to hurt Kào for being an alien, they were going to find themselves on the wrong end of a mob of angry passengers and one pissed-off overprotective fiancée. With a war raging in the rest of the galaxy, and Kào the only one who could offer advice, she was hopeful that the government would see the light, get what information they needed from Kào, and leave them in peace.

"United Flight Fifty-eight, this is San Francisco radio. Go ahead, ma'am."

She took a breath. "We've been gone awhile," she began. "And, boy, are we ready to come home."

Epilogue

The early spring morning was crisp and bright. Frosty dew coated the thick grasses that grew around the shed. Kào lugged two pails of grain out into the sunshine. His youngest of three sons, Joshua, dark-eyed and skinny, scampered along beside him, tugging on the bucket's handle. "Let me help, Daddy!"

Kào smiled. "Josh, settle down or you'll spill it all before we reach the barn." The three-year-old tried, but for all his effort, he bounced along the path as enthusiastic as before. Sparrows dove down from the trees to peck at the fallen grain. Smoke and the scent of breakfast cooking filled the air. Sunday mornings were peaceful at the ranch, just the way he preferred them. Not a day, or even an hour, passed without him pausing to appreciate what he had: four children, three of them his own sons, and a wife whose love had changed his life. Yes, they argued from time to time—when the woman refused to see logic, he thought with a smile—and they disciplined their children for various infractions, but Kào understood that his was a charmed life. Every year of the past ten had been stolen out of time.

An entire decade had passed without a word from the deep reaches of space. What had happened to Trist Pren? Had she died fighting? And what of the Empire—had the Talagars been victorious in the end? Or had the Alliance triumphed? Kào was afraid to know, as no one had yet come knocking on Earth's door.

The hairs raised on the back of his neck. He tipped his head back and peered at the sky, a cloudless blue dome crisscrossed by the condensation trails of atmospheric craft. Who would it be, making contact when that day came?

Joshua's fingers slid off the pail's handle and more grain spilled. "A spiderweb!" he cried and darted away to a fence post in the clearing in front of the barn.

Wearing a smile of resignation, Kào set down the buckets and followed. As men who had cheated death often did, he tried to remember to stop and savor the simple pleasures, like sharing in the delight of a small child.

He crouched next to Joshua. Head to head, they observed the web glowing with dew. "Look at the way the water outlines the silk."

Joshua touched his finger to the center. The web quivered, and the spider took offense, rappelling down to the ground. Joshua shrieked with surprise and threw his arms around Kào. Covering the back of the boy's head with his hand, Kào held him close. He felt a thumping that at first he thought was Joshua's heart. Then he realized it was the sound of a horse's hooves coming up the dirt path.

He stood, hoisting Joshua onto his shoulders, and they looked to the road. Roberta appeared over the crest, her long blond hair bouncing around her shoulders. "Dad!" she cried, her face tight with alarm.

He lowered Joshua to the ground. "Go inside," he told his son.

"But I don't want—"

"Go, Josh," he said, using the forbidding scowl he knew ensured compliance one hundred percent of the time. Joshua ran toward the sprawling cedar home. As he watched the boy, Kào couldn't help wondering what wrenching moments his own father had experienced trying to protect him when he was that age.

Roberta's chestnut mare cantered up to him. The girl pulled the horse back on its haunches. Kào caught the reins. "A car's driving up the road," she gasped. "With the kind of men you told us about."

Government men.

Ten years ago, after several months of debriefing by all levels of government officials, some shadowy, some domestic and others international, the President of the United States offered to keep Kào on the payroll if he'd remain available to consult on all matters alien. He did, and it had given his family the financial freedom that enabled Jordan to leave the airlines, as well, as giving them their dream of building and living on the land in Colorado. But in the back of his mind, Kào knew the day would come when payment would be due.

Roberta jumped down from the horse. "Are they coming to tell us about contact?"

As she spoke, Kào could see the black sedan on the winding road that led from the highway miles back. He answered immediately. "Yes."

Her nostrils flared in that same way Jordan's did when she was frightened. He grabbed the girl's shoulders and bent his head to look into her eyes. The agonizing worry he felt for his children was only a hint of what his parents must have endured the day the Talagars had come to Vantaar. "Boo, I want you to go inside and look after your brothers. Don't let them come outside. But tell your mother to come out here."

She nodded. "Okay, Dad," she whispered.

To this day, his heart squeezed from the sound of that particular word on this girl's lips. He gave her a powerful hug. "I love you. Now go—run."

She bit her lip and headed for the house. He watched her go until she was safely inside. Then he turned to face the car that had parked by the barn. Three agents donned suit jackets as they disembarked from the vehicle. Those he dealt with in these matters always dressed this way. He'd grown used to it. But they had never come here, to the ranch. He knew it meant that the news they had was what he'd both hoped for and dreaded for ten years.

The tallest man walked toward him, his arm extended. "Mr. Vantaar," he said, shaking his hand. "Han Richards, Office of Homeland Security." Introductions went around: Richards, an older man named Al Gutierrez, and Mel Lee, a woman.

Kào heard his front door slam closed. Jordan ran across the front yard. She was wearing one of his sweaters. It swallowed her slender body and fell halfway to the knees of her faded jeans. She took one look at the well-dressed trio, Kào's expression, and went pale under her freckles. But she acted fully composed as she walked to Kào's side.

His hand went in search of hers. Their fingers tangled. Hands clasped together, they waited for Richards to speak. "I have news," the man said.

Kào asked simply, "The Alliance or the Talagars?"

Richards swallowed. "The Talagars—they were defeated."

"*Yes.*" Jordan's fingers convulsed over his, and she released a loud breath.

"First contact was made yesterday with officials of the Alliance."

Kào shuddered and briefly squeezed his eyes closed. *Thank the Seeders.* "Have they landed?"

"No, nothing like that's been cleared yet. The ships are in orbit between us and the moon. There's going to be a lot to do between now and then. We'll need you to come to Washington."

"When?"

"Tomorrow. We'll fly you there. You and your family. You'll be at the president's side when we announce the news to the public."

The woman handed Kào a heavy-looking binder. He hefted it into his arms. There were times he missed the convenience of handheld computers. "There are several transcripts contained within that you might be interested in reading, sir," she said. "Particularly the dialogue with Colonel Tristin Pren."

Jordan punched her fist in the air. "Wa-hoo! It's Trist!"

Although it wasn't Kào's nature to let loose his joy in a similarly vocal fashion, no one could say he didn't know how to celebrate. Not caring that the agents looked on, not caring if he made a spectacle of himself, he swept Jordan off her feet and spun her around and around as he threw back his head and laughed out loud with a happiness he hadn't felt in all his life.

The wildflowers blanketed the meadow later that spring. Three horses and a pony were already grazing in the soft new grass when Jordan and Roberta dismounted, leaving their mares to forage with their stable mates. A breeze carried birdsong and the sound of children's laughter from a copse of aspens. "The boys are stealing all the strawberries," Jordan said and looped her arm over Boo's shoulders, her daughter, who had never given up that she'd come home, and who had inexplicably felt so much of what she experienced during her time on the *Savior.*

"Hurry, Mom, or they'll get all the ripe ones."

"Then we'd better run." Jordan dashed ahead.

Boo's laughter sang out. She was a sixteen year-old with an appreciation for life that rivaled her adoptive father's. She raced her mother across the meadow. Then, hands clasped, they whirled in circles and spun away into the trampled grass. Sprawled on her back, Jordan flung her arms wide and gazed up at the cloud-dotted sky. So much lay beyond that blue. But she had no desire to see any more of it than she already had. Her children, though, especially the boys, she suspected would someday want to find their roots.

Boo sprawled next to Jordan, and Jordan hugged her close. Then the boys arrived, tumbling all around them like falling coconuts. Jordan grabbed them all at once, Nick, Eddie, and Joshua, kissing and tickling. They tasted sweet. Like strawberries.

"I wondered where all of you went," a deep voice said a few moments later.

Joy welled up inside her. Kào . . . her husband, the love of her life. He stood over them, his dark form ringed in a corona of sunshine, like some god from the stars. She threw open her arms, welcoming him, too.

The boys squealed and rolled away. Boo rose to her feet, smiling indulgently at her parents from under her lashes before she followed her brothers, who had scampered back to the berry patch.

Kào settled his long body next to Jordan's and nuzzled her neck. His cheek was scratchy; his soft lips warm as they nibbled and nipped all the exposed places he'd long ago learned were the most sensitive.

Warmth began to pool low in her belly. She'd been drowsy, lazy, content, but Kào's affectionate caresses made her sharply aware of his body—and her own.

With the laughter of their children ringing in the distance,

Contact

they kissed, deeply, languidly, with banked passion. It was always like this with them. They could never get enough of each other, even now. After ten years, it was crazy to feel this way, but she still did. Maybe it would change now that they learned they had nothing more to fear from the skies.

But then his strong arms folded around her, molding her to his body as his mouth loved hers. Sighing, she smiled. *Hmm*, she thought. *Maybe* not.

SUSAN GRANT
THE STAR PRINCESS

Ilana Hamilton isn't an adventurer like her pilot mother, or a diplomat like her do-right brother; she's a brash, fun-loving filmmaker who'd rather work behind the camera than be a "Star Princess" in front of it. Heiress or not, she's a perfectly normal, single woman . . . until Prince Ché Vedla crashes into her life.

With six months to choose a bride, the sexy royal wants to sow his wild oats. Ilana can't blame him—but fall for the guy herself? Hotshot pilot or no, Ché is too arrogant and too old-fashioned. But when he sweeps her off her feet Ilana sees stars, and the higher he takes her the more she loves to fly. Only her heart asks where she will land.

Dorchester Publishing Co., Inc.
P.O. Box 6640 _____52541-0
Wayne, PA 19087-8640 **$6.99 US/$8.99 CAN**
Please add $2.50 for shipping and handling for the first book and $.75 for each book thereafter. NY and PA residents, please add appropriate sales tax. No cash, stamps, or C.O.D.s. Prices and availability subject to change.
Canadian orders require $2.00 extra postage and must be paid in U.S. dollars through a U.S. banking facility.

Name _____
Address_____
City_____ State _____ Zip _____
E-mail _____
I have enclosed $_____ in payment for the checked book(s).
Payment <u>must</u> accompany all orders. ❏ Please send a free catalog.

CHECK OUT OUR WEBSITE! www.dorchesterpub.com

UNLEASHED
C. J. BARRY

Lacey Garrett was about to be free. Her fiancé had run off with her business, her savings, and stuck her with his cat. What had she done to stop him? Nothing.

But she'd just been beamed to another planet. Here, she wasn't an ordinary Earthwoman; she was part of a team. Here she could help a man like the roguish starship captain Zain Masters. Here, she could face *krudo,* interplanetary defense systems, and galaxy-wide conspiracies. She could even defeat the monstrous Bobzillas that looked like her ex-fiancé! For Zain, Lacey could do anything—because his kisses, his touch, everything about him felt like destiny. And that destiny was the true Lacey Garrett . . . *UNLEASHED.*

Dorchester Publishing Co., Inc.
P.O. Box 6640
Wayne, PA 19087-8640

_52573-9
$6.99 US/$8.99 CAN

Please add $2.50 for shipping and handling for the first book and $.75 for each additional book. NY and PA residents, add appropriate sales tax. No cash, stamps, or CODs. Canadian orders require an extra $2.00 for shipping and handling and must be paid in U.S. dollars. Prices and availability subject to change. **Payment must accompany all orders.**

Name: _____

Address: _____

City: _____ State: _____ Zip: _____

E-mail: _____

I have enclosed $_____ in payment for the checked book(s).

For more information on these books, check out our website at www.dorchesterpub.com.
_____ *Please send me a free catalog.*

SHADOW FIRES

CATHERINE SPANGLER

Jenna dan Aron lives a solitary existence, shunned by her people because she can see the future. She even foresees her own destiny: to be a human offering, a mate for a savage Leor warlord. When two Shielder colonies have to be rescued and the Leors who are their only hope demand a bride for their leader in return, Jenna steps forward.

Arion of Saura finds mating outside his race abhorrent, but he has no choice, as his kind faces extinction. Bound to him, Jenna faces a life of barbarism with a mate who seems more beast than man. Jenna and Arion wage a battle of wills until they discover that the heart is mightier than any weapon—and that love will forge shadow and fire together.

Dorchester Publishing Co., Inc.
P.O. Box 6640   ___52525-9
Wayne, PA 19087-8640 $5.99 US/$7.99 CAN

Please add $2.50 for shipping and handling for the first book and $.75 for each additional book. NY and PA residents, add appropriate sales tax. No cash, stamps, or CODs. Canadian orders require $2.00 for shipping and handling and must be paid in U.S. dollars. Prices and availability subject to change. **Payment must accompany all orders.**

Name: _____

Address: _____

City: _____ State: _____ Zip: _____

E-mail:_____

I have enclosed $_____ in payment for the checked book(s).

CHECK OUT OUR WEBSITE! www.dorchesterpub.com
_____ Please send me a free catalog.

Whispers in the Stars
PATRICIA WADDELL

The only female sovereign in the galaxy, Lady Zara is descended from women who can telepathically sense people's emotions. But her gift feels more like a curse as she faces the raw strength of her betrothed—a stranger sent to uncover her secrets, to breach her defenses both as a monarch and a bride.

As Commander of the Galactic Guard, Logan has sacked many a stronghold, and the defiant ruler of Nubria will be merely one more conquest. As he schools his new spouse in the ways of passion, though, Logan longs to trust the whispers in the stars that speak of a warrior and a priestess joined by the love that links their very souls.

Dorchester Publishing Co., Inc.
P.O. Box 6640   ___52522-4
Wayne, PA 19087-8640   **$5.99 US/$7.99 CAN**
Please add $2.50 for shipping and handling for the first book and $.75 for each book thereafter. NY and PA residents, please add appropriate sales tax. No cash, stamps, or C.O.D.s. Prices and availibility subject to change.
Canadian orders require $2.00 extra postage and must be paid in U.S. dollars through a U.S. banking facility.

Name _____
Address_____
City _____ State _____ Zip _____
I have enclosed $_____ in payment for the checked book(s).
Payment <u>must</u> accompany all orders. ❏ Please send a free catalog.
      CHECK OUT OUR WEBSITE! www.dorchesterpub.com

ATTENTION
BOOK LOVERS!

Can't get enough of your favorite **ROMANCE**?

Call **1-800-481-9191** to:

✳ order books,

✳ receive a **FREE** catalog,

✳ join our book clubs to **SAVE 30%!**

Open Mon.-Fri. 10 AM-9 PM EST

Visit **www.dorchesterpub.com**
for special offers and inside
information on the authors you love.

We accept Visa, MasterCard or Discover®.
LEISURE BOOKS ♥ LOVE SPELL